TIME FOR A CHANGE

Also by Lynda Page and available from Headline

Evie
Annie
Josie
Peggie
And One For Luck
Just By Chance
At The Toss Of A Sixpence
Any Old Iron
Now Or Never
In For A Penny
All Or Nothing
A Cut Above
Out With The Old
Against The Odds
No Going Back
Whatever It Takes
A Lucky Break
For What It's Worth
Onwards And Upwards
The Sooner The Better
A Mother's Sin

TIME FOR
A CHANGE

Lynda Page

headline

First published in 2008
by HEADLINE PUBLISHING GROUP

1

Cataloguing in Publication Data is
available from the British Library

ISBN 978 0 7553 3879 5

Typeset in Stempel by Palimpsest Book Production Limited,
Grangemouth, Stirlingshire

Printed and bound in Great Britain by Clays Ltd, St Ives plc

HEADLINE PUBLISHING GROUP
An Hachette Livre UK Company
338 Euston Road
London NW1 3BH

www.headline.co.uk

For my beautiful granddaughter,
Frankie Burnett Page,
who joined our family on 17th January 2007.

The promise I made to your brother Liam, I now make to you:
to be the best grandmother I can possibly be.
To love you, guide you, have fun with you and spoil you rotten.
I wish you a long, healthy and happy life.

Your devoted gran'ma

Acknowledgements

With grateful thanks to Eric Vardy, The Bookmark, Syston, not only for pushing my books on the unsuspecting public but also for the number of times I have called upon your expertise in respect of your previous occupation as a policeman. You have never failed me.

Well done, Liam, for achieving such good grades in your SATs – we all knew you could do it. The future is so bright for you, my darling grandson, and I know you are going to make your mark on the world. Well, how can you possibly fail with your good looks and exuberant personality! You obviously take after your gran!

CHAPTER ONE

The men's mood was murderous.

Inside the cramped factory-floor office, engrossed in paperwork, the rhythmical pounding of boots on the concrete floor had Gil Morton lifting his head. He frowned in confusion to see a group of workers storming towards him down the aisle between two rows of noisy machinery.

Something had obviously happened in the factory and his intervention as works manager was needed. He couldn't think what, though. He'd not long ago completed his regular tour of inspection and all had seemed in order then. Judging from their faces, though, whatever it was, the men were far from happy about it. He grabbed his suit jacket from off the back of his chair and pulled it on as he covered the short distance between desk and door.

'What's going on, lads?' he asked peremptorily.

The leader of the group, Cyril Breville, thickset and forty-nine, a staunch trade unionist who never let any opportunity to wield his authority as shop steward pass him by, puffed out his barrel chest importantly and said, 'You're to come with us, Mr Morton.'

Gil looked at him, bemused. 'Come *where* with you?'

'The old man's office. He wants to see you now.'

Gil was not amused by the manner in which Breville was addressing him, and snapped, 'If Mr Brenton wished to see me he'd have got his secretary to telephone me. Now what exactly is going on?'

Breville's barrel chest swelled even more as he said smugly, 'I'm not at liberty to say why. Only that we've been sent to escort you, to make sure you get there.'

'Escort me? Now, look here, I want to know what's going on, Breville?'

Dan Watson, Cyril's second-in-command, angrily raised one fist and blurted out, 'As if you don't know, Mr Morton.'

Gil glared over at him, incensed by his impertinence. Why were all the men suddenly acting so disrespectfully towards him? 'I can assure you, I don't,' he retorted, annoyed. 'Now if you've got a grievance or a demand for something, you know the correct procedure. You approach me as works manager, and if I think it's valid then I approach Mr Brenton and we take it from there. This isn't the way to go about things and you all know it – especially you, Breville. So tell me why you're here and not at your machines, where you should be?'

'There's a matter that needs sorting out by you, that's all I'm prepared to say,' Cyril told him cagily. 'Now are you going to come quietly or do the lads and me have to force you to come along with us, Mr Morton? The choice is yours.'

Gil stared at him thunderstruck. Cyril and his entourage were giving him the sort of treatment they would show towards an employee who had been caught in a serious misdemeanour against the firm. He couldn't understand why as he'd done nothing to warrant such behaviour. Then a thought occurred to him. He'd got on well enough with his then fellow foreman Breville until five years back when Gil had been promoted by Mr Brenton to the prestigious position of works manager, Breville's direct superior. From the moment he had taken up his new appointment, Cyril had made it very clear that he did not perceive Gil as an ally any longer. Since then he'd done everything in his power to impede Gil, making it hard for him to introduce any changes he wanted to put into place, despite the fact that these changes were intended to help the workforce. In essence, Cyril's mission in life was to be a thorn in the side of his superiors, and as shop steward he had plenty of opportunities.

It was all credit to Gil that on most occasions, through tact and diplomacy, he'd managed to avoid all out industrial action. He was in no doubt that Cyril was inciting the men to down tools purely out of his own personal need to best the works manager and factory owner, and not because he thought such union action would help them.

In all likelihood he'd merely been requested to go and fetch Gil to the main office, but had chosen to present this as a terse demand in order to make himself appear more important in the men's eyes. Typical of Breville. What didn't make sense, though, was the fact that the rest of his entourage were also treating Gil in such a disrespectful manner.

Giving Cyril Breville a look that warned him he would be taken to task for this at a later time. Gil said, 'OK, let's go.'

Within seconds the men Cyril had brought with him had surrounded their works manager. Gil was bewildered by their action. It felt like they were frogmarching him to the firing squad for fear he would try and make a sudden escape bid. He was also aware that as they moved down the aisles, the machine operators they passed were stopping work and beginning to whisper amongst themselves. Furious at this treatment, Gil abruptly came to a standstill and grabbed Cyril Breville from behind, forcing the other man to turn around so he could address him face to face.

'You're taking liberties! I'm sure Mr Brenton merely requested you to fetch me. I will *not* be force marched to his office like a criminal just to satisfy your pathetic need to score points off me. Now stand aside, I know the way.'

Cyril Breville's eyes narrowed darkly. 'I was asked by Mr Brenton to escort you to his office so that's what I'm doing, *Mr Morton*.' Before Gil could protest further Cyril and his men had picked up their pace and he was forced to follow suit.

Miss Clara Harris, Maurice Brenton's prim and proper secretary, jumped to her feet as soon as they arrived in her office. It was obvious she had been waiting for them. Gil couldn't fail to notice also how grave her expression was. Considering they'd always enjoyed a very affable relationship, the fact that she did not so much as acknowledge him but addressed her words to Cyril only was confusing. 'I'll tell Mr Brenton you're here, Mr Breville.'

Tapping on a door to the side of her desk, she entered her boss's office. Seconds later she returned, again addressing Cyril Breville. 'Mr Brenton will see you now.'

With Cyril leading the way, they all marched into Mr Brenton's office.

Sixty-year-old Maurice Brenton was sitting behind his large mahogany desk, as smartly suited as always but stern-faced today. By his side was his sixteen-year-old son, Julian, a slight, blond, pasty-faced youth who nevertheless retained a strong sense of his own importance. He had started work that very morning after his father had finally realised that the money he was paying out on an expensive private school was money down the drain. Surrounded by an entourage as he was, Gil could not see that Maurice and his son were not the only ones waiting in the room.

As soon as the door was shut by the departing Miss Harris, Maurice addressed Cyril. 'Your men can return to their work stations now that Mr Morton has been safely delivered.'

Gil frowned, confused. Safely delivered? Just what did Brenton mean by that terminology?

While Cyril addressed his men, Maurice turned to his son. 'You can leave too, Julian. Wait outside with Miss Harris while I deal with this matter.'

The look on the boy's face said that he was not going to be dismissed so easily. In a whining voice he protested, 'But, Father, how am I supposed to learn how to run this place once you retire if you don't show me first-hand how to conduct myself in serious situations?'

Gil's concern mounted. What was so serious about this meeting? What hadn't he been told as yet?

Maurice Brenton conceded that his son had a point. 'All right, you can stay.'

As Cyril's entourage trooped out of the office Gil finally noticed there was someone else in the room. Perched on a chair before Maurice's desk sat Miriam Jones, one of the four clerk typists from the general office. She looked wretched. Her head was bent low and she was wringing a wet handkerchief between her hands and visibly shaking.

Obviously the serious situation involved Miriam Jones. Gil wondered what she had done that was bad enough to warrant her being brought before the owner, works manager and union representative. She had been acting as his own clerical assistant for the past six months, taken on by the firm to replace Sally Little who had left to have a baby. Gil was usually too busy dealing with the pressures of his own job to engage in social chit-chat so he did not know much about Miriam on a personal level. She was in her mid-thirties, he guessed, reasonably attractive, shapely and blonde. Most importantly, she did her work efficiently and that was what mattered most to Gil.

He looked at Maurice Brenton expectantly.

Maurice cleared his throat and fixed Gil with his eyes. 'I'll come straight to the point, Gil. Mrs Jones claims she was molested this morning.'

He was stunned by this revelation. 'Molested! And obviously by someone who works here. This is serious, very serious indeed. Have you questioned the man to get his side of the story yet, Mr Brenton?'

Maurice looked uncomfortable. 'That's what you're here for, Gil. You see, Mrs Jones claims it was you who did it.'

The ground seemed to give way beneath Gil. His jaw dropped as he exclaimed, 'What!'

The woman in question looked up at him and cried, 'You did molest me, Mr Morton. You know you did!'

He was reeling in total shock before such a serious allegation. 'But . . . but I did no such thing, Mrs Jones.'

'Well, if putting yer hands on my private parts ain't molesting me then what is it called then?' she shouted, and threw him a look of pure disgust. 'You come across as such a nice man when in truth you're nothing but a filthy . . .'

'That's enough, Mrs Jones,' commanded Maurice. He then addressed Gil. 'Mrs Jones approached Cyril for his advice on this matter. In his shop steward's capacity he brought it straight to me.

You must appreciate that we have to get to the bottom of this, Gil?'

'Yes, indeed, Mr Brenton,' he confirmed.

Maurice Brenton cleared his throat. 'Now, Mrs Jones has told me that she went across to your office as usual this morning to see what you needed doing. She had just begun to do the filing, apparently, when she realised you were standing beside her. She was about to ask you what you wanted when the next thing she knew you . . .' he paused for a moment before adding uncomfortably '. . . had one hand on her . . . er . . . bosom and the other on her . . . er . . . bottom, squeezing it. She was so shocked by such unwarranted attentions that she pushed you aside and ran out screaming. One of the other women found her in the lavatory, very distressed, and eventually got her to calm down enough to explain what had happened. It was she who advised Mrs Jones to seek union advice.'

Gil's face was ashen by now. 'I agree that Mrs Jones did run out of my office screaming this morning, but it certainly wasn't due to anything I had done. I was shocked, I'll admit, but I put it down to her having seen a mouse. It's happened before after all. I was so busy calculating figures for that urgent tender to the Ministry of Defence, I wasn't aware what was happening. I was meaning to call the maintenance department to come and put down a couple of traps but just haven't got round to it yet . . .'

He looked askance at his accuser then. 'I was sitting at my desk the whole time you were in my office this morning, never got up once, so how can you say I behaved like that? Why are you lying, Mrs Jones? What do you hope to gain by accusing me like this?'

'I'm not lying!' she shouted back at him, then turned her eyes to Maurice Brenton beseechingly. 'You have to believe me, Mr Brenton. Mr Morton did behave in that way to me.'

'And I'm saying this woman is lying,' said Gil with quiet conviction. 'I have never laid a finger on her in an intimate way. Absolutely not.'

Maurice gave a heavy sigh. 'Oh, what a mess.' He looked

thoughtful for a moment before he returned his attention to Miriam Jones. 'I can't find any reason to doubt you, Mrs Jones, but I can't bring myself to believe that my works manager is capable of such a thing either. He's a happily married man and has always shown a great natural respect for women, at work and in a social context. I can only presume that this has resulted from some sort of misunderstanding on your part. Mr Morton's office isn't that large. Maybe as he was moving past you to get something out of another filing cabinet, he accidentally came into contact with you.

'The only solution to this impasse I can suggest is that someone else from the general office is assigned to do Mr Morton's clerical work from now on. There need be no future one-to-one contact between you both. Now, let's all put this matter behind us, shall we, and get back to work?'

Cyril Breville spoke up then. 'I'm not at all happy with the solution you propose, Mr Brenton, he said officiously. 'You could just be putting another woman at risk. How do we know Mr Morton hasn't done this before but it hasn't been reported because the women are too scared? When the workforce get wind of this, they'll come down on the side of Mrs Jones. I mean, why should she make such an accusation for no reason? I'm sure I don't need to tell you what they'll be expecting, Mr Brenton. I can promise you my men will take action until you treat this accusation with the seriousness it deserves.'

Gil froze as his world crumbled around him. At Breville's instigation the men would down tools and not pick them up again until the works manager no longer posed a threat to the women who worked here.

'I don't see that you have any other option but to let Mr Morton go, Father,' piped up Julian Brenton. 'This wouldn't do the company's name any good if the newspapers got hold of it and you are seen to be taking the side of a sexual predator.'

His father shot him a thunderous glance. 'Shut up, Julian! You're here to observe only.'

'Young Mr Brenton is right,' said Cyril Breville unctuously.

'Unless Mr Morton can disprove Mrs Jones's claim you'll need to ask him to go – unless you want a long drawn out strike?'

Gil caught sight of the satisified smirk that played over Julian's lips when the shop steward sided with him. He was a daft lad, seeing all this as a bit of fun, something to giggle over later with his mates. Gil felt deeply hurt by such a juvenile attitude after all the times he himself had gone out of his way to help the boy, not informing Maurice Brenton of the numerous times he had caught his son up to no good in the factory. Some of those escapades could have resulted in serious harm, not only to Julian himself but to the friends with him at the time, had Gil not been such a vigilant works manager.

He became aware that eyes in the room were on him, awaiting his response, and a feeling of utter doom descended on him. He knew he had no other defence but his own word, which he could only hope was accepted. With his back ramrod-straight and eyes unblinking, he said, 'I can only reiterate to you all that I'm not guilty of what Mrs Jones accused me of. I did not do it.'

Maurice pushed back his chair and walked across to the window, staring out over the factory yard below. He stood there for several long moments, deep in thought, before he turned back to address them all. 'I want to speak to Mr Morton alone. The rest of you, please wait outside.'

As soon as they had departed his grave-faced boss told Gil, 'I believe you, I want you to know that. I've never had any reason to doubt your integrity, and the last thing I want is to lose you as my works manager. You've done an exemplary job for me, and you'll be a very hard man to replace. You do see, though, that my hands are tied? I have no choice but to let you go.'

Gil couldn't believe that after all his years of loyal service, Maurice Brenton was not going to stand up for him. The threat of industrial action was the clincher, though, because that would hit Brenton where it hurt most: in the pocket. It seemed it didn't matter how good a job was done, how much loyalty was shown by any individual, when it came down to it, to Maurice Brenton any worker was just a commodity and one that could be easily replaced.

Fixing his former boss with a clear-eyed gaze, Gil said, 'I'll clear my desk and be off the premises as quick as I can, sir.'

CHAPTER TWO

Several streets away, in the kitchen of her neatly maintained three-bedroomed palisade terrace house, Gil's wife Alexandra was in the middle of a confrontation of her own.

Arms folded tightly across her flat chest, her sharp-featured face screwed up in fury, Doreen Green was aggressively shouting at her: 'You'd no business advising my daughter to stand firm against me and her father over that ... that ... brainless individual she's seeing! Thanks to your so-called good advice, she's given me and my husband an ultimatum: either we make an effort to get to know him, or she'll leave home to set up with him and never speak to us again. So in future I'd appreciate you keeping your advice to yourself.'

Before Lex could respond, the back door flew open and another woman burst in. 'Good Lord, what on earth is going on, Lex? I could hear shouting as soon as I entered the back gate.'

Before Lex could respond, Doreen Green had spun to face the new arrival. 'I was just telling Mrs Morton to keep her nose out of my family's affairs in future. I'm quite capable of sorting out any problems we might have without her bad advice making matters worse!'

'Now you look here ...' the newcomer began.

'Thelma, please, let me handle this,' Lex interjected. 'Mrs Green, if you'll just let me explain ...'

'I've heard enough of your words coming from the mouth of my own daughter! Now *I'm* going to give *you* some good advice: stick your nose in again when it comes to her ... or my other two daughters for that matter ... and you'll wish you hadn't. I hope I've made myself clear?'

'You've made yourself *very* clear,' erupted Thelma Reader, a mousey-haired, homely-looking woman of medium height, her once youthful figure thickened after bearing four children. She was incensed on Lex's behalf. 'Now you listen here, lady. My friend would never intervene in anyone's private affairs unless she was personally invited or felt it right to do so. She obviously felt it right in these circumstances. Now she's done you the courtesy of hearing you out, the least you can do is give her the courtesy of listening to her side of the story.' It was apparent to Thelma, though, that the uninvited visitor was in no mood to sit and listen to anything, and was about to take her leave. So Thelma slammed the back door shut, turned the key and put it in her pocket. 'You ain't leaving until you've heard Lex out, so you might as well sit down and make yourself comfy.'

The two women glared at each other. Doreen Green saw that Thelma wasn't going to budge, however, and short of barging her way through to the front of the house, she was trapped. Grabbing a chair, she sat down on it. 'Say your piece and I can get out of here,' she snarled.

Lex sat down opposite her and took a deep breath. 'Mrs Green, I know we're only on nodding terms but last night I came across your daughter Gillian sobbing her heart out on the Simmons' garden wall. Her boyfriend was with her and he looked most upset too. I did what any woman would in the circumstances and stopped to ask them if they needed any help. I assumed by your daughter's state she'd suffered an accident or something.

'Then it all came out: how her parents flatly refused to accept the young man she was with as her future intended. She said she'd finally managed to get you to invite him round for tea, but he never got over the doorstep. You sent him away with a flea in his ear, without so much as attempting to get to know him. By the time I came across her she was so worn down by all the constant arguing that . . .'

'That specimen she's landed herself with was persuading her it'd be best she turn her back on us and set up home with him, I assume?' Doreen Green interjected knowingly. She pulled a digusted face. 'I saw what he was all about as soon as I clapped eyes on him so I refused to have him in my house. I bet he couldn't believe his luck when he met my daughter, knew he'd never get anyone better and was determined to hang on to her at any cost. Well, he'd reckoned without her parents. He's obviously as thick as two short planks. He was stuttering and stammering all over the place, couldn't string a single coherent sentence together. My daughter told me he had a responsible job with Leicester Council – good prospects an' all. She obviously exaggerated about *that*. I doubt he's got anything more responsible than road sweeping to do, the way he came across.

'Gillian obviously fell for his looks and became so besotted with him that she can't see him for the blithering idiot he really is. All she can expect married to him is living in some hovel, hardly able to feed and clothe the children they produce, while deeply regretting her parents never intervened and put a stop to the relationship before it was too late.' She made to get up. 'This is all a waste of my time. I came to say what I have, and I hope you took note. Now I'm ...'

'You're not going anywhere,' Thelma commanded. 'I meant what I said, you ain't leaving here until you've heard Lex out. Or do I need to tie you to that chair?'

Doreen Green stared at her thunderstruck for a moment before she settled back into her chair and demanded of Lex, 'Well, get on with it then. You might not be, but I'm a busy woman.'

Lex flashed a grateful look at Thelma, standing guard by the back door, before she continued, 'You've got it all wrong, Mrs Green. Terry ... with due respect to him let's give the lad his proper name ... was being very reasonable. When Gillian insisted she was leaving home to set up with him, it was he who told her he'd rather they finished the relationship than that it caused a rift with her family. He said he'd wait for her and they could take up again when she was old enough at twenty-one to make up her own mind about marrying without parental consent.'

'Gillian wouldn't hear of it. She said she couldn't bear to be parted from him for two years. She was going to pack up her stuff when you were all asleep that night and go to live in a hostel until they could get a place of their own.

'Mrs Green, I really do feel you're in the process of making the biggest mistake of your life by asking your daughter to choose between her family and her boyfriend. I believe you formed totally the wrong impression of Terry when you first set eyes on him. You didn't exactly meet him in normal circumstances, did you? Did it ever strike you that the reason he was stuttering and coming across like a blithering idiot was simply because he was nervous, given the importance of the meeting?'

The woman's jaw dropped. 'Er ... no, it didn't.'

'Well, he was, Mrs Green. Terry told me he was so desperate to make a good impression on you, he just fell apart as soon as you opened the door. He feels terribly guilty that he's the cause of all this trouble between you and your daughter. And Gillian didn't exaggerate about his job. He's a clerk in the Town Planning department, and studying at night for qualifications to help his case for promotion when the time comes.

'Mrs Green, I'm sure that if you'd just relent and agree to meet him again, and make proper allowances this time for his nerves, then you would see for yourself he's really a very intelligent young man who deserves the chance to prove he could be a suitable husband for Gillian.'

Doreen Green gawped at her, totally stunned. 'Oh! It never crossed my mind that his nerves were getting the better of him when I first clapped eyes on him.'

Lex smiled kindly at her. 'That's what I thought. And why I persuaded Gillian to try her best to get you and your husband to agree to meet Terry properly, so you could see for yourself that your first impressions were totally wrong. I interfered, I admit it, but I hope you can see that it was with the best of intentions? Family rifts can be so hard to heal, and they usually start from some silly misunderstanding.'

Doreen Green looked mortified. 'What an idiot I've been! I feel so stupid now. From what Gillian had told me and her father about ... Terry ... I was expecting a confident young man to greet me. When I opened the door to a bumbling buffoon, I couldn't see the point in introducing him to the rest of the family, because as far as I was concerned he wasn't ever going to join it.'

She looked apologetically at Lex. 'I'm so sorry I jumped to the wrong conclusion about your well-meant advice to Gillian. I thought you were just an interfering busybody, couldn't understand how a woman with a morsel of integrity could incite a young girl to defy her own parents. How wrong I was! I'm still not sure Terry's the right one for Gillian but I'm willing to give him another chance, and I'll make sure my husband does too. And we will make allowances for his nerves next time.'

Lex looked relieved. 'I'm very glad to hear that. Gillian and Terry are right for each other, though, Mrs Green. I'm confident of that.'

'You can't possibly know from the short time you were with them both,' Doreen Green challenged her.

'Lex can,' piped up Thelma. 'It's a knack she's got. Her mother was the same, God rest her soul. She was a great matchmaker. She knew Gil, Lex's husband, was the right one for her before Lex even met him. Isn't that right?'

Lex smiled and nodded. 'He worked alongside my dad at the factory,' she informed Doreen. 'Gil was his apprentice. My mother took one look at him when she'd gone to meet Dad out of the factory one night, took my father aside and told him this was the one for their daughter. She invited Gil for tea the following Sunday. Of course, if I'd known then my mother was matchmaking, I'd have been mortified and more than likely gone out before he was due to arrive. Clever Mum knew that, though, and only told me a friend of Dad's was coming for tea when I queried how many places she'd asked me to set at the table.'

Lex's eyes turned faraway and she smiled as a vision of that tall, handsome young man she'd unexpectedly found on the doorstep that fateful evening flashed before her. She remembered how stupid she had felt when she'd realised she was gawping wide-eyed up him, unable to find her voice, painfully conscious she was looking far from her best in a pair of old slacks and a baggy hand-knitted jumper, her unwashed hair hanging loose and her face devoid of make-up. Why hadn't her mum warned her?

But she quickly forgot any annoyance she'd felt when Gil came inside and they immediately fell into an easy conversation that lasted throughout the meal. When she saw him to the door much later there was no awkwardness between them and he asked her out on a date. Lex readily accepted as she had been secretly hoping for this. Gil told her later that as soon as he'd clapped eyes on her at the door that night he'd been smitten, knowing instantly that she was the one for him. Lex agreed it had been just the same for her.

'We've been happily married for twenty-five years now,' she told Doreen. 'And every anniversary Gil and I raise a glass to my mother for bringing us together.'

Thelma chipped in, 'I've lost count of the number of times Lex has made a prophecy about people we both know who've started new relationships. Nine times out of ten she's right. There was the time my son Graham started courting a girl called Rosalyn. Such a pretty outgoing young woman. Just my Graham's sort, I thought. I was planning the wedding the minute he brought her home, but Lex told me not to buy my hat just yet as Rosalyn was just a bit of fun for him and she couldn't see it lasting that long.

'I was adamant it was Lex that was wrong for once and that she'd eat her words at their wedding. Well, it turned out it was me who had egg on my face. Just over a year later, out of the blue and for no apparent reason, Graham finished with Rosalyn to take up with a quiet little thing called Maureen and as soon as he did, Lex told me I could buy that hat now. I scoffed, didn't I, Lex? It was my opinion Maureen was much too timid for my Jack-the-lad son and nowhere near as good-looking as the women he usually took up with. But Lex was right, as usual. Maureen proved to be a calming influence on him. They were engaged and married inside a year and now they're as happy as Larry together.' She beamed broadly. 'In fact, I learned last week I'm to become a granny in seven months' time.'

'Oh, then I congratulate you,' said Doreen sincerely. She looked at Lex enquiringly. 'Have you children, Mrs Morton?'

Lex answered her proudly. 'Two boys. Martin is twenty-three, Matthew just turned twenty-one.'

Doreen said, tongue-in-cheek, 'Then I pity your sons as far as women are concerned, with a fortune-teller like you breathing down their necks!'

Lex pressed her lips together. A couple of years back she had learned to her cost, not to interfere in her sons' relationships. Having seen their taste in girls – the showy sort who lived to dress up and be shown a good time – she'd found herself dreading to think how their lives would pan out if they tried to settle down with women like that.

Lex felt it was her duty, her purpose in life, to open her sons' eyes to the kind of women she felt they should be looking at as potential wives. She went about seeking two women who fitted her bill and found them in her dentist's nurse and the daughter of a friend at the W.I. Lex invited them both to tea one Sunday, telling Gil and her sons her guests were considering joining the W.I. and she was showing them how friendly the members were. Her hope was that in a congenial setting her sons would see for themselves that such steady, sensible young women were infinitely preferable to their usual girlfriends.

Everything went swimmingly at first. The spread she had laid on of cold ham and tongue, crisp salad, bread and butter, tinned fruit and evaporated milk, was being enjoyed by all and conversation between her sons and the guests was flowing amicably . . . until it came to clearing the table. Accepting her sons' offer of help while Gil entertained their guests in the lounge, Lex made the huge blunder of asking her offspring what they thought of their guests as opposed to the women they usually mixed with.

Martin immediately looked at her knowingly and shot back, 'Oh, so that's your game, is it, Mother? These two aren't really candidates for the Women's Institute at all, but potential wives for me and Matt.'

Gawping at them both, she blurted out, 'No, sons, that's not it at all. I was just . . .'

But Matt did not let her finish. In hushed tones, so that there was no fear of the women in the lounge overhearing, he snapped, 'Just because our gran chose Dad for you doesn't mean we'd allow our parents to choose wives for us. We're capable of finding our own. Other people might be happy with you playing matchmaker for them, but I'm not. I'm my own man.'

'And so am I, Mam,' growled Martin. 'As a matter of interest, do those women in there have any idea this get together is a put up job?'

'No, they don't . . . because it isn't! Look, by inviting them here, all I was hoping to do was open your eyes . . .'

Again she wasn't allowed to finish. Grabbing his coat off the back of the door, Martin announced, 'I've just remembered, I've got an arrangement with a friend. Pass on my apologies for my absence to our guests, won't you, Mam?'

Matt then took his coat off the back door. 'And mine too.'

Lex had been really annoyed with herself as she watched them depart. If she hadn't opened her mouth . . . All she could hope for now was that her sons did eventually see the light before it was too late and they tied themselves for life to unsuitable partners.

Doreen was addressing Thelma while Lex wool-gathered. 'I trust you'll let me out now I've done what you asked me to?'

Thelma grinned. 'Be glad to.'

'Phew, that was a close call!' Lex said to her friend as she shut the back door after seeing Doreen out.

Thelma looked shocked. 'Do you think Mrs Green would have physically attacked you then if I hadn't shown up? If that's the case, thank God I did.'

'No, I don't think she'd have resorted to violence, however mad she was with me. She's not the violent sort. No, I mean she came close to heading down the road to heartache there, if you hadn't forced her to listen to my side of the story before she left.' Lex smiled warmly at her friend. 'Thanks for making her do that.'

'Well, there was no way I was going to stand by and let her

call you black and blue when I knew you'd never have spoken up without a damn good reason.' Thelma flashed a look at the clock then. 'Goodness, is that the time?' She pulled a disgruntled face. 'My brief chance to have a cuppa and a chat with you has been spent putting Mrs Green straight. I've promised to go into work early today to cover for one of the gels who's a funeral to attend.'

She heaved a sigh. 'Pity I didn't know you or your mother when I first met my Des. Then I could have asked if either of you could see him making a fortune from fixing broken generators. Then, when you said, no, I'd never live a life of leisure but end up slaving four hours every afternoon and Saturday mornings behind the counter of the local barber's, maybe I'd have thought twice about marrying him!'

Lex gave a disdainful tut. 'My mother wasn't a clairvoyant and neither am I, Thelma, so neither of us could have predicted how much money Des would earn. Besides, even if we had been able to, you'd still have married him regardless. You two were meant for each other, and you know it.'

Thelma grinned. 'Yer right, I wouldn't swap him for the world. My Des is a good man.'

So is my Gil, thought Lex. Good in every way. He had never once during their years of marriage given her cause for concern, not like some men gave their wives: sleepless nights over their womanising ways, or money worries through their penchant for drink or gambling. Nor had she ever had reason to doubt his honesty and trustworthiness. He'd proved a good role model for their two sons who both respected and looked up to him, and in turn they were proving to be as steady as their father was, apart from in their dubious taste in women. Lex looked meaningfully at Thelma. 'Do I need to remind you that you encouraged Des to start up on his own when he discussed it with you? He was fed up working all hours for Brenton's and felt he could make just as much working for himself. It was you who offered to work part-time to help out while he secured enough regular work to meet the bills. Well, he managed that a couple of years back but

19

you've kept on your job since because the money you make helps pay for luxuries such as holidays.'

Thelma gave a shrug. 'Yeah, okay, you've made your point.' She headed for the back door then turned to face Lex. 'We still on for Saturday night?'

'Yes, about seven. I'm doing a casserole for supper before we settle down to play cards.'

Thelma licked her lips. 'We'll be here prompt then, bellies empty. We'll bring the booze. Oh, and Des said to tell Gil to be prepared for a thrashing this time.'

Lex laughed to herself as her friend closed the door behind her. Des was not the card shark he thought himself to be. Lex could read him by the little gleam that sparkled in his eye the instant he suspected he had been dealt a winning hand. Des might be excellent at keeping a poker face, but that gleam that others didn't appear to notice gave him away every time to Lex. But when she detected this spark, especially after Des had suffered a run of losses, fair-minded Lex, even with a potential winning hand herself, would purposely play badly to give him a chance of winning. If Gil suspected she did this, he'd never commented. He was as fair-minded as his wife and, after all, their games were only friendly, played for matchsticks.

Every Saturday night the two couples enjoyed supper and friendly games of cards over glasses of beer for the men, sherry or port for the women. And these were not the only social events the couples shared. From time to time they'd abandon their Saturday night supper and cards for a visit to the local or to Brenton's social club when a good act was on. And as their money worries had eased, the two couples also started to share holidays together in boarding houses on the east coast. As they hadn't as yet got around to discussing which coastal town they would go to this year, Lex thought that maybe that was something they could do while they were all together on Saturday night.

She considered herself very fortunate to have a such a friend as Thelma. They'd first met in 1940 while queuing together at the local Co-op for their provisions, worried about the time it was taking as both had young babies outside in prams and wanted to get back to them. As their conversation had progressed they had been surprised to discover that both the husbands they worried about, fighting abroad for their country, had worked for Brenton Engineering before joining up so could possibly be acquainted with each other.

Lex had taken an instant liking to plump, pleasant-faced Thelma and immediately made up her mind to ask her back to the house for a cup of tea, hoping she would have time. Much to her delight, Thelma said she did. At the time Lex had plenty of friends but was happy to welcome another into the fold. As the pair had become better and better acquainted, they discovered they had so much in common that soon they were each other's best friend. The truth was they'd just clicked.

When Gil received his well-deserved promotion to works manager along with a substantial enough pay rise to enable the Mortons to buy a home of their own five years ago, Thelma could have become envious of Lex and jealous that it wasn't her life that was taking a turn for the better. But instead her joy for her was genuine and, not that she had ever doubted it before, this reaction proved to Lex what a good and true friend she had found that day while waiting for her turn to be served in the Co-op.

After Thelma's departure, Lex had just started to busy herself with her chores when to her surprise her eldest son came crashing through the back door. The sudden shock of his unexpected arrival had her exclaiming, 'Martin, for goodness' sake, you nearly gave me a heart attack. What are you doing home?' Then, looking at him searchingly, she added, 'Are you ill?'

'No, Mam, only I forgot to take my football kit with me to work this morning and I've got practice straight after work. We've got a league match on Sunday morning against the team from Anstey, and if we don't win this we're positioned bottom in the Sunday League table.' He pulled a disparaging face and grumbled, 'It's our goalie's fault. He can't seem to understand that his function is to stop the balls going in, not the other way around. He's utterly hopeless.'

'Can't you get another one then?'

'If only we could. Sunday morning, most lads like to lie in after a heavy Saturday night so we've no choice but to stick with Roger.'

Lex looked at him enquiringly. 'But why come home now when you could have collected your kit when you came back for your dinner at one?'

'Oh, because I forgot to tell you this morning, I won't be coming home for dinner today.'

She gave an annoyed tut. 'Well, I wish you had. I've prepared a meat pie big enough for the four of us.' Then her face softened. 'I'll put yours aside to heat up after your football practice tonight, and I'll do you some chips to go with it.'

'Better do that for our Matt too 'cos on the way to work he told me he forgot to tell you but *he* isn't coming home this dinner-time either.' Then Martin looked excited. 'After we've grabbed something from the canteen, Jimmy Paterson is giving me and Matt a ride in the Sunbeam Mark 3 Rally he's just finished doing up. You should see it, Mam! It's fantastic considering it was almost a wreck when he bought it off the scrappy last year. We all thought he was mad at the time, throwing his money down the drain, but he's proved us all wrong.'

Lex looked worried. 'Make sure Jimmy doesn't drive too fast when you and Matt are in his car.'

Martin laughed. 'Don't worry, you can't get much speed up around the streets by the factory.' Then he added mischievously, 'But it'll be a different matter when we take it down the disused airfield in Leicester Forest East one night . . . I won't tell you about that until afterwards. So, where's my footy kit?'

Despite her annoyance at him for his laxness, Lex looked fondly at her tall, handsome, eldest son, at twenty-three the image of his father at that age. 'Where you usually find it – clean and pressed in your chest-of-drawers. Er . . . as a matter of interest, just how did you get permission from your foreman to come home for it in the middle of your shift?'

'I didn't.'

She gawped at him. 'You just walked out? Oh, Martin, you

shouldn't use your father's position with the firm to come and go as you please. You know he won't take into account the fact you're his son if it comes down to you being disciplined for misconduct.'

'Stop fussing, Mam. I won't be missed for the few minutes it's taken me to run here and back.'

'Of course you'll be missed. Who's operating your machine?'

'No one. As far as anyone's concerned, I've gone for an extra long trip to the lavvy.'

'Toilet,' she corrected him. 'But what if you're missed and ...'

Martin cut her short by grabbing her to him and giving her a hug. 'Mam, stop whittling, will you? My foreman won't miss me because just before I legged it back here, I saw him with Dad and a few of the other men, heading off towards the old man's office.'

'Old man's office? Oh, you mean Mr Brenton's office.' Lex was frowning and bothered as she pulled herself from his embrace. 'Your foreman is the shop steward, isn't he? And you said there were a few other men with them too?' She eyed him in concern. 'Oh, dear, trouble, do you think?'

Martin gave a nonchalant shrug. 'Dunno. Dad did look kind of ... well ... angry but puzzled, if that makes sense, and Breville looked full of his own importance as usual so something's afoot. All I could think of was that with them both out of the way, I could fetch my kit, save me missing any of my dinner break. Anyway, best do what I came for and get back.'

She watched as Martin headed for the stairs, listened to him thunder up and down again, reappearing in the kitchen with the football kit she had so carefully ironed, screwed up under his arm, boots dangling by their knotted laces around his neck, stopping just long enough to give her a quick affectionate peck on the cheek before charging out of the back door.

Lex closed it after him, hoping that he did indeed manage to return to his work station before he was missed as she didn't like to think of the possible consequences should he not.

CHAPTER THREE

Agood while later Lex looked at the clock and frowned. Gil was always home prompt for his dinner at nine minutes past one. It was now quarter past. If her husband wasn't going to manage to get back due to an incident at work, he never failed to telephone and let her know. Then she heard the noise of the back gate opening. Here he was at last! She rose to fetch the plates of food keeping warm in the oven but was stopped short by the sound of the back door bursting open and her two sons charging in. They had obviously been running hard as both of them were panting heavily, and both had obviously changed their mind about not coming home for their dinner.

Before she could tell them that she hadn't done enough vegetables or potatoes to go with the pie, but would eke out what she had done between them all as best she could, Martin blurted, 'Has Dad been home yet, Mam?'

She shook her head. 'He always telephones me to say he isn't coming, and as he hasn't he can't be far behind you. His car was playing up when he went off to work this morning, something to do with the battery, he said, so maybe he's having trouble starting it. I thought it was him when I heard the gate just now.' Then it registered with her that both her sons looked deeply worried. Much to her surprise, before she could question them as to why, they turned abruptly and ran out again.

She stared after them. They were both behaving very strangely. Then a possible reason for this struck her. Martin must have been caught this morning, leaving his machine without permission when he'd dashed home for his forgotten football kit, and obviously his

25

foreman Cyril Breville had not been pleased and was going to bring him before his father for disciplinary action. Had Martin been hoping Gil hadn't heard about his misdemeanour yet, and come home to beg for leniency when it was brought to his attention? Well, he should know by now he'd be wasting his time with any such request. Their father had left them both in no doubt when they'd started at Brenton's that they would be treated the same as any other worker. Regardless, the boys had obviously gone to waylay him and plead Martin's case, but why they couldn't have waited for him to arrive home first she couldn't fathom.

A while later Phyllis Watson said gratefully to Lex, 'It really is good of you to get my shopping in and do a few chores around the house for me.'

Lex, in the process of putting the said shopping away in the pantry, turned and smiled at her neighbour who was leaning on a pair of crutches, having broken her wrist and ankle four weeks previously. She'd fallen over a child's trike that she hadn't seen in her way as she'd been coming back from the shops laden down with heavy bags.

'It's my pleasure, Phyllis. It was no trouble picking up your few bits along with my own. Once I've done this, I'll get cracking on that washing for you.'

Phyllis looked a bit bemused. 'You brought my washing up to date for me yesterday afternoon, Alexandra. It was my hair I asked if you'd be good enough to wash, if you'd time.'

An embarrassed look filled Lex's face. 'Oh, I'm sorry, I knew it was something you wanted washing. I'll be right with you when I've finished this.'

Then Phyllis noticed her friend was putting a packet of Mirro scouring powder on the shelf with her food items, not under the sink where she kept her cleaning materials, and looked at her quizzically. 'Er . . . I have to say you seem a little preoccupied today, Alexandra. Is everything all right?'

Then Lex noticed what she was doing and understood the reason for Phyllis' question.

'Oh, goodness, how silly of me!' She heaved a sigh. 'I have to admit, my mind isn't completely on what I'm doing. It's just that Gil didn't turn up for his dinner today, and it's not like him not to telephone and let me know. Martin did tell me that he saw his father, the shop steward, and a few other men all heading towards the boss's office this morning. I'm just praying the workers aren't up in arms about something that could result in strike action. It's always the women I feel for, it's them that have to manage when their men's pay packets are short. All you seem to read about in the newspaper these days is strikes around the country, and usually they're over such paltry things. Plus I fear one of my boys has got himself into a spot of bother at work. I'm just hoping he can talk his way out of what he did and not end up sacked for it, Phyllis.'

'Before I was married I worked for Corah's as a machinist and I know there could be any number of reasons why Gilbert and the rest of those men were heading for the boss's office, Alexandra,' Phyllis told her. 'It might not be due to any problem at the works at all. Maybe the boss called a meeting with them to tell them of a big order they've just landed, how to work it in with all the other orders they have on their books, and it's overrun into the dinner hour.'

Phyllis abhorred the shortening of Christian names and insisted on addressing her friend as Alexandra. Lex had no problem with this. But despite her having several times corrected Phyllis when they had first become acquainted, telling her that Gil's name was not a shortened version of Gilbert but was in fact his name in full, Phyllis could not seem to take this on board. Ironically Gilbert *was* supposed to have been Gil's name, in honour of his paternal grandfather, but when his own father had gone to register the birth he was so drunk with elation at the arrival of what was to be his only child, as well as all the congratulatory drinks he had received from well-wishers en route in all the public houses he had called in, that he could only get out the 'Gil' part of the name to the Registrar.

'Oh, I do hope Gil and the others were called into the boss's office for a good reason like that and not what I fear, Phyllis. But I don't understand why he wouldn't have called me, to tell me he couldn't manage to come, home.'

'There could be any number of reasons why he hasn't, Alexandra. Have you checked that your telephone is working, for instance? Maybe your line is faulty and Gilbert couldn't get through. Or maybe the firm's lines have all gone faulty and they're waiting for the engineers to come and fix them?'

'I never thought of that either, Phyllis. Yes, maybe that's why I haven't heard from him. I'll check the telephone when I get back.'

'And as for your son who's in bother, dear, well, you worrying about that won't make any difference to the outcome, will it? If that lad of yours is in trouble, the damage has already been done and he'll just have to face the consequences.'

Smiling at Phyllis, Lex said, 'You're right. And hopefully it'll teach him a lesson about not taking such risks in future. Trouble is, however old your children are, to you they're still your babies and you automatically want to fight their battles for them, don't you?'

'Mmm,' mused Phyllis. 'Like I want to grab hold of a lovely young woman for my Derek and tell her what a good husband he'll make for her, and to get her claws into him fast. I fear he'll never meet the right woman to settle down with. He just doesn't seem interested in going out and finding one. At least you've not that fear with your two lads, Alexandra. Out most nights, aren't they, off to some place or other socialising, and every time I see them out it's never with the same girl more than twice.

'My Derek seems quite happy to spend most of his evenings at home watching the telly with me and his dad, or upstairs in his room playing his records, reading or building them bloomin' Airfix kits he loves doing. Getting my daughters off my hands wasn't such a problem! Always a string of lads calling for them as soon as they were of age, but no sign of any women calling for my son. He's twenty-four, I can't understand why he's not out sowing his wild oats. I'm fed up with thinking of ways to try and persuade him down the pub or off dancing, putting himself about so to speak.'

Lex shook her head. 'I wish you knew how worried I am about the type of girls my sons seem to run after, not the sort at all I'd like to see them looking towards settling with. Not that me or their father have ever actually been introduced to any of them, but from what I've observed when I've caught a glimpse of them, I doubt any of them know what a cooker is, let alone know how to use it. It seems to me my sons are far too concerned about good looks and fashion sense to be bothered about whether their girlfriends are capable of holding an interesting conversation or have the necessary skills to make a good wife. Still, mustn't interfere. I tried to once and it didn't go down well.'

She looked at Phyllis meaningfully. 'Have you thought that maybe Derek isn't into sowing wild oats, but would prefer to sow his oat only with the right woman, when he meets her?'

Her friend looked taken aback. 'Eh?'

'What I mean, Phyllis, is I've never thought of your Derek as the philandering sort. He's a very thoughtful, considerate young man. Maybe he just can't be bothered with all the hassle and wasted money involved with taking out a string of girls, just to see if one of them might turn into the one for him, and would prefer to spend his time at home until he meets the right one. You don't just meet people down the pub or dancing, you know. You can meet them in everyday life, too. He could just as well meet the love of his life going about his daily business as a plumber. You never know, one day a woman may appear out of the blue and that will be that for him.'

Phyllis was looking flabbergasted. 'Oh, I never thought of it that way. Yes, my lad is the sensitive type, and now I think about it he is the sort to wait for things to come to him sooner than go looking for them himself. Thanks for making me see things in a different light, Alexandra.'

She smiled. 'Seems we've both helped each other today, to look at things from a different perspective.'

Having finished off her task of putting away Phyllis' shopping and spending a pleasant hour washing and setting her incapacitated neighbour's hair, leaving her with a promise to drop in the next afternoon to lend a hand where needed, Lex set off back home.

She was just about to turn down the entry splitting the Mortons' house from the one next door when she stopped and smiled a greeting to the young woman approaching her. Justine Baker was the twenty-year-old granddaughter of elderly neighbours several doors down from the Mortons, who came to visit them every Tuesday afternoon straight from Charles Keene College where she was studying to be a shorthand secretary. She was only months away from qualifying, and according to her proud grandmother doing extremely well, on course for a top grade.

Justine was of medium height, her curvy frame dressed typical student fashion in a pair of fitted black slacks and a long hand-knitted black jumper under her shabby-looking navy duffel coat. She wore her thick long dark hair scraped back in a ponytail. She couldn't be classed as pretty but had what Lex would describe as an 'interesting' face. As she came up to Lex it was very evident the young woman was excited about something. Lex couldn't help but ask, 'Have you won the pools, Justine? You look fit to burst?'

A delighted beam split her face. 'As good as to me, Mrs Morton. The college have told me they're so impressed they want me to consider a post with them when I qualify, as under-secretary to the secretary of the Principal. Of course, I'm thrilled to accept. My mum and dad are so chuffed, and so will Gran and Grandpops be when I tell them.'

'Oh, many congratulations, Justine. I'm so pleased for you. Give your grandparents my regards won't you?'

'I will, Mrs Morton. Gran's rheumatics are causing her bother just now so I'm going to do her shopping for her then cook them a casserole for their supper. Mam's given me the recipe so there's no danger I'll poison them,' she added, laughing. Then she paused for a moment before she asked Lex in a casual manner, 'How . . . er . . . is Martin, Mrs Morton?' Then added hurriedly, 'Matthew too, and of course yourself and Mr Morton?'

Justine's romantic interest in her eldest son had been glaringly obvious to Lex from the moment they had moved into this street five years ago. Justine knew a good catch when she saw one. Trouble was, despite her own many good qualities she was not superficially the type Martin looked at when it came to his girl-friends. Lex felt this state of affairs was a great pity as Justine could prove a real asset to him, if only he would open his eyes and see her worth before it was too late and another man snapped her up.

'We're all fine, thank you for asking, Justine.'

'I'm glad to hear that. Martin ... er ... still seeing that woman I saw him with the other week, going into the White Hart in town?' A wistful look settled on Justine's face. 'She looked just like a model from a magazine – so beautiful. Mind you, he is very handsome so I'm not surprised he was with someone like that.'

Lex shrugged. 'I've no idea if he's still seeing her or not, love. I'm just his mother, he never talks to me about his girlfriends. Men only bring girls home to meet their parents when they're serious about them, don't they? And as Martin hasn't as yet, I can only assume he isn't serious about the woman you saw him with.' Justine looked pleased to hear this and Lex assumed the young woman felt it meant she herself was still in with a chance. 'You courting, are you?' Lex asked her.

'I was seeing someone, Mrs Morton, but we finished last week as he'd found someone he liked better than me.'

'I can't imagine that, Justine,' Lex told her sincerely. 'Any man would surely be proud to have you as his girlfriend.'

A fleeting look crossed her face that Lex read as regret that Martin didn't seem to think so. 'Thanks for the compliment, Mrs Morton. I think my ex liked his new girlfriend better than me because she's got her own car. Her family are the well-off sort. Still, if he's only interested in a girl for what she can bring him I wouldn't want to be with him anyway, so he's no loss to me.'

What a wise girl, thought Lex. Hopefully one day her sons would be mature enough to realise that the sort of woman they chose to consort with now wouldn't bring them lasting happiness.

It was types like Justine they should both be looking towards.

'Well, I'd best be off or Gran will think I'm not coming. 'Bye, Mrs Morton,' she said cheerily as she went on her way.

Arriving home, Lex was relieved to find no evidence of Martin and felt this was a good sign as surely if he had been going to be dismissed for abandoning his post he would have been home by now.

Having prepared bubble and squeak, using the uneaten cold mashed potatoes and vegetables from earlier, and warmed up the meat pie along with fresh gravy, at just after half-past five Lex went to check her appearance in the mirror hanging over the grey-and-brown-tiled fireplace in the living room. As dusk was falling on this early-October evening, she switched on the gold-coloured, deep-fringed standard lamp positioned behind Gil's armchair and gave the matching cushion a plump up, ready for him to sit comfortably against once he'd had his meal. He'd watch the *Tonight* programme, hosted by Cliff Michelmore, and afterwards catch up with that day's local news in the *Leicester Mercury* which she had put ready on the arm of his chair earlier.

Despite having been with Gil as long as she had, and never being given any reason to doubt his feelings for her, she had never let her appearance slide through complacency, liking to look as attractive as she could for him at all times, just as he liked to look clean-shaven and smartly dressed for her. So just before Gil was due home from work each evening, Lex would change out of her workaday clothes for a fresh dress, skirt or blouse, depending on her fancy, tidy her hair and apply a light coating of mascara and lipstick.

The reflection in the mirror that looked back at her that evening was of a maturely attractive forty-five-year-old woman with a cascade of wavy wheat-coloured hair flowing down to skim her slender shoulders. She had just a faint trace of lines around her almond-shaped, thickly lashed cornflower blue eyes. She had been blessed with a peaches and cream complexion which she did her best to keep youthful with the help of Pond's cold cream. Tonight she had teamed a pale pink twinset with a light cream straight skirt which hugged her still shapely physique. After applying pink lipstick to her generous lips, Lex appraised herself. By no means a vain woman, she was however satisfied with her appearance, feeling she had made the best of herself.

Back in the kitchen, stirring the pan of gravy, she heard the click of the back gate latch heralding an arrival. Martin had already informed her he had football practice straight after work so his dinner was keeping hot over a pan of simmering water. As Gil still hadn't telephoned her to say he was going to be late – and she had checked the telephone – it would either be him or Matthew. She rested the spoon in the pan and turned to welcome whichever one of them it was.

And then she waited.

Whoever it was, they seemed to be taking an age to cover the short distance from the gate at the side of the house to the back door. She was just about to go out and see for herself what was keeping them when the door opened and Gil stepped inside to stand just inside the doorway.

The fact he didn't immediately come across to give her his normal greeting of a kiss on her cheek, that he wasn't even looking at her but down at the floor, puzzled Lex. Then the stricken look on his face, his whole aura of wretchedness, struck her and a surge of foreboding flooded through her. 'Oh, dear God, has something happened to one of our boys?' she exclaimed.

He muttered back, 'As far as I know they're fine.'

Tremendous relief flooded through her to hear this, but regardless something terrible must had transpired to have reduced her husband to this state. Deeply worried, she demanded, 'Something has happened though, Gil, so what is it?'

His silence sent cold fear through her veins. Highly perturbed, she watched him turn slowly to shut the back door behind him then slip off his coat, hanging it on the hook before turning back to her. The effort it took him to look her in the eye this time was not lost on Lex. Taking a deep breath, he began, 'I've ...' He paused then to swallow hard and it was apparent to Lex that he dreaded what he was about to tell her. 'I've ... been dismissed.'

She stared at him thunderstruck for several long moments, fighting to digest what he had just told her, before she finally uttered, 'What!' Then clamped a hand to her mouth. 'Oh, dear God, the firm's gone under, hasn't it, and everyone has lost their jobs?'

He gravely shook his head. 'It's just me that's lost my job, Lex.'

She was baffled by his declaration. 'But I don't understand ... Why has Mr Brenton dismissed you? He told me himself at the last firm's do that he wouldn't know what to do without you. He's come to rely on you so much, trusting your judgement, he's ...'

He cut her short. 'Lex, there's no easy way to tell you this but a woman at work ... she's ... well, she's claimed I molested her when she was in my office this morning. I had no way to refute her accusation, there were only the two of us in there at the time, so no witnesses can be called. Mr Brenton had no choice but to let me go.'

Lex's face became ashen. She exhaled hard and stared in stupefaction at her husband for several long moments, fighting to comprehend the shocking news he'd just delivered. Somehow she found her way to the kitchen table and sank down on a chair. Staring at him in shock, she begged, 'Please tell me it's not true? Please tell me ... tell me anything ... that this is some sort of bad joke?'

Gil's shoulders sagged in despair. 'I wish I could, Lex,' he uttered remorsefully. He walked across to sit down on the chair next to her and took her hand, looking imploringly into her eyes. 'I'm so sorry to bring this on you, love. Please believe me, I never touched that woman.'

'I know you didn't,' she shot back at him with utter conviction. 'I know you better than I know myself, Gil Morton, and you would never lay a finger on any woman inappropriately. I can't believe that Mr Brenton believes you did and took this woman's word, knowing you as well as he does.'

Gil sighed heavily. 'Mr Brenton had no choice but to take her side, Lex. If not the men, who *didn't* believe me incapable of such a thing, would have taken industrial action. It could have ended in a long drawn out strike before I was eventually dismissed.'

Lex's eyes narrowed darkly. 'So, when all's said and done, Maurice Brenton has proved he cares only about his bank balance. After all your years of loyalty and the fact that you never gave him or his father any reason whatsoever to question your worth, he should have stood by you, only conceded defeat if the men couldn't be persuaded the woman's claim was false.

'Well, Maurice Brenton might have shown his true colours in abandoning you, and it remains to be seen whether he lives to regret that, but your family won't be turning their backs on you,' she said fervently. 'I'll repeat what I said earlier – I know you better than I know myself, Gil. You would never mistreat a woman in any way.' She laughed bitterly. 'You even get embarrassed when Thelma has a little flirt with you after she's had a couple of drinks too many.' She looked at him questioningly then. 'This woman must have some reason for picking on you to make a claim against, though.'

He looked totally mystified. 'I've been walking around since I left the factory this morning, trying to get to grips with all this, to come up with a reason but I've no idea. Absolutely none.'

Lex's own thoughts were thrashing wildly. 'Who is this woman?' she asked.

'Miriam Jones.'

'The Miriam Jones you told me about who took over from Sally Little a while back when she left to have her baby?'

He nodded. 'Seemed happy enough to be doing it, too. Least, she's never given me any sign she wasn't.'

'Then she's got to have something wrong with her. No sane person makes such a damaging accusation against someone without good reason.'

'I've no reason to believe she's not as sane as you or me, Lex.'

'Then have you upset her in any way and this is her spiteful way of taking revenge against you?'

'Not that I can think of. As I said, I can't think of anything I've done to give her a grudge against me.'

Lex's face screwed up in bewilderment, her mind frantically searching for a plausible reason why Miriam Jones had made such an outrageous claim against him. Then a possible one presented itself. 'Did she have a fancy for you? Did she make advances towards you, and you spurned her? You're a very handsome man . . .'

If the situation hadn't been so serious, Gil would have laughed at his wife's suggestion. 'Lex, I'm forty-five, and I might be handsome to you but I doubt . . .'

She firmly cut him short, saying. 'You're a handsome man, Gil. You've no vanity so you don't see it. Now, did this Miriam Jones proposition you in any way? Could her claim be by way of getting back at you for any perceived rejection of her?'

He vigorously shook his head. 'The only conversations I have had with her have all been work-related. There's never been the slightest trace of innuendo from her to me or vice versa.'

With no other explanation for why the woman had done what she had presenting itself to her, Lex rose to her feet, saying, 'If you've been walking around all afternoon you must be desperate for a drink.' She went across to the cooker to pick up the kettle simmering on the stove and tipped boiling water from it on to the leaves in the teapot. As she was pouring milk into a cup a sound reached her ears and she spun round to look at her husband. To her horror, she saw that he was crying.

In all the twenty-seven years she had known Gil, she had only ever witnessed him cry after a bereavement, when their respective parents had passed away, and from euphoria on the birth of their sons. And each time he hadn't realised she was privy to such uncontrollable emotion. Had he been, he would have been mortified. Gil was the sort of man who took his role of head of the household very seriously. Such men were the backbone of their families, seeing it as their job to support everyone, show strength at all times. Openly showing their emotions was deemed to be unforgivable weakness, and that would never do. Lex was distraught, therefore, to witness such a disintegration in the man she adored, all because of one woman's inexplicable lie.

Violence in any form appalled her. Regardless she could not stop an overwhelming surge of anger from flooding through her. She fought desperately to quell her desire to seek out this woman and throttle the truth from her. Almost throwing down the milk bottle she was holding, she dashed over to Gil, to encircle his head with her arms and pull him close. 'We'll get to the bottom of this,' she said with conviction. 'We'll prove that woman is lying, if it's the last thing we do.'

'I don't see how we can,' he uttered. 'She insists I did what she says I did to her. I have no evidence to disprove it.' Then he suddenly exclaimed, 'Oh, God.' Pulling his head free from her embrace, he looked up at her, mortified. 'Our boys ... How are they going to take this? What will they think of me?'

They looked round as the back door burst open then and their two strapping offspring charged in, only to stop short and quickly size up the scene before them.

It was Martin who spoke first. 'So it's true then?'

'That a woman at the factory has made a false accusation against your father, and her despicable lie has cost him his job? Yes, it's true.' Anger against Miriam Jones still raging within her, Lex snapped, 'Neither of you believes your father guilty of what she's claiming, do you?'

They both looked hurt that she could even think it.

It was Martin who responded. 'How can you ask us that, Mam?'

His handsome features twisted with reproach, Matt added, 'It never crossed our minds it could be true.'

Their mother's face clouded over then. 'I should have known you wouldn't doubt him. I'm sorry for what I said.'

They both walked over to the table, pulled out chairs and sat down, looking worriedly at their father. They had never seen him look so desolate and it distressed them both greatly.

'You all right, Dad?' Matt asked.

His brother shot him a glance of disdain. 'That's a stupid question to ask. How can he be with this hanging over him?'

'That's enough,' Lex scolded them sharply. 'We've enough to deal with at the moment without you two being at loggerheads.

Of course your father isn't all right, but he will be. He's got his family to see him through this. We know he's innocent and that's all that matters.'

There was a fresh glimmer of tears in Gil's eyes as he looked at his wife. It was apparent he was far too choked up to make any response to these expressions of support. Clearing his throat, he addressed his sons. 'I suppose my dismissal and the reason for it are all around the factory by now? I'm so sorry you had to hear of it this way.'

'It was me who heard the gossip first, Dad,' Martin told him. 'Not long after tea break this morning, I noticed some of the men whispering together. They kept looking over at me so naturally I went across to ask them what was going on. They tried to fob me off, said they were discussing a girl that one of them had just started seeing, but I knew they were lying to me and insisted they told me what they were really talking about.

'Of course I didn't believe that you'd assaulted one of the office women and been kicked out, and the others there had to hold me back from punching the man's lights out for spreading gossip. But Archie Miller was adamant he had his facts right. I still wouldn't have it, though, saying it was nothing more than malicious rumour. I shot to your office but you'd already packed up your things and left. Obviously I knew then you'd been sacked for something, but I still never believed for a minute it was for what the men were saying. I went and found Matt and we came straight home, expecting you to be here, so we could get to the bottom of it.'

He looked at his mother. 'We hated shooting off like we did when we came back at dinnertime to see if Dad was here, but it was obvious to us you weren't aware that anything had happened at work. We didn't want to start worrying you with what we'd heard until we knew the truth ourselves. Even then it wasn't up to us to tell you, it had to be Dad himself.'

He fixed his attention back on his father. 'When we couldn't find you we were worried you'd done something stupid to yourself. We've been searching high and low everywhere we could think of. Finally we ran out of places and had no choice but to come home, praying you'd have come back meantime. You don't know how glad we both are to see you here, safe and sound.' He glanced at his brother for back-up then asked tentatively, 'So what is the truth about what happened today?'

As her husband began to relate this morning's events, Lex's maternal instincts rose to the fore. She went over to the stove and busied herself dishing up their meal. As Gil related the part where he was frogmarched to Maurice Brenton's office, Lex didn't need to turn and look at her sons to know how angry it was making them. Cyril Breville was beneath contempt in her eyes, and she knew her sons would be thinking likewise. Then her anger changed to a feeling of deep hurt for Gil as she pictured him facing his accuser while unable to disprove her claim. But even worse than that for a man like him, his whole integrity was now in question. She knew he would never be able to hold his head up in public again until his innocence was proved, something that probably wouldn't be the case unless Miriam Jones felt her conscience prick and came clean over why she had done what she had.

Gil had just finished his narrative when she put their plates of hot food before them.

He looked down at his own blankly for a second before apologising to her. 'It looks very appetising, my dear, but I'm sorry, I just couldn't eat a thing at the moment. You understand, don't you?'

Matt too pushed his plate away. He had no appetite either. 'So that's it? It's this woman's word against yours, Dad, and there's nothing we can do about it?'

Gil sighed. 'That's about the size of it, son.'

'But we can't take this lying down,' said Martin, his food too remaining untouched. 'We should go round and confront her, make her confess that she made it all up.'

'Yeah, force her to come clean,' snarled Martin, a murderous look in his eyes.

Appalled, Gil glared at them and in no uncertain terms declared, 'We Mortons have never resorted to violence to resolve our problems, and we're not going to start now.'

Both boys looked shamefaced.

Her own meal forgotten on the work surface by the cooker, Lex sat down at the table and said, 'Don't think I haven't considered violence against Miriam Jones myself.' Then she addressed her sons. 'Does either of you know this woman personally? I'm clutching at straws here but is there any possibility she has a grievance against either of you and has taken revenge on your father instead?'

They both shrugged and shook their heads.

'I know her by sight but can't remember ever talking to her. If I have, it would just have been to say hello in passing, so I can't see why she'd have a beef against me,' said Martin.

'Same goes for me,' added Matt.

Lex was totally at a loss and sighed despondently. 'The only other reason I can think of why she'd do this would be to extort money from you, Gil. But then, if that was her aim, she wouldn't have reported it, would she?' She stared thoughtfully into space for several long moments before an other idea struck her and she said, 'Just maybe Miriam Jones isn't lying about what happened in your office after all . . .'

They all looked shocked.

'You mean, you think I *did* molest her!' Gil exclaimed, horrified.

'No, I do not,' Lex said with conviction. 'I will never change my mind on that score. But as I can't think of any other reason why she would do this, it has to have happened just as Mr Brenton thought it did. Gil, you said you were concentrating on important work at the time Miriam Jones claimed the incident happened?'

He looked bemused, not clear where his wife's train of thought was heading. 'Yes, I was. I was working on a tender for a big job that Brenton was badgering me to get done. We'd be supplying engine mounts and piston rods for the Ministry of Defence. Brenton's landing that contract would mean the men's jobs were safe for at least three years plus the possibility of a decent increase at the next round of pay talks.'

Folding her arms, Lex leaned on the table, looking at him intently. 'Well, dear, what if you were so consumed by your work, you didn't realise you'd got up to get something out of one of the cabinets next to where Miriam Jones was standing. As you went to squeeze past her your hands may have accidentally come into contact with her. We all do things then forget we've done them when our minds are fully occupied with important matters, like getting that tender done. The times I've found myself some- where and not been able to remember how I'd got there . . . That might explain why you can't remember how you came into bodily contact with her, like she swears you did.'

Gil looked thoughtful and said distractedly, 'I can't remember leaving my desk . . . but I was so engrossed in my work, I suppose that could be how it happened.'

'And Miriam Jones just over-reacted like Mr Brenton suggested she did?' said Martin.

Lex nodded. 'It's the only explanation I can think of that makes any sense.' She looked bewildered as her son scraped back his chair and stood up. 'Where are you going?'

'To see this woman and make her . . .'

'Sit back down,' she ordered him. As he obeyed Lex continued, 'We must allow Mrs Jones to see sense by herself because if it got out that the Mortons had been to visit her, people would be bound to think we bullied or blackmailed her even into changing her story, and that would not help your father. Hopefully once the shock of whatever happened to her has faded, she'll see things more clearly and come to this conclusion by herself.'

'But what if she doesn't, Mam?' demanded Matt.

'We have no choice but to hope she does,' Lex responded firmly.

'But it doesn't seem fair that Dad should be the one to suffer for her mistake,' argued Matt.

'No, I agree, it doesn't, but then life isn't fair sometimes. And when you suffer a setback you have no choice but to get on with it,' Lex told them firmly.

Gil looked at her worriedly. 'The gossips are going to have a field day with this, Lex, and I can't bear the thought of you, Martin or Matt being subjected to that. I wouldn't blame you if you wanted to move away from it all?'

'Gossip doesn't bother me. I'll soon put people straight if I hear any. And I can't say as I like the thought of moving 'cos I like it round here, but I'd be happy to for your sake and Dad's, Mam,' offered Martin

'Me too,' Matt agreed.

Lex shook her head. 'Moving away is absolutely the last thing we're going to do. We do that and it's as good as putting a banner across the road, saying "Gil Morton has admitted he's guilty of molesting Miriam Jones". No, we've always faced our problems as a family head-on. The best way we can act now is to carry on as normal. We Mortons have nothing to hang our heads over in shame. This is just a terrible misunderstanding, and I will not be hounded out of the home you've worked so hard to provide for us, Gil, through neighbours' tittle-tattle. Those people who know you will be aware you're not capable of doing this. The ones who choose to think the worst aren't worth knowing.'

'Mam's right, Dad,' said Matt.

'Yes, she is,' agreed Martin.

It was glaringly apparent that Gil was fighting back tears when he addressed them. 'I'm just so sorry to have brought this on you all. Thank you for believing in me and sticking by me.' He gave a heavy sigh then, looking at his wife. 'But I can't see how we'll be able to stay in this house, though, now I'm out of work. I'm not going to find it easy getting another job when a possible employer learns how I lost my last one, am I?'

'No, I can't deny that. It's not going to be easy. But there's got to be an employer somewhere who will accept your word that you lost your job over a terrible misunderstanding,' she said optimistically.

Gil flashed her a wan smile. 'I do hope so, Lex.'

'In the meantime, you can have all my wages until you're bringing one in again, Dad,' offered Matt.

'Mine too,' his brother confirmed.

Lex stretched over and affectionately patted their hands.

A choked Gil uttered, 'Thanks, sons, but hopefully we won't need to take you up on your offer.'

They all knew they had a difficult time ahead of them in more ways than one. It would need all their individual strength as well as their strength as a family to deal with what lay in front of them.

CHAPTER FOUR

At just after nine the next morning, Lex was replacing the kettle on the stove after making the tea when her husband came into the kitchen. In the past, whether on weekdays or weekends, they'd always risen together and it had felt strange to her to leave her husband in bed that morning while she saw to it that her sons were fed before going off to work. She was a bit surprised Gil hadn't stirred when the alarm had gone off as he wasn't a heavy sleeper. Now she turned to greet him, and it distressed her to see how strained he looked. She knew he'd not slept much at all. In fact, as he'd restlessly tossed and turned all night, he'd kept her awake too. But it was hardly surprising after yesterday's catastrophic events.

Lex had worried too as she lay sleepless that their sons could be facing a barrage of abuse while they were out that night, and was rather annoyed with herself in retrospect for encouraging them to go out, with the argument that the way forward was for them to show a brave face to the world and carry on as normal. She had been relieved to hear them both arrive home safely and, from the whispered goodnights and stumbling footsteps she'd heard before each retired to their separate room, gratified to learn that they both seemed to be in good spirits, in more ways than one.

She had learned when they had come down for breakfast this morning that they had cancelled their arrangements to meet their friends, instead going for a drink together at a pub in town. She didn't comment but assumed they had wanted to discuss what had happened to their father and how they were going to handle the backlash they were bound to receive at work.

She wanted to do something to protect them from what she feared they faced at Brenton's, not only today but for a while to come until the sensational news of their father's dismissal became stale. But they were grown men, of an age when mothers no longer fought their battles for them. If they were worried about what faced them at work, neither of them showed it as they tucked into the bacon and eggs Lex had prepared for them. They informed her that neither of them would be home at dinnertime today but would grab something in the canteen. They claimed they both had things they wanted to do. She assumed this to mean they'd face things out with their workmates during the hour long break; show that they saw no reason to feel ashamed.

Now she smiled warmly at Gil and said brightly, 'Morning, love. Sit yourself down. Cuppa coming up. Your bacon's all ready and it won't take me a minute to fry an egg.'

As he was taking his seat Gil told her, 'Just a cup of tea, thank you. I'm not hungry this morning.'

She appreciated why he'd no appetite as she hadn't been able to face food herself but regardless said, 'You didn't eat much of your dinner last night, Gil. Please, for me, try and eat some breakfast?'

He hadn't the strength to argue and sighed, 'Just a small portion then.'

She put his plate in front of him and sat down opposite. Over her third cup of tea that morning, she asked, 'So what's your plan for today?'

He was pushing the food around his plate. 'I thought I'd take a trip down the Labour Exchange to see what's on offer, and I'll get the *Mercury* on the way back to study the Jobs section. Can't expect our sons to keep us so the sooner I get set on the better. I know I face knockbacks, Lex, but as you said last night, there's got to be an employer out there somewhere who'll accept my word that I was dismissed through no fault of my own. I'm prepared to go back on the tools if necessary, but hopefully I'll get a foreman's position.'

Her heart went out to him then. Gil had worked tirelessly to gain a management role and it upset her greatly that he was being driven back down the ladder like this. But he had never been a man to wallow in self-pity, and it seemed he wasn't going to now. She was proud of him for that. Regardless, she felt she should support him against any local hostility. 'Would you like me to come with you, Gil?' she offered.

He stopped absently stirring his tea when she spoke, and looked up at her sharply. 'I don't need you to protect me, Lex. If our sons can face the men at Brenton's today, then I can face a few neighbours.' His face fell then. 'I'm sorry, I didn't mean to snap at you. It's just . . .' His shoulders sagged. 'I still can't believe what happened yesterday, that's all.'

She leaned over and grabbed his hand, squeezing it reassuringly. 'I'm so proud of you, Gil, for having the guts to face them all. Look, maybe Miriam Jones has already reached the conclusion we did yesterday. Maybe she's in with Mr Brenton right now, putting him straight. He could be round here soon, offering you your job back.'

Pushing his untouched plate away, Gil retorted, 'Lex, let's stop fooling ourselves. I was so relieved last night when you came up with a plausible explanation for her actions that I couldn't think further than that. But I had plenty of time to, last night in bed. Even if Miriam has realised she made a mistake, why should she come clean? Living with the guilt of what she's done to me is still going to be easier for her than looking a right fool and maybe losing her own job.

'We have to face the fact that, rightly or wrongly, I've been branded a threat to women, and I'll have to learn to live with that.' He scraped back his chair, stood up and went across to take his coat off the back door. Having automatically patted his pocket to check that his car keys were there, he laughed dryly. 'Oh, stupid me. I forgot I'd no car now. I lost that along with my job, didn't I?' Then, yanking open the back door, he disappeared from Lex's sight.

She felt desolate. Gil was right. She *had* been so relieved to find a plausible explanation for what had happened in his office yesterday morning that it had never crossed her mind that Miriam wouldn't speak up. But if she didn't, it meant that Gil would never be cleared of this crime he had not committed; would forever have to live with the stigma. Some men did not care a jot what others thought of them but Gil was a man who very much needed to know he had the respect and trust of those around him. Now that was in doubt, Lex didn't know how he was going to cope. Hopefully securing himself another job would help to restore some of his faith in humanity.

Then she reminded herself that the rest of her family were braving the aftermath of yesterday's events and she was not doing her bit by sitting moping at the table. She was in the process of clearing it when there was a knock on the back door. Before she could respond, a heavily panting Thelma charged in.

'It's a lie what I heard in the corner shop this morning about Gil, isn't it?' she demanded. Then she saw the look on Lex's face, took in the fact that her friend looked like she'd the weight of the world on her shoulders, and her own face fell in disbelief. 'It's not a lie, is it?'

Lex shook her head. 'I wish I could say it was.'

Stunned beyond belief, Thelma found her way to the table and sank down on a chair, looking at Lex in bewilderment. 'I thought someone was just spreading a malicious rumour 'cos they'd n'ote better to do, and had picked on Gil for some reason. Some women were discussing it in the greengrocer's when I went in, and I told them without a by-your-leave that I didn't care a jot what they'd heard from their men, I'd known Gil Morton for over twenty years and knew without a doubt he'd never lay a finger on any woman in that way, so they must have heard wrong.' She looked defiant. 'I still can't believe he's guilty of that sort of behaviour. I *won't* believe it. Neither will Des when he hears.'

A lump filled Lex's throat, threatening to choke her. 'Oh, Thelma, thank you,' she uttered. 'You don't know how much it means to me to hear you say that. Gil will so appreciate our friends' faith in him. He needs all the support he can get right now. He's not guilty, Thelma, it's all just a dreadful misunderstanding. I'm sorry you found out about this through gossip. I should have come and . . .'

'Good God, you've had enough on your mind with the shock of all this without coming round to me,' Thelma cut in. Then she ordered, 'Pour me a cuppa, gel, and tell me exactly how this all came about?'

A while later she shook her head in disbelief. 'This is just terrible for Gil, You too . . . and the boys . . . all of you, in fact.' She leaned over and grabbed Lex's hand, squeezing it tight as she said with conviction, 'But you will get over this. You're a strong family. Anyone who believes Gil capable of molesting that woman ain't worth knowing, lovey. I want to go and throttle her meself for blowing things out of proportion and causing what she has. But, like you said, if she genuinely believes Gil purposely touched her where he shouldn't, then she can't be blamed for reporting it.

'I agree with you, though, that Maurice Brenton should have stood by Gil and not dismissed him so readily. Not without at least calling a meeting with the men to put the case to them, rather than automatically assuming they'd take industrial action and put his factory in jeopardy.' She pulled a wry expression then. 'I bet half the men at Brenton's mistreat their wives in private, but they'd show proper outrage in public and be quick to form a lynch mob against an innocent man! I expect Gil's in bed still, is he? Poor love. It'll take him a while to come to terms with this.'

'No, he's not in bed, Thelma. He's gone down the Labour Exchange to see what's on offer.'

Her friend looked most impressed to hear this. 'Good on him. Hiding himself away would have been the worst thing he could have done. Just fuel the gossip, wouldn't it?'

'My sentiments exactly. I offered to go with him but he wouldn't let me.'

'You can't protect him from what he's facing, Lex, as much as you want to. And what about your boys? How have they taken this? They love their father so much, I can't see either of them taking it lying down.'

'Well, as you can imagine, they both wanted to pay a visit on

49

that woman and force the truth from her. I can't blame them, I had a job from stopping myself going for the same reason, but Gil and I made it clear we've never resorted to threatening behaviour to resolve our problems and we're not starting now. They're both at work today.'

Again Thelma looked impressed. 'Good on them too. I can see you're worried about what faces them there, the other men will have a field day with this, but they're not little boys any longer, Lex. Them two can fight their own battles.' She looked at her friend closely. 'Now what are your own plans for today?'

Lex needed to shop for provisions for their evening meal. She had told her family that the way forward was to carry on as they normally would, but suddenly the thought of facing the accusing eyes of those who chose to believe her husband guilty was unbearable to her. She knew Gil was innocent but couldn't prove it, had no defence to offer his critics who would now revel in perceiving him as a sexual predator. Lex didn't know how she was going to cope with that.

As though Thelma was reading her thoughts, she said, 'I need to go to the Co-op and the butcher's, Lex, so if you've some shopping to do, we could go together?'

She opened her mouth to accept the offer gratefully, then it struck her that this could be perceived as hiding behind her friend. In a voice that sounded far more assured than she inwardly felt, Lex said, 'I really appreciate your offer, Thelma, but if I'm to show people we Mortons have nothing to be ashamed of, I won't achieve that by hiding behind your skirts, will I? I need to do this alone.'

Despite her bravado Lex was relieved to find the road deserted when she emerged into it a short while later and set off towards the shops. As she approached Phyllis Watson's house she remembered that she had promised her incapacitated neighbour to call in and check what shopping she needed that day. This would be the first hurdle she faced in testing people's reactions. Lex took a deep breath to steel herself before she turned in at the gate.

Phyllis welcomed her in enthusiastically with the offer of a cup of tea. It was very apparent to Lex from her manner that she had not heard what had gone on in the Morton household since she'd last seen her Well, it would be better coming from Lex.

After helping Phyllis make the tea, she said, 'I get the impression you haven't heard what happened to Gil yesterday?'

Her friend just stared at her, 'What's that? I can tell by your face it was serious. A works accident, was it? Oh, I hope it was nothing too bad?'

'He's not had an accident, Phyllis. If only he had ... it would have been easier by far to bear.' Lex took a deep breath and then proceeded to update her friend.

Her neighbour stared at her in disbelief throughout.

'What utter nonsense!' she said when she got the chance. 'Gilbert Morton is the most upstanding man, other than my own husband, I have ever had the pleasure of knowing. In all the years I've been in his company in social situations, I've never seen him treat a woman with anything other than the utmost respect. In fact, on more than one occasion I've seen women flirting outrageously with *him* while they were the worse for drink. He's a handsome man, there is no denying that, Alexandra, and those were very attractive women too. But his only reaction was to go hot under the collar, he didn't at all enjoy their attentions. It was quite comical, being a bystander and watching him beat a hasty retreat on such occasions.'

She fixed Lex's eyes with her own and said with conviction. 'Anyway, what possible need could Gilbert have for anything another woman could give him when he already has all he could ever want in a woman? It's obvious to everyone who meets you together that you're perfectly suited and very content with each other. I can only conclude the same as you have: that the woman at Brenton's grossly over-reacted to some chance bodily contact. Huh! Men only have to look at women like that and they cry rape. Now, if it was Vivian Rotherhide's husband Ronald we were talking about, I wouldn't hesitate to believe the accusation was true. I've never seen a man with more of a roving eye than Ronald's got, and I don't know how Vivian puts up with it because he's quite blatant about it. I've lost count of the number of times I've seen him disappear with some woman or other and reappear a while later, looking tousled and with a smug grin on his face.'

Phyllis patted Lex's hand sympathetically. 'So dreadful for all of you, lovey, Gilbert especially. But anyone who knows him like I do will realise he's no more the lecherous sort than the Pope is. You're doing the right thing, facing it out. And rest assured, lovey, should I hear anyone gossiping in a derogatory way about all this, I shall certainly put them straight.'

Phyllis' reaction did much to boost Lex's confidence. A short while later she once again set off for the shops.

Four women were standing in front of the counter at the grocer's, an assistant on the other side. They were all so engrossed in conversation, they did not notice the arrival of a new customer.

The stoutest and oldest of them all, with a face reminiscent of a British bulldog and sparse tightly permed grey hair encased in a hairnet, was saying to the others, 'We women ain't safe in these streets with people of the likes of that Morton man roaming 'em.'

The thin, sharp-featured woman next to her said, 'It's true. You can't judge a book by its cover, Mrs Birtle. Such a nice, polite man he always came across as, the sort you'd trust to change a light bulb in yer bedroom with no one else present, when all the time he's nothing but a beast, preying on innocent women! I wonder how many he's abused over the years and them too afraid to come forward?'

The woman next to her, black round-framed spectacles clamped over her round black eyes, chipped in, 'They've two sons, yer know. Good-looking lads like their father. But it makes yer wonder if they've inherited his other traits as well, if yer understand me?'

The middle-aged assistant behind the counter joined in then. 'I feel sorry for Mrs Morton. She seems such a nice woman. It must be awful for her, thinking she's got a good husband when all the time he's been up to all sorts behind her back.'

The British bulldog spoke again. 'Well, it makes me wonder if she didn't have her suspicions all along. After all, she lives with him. And that makes her just as bad as him in my eyes, not doing anything about him but leaving him free to carry on his despicable acts.'

A round-faced woman beside her coat straining over her matronly chest, responded, 'I don't think we need worry about our own safety as far as the Morton men are concerned. It's my guess they'll all have done a bunk during the night sooner than face the shame and the backlash from us locals, who won't tolerate their type living round here anymore.'

From her position just inside the doorway, a frozen-faced Lex stared at the gossips. She felt a desperate need to launch herself at them and lash out, screaming that Gil was innocent of the crime he had been accused of, but to do that would only result in humiliation for herself and would certainly not help the Morton cause.

Taking a deep breath, she raised her chin proudly in the air and walked over to join them. An onlooker would never have guessed that it was taking all her courage for her to do just this.

Lex smiled at them all politely and with forced lightness said, 'Good morning, ladies.'

The British bulldog looked stunned to see who the newcomer was and issued a disgusted snort. 'Well, you've got a nerve, showing yer face in public.'

Lex fixed her with her eyes. 'Oh, really, Mrs Birtle, and why's that?'

'Well, if my husband had been caught doing what yours has, I'd have died with the shame of it.'

Lex's eyes narrowed. 'And what if my husband is innocent of what he's been accused of, Mrs Birtle?'

The other woman smirked. 'Innocent, my foot!' she scoffed. 'You saying there's no smoke without fire, Mrs Morton?'

'Mrs Birtle . . .' she looked at each in turn of the rest of the gathering '. . . ladies, has any of you stopped to consider that the woman who accused my husband of molesting her may in fact have made a simple mistake? In a confined space, squeezed up beside the filing cabinets, is it not possible that she misinterpreted a perfectly innocent action of Gil's?' She saw the looks on their faces and added, 'No, I thought not. Ever ready, to believe the worst. We Mortons have nothing to hang our heads in shame over, and we'll not be hounded out of our home through pure ignorance. Now obviously none of you is in a rush to get your shopping, but I am. So if you don't mind, I'll go ahead, shall I?'

She knew every eye was boring into her as she stood and ordered her groceries from the embarrassed assistant. It seemed to take an awfully long time. As she finally turned to depart, Lex forced herself to smile politely at them all again and say breezily, 'Good day, ladies.'

Outside in the street she paused for a moment, heaving a great sigh of relief to be out of the lions' den. It had been a dreadful ordeal for her, and one she wasn't looking forward to repeating, but she wasn't stupid enough to think that would be the end of it. She hoped, though, that the gossips would at least start to consider Gil's side of the story.

She dropped off Phyllis' shopping and went home, believing it was far too soon to expect her husband back. Entering the kitchen, she stopped short in surprise to see Gil sitting at the table. Her surprise immediately turned to dismay when it registered with her that he was holding his head in his hands in despair.

Dropping her bag of shopping by the door, Lex ran to him. She crouched down before him, placed one hand on his thigh and asked in deep concern, 'Oh, Gil, what is it? We knew it wasn't going to be easy. I wish I could spare you what you're going through, but just because a possible employer didn't believe your word about how you lost your job doesn't mean that . . .'

He dropped his hands, cutting her short with, 'I never got as far as an interview, Lex. I never got further than the end of the street.'

The desolate expression on his face distressed her beyond belief. 'Oh, so it's not because you've been knocked back by a potential employer that you're upset then?'

He shook his head. 'It was the women . . . Mrs Crouch and her daughter.'

Kathleen Crouch lived at the end of the street and was a quiet, nervy type of woman, the sort that jumped a foot if anyone shouted

'Boo!'. Her husband worked in the stores at Brenton's and was a mild-mannered type. Their fifteen-year-old daughter, an unremarkable reserved type of girl, had just left school and was starting work the following Monday as an apprentice hairdresser. Lex assumed the Crouch women must have said something nasty to Gil, but it surprised her as they were hardly the vocal type.

'What did they say to you?' she demanded.

'They never said anything to me.'

She looked perplexed. 'Then how come they upset you so much?'

'By what they did.' He took a shuddering breath. 'I was just approaching their house on the way to the bus stop, and as they came out of their gate they saw me and . . . and . . .'

'And what, Gil?' she pressed him.

He swallowed hard. 'Kath Crouch grabbed her daughter's arm and pulled her against her protectively. They just stared at me like . . . like . . .' His voice lowered to a choking whisper. 'It was obvious they were terrified of me.'

Lex gasped in shock. 'I'm sure you're mistaken,' she insisted.

'I'm not,' he snapped back at her. 'Those two women were terrified of me. I came straight back here. Seeing Thelma had arrived, I waited in the outhouse until you'd both left the house. I just wanted to be on my own.' He cradled his head in his hands again. 'I can't bear it, Lex. The thought that women are terrified to come near me in case I attack them . . . I can't put them in such a position, it's not fair of me to do that.'

Lex was staring at him in horror. 'Just what are you proposing, Gil?'

He lifted his head. 'The only thing left to me – that I don't go out during daylight hours unless I have no choice, and then only if you accompany me. Other women won't see me as a threat if you're there, will they? I'm sorry to ask you to do this but it's the only way, Lex.'

Appalled she cried, 'What? But that's ridiculous!'

'You weren't there, Lex. You never saw the way Kathleen Crouch and her daughter looked at me. I don't ever want to see women look at me like that again. If it means I stay indoors while the women in these streets go about their daily business, then that's what I'll do. Women rarely work night shifts, do they, so it's a night job I'll concentrate my efforts on getting. I'd be grateful if you could fetch me a copy of the *Leicester Mercury* later so I can start looking. Sorry if that means you'll have to go out again.' Gil got to his feet. 'I don't want to discuss this anymore. I'm going upstairs for a lie down.'

A distressed Lex stared after him. She couldn't comprehend that he was serious about becoming a virtual hermit in order to ostracise himself as much as possible from women. He wasn't thinking straight at the moment. Hopefully his thinking would be clearer once he'd had a sleep.

Lex immersed herself in her housework and the preparation of their evening meal, the radio turned up louder than normal, trying to distract herself from the desperate plight of her beloved husband. At one o'clock it felt very odd not to be welcoming anyone home to their dinner, but then nothing was right about her life today, and wouldn't be for a while. She made herself and Gil a sandwich and ate hers alone when he didn't appear downstairs. Before she left to fetch the newspaper for him, she popped her head around the bedroom door to inform him she was off. He appeared to be asleep so she left a note for him propped up on the kitchen table.

Thankfully she didn't encounter any familiar faces on her outing so was spared any repetition of what she had received in the Co-op that morning As cowardly as she felt it was, the newsagent she went to was not her local one but, another much further afield where she wasn't personally acquainted with the proprietor.

Gil was still in bed when she returned half an hour later. Again she fought to busy herself with mundane chores while fighting to concentrate her thoughts on the topical discussions of *Woman's Hour*. Gil still hadn't made an appearence when the programme finished so while doing a pile of ironing she continued listening to the *Afternoon Play*. It was a whodunit, centred around the murder of a member of an amateur dramatics society in a small northern town, but Lex had enough trials and tribulations of her own to worry about so the gist of the play was lost on her. When it had finished and Gil still hadn't appeared, she went back upstairs to check on him to find that he still appeared to be asleep.

Back downstairs she made herself a cup of tea, spotted the *Mercury* on the kitchen table and sat down to read through it. She liked to keep up with the news, felt it was important to know what was happening outside her own four walls. As her eyes scanned the headlines a terrible thought struck her. The *Mercury* not only carried news of major happenings around the world, its primary function was to report local news about local people. She was suddenly panic-stricken that somehow word of Gil's dismissal would have reached the ears of the newspaper's reporters and then the story would be known to the whole of Leicester and the shires. With her heart pounding frantically, Lex quickly scanned through the pages and was mortally relieved to find nothing on the subject. She then tried to read through the news properly. It seemed the rise of the Berlin Wall would have dire effects for the German people; a massive ban-the-bomb parade had ended in violent clashes and the arrest of 850 protesters; film star Gary Cooper had died at the age of sixty from lung cancer; a baby had been accidentally left on a bus; this October of 1961 was proving to be the warmest recorded for fifty years and weather experts were predicting a bitter winter ahead because of this. But none of it could take her mind off her husband's predicament and the possible fall-out from it that her sons had faced today.

The dinner was ready to dish up when Matt and Martin arrived home and Gil still wasn't down. Lex was about to go and wake him when the back door opened and her sons entered. Matt was trying his hardest to disguise a limp; Martin, though, couldn't hide the bloodied split on his lip or the painful-looking bruise disfiguring his cheek.

'Oh, my God, what's happened to you both?' she cried.

'Calm down, Mam,' Martin told her. 'Just a game of football at dinnertime that got a bit raucous. You should see the bloke who tackled me. At least I can still walk.'

Matt opened his mouth to offer his mother a similar excuse but was stopped in his tracks. 'Don't take your mother for a fool, either of you. You didn't receive those injuries from any football game. You've both been fighting, haven't you? It was about your dad, I assume?'

Martin looked at her sternly. 'Well, me and Matt told you we wouldn't stand for anyone bad-mouthing him, Mam. We were both expecting something like this and so were prepared for it.'

She fought back a gush of tears, so hurt for them both, but seeing their mother cry in front of them would only cause them more grief and they had obviously suffered enough for one day. Without a word, she opened the door beneath the sink and pulled out the Huntley and Palmer's biscuit tin where she kept her medical supplies. Fetching a pudding basin, she put cold water and a good helping of salt in it. Breaking off a wad of cotton wool from the roll, she dipped it into the salted water and told Martin, 'This is going to sting. Now hold still.'

He yelped as the salt on the wadding met the open wound on his lip. 'Ow, Mam, that hurts!'

She snapped back at him, 'Stop acting like a child, Martin. I don't expect you cried like a baby in front of the man who did this to you, did you?' She put a smear of Germolene ointment on it next, then a dab of Witch Hazel on his bruise. 'Let me look at your leg,' she ordered Matt.

Obediently he pulled up his trouser leg. A huge bruise was forming on his shin with a bloodied gash above, though thankfully it wasn't deep enough to require stitches. After cleaning the gash and applying a smear of Germolene, covering it with plaster, then dabbing Witch Hazel on his bruise, she said to both her sons, 'You'll live,' then sank down at the table with them. Fighting back tears for what they had suffered today, she asked worriedly, 'How bad was it for you at work?'

It had been confirmed to them both that they were in for a rough time as soon as they joined the crowd of workers streaming through the factory gates that morning.

Lawrence Stanton, a lanky bully in his late-twenties with dark, greasy hair fashioned in a D.A., immediately shouted across, 'Oi,

Mortons, surprised you've both got the nerve to be showing yer faces. I'd be hiding me mug in shame if I were you.'

Anger had erupted within Matt then and he made to respond, but Martin stopped him.

Fired up for a fight, and egged on by his mates, Loz didn't take kindly to their lack of response and shot over to stand before them, blocking their route. Jabbing Matt on the shoulder, he snarled, 'Didn't yer hear what I said, you deaf fuckers?'

Tight-lipped Matt shot back, 'How could we not? No need for a Tannoy with a voice like yours. Now you listen to me. My brother and I have no reason to hide away in shame. You can think what you like, our dad did not touch that woman.'

Loz snorted, 'Oh, yeah? I heard his hands were all over her. When my dad told my mam about it, she said she always knew there was summat iffy about him. When they were all at the last Christmas do down the Works and Social Club, she saw your dad look at her in a funny way. Now she realises he was eyeing her up as a possible victim.'

His cronies had joined Loz by now and stood around him, all sneering mockingly at the Morton brothers.

Martin and Matt were not the type to be intimidated. Standing firm, Martin looked Loz in the eye and said, 'Your mam was badly mistaken. My dad probably couldn't believe how ugly she was, that's all. Now I ain't daft, Loz. I know you bear a grudge towards Matt over that girl in the office a couple of years back. She turned you down for a date because she was hankering after one with my brother, which made you look stupid in front of your mates. You've been spoiling for a fight with our Matt over it ever since.'

Loz shot Matt a murderous glare. 'You weren't interested in her until you knew I was.'

'That's not true,' he snapped back. 'You never made it known you was interested, so how could I have realised?'

'You've eyes in yer head, ain't yer? So you did know, you fucking liar,' Loz growled back.

At this unjust accusation Matt saw red. He clenched his fist and made to launch himself at Loz, but was stopped by his elder brother grabbing him bodily and saying to the aggressor, 'It isn't my brother's fault he's better-looking than you and all the birds fancy him. Why dont you just forget about it or you'll get us all sacked for fighting on factory premises? Me and Matt will get other jobs easily enough, we're fully trained engineers, but you're just a semi-skilled labourer. It won't be so easy for you.' Then, without warning, he released his hold on his brother and gave Loz a forceful shove on the shoulder which sent him careering back into his group of mates.

At any other time Martin and Matt would have found the scene funny but today they could not find it in themselves to laugh.

At the clocking in machine they became aware that many of their colleagues were throwing them suspicious glances, some whispering together. It was obvious that the topic under discussion was the Morton brothers. At their separate work stations, men they'd worked alongside harmoniously before either showed them the cold shoulder or constantly shouted taunts about them and their father. At dinnertime they were both shoved and pushed from behind in the queue in the canteen, and became very conscious that all the women were looking across at them warily. On finding some vacant chairs at a table and taking them, they were pointedly snubbed when the other diners stood up and moved away. Greatly to their credit, they managed to ignore all this and acted as though they hadn't a care in the world.

At leaving time, still smarting from the way they'd made a fool of him that morning in front of his mates, Loz caught up with them as they were making their way towards the gates. He began throwing nasty insults at them both. Now pushed to their limit and mortally fed up of turning the other cheek, Martin and Matt could no longer control their emotions. Fists started flying and a gathering crowd of hecklers urged them on.

Through his office window Maurice Brenton witnessed the fracas and came down to intervene, warning them all in no uncertain terms that he would not tolerate employees fighting on the premises, whatever the reason. He would be lenient this time but not a second. Anyone involved in further violence would be instantly dismissed.

Loz and his mates scarpered off then like naughty schoolboys but not before sending signals to Martin and Matt that they'd be fools to think this was an end to it, although in fact neither of them was under any such illusion. They both knew that they were in for a rough time ahead, at least until something else happened at the works to take the heat off them.

Feeling their mother had enough to contend with at the moment, however, on their way home they had made a pact not to tell her the true extent of what had happened to them that day.

Casually Martin told her, 'It wasn't as bad as we were expecting, Mam. A few of the blokes were a bit lippy towards us, but we just ignored them. A lot of others came and told us they didn't believe Dad was guilty of what that woman said.' Which was in fact true. The majority had chosen to follow the lead of the trouble-making few, to avoid reprisals, but several braver types . . . although not as many as Martin made his mother believe . . . had taken both boys aside privately and expressed their belief in Gil's innocence.

Lex looked thankful to hear this. 'Oh, that's so good to hear. But it's your dad that needs to hear this, you must tell him as soon as you see him.'

'Where is, Dad?' Matt asked.

'He didn't sleep much last night so went up earlier to have a rest.'

'And how is he?' asked Martin.

'Er . . .' She didn't want to tell them what had happened to their father that morning, nor of his decision to cut himself off from the outside world during daylight hours in future. She was hoping that he'd see his folly in making that decision and change his mind. 'Your father's going to need time to adjust to what's happened to him, and we need to be patient. He's always prided himself on being the sort of man you can both look up to. He hasn't said as much to me, but I know he feels you'll no longer see him that way now.'

'He's daft to think that,' said Martin resolutely.

'Yes, he is,' his brother fervently agreed. 'Our dad is the best father we could ever have wished for. Nothing he could do would change our opinion of him.' He looked at his mother expectantly then. 'What's for dinner, Mam?'

'Yeah, what is it, I'm starving?' agreed Martin.

Despite her distress Lex couldn't help but chuckle. Trust her sons to be thinking of their stomachs at a time like this! But she was thankful that in the present turmoil there was at least this measure of normality.

Having served their meal to them, she went upstairs to rouse her husband. Letting herself quietly into the bedroom, she tiptoed across to the bed. Only the top of Gil's head was visible to her. In a soft coaxing tone, she said, 'It's gone six and dinner is on the table.' Receiving no response she tried again, but her second attempt was as futile as her first. She wasn't convinced he was actually asleep and dearly hoped he wasn't hiding himself away from his family now, too. 'I'll keep it hot for you, sweetheart, you come down when you're ready.'

Gil's plate of food was keeping hot over a pan of simmering water. Lex had cleared away the rest of the dinner dishes and was just wiping over the kitchen table when there was a tap on the back door and Thelma came in.

'Hello, lovey. I've left Des doing the dinner pots as I wanted to come and see how you're all faring?' She took in the strained expression on her friend's face and added, 'Not so good, I take it?'

Lex said forlornly, 'I knew it wasn't going to be easy, Thelma, and what's happened to all of us today has proved that. I just wish that was going to be the end of it, but I know it's not. I don't mind for myself but it's hard not to be able to shield Gil and the boys from what they're having to go through. I'm beginning to think I was wrong to insist we stay put around here and brave this out.'

Thelma shot over to her then, wrapping her arms around her friend and hugging her tight. 'You weren't wrong, you've got to stay put,' she said with conviction.

At this show of affection, there was a gush of tears from Lex. 'Deep down I know that, Thelma, but at least running away would

62

have saved my men from going through all this. Seeing Gil this morning after he'd been out, then the lads in the state they came home in, I just wanted to cry.'

Releasing Lex from her embrace, Thelma stripped off her coat, hung it on the back of the door and sat herself down at the table. 'Come and join me, tell me all about it.'

When they both had cups of tea, Lex described the events of the day.

After she had finished, Thelma said, 'I know you don't approve of violence, Lex, and neither do Des and I, but in this instance you can't blame your boys for not turning the other cheek. Those brainless louts at Brenton's clearly get their kicks from taunting other people in their misfortune. You'll probably have to be prepared to bathe a few more cuts and bruises before you see an end to it. I know it's awful of me to say this but let's hope there's some new misfortune in store for someone at the works, and then the heat will be taken off Martin and Matt.'

Lex felt bad for agreeing with her.

Thelma continued, 'As for Gil's behaviour . . . well, lovey, he's obviously not thinking at all clearly. And is it surprising, in the circumstances? I remember when I fell off my bike . . . I was travelling quite fast at the time when a car pulled out of a side street in front of me and I had to swerve to avoid it. I hit the curb full pelt and toppled head first over the handlebars. My mam was picking grit out of deep grazes on my knees and elbows for days afterwards. No way was I going to repeat that performance, until Des forced me to get back on or risk always being terrified of riding a bike . . . and at the time we used to bike everywhere together to save on bus fares to put towards our wedding.

'Well, obviously, Gil's got a phobia about women now because of what's happened to him. Your husband is an intelligent man. I'm sure that given a bit more time to get his head around what's happened to him, he'll see that his proposal of living the life of a night owl in future is absolutely ridiculous, not only for himself but his family. The only way forward is to face his phobia, like I had to.'

Lex sighed, 'I hope you're right, Thelma.'

She affectionately patted Lex's hand. 'I'm sure I am.' Then she asked, 'How did you get on this morning on your trip to the shops?'

Lex gave her the details.

When she had finished Thelma looked most impressed. 'You handled those women in the Co-op better than I would have done! I wouldn't have been anywhere near as diplomatic, bloody, nasty-mouthed vipers, the lot of them. But good old Phyllis, I've always liked her, salt-of-the-earth sort. At least Gil will know there's three of us women who ain't afraid to be in his company. No need to turn into a hermit on our account.' She paused for a moment before telling her friend, 'I appreciate your need to go it alone today, but if ever you don't feel up to it you can call on me.'

Lex smiled at her appreciatively. It was very comforting to know she had her friend on tap to support her while she herself laboured to support her family.

At ten o'clock that night, Lex finally conceded defeat and took the simmering pan of water off the stove. She scraped the plate clean. Gil obviously wasn't going to show his face again today. She soothed herself with the thought that maybe she had been wrong in assuming he was hiding away in bed in an effort to avoid his family. Maybe instead he'd been exhausted, both mentally and physically. He did appear to be asleep when she gently eased herself in beside him a while later. Sleep evaded Lex, though, until she heard the sound of the back door opening and closing, heralding the safe arrival home of her sons at just after eleven. It was only then that she fell into an exhausted slumber herself.

CHAPTER FIVE

For the second time in their twenty-five-year marriage Lex rose before Gil the next morning, to see her sons off to work. The fact that her husband had been in bed now for nearly twenty hours, and still appeared to be asleep, seriously concerned her. Lex decided that if he wasn't showing any sign of rising by the time she was ready to go shopping, she would have to do something about it, fetch the doctor if necessary to check nothing was medically wrong with him.

She was just splashing fat over the eggs in the pan when her sons lumbered into the kitchen. Neither of them could ever be described as the full-of-life sort first thing in the morning so their subdued manner today was no special cause for concern. As they ate, she did manage to get out of them the fact that they had spent the previous evening in their local. They admitted to her that they had been on the receiving end of some derogatory glances from a few regulars, and Gil's sacking was obviously a topic of general conversation, but they had endured nothing worse than that. It was with mixed feelings that Lex eventually waved them off to work. Part of her was worried about what faced them there today, the other part proud of them for continuing to brave it.

They had been gone ten minutes and she was just about to go up and check on Gil when he arrived in the kitchen. She was gratified to see that he was dressed – although casually, as he would on a Sunday in slacks and a jumper – and shaved. His movements seemed laboured, though, and there was no spark in his eyes or usual morning smile for her. This drawn-looking man before her was not the strong, purposeful one she had fallen in love with twenty-seven years ago, the man who'd relished the day ahead for what it would bring and the contribution he could make to it. This Gil looked like he couldn't care less whether he actually woke up or not.

Regardless, Lex addressed him breezily. 'Morning, love. Breakfast won't be a minute.'

He obviously had his appetite back as he made no comment to this but walked out of the room to sit down at the table in the dining room. After cracking an egg in the frying pan, Lex made to go in and pour him out his cup of tea then reminded herself he was suffering mentally, not physically. He was quite capable of pouring his own tea like he normally would. Moments later she placed his plate before him and sat down opposite.

After stiltedly thanking her for it, he asked, 'Did you manage to get me the *Mercury* yesterday?'

The fact that he hadn't met her eyes when speaking was not lost on Lex. 'It's on your armchair, dear,' she told him.

'After breakfast I'll start looking through the Jobs pages.'

'I hope there's something you feel like applying for. I'm sure there will be for a man with your skills,' she said encouragingly.

'Hopefully,' he responded shortly.

Gil had always shown a lively interest in his family, wanting to know every detail of their lives on a daily basis. The fact that he hadn't asked, as he usually did, if she had slept well the previous night, what her plans were for that day, or anything at all about their sons and how they were faring, bothered Lex deeply.

'Gil,' she ventured. She waited for him to look at her but he didn't so she continued speaking. 'When you saw Kathleen Crouch and her daughter yesterday ... well, I really believe she wasn't acting that way because she was afraid of you but just politely standing aside to let you pass.'

He looked up then and snapped at her brusquely, 'You can assume what you like, Lex. You weren't there so you didn't see the look on her face or the way she pulled her daughter protectively to her. I *was* there and I *did* see. They were afraid of me. As I told you yesterday, I will not put Kathleen Crouch or any other woman in that position again. I never want to feel responsible for such fear. I won't change my mind about that.' Pushing away his food barely touched, he scraped back his chair and stood up. 'Now, I'm sure you've got things to do and I don't want to get under your feet so I'm going into the living room to look through the newspaper.'

Before she could stop him he had left her to it, shutting the door firmly behind him as if shutting her out.

Lex stared after him blankly. Hopefully Thelma would make him see on Saturday evening that not every woman feared him now. She would also get Phyllis to pay him a visit so she could confirm this. Surely that would help persuade Gil to change his mind about his self-incarceration during daylight hours.

Lex rushed around clearing away the breakfast dishes and tidying the dining room, then went up to make the beds and tidy herself ready go to out.

Back downstairs she went into the living room to find Gil still engrossed in reading the newspaper. 'Anything of interest to you?' she enquired.

Without looking at her he responded flatly, 'A couple of possibles. I'll telephone to enquire after them when I've finished checking through all the engineering vacancies.'

'I'll keep my fingers crossed for you,' Lex said in an optimistic tone, then took a breath before continuing, 'I'm going around to see Phyllis Watson in a minute. You remember, she broke her ankle and arm after falling over a child's bike in the street. I've been helping her as much as I can until she's back on her feet.'

He snapped back, 'I might have lost my standing in the community, Lex, but not my memory.'

Her face fell in dismay. 'Oh, Gil, I wasn't insinuating that you had. I was just going to ask if you'd come with me? Phyllis was very supportive of you when I told her about what had happened. You should have heard her. She didn't believe anything that was said against you. I thought it would do you good to hear it for yourself from her own lips, that's all.'

'Just one woman in the hundreds around this area?'

'Well, actually it's two, Gil. Thelma is of the same mind.'

His head jerked in rebuttal. 'You might choose to believe what Thelma and Phyllis say to you, but I'll never be sure they're not secretly, wondering . . . taking care to keep someone else with them at all times when I'm around. The same goes for any others who come forward saying they believe me innocent of abusing Miriam Jones. The only woman I'm absolutely sure believes me, and in whose company I'll feel comfortable, is you, Lex. I know you so well, I'd see in an instant if you weren't being honest with me. The same goes for our sons. I couldn't stay here if I had any doubt at all that my family believed me.' It was obvious to Lex that he was fighting to keep his emotions in check. He couldn't hide the tremor in his bottom lip when he added, 'The only thing keeping me going is the fact that my family are behind me.' His voice barely a whisper, eyes haunted, he told her, 'I wish you knew how guilty I feel for bringing all this on you.'

Her heart broke for him then. Fighting back tears of her own, she dropped down beside his chair to grasp his hand, squeezing it tightly. Looking deep into his eyes, she told him in no uncertain terms, 'We'll never stop believing in you or supporting you through this, Gil. I won't lie and say I agree with your decision to keep away from all women in future, but I do respect your wishes and will do all I can to make sure it happens.'

He was too full of emotion to respond.

A while later, with her mind fully occupied with her husband's plight, Lex emerged from the entry and began walking past the house in the direction of Thelma's. She realised then that she had left her shopping bag behind. Turning around to retrace her steps, a flash of some bright colour on their front door caught her eye. Across it was daubed in thick red paint, MORTON THE MONSTER LIVES HERE.

She stared at it, frozen. What nasty-minded person or persons had done this? Then a wave of sheer panic rushed through her. Gil must not know about this. His state of mind was fragile enough without this vile message sending him further into decline.

Thankfully her sons hadn't caught sight of it when they had gone off to work earlier or they'd have been straight back to deal with it.

Lex's mind raced frantically, seeking a way to remove the obscenity before her beloved family caught sight of it. She didn't need to go over and examine it to know that it was gloss paint that had been used. She wouldn't be able to erase that with soap and water. The only way of obliterating it was by painting over it, and quickly and quietly so as not to alert Gil. She remembered that when he had repainted the outside of the house the previous year, helped by their sons, half a tin of the green gloss used for the door had been left over. Gil stored such items in the outhouse.

Without further ado, she hurried back to the entry, lifted the latch and sneaked inside to creep over to the outhouse – praying that Gil wasn't looking out of the dining-room or kitchen window. The outhouse was an Aladdin's cave of assorted gardening para-phernalia and items used for the repair and maintenance of the house, accumulated throughout their years of marriage. Thankfully Gil was a meticulous man who always kept the place in order. She was quickly able to spot paint tins and several used but cleaned brushes standing in a jar of turpentine on one of the shelves to one side of her. Stacked on top of a tin of white gloss was the half-empty tin of green she was seeking. Lex collected it, along with a brush and a piece of old cloth, then stealthily let herself out of the shed.

Lex got busy with her task. If any passers-by observed what she was doing she wasn't aware of it, in too great a hurry to complete her chore. It took just over fifteen minutes. Standing back then to examine her handiwork she was confident that when the green paint dried no one would be any the wiser about what lay underneath.

Hiding the now empty tin of paint and dirty brush in the middle of some shrubs to collect later and secrete in the dustbin, she hurried back down the path and set off again on her original errand.

Consumed with a mixture of deep distress over what she had found and tremendous relief that she had managed to avoid her family seeing it, Lex almost leaped out of her skin when a hand unexpectedly clamped her arm and a voice boomed out, 'You seem to be in a world of your own, Mrs Morton, but then I suppose in the circumstances that's to be expected.'

The baritone voice belonged to Veronica Middleton, a horse-faced, immaculately dressed matron in her mid-sixties. Veronica was the chairwoman of the local branch of the Women's Institute where Lex was a valued member.

'I was just on my way to pay a visit to you, glad I've bumped into you,' the woman continued. 'I've just chaired an emergency committee meeting about arrangements for the Christmas party we organise annually for the elderly in the area. Your own predicament came up during proceedings. The committee appreciate you must have a lot of personal matters keeping you occupied at the moment. I've come to inform you that we all quite understand why you won't be able to volunteer your services for this year's function or attend weekly meetings for the foreseeable future.' She eyed Lex meaningfully then. 'You do understand me, don't you, Mrs Morton?' Before Lex had chance to respond she added, 'Well, I have to rush. Things to do, people to see. Good day to you.'

Dumbstruck, Lex stared after her as she purposefully strode off down the street and disappeared around the corner. Oh, she understood all right. Veronica Middleton had been blatantly lying to her. She had chaired an emergency committee meeting, but it hadn't been called to discuss the arrangements for the Christmas party for the elderly but Lex herself. The committee, no doubt egged on by Veronica, had decided they didn't want the wife of a man accused of molestation tarnishing the reputation of their branch. Lex felt so hurt, so humiliated and so furiously angry, that after all her years of loyal service to the organisation they hadn't allowed her the courtesy of letting her put her side of the story to them before they decided she wasn't fit to be a member any longer.

Thankfully Thelma answered the door to her immediately.

'Come on in, gel, kettle's just boiled.' Then she noticed the state of her friend's paint-stained hands, the strained look on her face, and urged, 'Want to tell me about it?'

'Some kind person left a message on our front door last night. Thankfully I noticed it when I left the house earlier, but only because I'd forgotten my shopping bag and had to go back and fetch it. I remembered we'd paint left over from when Gil did the outside last year and was able to get rid of it before any of the family saw it. I was hoping Des might have something to get this paint off my hands?'

Thelma's expression was thunderous. 'I take it the message wasn't a friendly one. People who leave messages like that are nothing but cowards. Evil, nasty-minded ... Huh! I just hope I never discover the culprit or God help them. We've some turpentine in the outhouse. I'll go and fetch it and hope it does the trick.'

Lex's hands were red raw by the time she had finished scrubbing them with Thelma's coarse floor scrubbing-brush as her softer hand-brush proved useless. After she had managed to remove the last speck of paint, she gratefully applied a liberal amount of the Atrixo hand cream Thelma gave her to soothe her skin.

'You've had an eventful morning,' her friend said to her as she placed a cup of tea in front of Lex at the dining table – the kitchen in her three-bedroomed, flat-fronted terrace house was too small to accommodate a table. Nor did they have a bathroom but still bathed in the tin tub before the fire every Friday evening, occasionally accepting Gil and Lex's invitation to make use of their modern indoor bathroom.

Lex took a sip of her tea before responding, 'That's not all that's happened to me since I left the house this morning.'

Thelma looked taken aback. 'Good God, what else could have?' Then she added knowingly, 'Oh, met some neighbours, did you?'

'Thankfully, no, but I expect I will when I go to the shops after I leave here. No, I bumped into Veronica Middleton on my way here. She was on her way to see me. It seems I'm no longer welcome at the W.I. She didn't put it that way exactly, actually for her she was quite diplomatic, but that was what she was telling me.'

Thelma's fury returned. 'Bleeding snobs, that committee lot!' she blurted. 'Oh, Lex, excuse my French, but they are. Call themselves a charitable organisation! What's charitable about them

71

ostracising you for something your husband has allegedly done? Didn't even pay you the courtesy of hearing your side of the story and putting it to a general vote, did they? Well, it's their loss, lovey. They ain't half going to miss your contribution to the branch. They'll soon realise just what a valued member you were when they haven't got you to call upon. And they ain't going to bloody have my contribution either! At the meeting tonight I'm publicly resigning, and I'll make no bones about telling all of them why. Let's see how they like *that*.'

'Oh, Thelma, you don't need to.'

'Yes, I do. You're my friend, Lex. If I can't stand up for you, who can?'

She fought back tears of gratitude. 'In that case, would it be all right with you if I came round here every week when we'd normally go to the W.I. meeting? Gil might ask me why I'm not going any longer, if I stay in and I don't want to him know the reason, as I'm sure you can appreciate.'

'Of course,' Thelma readily agreed. Then she looked excited. 'I'll make sure I have no other visitors popping in and we can make them our own girls' nights together.'

Lex smiled. 'I'd like that.' Then she took a deep breath, hoping her friend understood why she was about to request what she was. 'Thelma, there was another purpose in my coming to see you this morning.'

Her tone of voice made her friend look at her worriedly. 'Oh?'

Lex took another deep breath. 'Well, it's just that I have to ask you not to call at the house for the foreseeable future. Believe me, I've done my best to try and persuade Gil that you and Phyllis don't believe him guilty of molesting that woman, but he's still adamant about keeping himself totally away from all women in future, including you.'

Her bottom lip trembled as she added, 'Oh, it's just so awful. I feel this nightmare is just getting worse and worse. It only started two days ago yet it feels I've been living it a lifetime already. At the moment I can't see an end to it. If only we could be allowed to try and pick up the pieces, rebuild our lives as best we can. It's destroying me see Gil this way, frightened to go out, refusing to answer the door in case there's a female at the other side of it. I'll do anything it takes to make his life bearable, anything at all. If that means I have to reorganise my life around him, then that's what I'll do.' She looked at her friend imploringly. 'I'd really hate to lose your friendship, Thelma. Please say you understand why I'm having to ask you this?'

She erupted, 'You'll never lose my friendship, Lex.' Then sighed heavily, reaching over to place a reassuring hand on Lex's and saying, 'Of course I understand why you're doing what you are. If this had happened to my Des, God forbid, I'd stand by him regardless of what it meant to myself.' A look of sadness filled her face then. 'I just hope this situation doesn't last long. I'll miss all the things we four used to share.' She eyed her friend searchingly. 'Won't you change your mind about paying that Jones woman a visit, try and reason with her and put this all right? I'll come with you.'

Lex resolutely shook her head. 'I appreciate your offer but if Miriam Jones thought she'd made a terrible mistake, she would have come forward about it by now, wouldn't she? And besides, like Gil said this morning, she's got a lot to lose by owning up so why would she? It seems we have no choice but to get on with it, Thelma. And if I'm truthful, I don't really want to see her. I don't want to lie in bed at night picturing the woman who's devastated our lives, whether she feels she's justified in what she did or not.'

'No, I don't think I would want to either,' Thelma sighed in resignation as she pushed back her chair. 'Cuppa?'

'Yes, please, then I must let you get on as I've no doubt you've things to do before you go off to work.' Lex paused for a moment before she said meaningfully, 'Thank you for being such a good and understanding friend to me, Thelma.'

Tears glinted in her eyes. 'Oh, Lex, don't you dare think I ever won't be. At the moment you might not find a welcome at many doors, but you'll always, *always* find one at mine.'

*

73

Lex's visit to the shops was no less of an ordeal than it had proved to be the previous day. She was very conscious that people were whispering about her, and witnessed one woman she had previously been on friendly terms with purposely crossing the road to avoid her.

Arriving home, she found Gil still sitting in his armchair in the living room, looking through the previous day's copy of the *Mercury*, though she spotted it wasn't the Jobs columns he was looking at but the news pages.

'I've got you the early edition of today's,' she told him, holding it out for him to take.

Folding up the previous day's copy and accepting the new edition his wife had bought him, he muttered, 'Thanks, Lex.'

'Any luck with the couple of jobs you rang after?'

He was studying the headlines by now and his tone was flat when he responded. 'I haven't got round to applying for them yet.'

She wondered if he was stalling, not yet mentally prepared for the reaction he might receive when quizzed by potential employers as to his reason for leaving his last post. Well, she couldn't blame him for that.

'I was just going to do a light lunch for us today as the boys told me they're joining their mates for a game of football at dinnertime.'

Her sons had informed her of that before leaving this morning, but she suspected they were in fact doing exactly what they had yesterday: facing up to the gossip and putting on brave faces. 'Is that agreeable to you, Gil?' she asked.

'I'll go along with anything you decide.'

That sounded as if he felt he had no right to any say in the household decisions that were made, which was nonsense. Neither she nor their sons had treated him in any way that would lead him to that conclusion. Sounding just as subdued, Lex asked, 'Would you like a cup of tea?'

'If you're making one, but please don't go to any trouble on my account.'

Despite herself, her patience snapped then. 'Gil, nothing I have ever done for you was any trouble to me, and it never will be. You're still the head of the house as far as your sons and I are concerned.'

With that she spun on her heel and left him to consider what she had said.

CHAPTER SIX

Lex was mortally relieved to see that both her sons appeared to be no worse off when they arrived home from work that evening. After they had both given her their customary peck on the cheek, she tentatively asked, 'How was your day?'

On the way home they'd made a pact not to divulge to their mother what had in fact transpired at work that day. Fuelled by his failure yesterday at the factory gates due to Maurice Brenton's intervention, Loz Stanton, roping in his mates, had spread it around that it had been the Mortons who had instigated the fight, offering his swollen bloodied nose, bruised chin and a fabricated limp as proof. Several of his mates claimed false injuries too, and consequently many of the shop-floor workers had fallen for the lie and responded by sending Martin and Matt to Coventry. Now it seemed that a third of the workforce weren't speaking to them, a third were throwing out nasty taunts and playing potentially dangerous tricks on them at every opportunity, and the remaining third were timidly offering the boys their support – but only when no one else was around.

It was Matt who responded, 'All was quiet on the Western Front. I think the blokes know they'll never get the better of me and Matt so they're not wasting their time trying.'

Martin saw his mother open her mouth to query this so cut her short by asking, 'How's your day been then, Mam?'

Lex looked at them. It was very apparent to her that they did not want to upset her unnecessarily by telling her what they had really suffered today. She smiled at them warmly and fibbed, 'All was quiet on my Western Front too.'

Her sons flashed each other a knowing look. Their mother's day had obviously been as eventful as their own.

'How's Dad?' Martin asked her.

'Where is he?' asked Matt.

'He's in the living room.' She paused, taking a breath before continuing, 'Look, sons, he isn't thinking at all straight at the moment. He's ... well, he's decided that all women are terrified of him now so he owes it to them to keep away from them in future.'

Both of the boys looked confused.

'And just how does Dad propose to do that?' Matt demanded.

'By not going out during the day unless he absolutely has to, and then only as long as I accompany him. He says he'll get himself a night job where no women at all are employed.'

Both her sons looked appalled.

Martin snapped, 'And what kind of life is that for him to be living? It won't prove much fun for you either, Mam.'

'You're right, Dad's definitely not thinking straight to have come up with that,' Matt retorted.

Lex told them sternly, 'Whether we feel your father's decision is right or not, we're his family and we'll support him. I trust I can count on you both.' It was taken for granted, not a question. 'If you'd both like to wash your hands, I'll be dishing up.' Then she went over to the kitchen door and called out, 'Gil, dinner is about to be put on the table.'

Presently he arrived in the dining room. Both his sons were shocked to see how haggard he looked. Nodding an awkward greeting to them both, he looked hesitantly at the carver chair at the head of the table, the one he'd occupied for the last twenty-five years. It was clear he didn't feel he warranted that honour any longer. Lex arrived in the room carrying two filled plates, took one look at her husband and realised what was going on. Putting his plate down in its usual place, she told him to tuck in before it went cold.

Unlike many other families who still held on to the Victorian rule that mealtimes be conducted in silence, the Mortons had always perceived them as times to catch up with the family's individual developments and to discuss both local and wider issues. Out of respect, the rest of the family would always wait for Gil to strike up conversation first, once they were all seated. He had always done so by asking his sons about their day and what plans they had for that evening. Tonight he made no such attempt and the meal was spent by them all in awkward silence. Although this state of affairs bothered them greatly, his sons were both relieved that at least Gil had not enquired after their day as neither of them wanted to lie to him about their treatment from their colleagues at Brenton's since his dismissal.

It was Lex who broke the silence by asking, 'So, what are you both up to tonight?'

Martin responded, 'I'm meeting a friend.' He grinned cheekily at his mother. 'Before you ask, yes, a girl. I met her down the local last week. She and her family have just moved into the area from the other side of town.'

Naturally Lex asked, as all mothers would, 'Oh, do you think it might become serious?'.

With a twinkle in his eye, he said, 'Mother, I haven't got your gift for knowing instantly whether someone is right for me or not, so how would I know? But I'm certainly having fun in the meantime, finding out.'

'Well, I hope you have a good time.' Then she looked at Matt. 'What are your plans?'

He looked bothered for a moment before saying, 'Well, as I'd nothing else planned, I thought I'd go with Dad down the snooker hall for a few games.' He looked expectantly at Gil. 'How about it, Dad?'

Lex held her breath. It had temporarily slipped her mind that it was Thursday. While she attended her W.I. meeting, Gil usually went down the local snooker hall for a few games and to catch up with several men he'd been friendly with for years, including Thelma's husband Des. If they had nothing better on, his sons would join him. Trouble was, a handful of womenfolk also frequented the snooker hall. Matt had obviously forgotten this fact.

Gil responded flatly, 'I'll give it a miss, thank you, son.'

'Then I'll stay in and keep you company while Mam's out at her W.I. meeting. We haven't had a game of chess for a while, fancy one?'

'There's no need to stay in on my account,' his father brusquely replied. 'I'm not stupid. I know what they'll have been putting you through at work ... don't tell me you got those cuts and bruises on your face tripping over a mat in the kitchen. You're both enduring enough thanks to me without having your social life disrupted.'

The rest of the meal was spent in awkward silence, and all of them were inwardly grateful to leave the table that night and go about their business. Lex cleared away, both Martin and Matt disappeared up to their rooms to ready themselves for their respective evenings out, and Gil returned to the living room to watch the evening news on television.

Thelma's husband Des, a tubby, greying forty-four-year-old man of kindly disposition, welcomed Lex into his house a while later. Giving her a friendly hug, he exclaimed, 'Oh, lovey, it's good to see you. Dreadful business with Gil, just bloody dreadful. Thelma and I don't believe a word of it, naturally. Pass that on, love, won't you? So, how are you all coping?'

Lex smiled warmly at him as he took her coat. 'It's good to see you too, Des. And the lads and I would cope a lot better if people would just leave us alone, but it's a gossips' dream this, isn't it? And I suppose it would be uncharitable of me not to want them to have their bit of fun at the expense of an innocent man and his family. Sorry, don't mean to be sarcastic. It's just that Gil's not coping at all, Des, and it's breaking my heart seeing him like he is.'

Des hung up her coat, saying, 'Thelma told me that Gil's got it into his head all females are terrified of him now in case he makes inappropriate advances.' He shook his head ruefully. 'I've been friends with that man for over twenty years and never once seen him act in any way but with the utmost respect towards women, even when he's had a few too many pints of best bitter inside him.' He patted her arm reassuringly. 'If it's any consolation, I can appreciate why Gil's acting like he is, though. I'd be mortified if some woman accused me out of the blue like that. I'm sure when he's got his head around all this, he'll see the best way to silence his critics is to show his face to the world, not hide away by day. I was really upset when Thelma told me our social nights have been put a stop to . . . just for the time being, I hope.'

'I hope so too, Des,' Lex said in all sincerity.

He looked thoughtfully at her. 'Gil's always been what I'd call a doer. It can't be good for him to shut himself up in the house with all this time on his hands to dwell on things. When you've any troubles, let alone big ones like Gil is having to deal with, there's nothing like having something to take your mind off them. Best thing he can do is get himself set on in a new job, as soon as possible.'

'He's been scouring the *Mercury* for something suitable, but the trouble is he seems to have lost his nerve about enquiring after any. I can only assume that's because he's not ready to face the humiliation of rejection when he reveals to a potential employer why he lost his last job.'

'He's a family to keep, Lex, and for men like Gil and myself pride goes out the window when it comes to providing for our families. I'll have a word with him tonight at the snooker hall – encourage him. I'm sure the other chaps will be voicing their support too.'

Lex sighed. 'He's not going to the snooker, Des, tonight or ever again according to him. Some of the men take their women along to watch, don't they?'

'Oh! But none of our group does.' Des looked bothered. 'He really is taking this to extremes, isn't he? I'll call past yours on my way, see if I can persuade him to come along tonight.'

'Oh, Des, will you?' she enthused. 'I really hope you succeed.'

'I'll do my best,' he assured her then once again looked bothered. 'Thelma told me you'd been told you're no longer welcome at the W.I.' He patted her arm. 'If that's how narrow-minded them lot are then you're best out of it, lovey, and so is my Thelma.'

'Most of the members are good women, Des, it's just a handful who've caused this to happen.' Lex looked sad. 'I enjoyed all the good works I helped to do in the community, and will miss the social side of it too. I felt terrible, letting Gil believe I was off to a meeting tonight, but hearing I'd been expelled because of him would only make things worse for him. I felt I'd no choice but to keep up this charade until he's in a stronger frame of mind.'

'Sometimes we have to lie, Lex. Thelma's furious about the way you're being treated and I've been given my orders to make you comfy while she's off giving the committee a piece of her mind. Cuppa or something stronger?'

'I feel like diving into a bottle of port at the moment, Des, but I'd not be able to explain my inebriated state to Gil when I got home. Better have a cuppa, please.'

The kettle was just boiling when the back door was thrown open and Thelma charged in. 'Well, that's told that lot,' she blurted out triumphantly as she stripped off her coat. 'I wish I'd had a cine-camera then I could have played it back to you. Right after we'd sung "Jerusalem" I charged up to the front, got everyone's attention, then let rip about what I thought of the committee for deciding on our behalf to ask you not to come anymore. Then I said that *I* no longer wanted to be associated with the W.I. either. You should have seen their faces! Talk about gobsmacked.

'Anyway, Lily Saddleworth and Franny Jilks caught up with me as I left the building. They told me to tell you that they think what the committee has done in the name of the members is appalling and against W.I. rules. They should have put it to a vote. They both know Gil through their husbands working at Brenton's and have met him several times at works functions. They don't believe a word of it and they were going to let the committee know their feelings.

'It's that Veronica Middleton that's behind it. Just because her husband is a surgeon at the General Hospital, she thinks she's better than all the rest of us. She truly believes she's in sole charge of the branch and speaks for us all. Well, I don't think she'll be so ready to in future, after what I said and when Lily and Franny have finished giving her a piece of their minds too. I wouldn't be surprised if a vote's taken and she's asked to resign over this. And bloody well serve her right, in my opinion.'

Thelma addressed her husband then. 'I'll finish mashing a cuppa while you get yourself ready for the snooker hall, 'cos me and Lex are going to have a girly night.' She looked at her friend, giving her hair a pat. 'I was hoping you'd fancy giving me a perm, God knows I sorely need one. I bought a Prom from the chemist on my way to work this afternoon, just in case.'

Lex was only too happy to oblige her friend.

Arriving back home at just after ten, there was no sign of Gil and she was most surprised to see Martin already home, lolling on the settee, watching the television. He looked fed up.

'I didn't expect you home so early?' Lex said to him as she took off her coat, laying it over her arm ready to hang up.

Not having heard his mother come in, he jumped and looked startled. 'Oh, hello, Mam.' He stared at her worriedly. 'Any trouble?'

She stared back at him, nonplussed. 'Trouble?'

'From the other women at your meeting?'

'Oh, er . . . no, none at all.'

He still looked unconvinced. 'I don't believe not one of them has heard about it and reported it to the others. Are you being honest with me, Mam?'

She really ought to take Martin into her confidence over her expulsion from the W.I. but knew he'd be hurt and angry for her and he had enough on his plate without this. 'I am being honest with you, Martin. I didn't get any trouble from any of the women at the W.I. Where is your father?' she asked

'In bed. He'd already gone up when I came in.'

She was aware that Des had failed in his quest to persuade Gil to accompany him to the snooker hall earlier as she'd spotted Gil's coat on the back of the door when she had arrived in. She had thought there was no sign of him because he was merely paying a visit to the bathroom, however. 'Oh! What time did you come in?'

'About nine.'

Lex was deeply worried now. Gil seemed to be finding the solace of his bed preferable to his own family's company. She hoped this was just a phase, the same as his decision not to go out during daylight hours. A memory stirred then and she looked at Martin quizzically. 'I thought you had a date tonight?'

'It was cancelled,' he said offhandedly.

'Oh, I'm sorry to hear that. What was the reason?'

He felt his mother didn't need to know that his date had in fact turned up, along with a friend for support, informing him that her parents had banned her from associating with the likes of him. She hadn't even showed him the courtesy of asking if the accusation against his father was true or not. He had been too angry with her to care by then. If this was the type of woman she was, at twenty-two still obviously ruled by her parents and unable to judge people for herself, then she wasn't the type for him anyway.

Picking up the newspaper and making a show of looking at the television listings for the rest of the evening, he lied, 'She's in bed with the 'flu. All my other mates are doing their own stuff tonight and I didn't fancy going down the snooker hall so I came home.'

Lex knew Martin wasn't being honest with her, he couldn't meet her eye. Neither of her sons was a natural liar and only tried to with the best of intentions. She knew Martin was lying now to protect her from the real reason his date was cancelled at short notice. She felt sorry for him, but he was clearly better off without the girl.

She would offer motherly comfort in the best way she knew. Lex went across and perched on the arm of the sofa. 'Milky cocoa and a couple of my homemade raisin biscuits?' she suggested.

As he met her eyes, for an instant she saw him as a young boy again, when any childish trouble could be put right this way.

'Yes, please, Mam!'

The milk was just boiling when Matt arrived. Instantly seeing what his mother was doing, he asked, 'Got enough for me?'

She smiled over at him. 'Of course.' He at least seemed to be in good spirits, like he normally would be after an enjoyable evening out. 'Had a good night, son?'

Sitting at the kitchen table, taking off his shoes, he nodded. 'Apart from losing ten bob to Harry Carter. I can never win against him, but then neither can Dad who's an ace player himself so I don't feel too bad.' Shoes off, he got up and went across to her, helping himself to a biscuit from the tin and biting into it. Leaning against the sink, he told her, 'Dad was missed, Mam. They all told me to tell him that none of them believe that woman's claim, their wives either. If he doesn't show up next week, they'll come and fetch him themselves.'

Her son was looking her in the eye so she knew he spoke the truth. Lex allowed herself a moment of hope. Gil's snooker crowd and their respective wives knew what kind of a man he was. Maybe by next week he would have remembered it himself and begun to rebuild his life again.

CHAPTER SEVEN

The next morning Lex got up as usual to see her boys off to work. She hand-washed some things and had just begun to peg the washing on the line when she heard a noise coming from next-door's yard. Coal was obviously being shovelled into a bucket.

To one side of the Mortons lived an elderly couple, a retired greengrocer and his wife called Harry and Iris Hubert. They were a couple who valued their privacy but were friendly enough when they saw their neighbours. At the moment, the Huberts were visiting their only son and his family who lived in Brighton, having been persuaded to stay on for the festive season and return only after the New Year. Lex was keeping her eye on their house for them meantime.

Frank and Jane Higgins and their two school-age children lived to the other side. Frank was a schoolteacher. They were a friendly couple in their early-thirties, very modern in their outlook. They rented the house from the owner who had gone to work in London for his firm over a year ago and hadn't wanted to sell up in case it didn't work out for him there. Lex had been on very friendly terms with the owner, Robert Western, and his wife Carol, and then in turn with his tenants. She often minded the Higgins' children for them.

It was the Higgins' garden the noise was coming from. It would be Jane doing the chores as Frank would be at work at this time on a weekday morning. Lex hadn't seen either her or her husband since Gil's dismissal. With them living so close she should perhaps have gone round before now and informed them that there was no substance to the claim, but with so much to contend with it had not entered her mind. She was confident, though, that the Higgins knew Gil more than well enough not to have taken any gossip they'd heard for gospel.

The red-brick boundary walls were six foot high. Lex had to stand on an upturned crate purposely put there for having a chat over the wall with her neighbour.

'Hello, Jane,' she called over to the pretty, petite, flaxen-haired woman busily shovelling coal through a hatch in the shed which she was heaping up in an ornate brass bucket. Lex stood waiting while her neighbour turned around to make eye contact with her before she continued, 'I'm glad I've caught you. I'd like a word, if you've a moment. Is it all right if I pop around?'

To Lex's surprise there was no welcoming smile from Jane as there would usually be but instead a look of wariness. Lex instantly knew that she had learned of Gil's dismissal. Her neighbour's voice was very stilted when she responded, 'I'm afraid it isn't convenient for you to come around at the moment. I'm just about to go out after I've finished doing this.'

Regardless of her neighbour's frosty reception, Lex smiled warmly at her. 'When you come back then? I really would like a word with you, as soon as possible.'

The frosty tone turned icy. 'I'm afraid I'm not sure when I'll be back.'

Lex's face fell. 'I take it you've heard about Gil, Jane? I should have come around and explained myself but . . .'

'Well, I can imagine you've had too much on your mind to be thinking about the neighbours,' Jane cut in. She paused, shifting awkwardly on her feet. 'Look, Lex, I need to stress that neither Frank nor myself believe the gossip. Gil has never acted in any way improperly towards me, and I've never seen him do so with any other woman since I've lived next door to you.' She put down the shovel and wrung her hands. 'But Frank's worried . . . you see, why would the woman who accused Gil make such a claim if there was no substance to it? We have our daughters to consider. We've come to the decision it's best we don't have anything to do with you in future.'

Lex was gawping at her incredulously. 'You actually think my husband is a danger to your daughters! Jane, Gil never touched that woman in his office. It's all been a terrible misunderstanding. He's no more a danger to your . . .'

'Frank said you'd say that,' she interjected. 'You're his wife, you're bound to stand up for him. Since it happened we've seen you out and about but we haven't seen Gil at all, not even in the garden. And it's like Frank said: if he's nothing to hide, why is he hiding away? We've made our decision, Lex, and we're moving. Frank's been on to the letting people and we're going to see a house after he finishes work this afternoon, one that's well away from here. You're a mother yourself, you should understand.'

Lex would go to any lengths to protect her children from harm, even now, despite their age, and couldn't say she blamed the Higgins for doing what it took to protect theirs. But they had nothing to protect them from so far as Gil was concerned. Before she could respond, though, Jane announced, 'Must get on.' Leaving her half-filled coal bucket behind, she disappeared inside the house.

Lex stared after her. She couldn't quite believe that her neighbours were moving from fear that their two young girls could be in danger from Gil. She had mistakenly believed that as the days went by, and the initial sensation started to fade, things would get better for her family. But in fact it was all getting worse. Like the message on the front door, this was another thing she must keep from Gil for fear of what effect it would have on him. If he questioned her about the Higgins' move she would lie to her back teeth if necessary, sooner than tell him the truth.

It was with a heavy heart that Lex clambered down off the crate to resume her task of hanging out the washing.

Back in the kitchen she was relieved to find her husband had arrived downstairs, although it greatly distressed her to see he was wearing crumpled pyjamas under his dressing gown, was unwashed and unshaven, an air of sluggish fatigue about him making it obvious he hadn't slept well at all. In twenty-five years of marriage, out of his own inner pride and by way of setting an example to his sons and showing respect for his wife, Gil had never arrived down for breakfast in his night attire or without washing and shaving first. She supposed she should comfort herself with the fact that he was at least up and about.

She made to wish him good morning when to her absolute horror she registered the fact he was holding the bread knife and blood from a cut on his wrist was dripping on to the linoleum floor.

A wave of sheer panic consumed Lex then. Did Gil think life had no meaning for him now and that he'd be better off dead!

Dropping her empty washing basket and bag of pegs on the floor, she dived across, grabbing tight hold of the hand holding the knife and crying out in alarm: 'Things seem bad for you at the moment, Gil, but they will get better, believe me they will. There's no need for this.'

Gazing back at her, shocked, he snapped, 'No need for what, Lex? Just what do you think you've caught me doing?' Before she could respond he proclaimed, 'You thought I was trying to do away with myself, didn't you?' He shook his head in disbelief, yanking his wrist free from her grip and glaring in incredulity. 'Do you think I feel so little for you and our sons that I would take my own life, in our kitchen, where you'd find me? Don't you think I feel I've brought enough trouble on you all without doing that?'

Her face filled with remorse, she implored him, 'Oh, Gil, I'm so sorry, please forgive me. It's just that when I came in and saw you with that knife and the blood . . . well, what would you have thought if you'd been me?'

The cold look he gave her made her shudder. 'Not what you did, Lex. I know you well enough to realise that no matter how bad things were for you, you'd never bring such hurt on your family as to take your own life. You obviously don't know me as well as I thought you did. For your information, when I arrived down I saw you out in the garden hanging out the washing and presumed the sausages in the oven were for me. So, to save you the bother, I was making myself a sandwich. As I was cutting the bread, the knife slipped and caught my wrist.'

She gulped with shame and said, 'I'll get the medical tin and clean and dress the cut for you.'

'For God's sake, stop fussing, woman! I'm not a child, I'm quite capable of tending to it myself,' he barked as he threw the knife over into the sink and grabbed a tea towel to bind around his wrist.

His rejection of her help and the manner in which he'd just addressed her stung Lex deeply. 'Oh!' she exclaimed. 'I'll ... er ... finish making your sandwich for you, and while you're eating we could have a talk about ...'

'About what, Lex?' he sharply interrupted her 'On the wages I expect to earn now, providing I can get set on that is, we won't be able to afford a holiday anymore so there's no point in discussing where we're going next year. I won't be able to take you out to a nice restaurant on your birthday or for our anniversary either. And I dread to think of the amount of housekeeping you're going to have to manage on from now on. So you tell me what we've got to talk about, because there's nothing I can see.

'We've nothing to look forward to now except a life of scrimping and scraping and worrying if we've got enough coal to keep the house warm in winter, though I doubt we'll still manage to afford this house so it'll be back to renting some damp hovel for us. And in our old age we'll be dependent on the charity of others for our survival.'

While she stood frozen in horror at this prospect, he ripped off the rest of the slice of bread he'd been in the process of cutting then slapped it on top of the one containing the sausages. He picked up the plate along with a cup of tea he'd already poured himself and strode out of the kitchen, kicking shut the door behind him.

Lex issued a deep groan of despair, tears of desolation pricking her eyes. Her husband was becoming a stranger to her. He'd always been the optimistic sort, grasping what life offered him with enthusiasm, and never in all their years together had he spoken to her with such pessimism. She felt she was losing the man she knew and deeply loved, and didn't know what to do to bring him back to her again so that together they could ride out this storm and build themselves a better future than Gil had just pictured.

She jumped as a hand touched her arm and a voice said, 'Are you all right, love?'

She spun around to see Des looking at her worriedly. 'Oh, Des, how lovely to see you.' She forced a bright smile to her face and said, 'I'm fine, thank you.'

He eyed her knowingly. 'I'm not blind, love. I saw your face through the window as I was walking over to the back door just now, and, to use one of my Thelma's sayings, you looked like death warmed up.' He eyed her with concern. 'Things seem bad right now but they will get better.'

At this her shoulders sagged, face started to crumple. 'Oh, Des, I keep trying to tell myself that, but it doesn't seem like things will ever improve for us now.' Miserable tears spurted then and she blubbered, 'My neighbour has just told me they're moving out because they fear Gil is a threat to their two little girls. I dread him finding that out, can't imagine what the news would do to him. I must keep it from him at all costs. As for Gil . . .

'Oh, Des, he feels we have no future anymore. He won't talk to me about it, so I don't know how to make him see that we do have a future. It might not be the one he worked so hard to give us all, but what does that matter as long as we all have each other?' Lex paused to wipe away tears with the back of her hand before adding, 'What kind of wife am I when my own husband won't let me help him through the worst time he's ever faced?'

Des's tone was firm. 'Now you listen to me, Lex. You're an exemplary wife to Gil. You've stood by him when others would have thrown him out without a by-your-leave after what he came home and told you. Your sons are a credit to you too. Not many lads would be braving what I deeply suspect they are having to at Brenton's, to prove their own belief in their father's innocence and unjust dismissal. Gil's still in shock over all this, Lex, can't yet see the wood from the trees so to speak. I'm hoping I might be able to help on that score.' He pointed in the direction of the dining room. 'In there, is he?'

Wondering just what Des was up to, she nodded.

Without further ado he went across, opened the door and disappeared. Lex heard him say jocularly, 'Hello, Gil. That sandwich looks mighty good to me against the bowl of porridge I had this morning. Thelma's never mastered the art of porridge-making and you can build bricks with hers, but I'd never hurt her by telling her.' It was an exaggeration as Thelma was really a good cook, but this was Des's way of breaking the ice.

Gil's reply was stony. 'I doubt you came here to discuss my choice of breakfast or your wife's culinary skills. What did you come for?'

His friend's tone was still breezy. 'I didn't think I needed an excuse to call on you. We all missed you at snooker last night. The chaps there told me to tell you that they know that woman's claim is nonsense, their wives all feel the same too, and if you don't come next week they'll be round here to fetch you, me included.'

'Then you'll all be wasting your time. I'm finished with snooker. No interest in it anymore. Was that all?'

'No, not quite. I also came to ask a favour of you. I'm a bit pushed, you see. Got an urget job on that I've promised to get finished today, and I've just had another desperate customer call me up with another urgent job. I was about to turn him away when I thought of you and wondered, if you've nothing else important on, if you could take the job on for me? It's nothing you can't handle, Gil. Just a generator that keeps cutting out. Of course I'll pay you what I was going to be paid for fixing it . . .'

Gil looked at him blankly. 'Only last week you were telling me you hoped things were going to pick up for you soon as you were slack and only just keeping your head above water. Now all of a sudden you're inundated with work? I've never accepted charity, Des, and I'm not about to start now. You know your way out.'

In a deeply offended voice, his friend said, 'I would never insult you by offering you charity, Gil. I've known you long enough to realise how proud you are. Now stop being stubborn, man. I really do need help.'

Gil's voice was resolute when he replied, 'I'm sure someone else will help you out and save you losing a customer. Now, if you don't mind, my breakfast is going cold.'

There was silence for a moment before Des said quietly, 'I never put you down as a quitter, Gil. If you want to cut your nose off to spite your face then I'll leave you to get on with it.'

Back in the kitchen he gave a helpless shrug and patted Lex's arm. 'It was worth a try, lovey. I really thought my offer of work would do the trick, help him out of the dark hole he's buried himself in, but it seems I was wrong. I'm at a loss now to know how to help him if he won't help himself. I'll see you soon, lovey.'

All she could say was, 'Thanks so much for trying, Des.'

As he saw himself out Lex's whole body sagged in despair. When she had heard him make his offer to Gil her hopes had soared. No one could refuse a cry for help from a friend in desperate need, surely. Gil had refused, though, and not only that, he had done it so rudely. She felt embarrassed about his manner towards Des. Suddenly any sympathy for Gil's plight was overridden by anger. Despite the way he was feeling, how could he have been so offensive to a man who had been such a good friend to him for over two decades? Gil's behaviour was unforgivable. Courtesy cost nothing. Gil well deserved it if Des never spoke to him again, Lex for one wouldn't blame him.

She rarely lost her temper but that thought caused it to boil over.

With a look of doom still about him, Gil was biting into his sandwich when Lex charged into the dining room and cried, 'How could you, Gil? How could you treat Des like that? He was offering you the hand of friendship and you refused to take it. I wouldn't blame him if he never bothered with you again! He only did what you would have if the circumstances had been reversed.' She was on a roll now, unable to stop herself. 'I've excused your behaviour for long enough. Worse things have happened to people, Gil, despite you thinking this is the end of the world for you. And they've picked themselves up and started again and definitely not treated their family and friends in the manner you're treating yours!

'You're so wrapped up in your own misery, you've not even thought to ask me or your sons how we're dealing with this. I dread to think what our boys have faced in the factory from the other men over this yet they're determined to suffer in silence what's dished out to them, to prove to everyone their belief in their father's innocence. Your family is doing their best to get on with things, Gil. What are you prepared to do to put all this behind you – or are you just going to sit there and fester in self-pity for the rest of your life?'

Sandwich poised in mid-air, he sat looking at her blankly. When he made no attempt to answer Lex shook her head, turned and stormed out of the room.

Back in the kitchen she clutched the edge of the sink and slumped against it in utter despair. If Gil could not find it within himself to make an effort to rebuild his life, what hope had they got as a family? She and their sons couldn't do it without his contribution. Then guilt reared in her. She had never spoken to her husband in such a way before, never had reason to, and felt remorse for her tirade. Any last morsel of inner respect and pride he'd had left, she feared she had just taken from him. There was a time and a place for home truths and this moment in Gil's life wasn't one of them. She should have kept her own counsel, or at the very least found a way to speak her mind in a more sympathetic way.

She was about to return and apologise for her outburst, beg his forgiveness, hope she could somehow put matters between them back to what they were before, when a sound reached her. Automatically she spun around to look in the direction of the dining room. The noise she had heard was that of a chair being pushed back. Was Gil coming through to give her a piece of his mind? She steeled herself for a verbal attack on her. But she heard his footsteps heading for the stairs, up them and across the landing and on into their bedroom. She had obviously upset him so much he had returned to the solace of his bed.

Acute remorse consumed her then. She needed to find a way to repair the damage she feared she had caused. But how could she do that when words spoken could not be retracted? She stared blindly out of the window, seeking for a way to redeem herself in her husband's eyes, but all it seemed she could do was hope that when he next came down he was in a more receptive mood and found it within himself to forgive her.

Turning on the radio in order to break the silence, she began to tidy away the remains of breakfast. She was running water into the washing-up bowl when she sensed someone had entered the room. She turned around and to her surprise saw Gil, washed and dressed in his old Brenton's work overalls, the ones he'd abandoned on becoming works manager but had kept to protect his clothes while tackling dirty maintenance jobs around the house.

As Lex looked on he walked across to the back door and took his coat off the hook. Clearing his throat, he turned to face her. 'Er . . . I don't know how long I'll be. Depends how long it takes for me to do the job Des asked me to help him with.'

She was flabbergasted by this turn of events and faltered, 'Oh, er . . . would you like me to make up a flask of tea and a sandwich for you?'

He awkwardly responded, 'Thanks for the offer but I want to be off and get cracking on the job. I'll see you later then.'

With that he turned and left.

She looked out of the window and watched him hesitate before the back gate before leaving the yard. It seemed her outburst had not had the detrimental effect on him she'd gravely feared, but quite the opposite, in fact. Oh, please God, let that be true, she prayed.

She wouldn't find out until he returned home.

CHAPTER EIGHT

Outside, Gil was just about to emerge from the entry when suddenly a vision of hordes of furious women, possibly men too, baying for his blood and waiting to pounce on him, made him stop short.

His wife's words to him that morning had shocked him rigid Throughout her tirade he had been very much aware that she had been reduced to such a state because of his own selfish behaviour.

And she was right. He had become so consumed in self-pity for the price he was having to pay for Miriam Jones' lies he hadn't considered what effect it was having on his family, too. Lex had brought forcefully home to him the fact that if he carried on like this, then regardless of anything else he had lost, he could also lose those most dear to him. That thought terrified Gil witless. His wife and sons were everything to him. How could he have been so cowardly as to allow his family to face the backlash of this alone while he gutlessly hid himself away inside their house, consumed by the fact that his honour as breadwinner was in shreds, cowardly avoiding the abuse he could receive from some members of the public. He didn't deserve his family, friends either for that matter. He had just been unforgivably rude to Des. His friend had taken the trouble to pay him a visit, offer him a lifeline, and Gil had thrown it back in his face. He wouldn't blame Des if he never spoke to him again.

Lex had just made him realise that what the outside world thought of him now wasn't important; what his family and close friends did, was. The future he could offer his family now might not match up to the one he had worked hard to bring them in the past, but the fact that they still wanted him as part of that future was what he needed to concentrate and build upon. He couldn't bring them any sort of future imprisoned inside his own house, wallowing in misery. He needed to do what his wife and sons were doing, and that was to get himself out and grab whatever opportunity was open to him now.

The trouble was that all the courage he had mustered to venture out into the world again, fuelled by his wife's earlier home truths, had suddenly deserted him now that he was faced with reality. Smartly dressed and standing proudly erect as he was, he knew no passer-by would ever guess the depth of the inner turmoil and nervous fear raging inside him.

He made to turn and hurry back inside the safety of his own four walls when another vision of Lex and his sons rose before him. Whatever he was feeling now, so must they have on their initial venture out after his disgrace. They hadn't been cowards and fled back inside. Neither must he.

Taking a deep breath, he thrust his chin out and mentally spurred himself on to step into the street and turn in the direction of Des's workshop. His eyes fixed firmly ahead, each step an effort to him, he forced himself not to consider the neighbours' eyes watching him from behind twitching curtains as he passed.

Approaching the Crouches' abode his heart began to thump wildly and he held his breath, willing neither Kathleen nor her daughter to make an appearance today and force him to face a repeat performance of three days ago. Much to his gratitude he passed by the Crouches' without incident and heaved a sigh of relief.

So far, so good.

But just as he approached the corner of the street, from around the corner, to his horror, he saw Julie Dawson tottering towards him on high stilettos. She was an hourglass-shaped, very attractive bleached blonde in her early-thirties, the third wife of sixty-six-year-old local bookie, Jack Dawson. As usual she was dressed in figure-hugging clothes: a low-cut blouse and black pencil skirt under a mock leopardskin coat. Martin and Matt unkindly referred to her as the 'local dumb blonde' and with just cause as she definitely had not been blessed in the intelligence department, but regardless she had enough wit about her to snare herself a man who could provide her with the expensive luxuries her slum-dwelling parents had been unable to. Contrary to popular belief, Julie had not married Jack to better herself but because she deeply loved the man. The Dawsons lived several doors down from the Mortons and, although they did not mix, socially were on friendly speaking terms.

Gil's heart pounded madly again, his mind whirled. This was just the kind of situation he had been dreading: a face-to-face meeting with a woman. It was too late for him to duck into an entry to avoid meeting Julie as she was almost upon him. He was in no doubt she would have learned of the accusation against him, if not through gossip then definitely through her husband as what Jack didn't learn about the locals over his counter wasn't worth knowing. The way she would react to meeting him in broad daylight wasn't all that worried Gil. He felt he must not give Julie any reason to feel he was coming on to her in a sexual manner, and the only way he felt he could do that was by completely ignoring her. Eyes still fixed firmly ahead, he quickened his stride to pass her by as fast as possible and put a safe distance between them.

As they approached each other a look of recognition lit Julie's eyes. Smiling, she stopped and greeted him in her girlish high voice: 'Hello, Mr Morton.' When he made no attempt to acknowledge her, she quipped, 'Oi, Mr Morton, gone deaf in yer old age? Oi, Mr Morton, it's me, Julie Dawson.' A look of astonishment settled on her face then as he walked by. Undeterred she tried again, calling after him, 'You all right, Mr Morton? Oh, but you wouldn't be, would yer? I've heard what's been said about yer. Jack said it's always the ones yer least expect that turn out to be the rum sort and told me I was to steer clear of yer, just in case the rumours about you are true, but I don't believe what's being said about yer, not one bit, Mr Morton. You're a proper gent, you are. You've always treated me with respect, not like some I could mention who think I'm a gold digger. Oi, Mr Morton, did yer hear what I said? Oh, obviously not,' she muttered. She stared bemused after him for several moments before she turned and resumed her journey.

Gil was by now round the corner of the street, still striding ahead like a man in a desperate hurry to reach his destination. Unfortunately Julie Dawson's declaration of belief in his innocence had not been made within earshot.

He had hardly travelled more than five yards from the corner and was approaching the parade of shops when Betty Turner came waddling out of the chemist. A stout childless widow in her early-fifties, Betty was renowned for her narrow mindedness. She always saw the worst in everyone but herself and most people avoided her if at all possible, so as not to have to endure her endless unjustified complaints about other local residents she had taken a dislike to for some petty reason or other. Of all the people for Gil to bump into today it had to be her! Again it was too late for him to dodge into an entry to avoid contact with her, she'd already seen him.

Steeling himself, his eyes still fixed firmly ahead, Gil tried to pretend he hadn't seen Betty and to walk straight by her. But as he came level with her, much to his shock she cleared her throat and spat some phlegm at him, before hissing at him with a look of outrage, 'You filthy beast! You should be ashamed to walk amongst decent folk. You should be locked up and the key thrown away for what you did to that poor woman.'

Despite his resolve to do his best to avoid any contact with women, this nasty attack on his person, and especially by this particular woman who constantly complained to everybody about the morals and manners of others, he couldn't ignore. Stopping in his tracks, Gil turned back to face her as he took a clean handkerchief out of his pocket to wipe away the filth from his coat. Fixing her with his eyes, he said in an even voice, 'I agree with you, Mrs Turner. If I were guilty of what's claimed then I should be ashamed to walk amongst you decent folk and be locked up and the key thrown away. But as I'm not guilty, I'm not ashamed to walk these streets and it'd be an injustice to lock me away.' Tipping his forelock he added politely, 'Good day to you.'

Leaving her staring after him open-mouthed he continued on his way. It wasn't until he was convinced he was out of her sight that he stood still to take several deep breaths to calm his racing heart. The incident had deeply upset him and he knew it probably wouldn't be the last time he felt like that, but still he felt proud of himself for the way he had handled it.

Apart from some whispers and stares, nothing else happened to him on the rest of his journey to Des's workshop.

The man himself was just about to climb into his ten-year-old battered Ford Transit when to his surprise he saw Gil arrive on his workshop forecourt. After their encounter that morning, this was the last person Des had expected to see. He stared in surprise for a moment before going over to give his friend a warm greeting, but Gil got in first.

With an ashamed expression on his face and shame in his tone of voice, he said, 'I deeply apologise for my behaviour to you this morning, Des.' Shifting uncomfortably on his feet, he added, 'Is ... er ... your invitation to give you a hand still open?'

A delighted Des slapped him on the back. 'Of course it is, mate. I'm so glad you've decided to take me up on it. Come through to the workshop and I'll show you what's what.'

Back at the Morton household, Lex was finding it difficult to concentrate on her housework. She was constantly on edge, waiting for Gil to return, worried witless that he had met with another situation on his journey to Des's workshop, similar to or worse than the one he had been in with Kath Crouch and her daughter a couple of days before. If he suffered another setback there was no telling what would happen to him as a result. In an effort to steer her thoughts on to something else she decided to make a shopping list. She had only written down the first item when the door burst open. Lex was fully expecting it to be Gil and, not knowing what to expect from him, was surprised instead to see that the arrival was not her husband but Thelma.

Before Lex could address her, Thelma excitedly told her, 'I know you asked me not to come round for the time being but I had to, Lex. I had to confirm I wasn't seeing things. It *was* Gil I saw going into Des's workshop about ten minutes ago, wasn't it?'

Lex was overjoyed to hear this news. At least her husband had got as far as Des's workshop without losing his nerve and returning. Smiling in delight she said, 'Seems we've had a breakthrough, Thelma. Well, hopefully we have. I won't know for sure until Gil comes home. We've your Des to thank for it.'

Thelma looked miffed. 'I knew that old man of mine was up to something. He was so distracted this morning and wouldn't say why when I asked him what was bothering him, just fobbed me off saying he was busy and needed to get to work. He rushed out without his flask and sandwiches, and that's how I saw Gil entering his workshop ... I was on my way to take them to him on my way to the shops. Obviously Des didn't want to tell me about his plan to get Gil out of the house in case it didn't come off.' She looked searchingly at her anxious friend. 'You're like a jumping bean, gel. You need to calm down or you'll make yourself ill.'

'I've never felt so on edge in all my life, Thelma. If Des's plan fails for any reason I doubt we'd ever get Gil out of the house again.'

'All you can do is have faith it will work, lovey. I'm intrigued to know what plan my old man came up with to encourage Gil over your doorstep?'

Lex smiled. 'Was one hell of a good friend to Gil, that's what. He paid a visit here this morning to ask if Gil could help out with fixing a generator that a client of Des's was desperate for. Des said he was too busy to do it himself and didn't want to turn the customer away.' She didn't enlighten her friend as to how rudely Gil had refused Des's charity at first, or about her own blast of home truths that thankfully had spurred him out of the house. She only prayed it proved to be a success. 'I can't tell you how grateful I am to Des, Thelma. I know he lied about being inundated with work and really could ill afford to hand over that job to Gil.'

'Friendship is worth more than money, Lex. Besides, if it weren't for Gil then Des would never have taken the risk of going into business for himself. Never forget that when Des was so desperate to try his luck on his own, but worried he might not be able to support his family and get the money together to start his business up, Gil persuaded him to go ahead. Told him he didn't want to reach old age with any regrets. Should it not work out Gil promised him a job back at Brenton's. He also didn't hesitate to offer to stand as guarantor for Des with the bank, so that he could get the capital he needed. Despite my own efforts to persuade Des to have a bash at it, it was that show of faith and belief from Gil that spurred him on to go it alone.

'One good turn deserves another, doesn't it, Lex? Besides, I've forgotten the number of times you've bailed me out over the years when I hadn't a pot to piss in while my kids were young ... a few spuds, the odd packet of tea, bag of sugar, loaf of bread, block of margarine. It all adds up. So it's a nice feeling for me to think that we've done something for you for a change.'

Lex reminded her, 'Aren't you forgetting the many times you've come to my rescue when I hadn't a penny in my purse myself while my boys were young? And I'll not forget how you never hesitated to share your black market stuff with me during the war, when you could have kept it all or made a bob or two by selling it on.'

Thelma waved her hand dismissively. 'Well, I only got what I did because of my brothers' contacts. If the boot had been on the other foot you'd have shared what you managed to get with me, I've no doubt of that. You shared the extra coal you got from your coalman Uncle Fred, thank God and rest his soul. I dread to think how many nights we'd have shivered if your uncle had taken up another occupation when he left school. Anyway, how could I ever forget you minding my kids so I could work in the ammunitions factory to help meet my bills? And you wouldn't take any money for it.'

'I enjoyed having your kids, they were company for mine. And I was lucky that Gil's rank of sergeant meant he received more pay than Des so I was able to manage better. And remember I only had two children to feed and clothe against your four.' Lex smiled warmly at her friend. 'The truth is, Thelma, we helped each other equally.'

She smiled back. 'Yes, we did, didn't we? We both had our families round us then but I don't think we'd have come through it as well without each other's support.' She gave a heavy sigh, her eyes glazing over. 'Is was all so dreadful, wasn't it?'

They both lapsed into silence as memories of those terrible years came flooding back, seeing themselves again as new mothers forced to survive on their respective husband's meagre Army pay, endlessly queuing for what little was on offer while deeply worried for their menfolk's safety, not even knowing if they'd see them again. Against the odds, thankfully they did and both men came through physically unscathed, though mentally it took both of them a while to adjust. That they succeeded was mostly due to the support of their loving wives.

With a shudder Thelma said, 'I never want to go back there again.'

Lex sighed, 'Me neither.'

Then Thelma saw her flash a nervous glance at the kitchen clock and said to her, 'Is that what you're going to be doing all day, Lex, clock watching?'

'Oh, Thelma, I never thought I'd see the day when I didn't want my husband to come home before it was time.'

She leaned over and gave her friend's hand a reassuring pat. 'If Gil'd lost his nerve or met up with a situation he couldn't cope with, he'd have been back by now. You need to busy yourself or you'll be a quivering wreck by the time he does come home, and if he sees you've been on edge while he's been out, it won't do his confidence much good, will it?'

Lex nodded. 'You're right. I've plenty of housework to do. I'm ashamed to admit it's been a bit neglected since this all began. And I've shopping to get for myself and Phyllis if she needs any today.'

'Well, if you've shopping to do, so have I. I'll come with you.' And with a fighting look in her eye, Thelma added, 'You just hope we don't meet up with any gobby sorts today because, by God, will I give them short shrift if I hear one word of untoward gossip about my friends!'

And Lex had no doubt she meant what she said.

They were not going to be so lucky as to have a care-free shopping trip that morning. Lex hadn't visited the butcher's since her troubles began. As soon as they entered the shop the three queuing women took one look at her and all pulled faces, as if a nasty smell had just wafted in.

Sensing trouble brewing, butcher Archie Haines, a rotund, ruddy-faced man, raised his meat cleaver warningly in the air and addressed his customers sternly. 'Now, ladies, it's my shop and I choose who I serve in it. Mrs Morton is as welcome in here as she's always been. If none of you likes that then you're welcome to leave and shop for your meat elsewhere.'

One woman huffed out her breath, turned and pushed rudely by Lex as she stormed out, announcing, 'I'll be back later.' The other two looked peeved but stayed put, making sure their backs were turned firmly against Lex by way of registering their protest against her presence.

It was an uncomfortable wait for her. Sensing this, Thelma constantly kept up a flow of conversation with her on trivial matters. When it came to Lex's turn to be served, she said to Archie, 'Thanks for that, Mr Haines.'

He smiled kindly at her. 'Mrs Morton, if I banned any customer from using my shop once I'd heard rumours about them, I'd have hardly any custom left. I haven't had the pleasure of meeting your husband personally but I've been acquainted with you for a number of years and I've always found you a very nice person. I can't imagine you being married to the sort that would act as it's claimed your husband did. Now, what's your pleasure today?'

Purchases made and back outside the shop, Thelma said, 'Well, that's another ally you've got, gel. Archie Haines ain't backwards in coming forwards, and if he hears any of his customers mouthing off, he'll give them a piece of his mind.'

Despite fighting hard to be positive that Gil was working happily away in Des's workshop, and that this was the beginning of his reinstatement, Lex could not stop feeling anxious that something had befallen him during his outing. It took her a great effort to appear bright and cheery during the rest of her shopping expedition and while lending Phyllis a hand with her housework that afternoon. She was genuinely glad to learn from her friend, though, that her casts were to be removed the following Friday, relieving Lex from her housekeeping duties, and equally glad to get home and let her bright façade drop.

At just approaching six, with the meal ready to be dished up, herself tidied, and still no sign of Gil, it was a highly charged Lex who awaited her menfolk's return.

Immediately she heard the latch on the back gate click, she dashed to the door and yanked it open. Although delighted to see it was her sons back safe and sound, she was disappointed not to see Gil.

As he stepped inside and pecked her cheek, Martin said reproachfully, 'You could look happier to see us, Mam.'

'Oh, I am glad, of course I am, sweetheart. Hello, Matt,' she greeted her other son, offering her cheek for his kiss. As she shut the door after them she asked, 'How did it go today?'

Nothing had changed at the factory. The majority of the shop-floor men were still blatantly ignoring them, and on arriving that morning they had found their clocking in cards ripped to shreds and scattered all over the floor. Regardless, they were both continuing to put on an act of indifference, to show that such childish behaviour would not achieve the effect hoped for.

'It's Friday, we got paid, so it was a good day, Mam,' Martin told her as he pulled off his work boots. He looked at her meaningfully. 'Stop worrying yourself how me and Matt are getting on at work. We're both old enough and ugly enough to look after ourselves. You just worry about getting Dad back to his old self.'

'Watch out who you're calling ugly,' piped up Matt with a glint of humour in his eyes. 'I've been told on more than one occasion that I'm handsome enough to be in films.'

Martin scoffed, 'It was me they were talking about, not you.'

'You're both as handsome as each another,' chipped in Lex. 'You've your father to thank, you both take after him.'

'Oh, I dunno, Mam, you're not a bad-looking broad yourself ... for your age, that is,' said Martin to her, tongue in cheek.

Lex chuckled, 'Cheeky monkey.'

'Talking of Dad,' said Matt, putting his empty lunch box on the draining board then taking off his working jacket and hanging it up, 'while he's not here, we can tell you that me and Martin have decided he's locked himself up inside this house for long enough. If we don't do something about that now there's a danger he'll never leave it again. We understand why he's terrified of being in female company, after what happened to him, but the only way to conquer your fears is to face them head on, like Dad's always told us. He made me get straight back on my bike when I fell off it, didn't he? I was terrified at the time ... well, I was only seven but still ...'

'Yeah, and he made me get straight back into the swimming pool when I nearly drowned,' piped up Matt.

'You never nearly drowned, you clot, you just breathed in when your mouth was underwater, that's all,' his brother chided him. 'Anyway, it's about time Dad practised what he preaches.'

'Yes, I agree, but ...'

'No buts, Mam,' Martin interjected. 'I know you're trying to protect Dad but it's no good us three doing our best to put this behind us and get on with things, if he can't bring himself to. Well, it's three days now and he doesn't seem to be coming to his senses so we need to take action.

'Me and Matt are going to make him come to the pub with us tonight, even if we have to carry him. We won't leave his side and we'll be there to protect him from any backlash. We'll continue going out with him until he gets back enough confidence to go out by himself. Forcing him out is the only way, Mam. Dad's a big man but he's not as young as he used to be. He won't be any match for me and Matt. He can think of us what he likes, we have to do this for him, Mam. Be cruel to be kind, so to speak.'

Lex felt fortunate to have such caring sons. 'I agree that your plan might have been our only option ... if your father hadn't gone out himself this morning.' They both looked shocked and delighted to hear this news. 'Des popped in this morning to ask your father to help him do a job he couldn't manage by himself, and I'm pleased to tell you that Dad accepted. As he's not back yet, I'm hoping it's a sign that all has gone well.'

Just then they all heard the back gate open.

'That must be him now,' Lex said, and eyed them both urgently. 'Now I think it's best we act like we normally would towards your father on coming in from work. Let him take the lead, do him the courtesy of telling us what he wants to, when he wants to. He already feels he doesn't deserve his position as head of our household any longer, and we must do all we can to prove to him that in our eyes he does. You do understand me, don't you?'

'Yes, Mam,' they responded in unison.

Martin and Matt shot into the dining room and sat down at the table. Lex grabbed hold of the pan of potatoes off the stove and was in the process of draining them at the sink when Gil entered.

She smiled over at him while quickly appraising him. She was mortally grateful to see he didn't look as though he'd suffered any physical hostility during his outing, and had lost the doom-stricken look he had been sporting earlier. There was a spark of life in his eyes. 'Hello, love,' she said breezily. 'Dinner won't be a moment.'

'It smells good.' He sniffed appreciatively as he came across to give her a kiss. She knew then that whatever had happened today, life had taken a turn for the better. Hope soared within her that it would continue to do so.

Stripping off his coat to hang on the back of the door, he asked, 'Lads home, are they?'

Lex nodded. 'Both at the table, waiting for their dinner.'

As she moved away from the sink Gil went to it, turned on the hot tap and picked up the bar of Cadam soap from the soap dish. 'I'll just freshen up then.'

She finished dishing up. Courteously he picked up two of the plates for her and followed her through.

'Looks good, Mam,' said Matt as she put his plate down in front of him.

'Yeah, sure does,' said Martin. 'Evening, Dad,' he said in a casual tone.

Without hesitation this time, Gil sat down in his normal place at the head of the table and sprinkled salt from the salt cellar on to his meal. He picked up his knife and fork and made to tuck in but hesitated then and looked at each of his sons who by now were busy tucking in themselves. Laying down his cutlery, he asked in a stilted tone, 'How . . . er . . . are things at work? I don't expect you're getting an easy time of it?'

It was obvious to Lex that he had taken in what she had said that morning about him not showing a bit of interest in how his family were coping, and was now making an effort to rectify that.

It was Martin who answered, 'Nothing we can't handle, Dad, so don't worry yourself on that score.'

Gil was looking searchingly at his son's face, at the healing cuts and bruises he'd sustained from the fight he'd had with Loz and his cronies outside the factory gates. 'You look to me like you handled yourself pretty well, son. I don't hold with the use of fists, you know that, but I suspect you only resorted to them while defending my honour, and for that I thank you.' Then he looked pointedly at his younger son. 'I can't see any visible signs of you being in a fight, but I can't imagine you stood back either, so thank you too.'

He paused for a moment to take a deep breath. 'I won't lie to you all and say I've come to terms with what's happened to me, because I haven't and never will, but I know it's something I have to learn to live with. I've been acting very selfishly these last couple of days, been far from thinking straight. I do want us to continue to be a family and have some sort of future together, very much so, and I apologise for my recent behaviour and hope you can forgive me. It would have served me right if I'd lost you all.' He flashed a look at his wife then and said gratefully, 'Thank God I was made to come to my senses before it was too late.'

Lex leaned over to grab hold of his hand and squeeze it tight.

'You'll never lose us, love, never. I wish I could put into words how proud I ... we ... all are of you. We know what it took for you to do what you did today. Whatever future we have now, we'll all make the best of it. We've got each other and that's the main thing.'

'Yes, it is,' he agreed huskily.

Martin felt that since his father had enquired of his sons how their day had gone, he was now at liberty to return the compliment. Besides he was keen to know. 'Mam told us you went to help Des on a job. Go all right, did it?'

Gil nodded. 'Des seemed pleased with what I did.'

'I should think he was, Dad, you're the best engineer I know. I bet it felt odd getting your hands dirty again, though?' said Martin.

Gil smiled. 'Truth be told, I thoroughly enjoyed myself, son. I relished my job as works manager, despite how stressful it could be, and there's no denying I enjoyed the financial benefits it brought us, but I'm an engineer at heart and to me there's nothing more satisfying than knowing you've managed to bring life back into a seemingly dead machine, or had a hand in making some of the parts that've gone into making that machine work.' He asked Lex then, 'Did you happen to get a local paper for me today, love?'

She nodded. 'It's on the arm of your chair.'

'Thank you. I'll have a look through it when we've finished dinner, see what's on offer. Keep your fingers crossed that one of those jobs has my name on it.'

This news was music to Lex's ears. This morning she'd never thought she would hear those words from his lips again.

'What about ... er ...' Matt began.

Gil looked at him quizzically. 'Yes, son?'

He looked awkward. 'Well ... er ... you said you didn't feel comfortable being around women any longer, and most factories have women working in them in some capacity, so have you changed your mind?'

Gil gave a heavy sigh, his face suddenly bereft. 'No, son, I haven't,' he said with conviction. 'While this is hanging over my head, I'll never feel comfortable in an unknown woman's company again, not unless a miracle happens and my name is cleared, but whether I like it or not I have a family to keep so I have to go out to work.

'I've come to my senses and know I'm in no position to be choosy so will have to stomach the fact that females could be employed wherever I'm lucky enough to be set on. I'll just have to keep myself to myself so that I'm never in a position to be accused again. And if all the other workers think I'm the unsociable sort, then so be it.' Gil looked remorsefully at his wife. 'I know you enjoyed our social life, I did too, and I don't expect you to give up going out with friends just because I have, love.'

She laid a hand on his arm for reassurance and told him, 'This rotten situation has changed our lives. I won't lie and tell you it's not going to be hard for me, adjusting to the way we're going to be living from now on, but I married you for better or worse and I meant my vows when I said them. That hasn't changed.' She could see he was having to fight hard to keep his emotions in check and quickly changed the subject by ordering them all, 'Let's eat up before it gets cold.'

A while later she was in the kitchen, running water into the bowl to wash the dishes, when to her surprise she heard Martin ask, 'Want a hand, Mam?'

In shock she turned to see both her sons looking back at her enquiringly. Lex couldn't remember the last time either of them had offered their help with a domestic chore, and she wasn't about to turn this offer down. 'That would be much appreciated. Grab yourselves a tea towel each.'

As they did she said to them, 'So what's brought this on? Usually you two are the first to voice your opinion that anything that needs doing in the kitchen is women's work.'

There was an awkward silence for a moment before Martin responded. 'Well, maybe this business with Dad has made us realise how lucky we are to have a mother like you.'

'Yes, that's right, Mam,' piped up Matt. 'We've realised how much you do for us, and that it wouldn't hurt us to offer you a hand now and again. But it's how you've supported Dad through this awful time that's really made us see . . . that, well, you're the sort of woman we should bear in mind when we choose girls to settle down with.' He then made an announcement which absolutely stunned her. 'The sort who'll stand by us through thick and thin if anything bad happens, though God forbid it does.'

'And can cook a decent dinner,' quipped Martin. 'I doubt any of the birds I've ever been out with know how to boil an egg, let alone how to do a roast with crispy spuds like you do them, Mam.'

She stared at them both, shell-shocked. What an accolade, to be told by your own sons that they wanted a relationship just like their parents had. This terrible situation with their father had its bright side if it had made her sons start to look at life in a more mature way. They'd obviously discussed much more than how they were going to help their father over this terrible episode. 'So you've both realised that a pretty face and nice figure don't necessarily make for a lasting relationship?'

Matt nodded. 'Something like that, Mam.'

Hopefully this meant she was going to end up with two daughters-in-law she wouldn't need to worry about. 'You don't know how relieved I am to hear that!'

Matt put a dried plate on the kitchen table and then proceeded to pick up a saucepan and begin drying that. 'Though where we'll meet such women is the real question. Certainly not the sort of places I usually go to.'

'No, me neither,' said Martin.

'Oh, I'm sure you do mix with them all the time,' Lex told him positively. 'It's just that you haven't been looking too deeply up to now.' Then a thought struck her. Now Martin had expressed his desire to meet women with depth to them, was there a chance he'd start to see Justine's potential and not just perceive her as the unsophisticated student he had seen up to now? She felt sure her son and Justine would get on famously together, given half a chance. If only she could get them together long enough in a social setting for him to see this for himself. But how was the problem to be solved when they moved in such different circles? She could invite Justine for tea, but then she had tried that before and been accused of matchmaking by her angry sons.

With her mind whirling Lex returned to her task of washing the dishes. She had just about conceded defeat when an idea came to her and she only barely managed to stop herself from crying out: Eureka! It would mean blatantly lying, but if that lie brought two people together in a lasting relationship, she felt the Almighty would forgive her.

'Oh, Martin, there's a favour I'd like to ask of you ...'

Picking up a handful of cutlery to dry, he looked at her askance. 'Yes?'

Lex took a deep breath and in a casual tone said, 'Well, it's just that I was talking to old Mrs Tuttle today and she was telling me that her granddaughter Justine is very upset at the moment because she's discovered her boyfriend was cheating on her. Well, you can imagine.'

He shrugged. 'I suppose she would be, but what's all this got to do with me doing you a favour?'

'As you can probably guess Justine is badly in need of cheering up. It was just an idea but if you haven't anything better to do while you're looking for someone special to take out, I wondered if you'd play the Good Samaritan and offer to take Justine?'

He looked utterly appalled at the thought. 'Oh, I don't know about that, Mam. She's not my type at all.'

'I'm not asking you to marry her, Martin, just cheer her up.' Then Lex added casually, 'Anyway, how do you know Justine isn't your type – because as far as I know, you've never spent any time in her company?'

He scoffed, 'She's a student, Mam. All students are into skiffle clubs, ban-the-bomb marches, and wearing scruffy clothes that don't look like they've been washed for weeks. Well, that's not my thing at all.'

'Justine always looks clean and tidy to me whenever I see her. And I take it you've never been to a skiffle club so how can you possibly know you wouldn't actually enjoy it?

Martin looked blankly back at her. His mother had a point. The thought of spending an evening in Justine's company still didn't appeal to him, though. 'I don't think she would be very keen to go out with me. I mean, she can't get away from me quick enough every time our paths cross.'

Oh, how blind men are, thought Lex. Her son believed himself to be a man of the world, but clearly wasn't that much of one because he couldn't see that Justine behaved as she did for fear of embarrassing herself in front of him, when she was deeply attracted to him. It appeared that Martin was not going to agree to her request even when it would bring him together with the one woman instinct told her could prove to be his perfect match. In frustration Lex snapped, 'Well, it's obvious to me you're far more worried what your mates would think of you, should they see you out with someone not so glamorous, than you are about helping a poor young woman get over a broken relationship. I mean, what's a few hours of your time, taking her out?'

Matt meanwhile was showing a keen interest in the events being played out before him. Grabbing hold of his brother's arm, he said, 'Have you got a sec?'

Looking puzzled as to why it was suddenly so important that Matt should have a private word with him, Martin nevertheless followed him into the dining room. Lex heard them whispering in there for a moment before they both came back into the kitchen. To her surprise Martin said to her then, 'I suppose I could act the Good Samaritan for you, just this once, Mam.'

She stopped herself from blurting out, 'Oh, good,' and instead smiled warmly at him. 'That's really kind of you, son. I happen to know Justine is at the Tuttles' now, so why don't you go and ask her? Oh, but don't mention anything about her boyfriend or you'll only embarrass her.'

As he departed to do her bidding Lex inwardly smiled to herself. That was one son taken care of in the happy relationship stakes. Now all she had to hope was that Matt would meet someone just as suitable. Thinking of her youngest son, she asked him, 'What was suddenly so important that you needed to speak to your brother in private?'

He pulled an innocent expression. 'I didn't mean to interrupt, Mam, I thought you'd finished what you had to say to Martin. If you must know I ... er ... was just reminding him that he borrowed ten bob off me last week and I want it back.'

Why Matt couldn't have done that with her present was beyond Lex, but what her other son was doing right that minute was of more interest and filled her thoughts.

She was mashing a pot of tea when Martin returned. 'Well, I hope you're happy now, Mam. I'm taking Justine out next Thursday night. Though I'm sure she's wondering why I asked her, and not that keen either. She stood staring at me with this idiotic look on her face for ages. I had to ask her again before she mumbled that she'd like to go. Some night this is going to be,' he grumbled as he disappeared off into the living room to join his father and brother.

The best night of your life, thought his mother confidently.

CHAPTER NINE

The following Thursday evening at just before eight, with Gil under the impression that his wife was attending her usual W.I. meeting, Lex was sharing a pot of tea with Thelma at her dining table. Unusually, they had the house to themselves as Thelma's two remaining children still living at home, eighteen-year-old daughter Paula and her sixteen-year-old sister Joanne, were both out. Their father, Lex assumed, must already have left for his night down at the snooker hall as there was no sign of him either.

Thelma had been convinced that life for both couples would soon return to normal and their social get-togethers resume now Gil had taken the initial step of venturing out in public again. She had been bitterly disappointed to learn from Lex that Gil still hadn't changed his mind about avoiding women's company as much as possible. But there was nothing she could do but accept the situation that, sadly, their social get-togethers were a thing of the past for now. What mattered most to Thelma, though, was that she and Lex's happy hours together would go on.

As she supped her tea, Thelma was looking at her friend quizzically. 'Why do you keep looking at the clock?' she asked.

Lex looked at it again. It was just on eight. 'They should be meeting about now . . . I'm on tenterhooks, hoping it goes well.'

An excited expression filled Thelma's homely middle-aged face as a memory stirred within her. 'Oh, of course, this is the night Martin is taking Justine out, isn't it? I'm sure it'll go really well as you're so adamant the pair of them are meant for each other. Where's Martin taking her?'

'I didn't ask him any details for fear I'd look too keen and then he'd twig I was hoping for more from this than I let on.'

Thelma looked thoughtful for a moment before she said, 'A pale blue costume and navy accessories. What do you think, Lex?'

She looked puzzled. 'For what?'

'Martin and Justine's wedding. Some do that will be, your eldest son's wedding, and I want to look my best. Well, it's bound to happen, I know how clever you are at matching people. What will you wear?'

A vision of that wonderful day rose before Lex then. She saw the bride and groom looking radiant surrounded by all their family and friends, dressed in their best. And, of course, the sun would be shining. Dreamily she said, 'If it's a summer wedding . . .'

A manly voice interrupted her daydream. 'Whose wedding are you two discussing?' Des asked as he walked into the room.. He looked enquiringly at his wife. 'I'm not aware of anyone we know getting married.'

'The couple whose wedding we're discussing don't even plan to marry yet, but they will soon because Lex has set her seal of approval on it,' his wife told him confidently.

Des looked knowingly at Lex. 'I'd better get my best suit to the cleaner's then.'

She laughed. 'I think you've plenty of time. It's only their first date tonight.'

The look on Des's face was a sight to behold.

Getting up, Thelma said to him, 'I'll fill the bowl with hot water for your wash and your dinner's in the oven keeping hot. You can eat on a tray in the living room, watching the television, so me and Lex can have some peace and enjoy our time together.'

Lex noticed then Des was still dressed in his grubby work overalls. As Thelma went off into the kitchen she enquired, 'Have you just finished work? I never asked Thelma where you were when I came in half an hour ago because I thought you'd gone off to snooker as usual.'

He gave a tired yawn. 'That was my plan but one of the jobs I had on today took much longer than I thought it would, then

I had to deliver the generator back to its owner, and when I got back to the workshop I was just finishing up when I got a call from another chap I'd done work for . . . well, actually it was his generator that Gil fixed on my behalf . . . who wanted me to go and see him on my way home. He'd something he wanted to discuss with me.' Des grinned. 'Thankfully I've got a wife who doesn't raise hell when I'm late home for my dinner.' He looked enquiringly at Lex. 'Has Gil had any luck being set on yet?'

A worried expression settled over her face. 'He's trying so hard, but as soon as it comes out why he left Brenton's after working for them all his working life, the interview is abruptly ended. I admire him so much for being determined to carry on regardless. That's why I've not told him yet about my being turfed out of the W.I. I feel very guilty for deceiving him, but he's contending with enough at the moment without me causing him more problems.' Then Lex looked at their friend. 'I just want to thank you very much for offering Gil that bit of work. I suspect you could have managed well enough without his help?'

'If friends can't help each other in times of crisis, then who can, Lex? Trouble is, though, Gil wouldn't take any money from me for doing it. We had a bit of a barney about it, in fact. He was adamant he'd come only to do a friend a favour, and I was adamant that it wasn't fair I should keep the money for a job he'd done. We were getting nowhere and I had to go out to price a job, was in danger of being late for my appointment, in fact, so I had no choice but to concede defeat. Anyway, don't take this wrong but actually I'm pleased to hear he hasn't been set on yet.'

'Oh, why?'

'Because I've a proposition I'd like to put to him, one I'm hoping he'll be interested in.'

Thelma came back in then. 'What proposition is that?' she quizzed her husband.

He tapped the side of his nose. 'If you don't mind, me darlin', I'd like to discuss it with Gil before I say anything else about it. After I've had my dinner and freshened up, I'll go and put it to him.' Des went off into the kitchen then, leaving the two women looking after him, wondering just what this proposition was he wanted to discuss with Gil.

Lex was eager to get home for two reasons that night. First to learn what Des had suggested to Gil, and secondly to find out how Martin's evening with Justine had gone.

Arriving at just before ten, her usual time for getting home from the W.I. meeting, she was glad to see no sign of her son. She took this as a sign that he was still out with Justine and their evening together hadn't been cut short for any reason. Matt, she knew, had gone to the snooker hall. Gil was in the living room, sitting in his armchair. His eyes might have been fixed on the television, seemingly watching *The Phil Silvers Show*, but she knew his thoughts were not on the hilarious antics of Sergeant Bilko but fixed firmly elsewhere. He hadn't even heard her come in until she said for the second time, 'I'm back, Gil.'

He looked startled to see her standing there. 'Oh, hello, love. I never heard you come in.'

'Good job I wasn't a burglar then.'

'Enjoy your meeting, did you?' he asked her as she walked in to take a seat in the armchair opposite his.

'More to the point, are you all right? You were miles away when I came in.' She wanted to ask him if his distracted state was anything to do with what Des had told her, but that would mean alerting her husband to the fact she had seen their friend when she was supposed to be at the W.I. meeting. Or something else entirely might have happened while she was out. 'There hasn't been any trouble while I've been gone, has there?' she anxiously enquired.

To her relief he said, 'No, not at all. But Des called around ... in fact, you've not long missed him ... and I was mulling over something he asked me.'

She leaned forward. 'Oh, what was that?'

'Well, it seems the owner of the generator I fixed last Friday was very impressed with how well it worked when Des took it back. All I did was rewire it differently to get more output out of the KVA, it wasn't rocket science by any means, and give it a good service while I was at it, but the owner said it works better now than it did when he bought it new twenty years ago.

'He asked Des over for a chat this evening to see if he would take on the servicing and repairs of his other five generators. He also asked if Des wanted him to spread word around about the good service he gives – far better than the client has been getting from the last firm he used. They told him they couldn't look at his faulty generator for over a week as they had too much work on, and later he found out they'd shoved his business aside in order to do a more lucrative job for another firm. He wasn't happy so he rang around some of his colleagues in the trade to see if they could recommend another company, and the first one he tried told him about Des.'

Lex smiled proudly at her husband. 'Des knew he was on to a sure thing when he asked you to give him a hand.' She was desperate to know just what the proposition was that Des had now put to him. 'So apart from coming to tell you his new client was delighted with the work you did, what did he come to ask you?'

Gil took a deep breath. 'To see if I was interested in working for him ... well, as he put it, joining him in his business.'

Lex was stunned. 'Oh, really?' she exclaimed in delight. 'Why, darling, that's wonderful. When do you start?'

'Look, Lex, I was very shocked as well as honoured by Des's offer. As much as I'd like to take him up on it, though, it's a heck of a gamble.'

She looked perplexed. 'In what way?'

'Well, Des is only just managing to get by on what he brings in now ... in fact, he's not really, is he, as Thelma still works to help support them? It's not just that, though. Lex, I'm not so stupid I didn't realise that Des could ill afford to give me that work last week. It was his attempt to stop me from hiding myself away and it worked, but that's why I wouldn't take any money from him for doing it.' Gil gave a forlorn sigh. 'I feel he's offering me this job out of pity because he knows it's going to be difficult for me to get set on elsewhere.'

Lex looked aghast at this. 'Des has always admired you, Gil, but feel sorry for you? I can say without a word of hesitation, definitely not. I know him well enough for that and so do you. He'd never be suggesting you two work together if he thought he was putting his own family's livelihood in jeopardy. And may I remind you that if it weren't for your support of him in the past, he wouldn't have a business now. Has it crossed your mind what pleasure it would give him to be able to repay you for that?'

It was apparent by Gil's expression that it hadn't. 'God knows, this is the answer to a prayer, Lex,' he mused. 'I could work happily in the workshop while he's out and about fixing generators on site as well as touting for other business along the way. Main thing is there are absolutely no women around.

'Des has always been aware there's business out there he hasn't been able to go after as a one man band, and he's not been able to get himself into a position money wise where he can fund another wage. He could have taken a gamble and gone to the bank to see about another loan to cover a second man, but if it didn't work out then he'd be in the horrible position of having to get rid of the bloke he'd taken on, as well as coping with the repayments. It's been frustrating for him.

'If I accepted his offer it would mean a struggle for us financially for however long it took for Des to bring in enough new business to cover my wage. I wouldn't take money from him until I knew that was the case. But it could take a few weeks, months even, for enough to start coming in to support two families, and some weeks we might not make as much as others. We'd also have to build up a contingency fund to meet such times. I've already lost one week's pay, Lex, and we've had to dip into our savings to meet our bills. What we've got left if I don't get set on soon will quickly be swallowed up, even taking into consideration extra contributions from the boys which, like you, I'm loath to take off them.

'So, you see, it's not possible for me to take up Des's offer as matters stand. I need a steady full-time wage coming in as soon as possible, that's where I must concentrate my efforts. I told him I'd give him my answer tomorrow, and after serious consideration it's got to be no, but I will tell him that if ever he needs help in future, I'd be glad to oblige in between my normal working hours. That way he'll be able to accept some work he'd otherwise have to turn down, and it'll be a bit of extra money for us to add to the reduced income I'll be getting in future.'

Lex sat staring at her husband blankly, her thoughts seeking frantically for a solution to this situation. She didn't care how much they struggled financially, how far they had to lower their standards, if it meant her husband could live a day-to-day life free from constant worry.

Then the answer became glaringly obvious to her.

'You can accept Des's offer, Gil,' she said.

'I told you, I can't.'

'You can, Gil, if I cut our household expenses down to the bone and bring in some money to help meet the bills.'

He looked taken aback. 'You mean, you're proposing to go out to work? But I've always supported our family, Lex, I won't hear of that. Besides, you've already got a full-time job, looking after us.'

'Thelma looks after her family more than adequately as well as working. If thousands of other women do, so can I,' she said resolutely. 'Our sons aren't babies anymore, and I easily found time to help the likes of Phyllis and regularly pay a visit to Thelma in the morning for tea and a chat, so in truth I do rather live a life of leisure compared to other women. Gil, I'd like to do this,' she said with conviction. 'Surely it doesn't matter how the money comes into this house so long as it does? We're a family, and when needs must, we all pull together.'

She could see he was still struggling with his principles. To the likes of Gil it was the man's job to provide the money, the wife's to look after the household. She was so afraid he was going to let this opportunity slip through his fingers that she implored him, 'Are you seriously going to turn Des's offer down from misguided pride? Have you not thought that maybe he sees this as the perfect opportunity to build up the business, being able to work with someone he likes and trusts'

Gil looked surprised by that. He had been too caught up with the notion that Des was taking pity on him to look for any other reason behind this offer. Lex desperately wanted to plead with him to reconsider his decision, at least give it a chance to see how it worked out, but she had voiced her views on the matter and out of respect for him must now leave him to decide what was best. She had to go along with whatever he decided.

'I'll go and make us a cup of Ovaltine.'

The milk was just coming to the boil when Gil came in and made his way over to the pantry. Assuming she knew what he was going in there for, she said, 'I've already got out the biscuit tin to bring through, in case you fancied one.'

'It wasn't a biscuit I was after. I'll be needing to give my flask and lunch box a wash out. They've not been used in the five years since I was promoted off the tools.'

Lex's heart raced. She knew this was her husband's way of telling her that he was after all going to take up Des's offer. Matter-of-factly she said, 'They're both on the top shelf next to the spare light bulbs. If you get them out, I'll leave them to soak overnight in bicarbonate of soda.'

He smiled at her tenderly. 'Thanks, Lex. And, look, please don't think for a minute I'm saying you wouldn't be able to cope. You're the most capable woman I know, but you haven't worked for over twenty years and . . .'

She placed her fingers on his lips to silence him. 'If it all proves too much for me, you'll be the first to know.'

'As long as you remember that.'

He was just emerging from the pantry, flask and lunch box in hand, when the back door opened and Martin and Matt entered.

Lex smiled a greeting at them both. 'Had a good night, the pair of you?' It was really Martin's evening she was interested in.

'I did, Mam, thanks,' Matt answered her, slipping off his shoes. The truth was, though, that he had and he hadn't. He'd been enjoying his game of snooker with the usual crowd, the other members having once again expressed regret to him about his father's absence. They said they hoped that the situation would change in the future. As the evening had worn on, though, it became glaringly apparent to him that an attendee from another group of men who frequented the snooker hall on the same night as they did had learned of his father's trouble, was aware that Matt was his son, and when he became the worse for drink, began throwing out snide comments. The crowd he was with tried their best to persuade him not to but it was obvious to Matt that he was spoiling for a fight and he'd felt it best to leave early. He wasn't going to let on to his parents about this, though.

'What about you, Martin?' Lex asked him keenly.

His answer was far from the one she was hoping for.

In a disgruntled tone he told her, 'I had an awful night, Mam. Me and Justine have nothing at all in common. I couldn't wait until a reasonable enough time had passed for me to make an excuse to see her to her bus stop. It was obvious she felt the same way – she couldn't grab her coat quick enough. I met Matt on the way back and we had a pint together in the local.'

His mother was staring at him flabbergasted. She couldn't believe she had been so wrong.

'Oh! Well, I'm sorry it was such a disaster. Er ... Ovaltine, both of you?'

But her question was lost on her sons as their interest had been taken by what their father was holding in his hands.

'Cleaning out your flask and lunch box can only mean one thing, Dad. You've got a job.'

He grinned at Martin. 'I have, son, yes. I'm going to be working for Des.'

They both leaped over and patted him on his back.

'This is brilliant news,' Matt enthused.

'So when did this come about, Dad?' Martin asked him keenly.

As Lex added more milk to the pan she was only half attending to Gil's story. Now she knew that he had got a purpose back in his life, she was keen to regain her own. She'd been so sure about Martin and Justine ... it was quite a shock to find her match-making skills were on the wane. Just as well she had something else to distract her.

The thought of working again excited her. She hadn't held a paying job for over twenty-three years, not since she was six months pregnant with Martin and had given up her position as a shorthand typist for a cardboard box-making company, to await his birth. Her role as housewife and mother had brought her a great sense of satisfaction and pride, but it was a completely different feeling from that she had experienced as part of a thriving company, knowing that her contribution was playing a part in the general success. It would be good to get back into the working world again and all it brought with it.

CHAPTER TEN

To Lex it was as if the terrible events of the previous week had not happened and she'd been transported five years back to before Gil had been promoted off the shop floor. In the morning she saw all her men well fed, their flasks and lunch boxes filled . . . they had all decided to revert to having their main meal in the evening in light of the fact that Lex would hopefully be out working soon and therefore not at home to prepare anything at midday.

Having tidied up the remains of breakfast and tackled the immediate housework, she collected the previous day's copy of the *Mercury* from the side of Gil's armchair, settling herself at the kitchen table to study the Situations Vacant pages in her quest to get herself a job. She had hardly begun when a tap on the back door heralded Thelma, an air of great excitement about her.

'I know it's safe to come because Gil's at Des's workshop,' she said, sitting down opposite Lex. 'Des popped home on his way to a job to tell me Gil's accepted his offer. Lex, it's awful the way this has come about but I'm so pleased Gil is joining him! And Des is over the moon. He couldn't have wished for a better person to come in with him. Until now it's just ticked along, but now Gil's on board Des is positive the business is really going to flourish. I am too. Des's been desperate to expand since he realised there was far more work out there than he could handle on his own, but getting someone good like Gil to help him has been the problem. I mean, it's like Des says, anyone can tell you anything in an interview. It's not until they're actually working on a job and you can see for yourself that their skills are up to the standard they say they are, that you can be sure. He could have lost his business, trying to expand it.

'Now he's got the right man to help him, he's going to make an appointment today with the bank manager, to see about getting a loan to cover Gil's wages until Des finds them new clients. Oh, and he's got me on strict instructions to steer clear of the workshop out of respect for Gil. Not that I ever went down there much anyway, except to take Des's lunch when he forgot it. He'll just have to remember from now on or go without, won't he? Anyway, now Gil's taken this step, I'm hopeful it won't be long before he comes to his senses about mixing with women again and then we'll all be back to normal. We can certainly carry on with me popping in for a cuppa and chat some mornings before I go to work, can't we?' Her face split into a broad beam of delight. 'Oh, isn't it just great that our husbands are working together?'

Lex vigorously nodded. 'Yes, it is. It's the answer to all Gil's worries about his work situation. I can't tell you what it means to me to know he's going to feel happy about his new place of work, which he wouldn't have been if he'd had to take a job in another factory. But, Thelma, Des doesn't need to take out a loan to cover Gil's wages. Gil's adamant he won't take money from Des's own pocket.'

Thelma looked worried. 'I appreciate his reasons, and it's very commendable of him, but how will you be able to get by in the meantime?'

'We've our savings to fall back on. The extra Martin and Matt are handing over on top of their normal board helps too. I'm going to cut down on household expenses as much as I can . . . and my wages will make all the difference.'

Thelma stared blankly at her. 'Your wages?' Then she exclaimed, 'You mean, you're going to get a job?'

Lex laughed at the comical expression on her friend's face. 'Don't look so shocked!' Then she asked seriously, 'Don't you think I'll get one? I mean, I know I haven't worked for well over twenty years but surely I'm capable of doing something.'

'Eh, gel, I think you'll land a job easy,' Thelma told her in no uncertain terms. 'I wasn't surprised or shocked. What I was . . . well, if you want the truth, I was being selfish. You working means I'll get to see less of you and . . . well, I'll miss you. So what do you fancy doing job wise?'

Lex shrugged. 'I'm not fussy. Anything that pays a wage. My secretarial skills are too rusty to apply for jobs using those so I thought something in the clerical line – receptionist, filing clerk – or maybe a shop assistant like you. I was just about to check in the *Mercury* to see what's on offer.'

Thelma pulled over the newspaper from in front of Lex. 'You mash a cuppa while I start looking.' As Lex busied herself mashing the pot of tea, Thelma began scanning her eyes down the Vacancies columns. 'School cleaner. Fish gutter. Sausage stuffer. Taxidermist assistant . . .'

'Hang on a minute, don't dismiss any of those,' Lex called over to her. 'Do any of them state how much they're paying?'

Thelma looked over at her, appalled. 'You can't seriously be considering any of those? You've more to offer than cleaning floors. You'd permanently stink of fish, working as a gutter, and never look at a sausage again after stuffing them all day. And do you really want to work with dead animals?'

Lex shuddered at the thought. 'No, can't say as I do.'

'Right, then, you get back to making the tea and leave me to find you a suitable job.' She carried on where she had left off. 'Assistant in an alterations shop . . . no, you're not doing that. You've enough sewing of your own to do without tackling other people's. Florist . . . What do you know about flowers?' She answered her own question. 'About as much as I do, that you stick them in a vase and hope for the best. Shoe shop assistant? Oh, no, you don't want to be handling people's smelly feet all day.

'Well, I'll be blowed if there isn't a job offered here which is right up my street. It's in a sweet factory. Ohhh . . . just think of being able to sample all those yummy chocolates. Oh, but on second thoughts, it's bad enough me sampling all those goods when my boss's back is turned at the bakers. If I get any fatter, I'll burst. Right, back to a job for you. Packing crisps into boxes. Oh, God, that would drive you mad or make you brain dead ...' This commentary continued as she picked fault with every job she spied.

Lex was just putting Thelma's cup of tea before her when her friend suddenly exclaimed, 'Oh, my God, I've found the perfect job for you.'

'Really! Oh, Thelma, what is it?' she keenly asked, sitting down opposite her.

Her friend blurted out excitedly, 'Receptionist at a marriage bureau.' Lex was staring at her as if she'd suddenly sprouted another head. 'You know, one of them matchmaking places for people who can afford to have someone find them a husband or wife.'

Lex tutted. 'Yes, I do know what a marriage bureau is, Thelma. I just hadn't realised there was one in Leicester.' An eager expression filled her face then. 'Oh, I really do like the thought of helping match people together. Do you think I'd stand a chance of getting the job?' Then a thought struck her and she gave a despondent sigh. 'I don't think there's any point in me applying for it, really.'

Thelma looked flabbergasted. 'Whyever not? This job's absolutely ideal for you.'

Lex sighed, 'I might have thought so myself before yesterday, but in light of how off my instincts were about Martin and Justine ...'

'What do you mean? Didn't they hit it off after all?' Thelma cut in.

Lex shook her head. 'Martin told me he had an awful time, and it seems Justine did too. Apparently she couldn't wait to make her escape from him when he suggested they call it a night.'

Shocked, Thelma exclaimed, 'Oh, I can't believe it. I've never known you be wrong before, Lex.' She tutted with irritation. 'Oh, and I was so looking forward to their wedding an' all.' Then she leaned over and gave her friend's hand a reassuring pat. 'You can't win them all, lovey. No one gets things right all the time. We're only human after all.

'Anyway, the job advertised at the marriage bureau is only for a receptionist. It asks anyone who's interested to telephone for an appointment for an interview.' She pushed the newspaper towards Lex, stabbing her finger on the advertisement. 'There's the number, what are you waiting for?'

What was she waiting for? She could do that job easily, and enjoy it too. She really liked the thought of helping lonely people find happiness even if it was only making appointments for them, greeting them with a friendly face and putting them at their ease on arrival. Picking up the newspaper, Lex went off into the hallway to make her call. She returned to rejoin Thelma several minutes later and jubilantly announced, 'I've got an appointment at two this afternoon with a Mrs Landers.'

Thelma looked delighted to hear this. She stood up and hooked her handbag over her arm. 'I'll leave you in peace to tart yourself up then. You'd better call around tonight, let me know how you got on.'

It felt strange to Lex to be dressing herself for a job interview. The last time she had done so was nearly thirty years ago when she had attended one at the box-making company right after leaving school. It was her very first interview and she'd been fully expecting to have to attend many more before she landed herself a job. She experienced the same apprehension now as she had then: worried if she had dressed right; if she would give the right answers to the questions she would be asked; if she had all the skills expected for the job. Regardless, she had been successful at that first interview and dearly hoped she would be this time too.

At just after half-past twelve she was smartly attired in a plain black straight skirt and white blouse, her navy winter coat and low-heeled court shoes. She wore her hair neatly rolled up into a French pleat, and lightly applied mascara and pale pink lipstick before she set off to catch the bus into town.

With head held erect, eyes fixed firmly ahead of her, she walked purposefully down the street. She was just approaching the bus stop when she spotted Phyllis coming out of the baker's, using a walking stick. As soon as her neighbour saw her she smiled a greeting and waited for Lex to reach her before saying, 'Hello, me old duck. Oh, it's good to be out and about again, doing me own shopping. Not that I can carry much while I still need to use this stick. The hospital said I'll need it for a couple of weeks while I build the muscles in me leg back up again, but at least I'm not having to rely on the likes of yourself to do it for me, and taking up your time.'

'It was no bother to me, Phyllis. I was glad to be of help.'

She smiled appreciatively at Lex then looked her up and down. 'Where are you off to, all togged up?'

'I'm going for a job interview.'

Phyllis gave her a knowing look. It was obvious she understood perfectly why her friend needed to return to work. 'Well, best of luck, lovey. Whoever your interview is with, it's my opinion they'd be mad not to take the likes of you on.' She lowered her voice and asked, 'What's the work situation with Gil? Any luck for him yet?'

She nodded. 'I'm glad to say he's working for Thelma's husband now, fixing generators.'

'Well, that's good news! Getting a job is the best way of putting all that terrible business behind him. Is it all right now for me to go back to calling in on you when I'm passing?' Phyllis hopefully enquired.

Lex sighed. 'I'm sorry to say that hasn't changed yet, Phyllis. Gil's still terrified of finding himself in a situation where he could be accused of doing something he hasn't. But hopefully, come time, that will change.'

Phyllis looked sympathetically at her. 'Oh, I do hope so, lovey. It must be hard on you, having to put your friends off like this. But if what happened to Gilbert had happened to my husband, I'd have been just like you, doing all it took to support him through it.'

Just then from out of the haberdasher's behind them two middle-aged women appeared. Hilda Price, recognising Lex, gave a disdainful sniff and fixed her beady eyes on Phyllis. 'Well, you obviously haven't heard what Mrs Morton's husband has been up to, you being tied to your house after yer accident,' she commented.

Phyllis stared back at her. 'Oh, but I have, Mrs Price.'

The older woman looked shocked. 'And you're that desperate for friends yer reducing yourself to associating with the likes of *her*, a'yer, Mrs Watson? I'm utterly disgusted with you! Well, me and Letty are very particular who we associate with, so while yer feel the need to have *her* type as yer friend, you can count me and Letty out.'

To Hilda Price's obvious shock Phyllis responded tartly, 'Fine by me, Mrs Price. I've never counted you amongst my friends anyway, considering you as I do to be a narrow-minded bigot. I prefer the open-minded sort who appreciates we're all entitled to our own opinion, though I've listened to your prejudices out of politeness whenever I was unfortunate enough to cross paths with you. Now I need no longer endure your endless whinging. Well, good! Now, if you don't mind, Mrs Morton and I are having a private conversation.'

Face tight with indignation, Hilda Price hissed back, 'I certainly won't be wasting my money on a Christmas card for *you* this year! And neither will Letty.' She then looked disgustedly at Lex. 'I expect you know you won't be getting one either? Women ain't safe in their beds with the likes of your husband still walking the streets. He should be locked up for life for what he did to that poor woman.' She gave her companion a push in the back. 'Come along, Letty.'

Phyllis and Lex watched both of them disappear inside the greengrocer's.

Lex heaved a deep, sad sigh. 'I don't know what I'd do without the likes of you and Thelma championing our cause, Phyllis. We're trying so hard to make the best of things, but being constantly attacked like this by people we used to get on well with . . . well, I just wonder if it will ever end.'

Phyllis smiled kindly at her. 'As matters stand, I can't promise you it ever will, lovey. All you can keep doing is ignoring the likes of Hilda Price and concentrating on making the best of what you've got.'

Just then they both sensed another presence and turned their heads to see an anxious Letty Morgan had returned. 'Er . . . excuse me for butting in,' she said timidly, then turned and flashed a worried glance across to the greengrocer's before bringing her attention back to Lex and Thelma. 'Hilda always assumes she can speak for me, but it's not true. It's just . . . she can cause such a lot of trouble for me, being my next-door neighbour, and I'd sooner be on the right side of her than the bad. She's not a nice person at all if you upset her. She got the Clarks evicted several years back after their young son accidentally broke her window when he was playing with his ball. Even though the Clarks repaired it, Hilda still plagued the landlord with her exaggerations until he had no choice but to give them notice. If she got me evicted, I don't know what I'd do. I've nowhere else to go.'

She then smiled kindly at Lex. 'I don't in the least believe Mr Morton guilty of what is claimed. People with that sort of tendency always have a roving eye, just like my Uncle Francis had . . . and what a womaniser he was! But I have only ever seen Mr Morton look at one woman in that way, if you understand me, and it was yourself he was looking at, Lex. Anyway, I just wanted you to know, not all us locals think like Hilda does.

'Better get back. I slipped out without her seeing me . . .' With that she hurried off back into the greengrocer's.

'There you go, Alexandra, you've got more allies than you know,' Phyllis said to her.

'Yes, we have. I feel really humble that Letty braved Hilda Price's retribution to come and tell me what she thinks. It's made me feel so much better, and hopefully it will Gil too, when I tell him.' She recognised the sound of the bus then. 'I don't want to miss this. You will excuse me, won't you, Phyllis?'

As Lex darted across to the bus stop, Phyllis called after her,

'Good luck with your interview. Remember to drop by on your way home and tell me how you got on. I'll be keeping everything crossed for you!'

CHAPTER ELEVEN

Lex was out of puff by the time she had climbed the three flights of stairs to the attic offices of Cupid's Marriage Bureau. They were situated in a narrow four-storey Victorian building on Halford Street in the centre of town, which housed a number of other businesses. On the narrow landing she arrived at a brass plaque on the wall to one side of a half-glazed door which told her she had arrived at the right place.

Tapping politely on it, Lex went inside.

The room she entered was not large but spacious enough to house a desk and chair which she assumed was the receptionist's work station. On the wall opposite five straight-backed chairs were lined up, plus a small table holding a selection of magazines and a coat stand in the corner. There was no sign of the receptionist. In fact, the desk showed no visible evidence of anyone working from it as all it held was an empty Remington typewriter and a black Bakelite telephone. Across the room was another half-glazed door which was closed. Lex could hear the muted sounds of voices behind it. The woman she had come to see obviously had someone else in with her. Lex wondered if it was a client or a competitor for the job she had come about? Desperately wanting the job for herself, she hoped it was a client.

Shutting the outer door behind her, she made her way across to the row of chairs and sat down on the one in the middle to wait her turn. She was just about to pick up a magazine to occupy her when a sudden anguished cry resounded from inside the other office. Almost immediately the door swung open and a young woman came charging out. She was crying hysterically. Open-mouthed and wide-eyed, Lex watched her sprint over to the outer door, wrench it open and run out.

All her motherly instincts rushing to the fore, without hesitation Lex jumped up from her chair to chase after the distraught young woman. She felt she had to offer her some support when she was so upset.

Seemingly hell-bent on getting out of the building, the young woman didn't appear to hear Lex calling out to her as she belted down the three flights of stairs. It wasn't until she had dashed out and into the street that Lex finally caught her up.

Catching hold of her arm, breathlessly she said, 'Look, excuse me, but are you all right? Well, obviously that's a stupid question. I just wanted to know if you need any help?'

The young woman was wiping her eyes with a handkerchief, still distraught. 'There's no help you can give me,' she sobbed. 'If I'm not good enough to be accepted as a client by a marriage bureau, then I'm beyond help, aren't I?'

Lex was taken aback. This young woman was in her mid-twenties, she guessed, not beautiful but pleasant enough. She was a little on the plump side which made her appear smaller than her height of five foot three or so. She was dressed neatly in a plain skirt and blouse under a grey winter coat, her pale brown hair cut into a chin-length bob. She had an old-fashioned air about her. Lex's fussy sons wouldn't give this girl a second look, despite their new resolve to seek out young women with more to offer than mere physical attractions, but Lex had no doubt there were many men who wouldn't pass up a chance to take her out.

'You must be mistaken. I can't see any reason why you'd be turned down as a client. Though, I have to say, I can't understand why a nice young lady like you would ever need the services of a marriage bureau anyway.'

A flood of fresh tears gushed down her cheeks. 'It was my last resort,' she sobbed.

'Nonsense!' Lex exclaimed. 'I can't believe you're not inundated with requests from men wanting your company. I'm sure you must have misunderstood what was said about not taking you on?'

She shook her head. 'How could I have mistaken being told, "I can't be of any assistance to you as you're not the type I have as a client".' Another fat gush of tears spurted out of her eyes. Burying her face in her handkerchief, she wept aloud.

Lex stared at her helplessly. She felt positive this young woman had misconstrued what had been said to her. Her own interview for the vacant receptionist's position was completely forgotten as the other woman's plight preoccupied her. Smiling kindly, she offered, 'Look, why don't we go back upstairs and sort out this misunderstanding?'

A look of pure horror filled the younger woman's face. 'Go back! I'm never going back in there to be humiliated by that woman. I thought the idea of a marriage bureau was to bring people together from all walks of life, but the one Mrs Landers runs obviously doesn't operate like that. She gave me the impression she thought I wasn't nearly pretty enough or with the right sort of figure to be one of her clients.'

Anger erupted within Lex then. She felt a terrible desire to go back to Cupid's Marriage Bureau and give the woman who ran it a piece of her mind. If it was indeed the case that certain criteria had to be fulfilled before clients were accepted then it was a despicable way to operate such a business, but the quelling of her own wrath would have to wait. She couldn't bring herself to leave this young woman in such a state. Lex glanced around. Opposite was a café. 'I could do with a cup of tea. Do you fancy joining me?'

Her companion looked at her for a moment. It seemed that after such a cruel rebuff she was shocked anyone at all would request her company. Eventually she said gratefully, 'If you've time, yes, please.'

A few minutes later they were sitting opposite each other, cup of tea in hand.

The young woman had by now stopped crying at least, although she looked as wretched as she would on learning of the death of someone very dear to her.

'Not the best tea I've tasted but it's hot, I suppose,' Lex said to break the ice. 'My name is Alexandra, people call me Lex.'

'Amanda Hopkins. I like to be called Mandy,' she responded dully.

Regardless Lex responded brightly, 'Well, I'm very glad to meet you, Mandy. Are you feeling any better?'

The girl put down her cup, shook her head and said miserably, 'If you want the truth, I just want to die. I feel so . . . so . . . well, as if I've nothing to look forward to.'

Lex was appalled to hear this. 'Oh, but a young woman like you has her whole life ahead of her.'

'Other women of my age may have but I certainly haven't. All I do is get up in the morning, go to work, then come home again to sit on my own. I hate the weekends because I never see anyone apart from when I go shopping on Saturday morning and have a chat with the locals – if they're not in too much of a rush to spare me the time, that is. The old lady who lives in the flat below mine likes to keep herself to herself so I can't even go and see her to break the monotony.'

'But what about your family? Friends? People you work with?'

Mandy gave a shake of her head. 'From the age of twelve I lived in an orphanage. My father died in the war, my mother from tuberculosis, after that and what family they had between them didn't want the responsibility of me. I was shy as a child and found it difficult to make friends. All the other kids in the orphanage picked on me, and to avoid their bullying I kept myself to myself as much as I could.

'I was so glad to leave the home when I was fifteen. So excited when I thought I'd make lots of new friends at work and wouldn't be lonely ever again. I told the social worker when she came to help me get a place to live and a job that I really wanted to work in a big company that employed lots of people, but she said she didn't think that environment would suit my personality and got me a job working in small office for a man old enough to be my father who imports fabric from abroad. She made me accept it.

'There's just myself running the office, and Mr Foster is out most days on business so most of the time I'm on my own. When he is in the office, he's always talking about his wife and children which makes me feel even more lonely and worried I'll never have a family of my own. I've often thought of finding myself a job in a bigger firm now I've some experience behind me, and I know Mr Foster would give me a good reference, but he's been good to me in his way. He's always telling me how lucky he was to get someone like me and how much he relies on me. I just can't bring myself to go as I know how upset he'd be.

'I'm not comfortable about going into pubs or out dancing on my own to meet people. To be honest, I know I must come across as boring but I don't really enjoy that sort of thing. You see, I like going to museums and looking around old houses, reading, going to the cinema, having friends . . . well, if I had any . . . round for a meal as I love to cook. I have made lots of efforts to make friends by joining clubs, I love knitting and embroidery, but all the other women who went to the clubs I joined were years older than me. I've gone to coffee bars, hoping to get chatting to women of my age who are looking for a friend. I did meet a couple, but no sooner did I seem to start getting on well enough with them to suggest we go out socially together than they met men and obviously wanted to spend all their spare time with them. And so here I am, left high and dry on my own again.'

Mandy gave a wistful sigh. 'I did get chatting to a man once in a coffee bar. There was no other seats so he asked if he could sit at my table. He was very nice, the gentlemanly sort. He told me he was a bus driver and in his spare time made wooden furniture on commission from friends in his dad's shed. One day he hoped to have his own furniture-making business.' She cast down her eyes to fix them on the contents of her cup. 'He was just the type of man I'd dreamed of meeting and I desperately hoped he liked me enough to ask me out. I can't tell you how disappointed I was when it turned out he was just passing the time with me while waiting for his girlfriend to come in as they were going to the pictures. It was a film I'd very much wanted to see but couldn't bring myself to go to on my own.' She lifted her head and looked

Lex in the eye. 'It's no fun watching a film by yourself with no one to discuss it with afterwards. Or a hand to hold in the scary parts,' she added wistfully.

'When I read the advert for Cupid's Marriage Bureau in the *Mercury* ... well, it was like the answer to my prayers. I can't seem to meet a man in the usual way so why not pay for someone's help to find me one? I was so excited about going to that appointment. I wasn't stupid enough to be expecting to be told there was hordes of men on their books looking for someone just like me, but maybe one or two might be.

'As soon as I walked into the reception area I saw the disappointed look Mrs Landers gave me. I can't tell you how shocked I was by what she said to me then and how it made me feel.' She paused and gave Lex a sidelong look. 'You must think me a pathetic woman who can't make any friends or get a man for herself?'

'Absolutely not,' Lex told her resolutely. 'What I do think is that you're a lovely young woman who's tried her best to make a social life for herself, but failed because of the small circle you move in.'

Lex's heart went out to this girl. She couldn't imagine her own life without family and friends. Mandy was desperately lonely and the need to do something for her overwhelmed Lex. How dearly she wished she herself knew of a single young woman around Mandy's age she could pal her up with, but all the possible candidates she knew of were attached in some way or other already. And besides, Mandy had her own very particular interests and Lex didn't know many other girls who shared them. If only she knew a nice steady young man, the sort to appreciate Mandy's quiet considered ways.

Then suddenly a vision of the very man for Mandy danced before her: Phyllis's son Derek. He was quiet and self-effacing too. They should get on very well together, Lex felt sure. And even if no romantic spark ignited between them, friendship could well develop through their common interests. Then she remembered how sure she'd been about Martin and Justine ... But, like Thelma said, no one could get things right all the time. With such a strong feeling that two people were compatible, as she had about Derek and Mandy, it would be wrong of her not to try and instigate a meeting between them, wouldn't it? How to get them together without making it obvious, though, was a real problem. She felt sure she could persuade Mandy to meet Derek on a blind date, due to the lengths she had already gone to meet people, but what if Derek wasn't receptive to that idea? She didn't like the thought of dashing Mandy's hopes again. Lex racked her brains for another way to bring them together.

In desperation she asked, 'I don't suppose you have need of a plumber's services, have you?'

Mandy obviously thought this strange. 'My landlord sees to that kind of thing. Well, when he gets around to it, that is. Why have you asked me that?'

Lex tried not to let her disappointment show. Her hope had been that while Derek was fixing, say, a leaky tap, they'd start to chat and find they had a lot in common. Then, wanting to get to know more about Mandy, Derek would ask her out. Getting this pair together wasn't going to be that simple, though.

'Oh, er . . . I suddenly remembered someone had asked me if I knew of a plumber and I thought it was you.' Lex gave a little laugh. 'Your mind playing tricks on you is one of the hazards of getting older.' Her thoughts whirled into motion again and suddenly it occurred to her that Mandy herself had already shown her the way. She took a deep breath and offered, 'If you'd like to go to the pictures one night, I could go with you?'

Mandy stared at her for a moment before she beamed with delight. 'Really?' she exclaimed. 'Oh, I'd really look forward to that. I'm free any night that would suit you.'

'What about tonight?' Lex suggested. 'I could meet you outside the Odeon on Belgrave Gate at seven-thirty. I'm not fussy what we see. Hopefully they're showing something you'd like to watch, but if not we could try the other picture houses in town.'

'I'll be there,' Mandy responded eagerly.

Lex felt elated. Phase one of her plan was in progress. Now all she had to do was make sure phase two went as smoothly, and then hopefully she'd be able to bring some happiness into Mandy's lonely life.

'I'd better get back to work,' the girl told her, then added excitedly, 'Oh, I can't wait for tonight.'

Hopefully it won't be me you see, Lex thought, but just smiled at her.

After parting company with Mandy outside the café, Lex decided she had to meet the woman who ran Cupid's Marriage Bureau and who had behaved so cruelly to her vulnerable would-be client. How many other women, men even, who didn't fit her criteria had seen their hopes callously trampled on? The woman needed to be brought to task for her merciless operating methods and Lex was angry enough to do it.

After her long climb back up the three flights of stairs she again arrived breathlessly on the landing and stood there for a moment to prepare herself for what she was about to do. Then, thrusting her chin determinedly in the air, she walked purposefully into the reception area. As earlier the room was empty. She could hear no voices coming from the inner office. The door to it stood ajar so she went across and entered the other room.

It was larger than the reception area, with eaves windows in the sloping attic roof. The white-painted walls were bare, creating a clinical feeling. Lex's sudden arrival caused the woman sitting stiffly at a desk in the middle of the room to raise her head and look enquiringly at her. She was in her early-thirties, a grey suit and white blouse hanging off her skinny frame. Her long thin face was dominated by a large nose; her eyes were grey and set close together. She wore her straight fine brown hair pulled tightly back, and no makeup or jewellery except for a thin gold band on the third finger of her left hand.

The woman looked startled for a moment before addressing Lex in a sharp tone. 'If you'd care to take a seat in reception, I'll be with you in a moment.'

Lex had been fully expecting to face a mature woman whose journey through life had equipped her with the insight to be able to assess other people. In such a business surely she should also be emitting a warm and welcoming aura, to calm the nerves of clients who found their initial visit daunting due to its personal nature. This severe-looking, abrupt young woman was more the type Lex would expect to find sitting in judgement on a magistrates' bench.

'If you don't mind, I'd like to say what I've come to and be on my way.' Lex thought it would be a good idea to check she was facing the right person before she proceeded. 'I presume you are Mrs Landers?'

There was a quizzical expression on her face when she responded, 'Yes, I am.'

Lex pulled herself up to her full height, reared back her head, took a breath and began. 'Well, Mrs Landers . . .'

'Who exactly are you?' Christine Landers interjected.

Lex's mouth snapped shut. She had returned to give this woman a piece of her mind for the way she had treated Mandy – and yet she had not had the foresight to introduce herself before she launched into her tirade. 'Oh! I apologise for my lapse. I'm Alexandra Morton. I . . .'

Before Lex could go any further Christine Landers exclaimed, 'Oh, the lady about the receptionist's job?' She pulled a face. 'Well, you're late,' she scolded. 'Nearly an hour late to be precise.' She shot Lex a disparaging look. 'Not a good way to impress a possible employer. In fact, I'm not impressed at all. After speaking to you on the telephone this morning, I had high hopes that you were just what I was looking for, but you're no better than all the others I've interviewed for the position. One of the women I saw had the nerve to inform me she was hoping to get the job here so she could find herself a husband and not have to pay the bureau's fees! I'm beginning to think I should just continue to try and manage to run things on my own, as I have been so far. Now, if you'll excuse me, I'm busy.'

But Lex was not leaving until she had done what she came for. 'Mrs Landers, for your information I was here on time for my interview. In fact, I was early. I set out this morning hoping to impress you, but after what I saw of the way you treat your possible clients, impressing you is the last thing I'm interested in doing. In fact, I wouldn't work for you if my life depended on it.'

The look of astonishment on Christine Landers' face was almost comical. 'I beg your pardon!'

Lex's tone was cold. 'It's not *my* pardon you need to be begging but Amanda Hopkins', the young woman you just sent out of here feeling devastated. Thankfully I was waiting to see you at the time. It upset me so much to see the state she was in that I went after her to see if I could help.'

'I just told Miss Hopkins the truth – that I couldn't be of assistance to her.'

'The type of people you choose as clients is your business, Mrs Landers, but have you any idea how you made Miss Hopkins feel when you turned her away in that manner, informing her she didn't meet your criteria? Worthless would be putting it mildly. You certainly left her doubting that any man would ever look twice at her.'

The other woman was visibly shaken to hear this. 'Oh! I never purposely set out to upset Miss Hopkins.' There was a bitter edge to her voice when she continued, 'But in my experience all men want a good-looking woman on their arm, someone with a shapely figure who'll attract attention and boost their ego. Unfortunately Mandy Hopkins isn't that sort at all. It wouldn't have been fair of me to have taken her money and given her false hopes.'

Lex looked at her askance. 'Then your experience must be very limited for you to have come to that conclusion. In my own experience, men fantasise about having a film star on their arm, but when they marry they choose someone who won't run off with the first person who comes along who's more affluent and better-looking than they are themselves. A man wants a woman who can make a nice home for him, look after him and their children properly. Beauty is in the eye of the beholder, Mrs Landers.'

She just stopped herself from telling this woman that it wasn't as though she was a beauty herself. Obviously her husband must find her attractive. Instead she said, 'What we may deem good-looking, someone else may well perceive as ugly. Maybe you should have the decency to state in your advertisement that only people of a particular shape and appearance need apply. That way you'll save the likes of Miss Hopkins all the pain and hurt of rejecting them as clients.

'Thankfully, though, in Miss Hopkins' case I happen to know of a single man I'm positive will find her attractive. I'm going to do my best to bring them together, hopefully help her to regain the sense of self-worth you took from her. I wish you every success with your business, Mrs Landers, but it's my opinion you're too blinkered in your own views to make a success of it. Good day.'

Lex made to depart but was stopped in her tracks by Christine Landers. Her voice was almost begging in its tone. 'Please don't go, Mrs Morton. Believe me, I really didn't mean to hurt Miss Hopkins' feelings. I'll send her a letter expressing my deep regret. And I do hope you manage to get her together with the man you have in mind and that it works out for them, really I do.' She looked quizzically at Lex then. 'You seem to know a lot about the matchmaking profession, Mrs Morton. Have you worked for a marriage bureau before? I understood my bureau was the first of its kind in Leicester, so in another major city perhaps?'

Lex shook her head. 'No, but my mother had a talent for match-making and I seem to have inherited the gift. Over the years I've had a number of successes.' Reminded of her recent failure she owned up, 'I haven't always succeeded, but like my friend says, you can't win them all. But the joy I feel when I've had a hand in getting people together who might not otherwise have paired up is something I just couldn't describe. That's why I was so keen to get the job as your receptionist, even if I was only making appointments for clients and showing them a welcome when they arrived. I mean, it must be very daunting for them when they first come, knowing that they're going to be admitting to a stranger that they need help in securing themselves a close relationship, whatever the reason.'

The younger woman was staring at her intently. She heaved a deep worried sigh. 'I blindly thought all that was entailed in successfully matching two people together was a male client telling me he was looking for a shapely blue-eyed blonde, and a shapely blue-eyed blonde client wanting to be introduced to a man with the means to keep her in style. I thought if I could get the pair of them to meet up at a suitable venue, I'd have two satisfied clients.'

Lex looked at her aghast. 'You should know yourself, as a married woman, there's a bit more to it than that, Mrs Landers. There has to be a physical attraction between two people, true, but they also need to share common interests, likes and dislikes, a joint vision of the future, else you've no hope of a bond forming between them. And, of course, two people can be ideally suited to one another in every way, but if that magic spark doesn't ignite between them, then there's nothing you or anyone else can do to bring it about. Also, sometimes the most unlikely couple, people you'd never imagine could be in the same room together, let alone get on well enough for marriage and children, make the most solid alliance against all the odds.'

Christine Landers sat deep in thought for several moments before finally giving a groan of despair. To Lex's bewilderment she said, 'It's the wrong way round.'

Frowning, she asked, 'What is?'

'Well, it seems I should be the receptionist, and someone with your experience and insight into people should do the actual match-making. Look, I know you said you wouldn't consider working for me but is there any possibility you'd change your mind?'

Lex stared at her blankly, thinking she had surely misunder-stood. 'Are you . . . well, are you suggesting I take over your role and you become the receptionist, or have I got that wrong?'

'No, you haven't.' Christine took a deep breath. 'I'm very embarrassed to admit that you've made me see I won't have a business at all if I carry on running it the way I am. I need someone with your special talent to join me here. It's a talent I haven't got, and if I don't get someone like yourself on board then I won't have my business for much longer. I'm sure we can reach an arrangement about proper recompense for your duties.'

Lex was speechless. She had only returned to give this woman a piece of her mind and, having done so, had fully expected to be ordered off the premises for her audacity. Instead she was being offered a job, and not just any old job but her dream job. She still wasn't sure about having the likes of Christine Landers as her boss, but the thought of being paid for doing something that came naturally to her, and the joy and satisfaction it would afford her to know she was bringing happiness to lonely people, overrode all that. 'I'd love to accept,' she said in delight. Then a thought struck her and she added, 'On one condition though, Mrs Landers. In future we don't turn anyone away who comes in seeking our help, no matter what their shape, size, age or looks.'

Without hesitation Christine asked her, 'How soon can you start, Mrs Morton?'

CHAPTER TWELVE

As Lex made her way home, walking on a cloud of euphoria, desperate to tell her family her surprising news, Gil was whistling as he worked, servicing a generator. He was completely absorbed in the task and had eyes and ears for nothing else. Across the workshop meanwhile, having just finished a telephone conversation, Des got up from his battered old table and chair and made his way over to Gil.

'How goes it, mate?'

Gil stopped what he was doing to wipe his greasy hands on the rag he took out of his overall pocket. 'Just finished the servicing, then I'm going to put some oil in and fire her up. Pray it works.'

Des slapped him on his back good-naturedly. 'It will do with you in charge of it,' he said positively. 'Anyway, I'm glad you're about finished this job because that was Sam Kipple on the blower. He's bringing Bessie in . . .' He stopped abruptly when he saw Gil stiffen and a look of sheer panic flood his face. It really grieved Des to see this once proud, and still highly principled, man react so badly to the introduction of a woman's name into the conversation. He quickly explained, 'It's okay, Gil, Bessie is Sam's nickname for his generator.'

Gil's whole body sagged in relief. 'Oh, I thought . . .'

'I know what you thought,' Des interjected, 'but you're totally safe here. The only woman who's ever been in this place since I've had it as my workshop is Thelma and she fully respects your wishes. Rest assured, you'll never be placed in any compromising situation while we're working together. Until you tell me otherwise, I'll see to that.' They heard the noise of a van pulling on to the forecourt then. 'That'll be Sam now.'

Sam Kipple, a stocky man in his early-forties wearing grubby brown workmen's overalls, was just climbing out of his rusting Ford transit when Des came out to greet him.

'She's up to her old tricks, Des,' Sam said to him, slamming shut the van's door. 'She's more temperamental than me bloody wife is, and that's saying summat. Can you work your usual magic on her by early this afternoon? I've a rush job on for a window frame that I promised for this evening. I won't get it finished without Bessie in action as she powers my outdoor saw.'

Des pulled an uncertain expression and scratched his chin. 'I told you the last time you brought her in, Sam, she's long overdue for the knacker's yard. She's got more parts on her than original pieces, and a lot of those I salvaged from scrap.'

'I ain't spending good money on a new one while you can still breathe life into my Bessie, Des. I've had her since I started up in me own business twenty years ago. I feel she's like part of my family. If yer want the truth, I'd feel like I was putting her down unless I knew for certain there was absolutely nothing more you could do for her. So, can I expect her back this afternoon?'

Des sighed, 'I'll do my best.'

Sam's attention was caught then by a movement inside the workshop and he looked quizzically at Des. 'Is that Gil Morton I see? What's he doing here?'

'Working.'

'Working! Listen, mate, you do know why he was dismissed from Brenton's?'

Des nodded.

Sam eyed him incredulously. 'And you're happy to employ someone who's been accused of attacking a woman?'

Des' tone was resolute. 'Gil never touched that woman in any way he shouldn't have, Sam.'

His customer gave a sardonic laugh. 'You're bound to say that, you're his friend Look, a bit of advice, mate. Showing loyalty to a friend is one thing, but standing by a man who's been branded what he has . . . well, you could put your business at risk, because in my book there's no smoke without fire. I've a wife and three daughters to consider, and I ain't happy about you enabling him to stay around here putting my women folk at risk. I suspect a lot of your other customers will be of a like mind when they find out.'

Tight-faced, Des responded, 'I've a wife and daughters too, Sam. Do you think I would put those I cherish in any danger, merely out of loyalty to a friend? I didn't just take Gil's word about his innocence, I've had over twenty years of friendship with him to illustrate it. The hundreds of times we've been out together as mates or with our wives on social occasions; the holidays we've all spent together. I've never once witnessed him do anything questionable in all that time, and I know without asking you that you'd never heard any breath of suspicion about him either before that woman made her false accusation. Now you and any other of my customers who don't like the fact Gil is working here are entitled to take your business elsewhere. He's staying put.'

Sam looked uncomfortable. In a different tone he said, 'Well . . . er . . . maybe I spoke a bit hastily before I thought about it all. I've done business with you long enough to know what an honourable man you are, Des. I've no reason to believe you'd have a friend whose integrity didn't match your own. I'll give you a hand offloading Bessie, shall I?'

Several minutes later when Des returned to the workshop he was surprised to find Gil with his jacket on, the haversack containing his lunch box and thermos flask slung over his shoulder. 'Going somewhere?' Des asked him, puzzled.

Gil shifted uncomfortably on his feet. 'Look, Des, don't think I'm not grateful to you for giving me this opportunity, but I can't risk you losing your business on my account. I didn't mean to eavesdrop but I heard what Sam Kipple said.'

'Then you obviously heard what I said back to him. We've an agreement, Gil, one we shook hands on. You will work here with me and I'll start to put word around that I'm in a position to handle more jobs. It wouldn't be like you to leave me high and dry and looking a fool just because someone like Kipple spouted his mouth off before considering the facts, would it? Now, while you get your coat off, I'll mash us a brew. Then I'd appreciate you giving me a hand getting Bessie inside so I can take a look at her. And maybe you can help me diagnose what's ailing her . . .'

A few streets away, hidden behind a wall in Brenton's yard, Matt had opted to swap his afternoon tea break in the canteen for a blow of fresh air in the yard. Puffing on a cigarette, his attention was caught by a woman who had left the general office building and was making her way to another a few yards away that housed the stores. An expression of distaste on his face, he watched her closely and then jumped when he felt another presence by his side. He spun his head to find his brother looking very relieved to see him.

'When you didn't turn up in the canteen, I wondered what had happened to you.'

Matt took a long drag from his cigarette before answering, 'I'm just fed up with this being sent to Coventry business, and all the black looks and nasty comments, so I decided to give it a miss this breaktime. It's bloody hard turning the other cheek, isn't it, broth? When I got back to my work station after dinnertime, after having to turn a blind eye to those two pigs who spat in our food as they passed our table, some bastard had cut almost all the way through the pulley belt on my machine. When the friction caused it to snap it nearly took my bloody head off as it came whipping by. That lot I work with all stood about laughing 'cos they thought it was funny, but that "prank" could have caused me serious damage, Martin, could have killed me, in fact. It's been over a week now. You'd have thought this vendetta business would have eased up a bit, but it doesn't look like it's ever going to.'

Martin agreed. 'I know it's hard, broth. I'm going through the same as you are. But, remember, we're doing this for Dad. It can't go on forever. Sooner or later something else will catch everyone's attention and then that lot in there will be focusing their jibes on some other poor sod and they'll forget all about us. Just make sure you always check over your machine before you start her up while this is going on.'

Matt sighed. ''Course I will. I've made a decision, though, Martin. The minute we've proved our point here, I'm kissing this place goodbye. I used to enjoy my job, felt really part of things here, but now I feel like a leper. Even when things are back to normal, it won't be the same for me. I was pals with many of that lot who've turned against us, and after this is all over I can't go back to that as if nothing's happened. They might all be two-faced, I'm not.'

'Most of them aren't either, Matt, it's just that they're scared of all the sorts like Loz and his mates, Stan Jenkins in the moulding shop and his bully boys. They know what'll be done to them if they don't show proper allegiance.'

'Yes, I know, but it's not just that. This business has proved to me that when it comes down to it, Maurice Brenton doesn't give a toss about his workers. All he cares about is his profits. I'll never forgive him for not putting up even a bit of a fight for Dad, after all the loyal service he's showed the firm.'

Martin pulled a wry face. 'I agree with you there, Matt. Okay, as soon as things look set to return to normal, me and you are high tailing it out of here.' He took a cigarette from a packet in the top pocket of his overalls and lit it before saying, 'If things carry on the way they are here, it won't be just us two looking for other jobs.'

Stubbing out his own cigarette, Matt looked at his brother quizzically. 'What do you mean?'

'I was in a cubicle in the Gents this morning when Cyril Breville and Wal Summers, his union sidekick, came in. I overheard them talking. It seems the new works manager who was brought in to replace Dad, Mr Minton, finished off the tender for the Ministry of Defence but made a right cock up of it. According to Breville, Brenton's haven't been awarded the order the old man was desperate to get. It would have secured all our jobs for the next three years at least. I don't know where Minton was works manager before but it certainly wasn't for a big firm like ours. He's no match for Breville, not like Dad was, and I tell you, broth, there's going to be fun and games here shortly 'cos Breville is going to have us men out for something or other, just to prove how powerful he is. Minton won't be able to handle it like Dad could, so whatever Breville finds to get us all out on, it's going to be a long drawn out strike, you can bet your life on that. Hopefully we'll both be long gone by then. I prefer to get a pay packet at the end of each week.'

'If anyone should be long gone, it's her,' Matt snarled, indicating with a nod of his head the stores building and the woman standing outside it now. 'That brazen bitch just waltzed across the yard like she'd not a care in the world. No one would think that just over a week ago she wrecked Dad's life and made his family's hell along with it.'

Martin looked over in the direction Matt was staring. 'Oh, the infamous Mrs Jones. I wish we knew why she accused Dad of what she did. She doesn't appear to have had anything to gain from it, does she, or it would have come to light by now?'

Matt sighed heavily. 'If I didn't know Dad as well as I do, I'd probably be thinking he was guilty. But I do know him, and I know he's not. It can only be like Mam suggested. That woman was besotted with him, and he being the type he is never noticed her advances. She took it he was spurning her, and what she did was just through her spite.'

'Well, why would Dad look at another woman when he's got the likes of our Mam? There's plenty more men in this factory, mind, why did the Jones woman have to pick on him to take a fancy to? Anyway, I still think we should have gone to see her and wrung the truth from her, made her come clean to old man Brenton.'

'I'm with you there, broth, but we can't go against Mam and Dad's wishes on that. We've got no choice but to get on with it.'

Just then a head popped around the wall and Loz sneered at them both. 'Oh, this is where yer hiding, is it?' He came barrelling up to them with six of his cronies, all sniggering like silly schoolboys. 'Too fucking cowardly, I take it, to face us all in the canteen this tea break.' He threw a butt end on the ground, stamping it out with his boot then flipping strands of greasy hair away from his mean blue eyes before adding sarcastically, 'All getting too much for you, is it?'

Both Matt and Martin issued fed up sighs. It seemed nowhere in this maze of factory buildings was free from their tormentors.

When Loz received no reply from either of them, he gave Matt a forceful shove on his shoulder, sending him careering back to land hard against the wall behind him. 'You fucking deaf as well as a coward? Don't you fucking ignore me!'

After days of this kind of treatment and the serious harm he'd only narrowly avoided after someone had tampered with the pulley belt on his machine that morning, Matt could no longer contain himself. Before Martin could stop him he'd righted himself, swung back his arm and landed a punch on Loz's chin, knocking him to the ground. Going to stand over Loz, Matt bellowed down at him, 'Who are you calling a fucking coward? It's *you* that's the coward, hiding behind your mates. Never approach me when you're on your own, do you? I've seen you dodge behind a machine when you've seen me coming towards you and you've none of your cronies with you. So aren't you in fact the pot calling the kettle black?'

Mortified at being humiliated in front of his mates by Matt's unexpected attack, eyes blazing furiously, Loz scrambled up and was just about to launch a retaliatory attack when Cyril Breville appeared next to them.

Quickly sizing up the situation, he demanded, 'What's going on here, lads?'

Before Matt or Martin could respond, Loz erupted, 'Me and me mates were just making our way back to work from the canteen, minding our own business, and the Mortons set about us, that's what, Mr Breville.'

Cyril fixed his attention on Martin and Matt. 'Is this true?'

'No, it's not, Mr Breville. We were minding our own business, having a fag. It was Loz that set on Matt,' Martin told him.

'Fucking liar!' Loz cried. 'I told you the truth, Mr Breville.

Ain't that right, lads?' he addressed his mates, looking at them all meaningfully.

'Yeah,' they all agreed. 'It was the Mortons what started it, Mr Breville, honest it was.'

The malicious spark in Loz's eyes flared brighter and a smirk played round his lips. 'So, Mr Breville, it's two against seven. The firm's rules are, no fighting on company premises, so you ain't got any choice. You'll have to take these two before the old man for disciplinary action, and he'll have no choice but to take our word that they started it and have 'em marched off the premises.'

Matt didn't see why he should give them all the satisfaction. 'As far as I'm concerned you're not going to have the pleasure of seeing another innocent man sacked,' he declared. Then, so sick and tired of this whole business that his common sense completely deserted him, he added, 'In fact, you can stuff your job right where the sun don't shine, Mr Breville. I've had enough of this place, I'm off.'

Loyal to his brother and very angry that he had been manipulated in this way, Martin blurted out, 'That includes me too. We'll clear our lockers and collect our cards and dues on Friday from the pay office.' He looked fixedly at Loz. 'My dad's always brought us up to believe that violence isn't the way to prove a point, but enough is enough. Now, I'm warning you, if me or my brother hear any lies or gossip about how we came to leave Brenton's employ, you'll wish you'd never been born. There's enough lying going on over my dad. Neither me nor Martin will stand for any more. Come on, Matt,' he urged.

They spun on their heel and stormed off back to their separate work stations to collect their tools before meeting up again in the locker room to recover their personal items.

Clocking out of Brenton's for the last time, a worried look clouded Matt's face as it struck him just what they had done. 'I don't regret getting out of here but the folks are relying on what we earn to tide them over . . .'

Martin looked worried too. 'Oh, shit, so they are! Well, we'd better get down the Labour Exchange post haste then and hope we get set on quick.'

A while later they were both scanning the job cards under the engineering section at the Labour Exchange. In this post-war boom factories producing all types of machinery and parts were crying out for qualified engineers, but all insisted on the one qualification the brothers hadn't given any thought to. When they had walked off the job today it hadn't crossed their mind that they were going without favourable references.

'No firm is going to give us a job without a glowing recommendation from the last business we worked for,' Martin said despondently.

'So what the hell are we going to do then?' asked a mortified Matt.

A balding, bespectacled man approached them. 'You'll have to leave, I'm afraid, we're shutting for the night.'

With a worried face Martin said, 'We'd better get home and break the news of what we've done to Mam and Dad. God knows, this is the last thing they need on top of everything else. They're not going to be very happy with us.'

'No, they're not,' muttered Matt.

The night was dark and cold. Both of them pulled the collar of their work jacket up to protect themselves from the biting November wind that greeted them outside. They walked towards the bus station, each lost in his own private thoughts. It wasn't until they were sitting on the crowded bus, waiting for it to depart, that Martin said, 'Well, I can see only two options left open to us, Matt. First, we could go cap in hand and beg Brenton's to give us references.'

Matt groaned. 'Oh, hell. But I can't see them giving us them after we walked out like we did.'

'Nor can I, but without a reference we won't get set on elsewhere, will we, so we'd just have to swallow our pride. Beg if necessary. Anyway, when I was looking down all those job cards it made me realise something, Matt.'

'Oh, what?'

'That I don't want to work for an employer anymore, putting money in his pocket that could go into my own. I want to work for myself.'

159

His announcement shocked his brother. Martin had never mentioned any desire to work for himself before. Matt responded negatively. 'Nice dream, brother, but not really possible for the likes of us. It takes money to start a business, much more than the few quid we've got in our Post Office savings. Besides, even if we had the money, the only work we could tackle with our qualifications is the same sort of thing Des does, maintaining generators. But that would mean we'd be in competition with him and Dad, and we couldn't do that.'

Martin shook his head, looking bothered. 'No, we couldn't, but surely there must be something else we could turn our hands to, something that doesn't need that much of an outlay to set up.'

Both of them lapsed into silence as the bus began its journey, each trying to fathom a service they could offer the general public that would make them both a living but wouldn't be in direct competition with Des and their father.

Finally Matt said keenly, 'I've got it! We can do window cleaning. Ladders and a barrow wouldn't cost that much.'

Martin looked horrified at the thought. 'That's maybe fine for you, Matt, but you know I can't stand heights.'

He looked disappointed. 'Oh, I forgot about you having a problem with being more than two inches off the ground.'

Martin snapped back at him, 'You make it sound like I've got a nasty disease. I can't help it if I suffer from vertigo. But at least you came up with something. I can't think of anything myself.'

Matt gave a defeated sigh. 'So we have no choice but to go and beg Brenton's for a reference. I was really hoping we could avoid that.'

Arriving at the back door of their home a while later, they looked at each other as if to say, Well, here goes, before Martin opened the door and they both trooped inside.

They stopped abruptly on the threshold at the sight that greeted them. The Servis twin tub washing machine was by the sink and their mother was just finishing mopping the floor. At their arrival she exclaimed, 'Thank goodness you're both home. Watch you don't slip on the floor, it's wet. Oh, no, is that the time! I haven't started the dinner yet.

'But what an afternoon I've had! I have the most exciting news to tell you all, and I was having such a job containing myself until you got home I decided to keep myself busy by doing some washing and putting the vacuum around. Well, I don't know what happened to the washer but all of a sudden water starting pouring across the floor . . . and the vacuum isn't picking up at all!

'I'm lucky, though, I've engineers for a husband and sons. As you're home first, you'll take a look at them for me, won't you? I pity the poor housewives whose men aren't as capable as mine. Getting a domestic engineer to call inside a week is a real problem. They never turn up when they say they will, and then they charge a fortune . . .'

Martin was looking thoughtfully at the washing machine. 'Sounds to me like something is blocking the pump, Mam. Probably a sock or a handkerchief, something small like that. If it is I'll have it fixed for you in a jiffy.'

'And it sounds to me like the belt has come off the vacuum else it's snapped and needs replacing, and that's why it's not picking up,' explained Matt.

Lex beamed at them both while giving the mop a wring out in the bucket of dirty water. 'I knew my men would come to my rescue.'

As she cleaned the dirty mop head under the tap she was not privy to the look exchanged between her sons.

'Are you thinking what I am, Matt?' Martin asked.

He grinned. 'I've got a feeling I am.'

Lex heard that. Propping the mop by the sink to dry, she asked, 'What are you both thinking?'

Much to her shock, her eldest son picked her up and swung her round, exclaiming, 'You're marvellous, our Mam!'

'Put me down,' Lex scolded him. When he had and she was straightening her clothes, she said, 'It's a bit premature for congratulations, I haven't told you what my good news is yet. How did you both find out?'

They both looked at her. 'About what?'

'About . . .' She stopped in mid-flow, catching sight of the time on the clock on the wall. It was just after six. 'Oh, goodness, I've got to dash, I've a quick errand to do,' she announced, taking off her apron and placing it over the back of a kitchen chair.

Grabbing her coat off the back door she continued, 'If your father comes home while I'm gone, tell him I'll be back shortly. Dinner won't be long after as it's liver and onions tonight. Hopefully by then you'll have my machines fixed for me and I can finish off the washing and hoovering later.' She opened the door and made to depart before something struck her. 'Oh, I'm sorry, I forgot to ask, how was your day?'

There was an underlying note in her voice that told her sons what she really wanted to know was whether their persecution by the other men was still going on, or it the gossip about their father had started to die down yet.

But she needed to be seated with a cup of tea, or preferably a stiff drink, in her hand when she learned what they had to tell her. Better still, their father should be here too so they could get it over with in one go. They were lucky to have parents who respected their children's right to make their own decisions, but they had always stressed the need for these to be responsible, and adults did not walk out of a job until they had another lined up.

'We'll tell you all about it when you get back from your errand,' Martin said evasively.

With the thought of that uppermost in her mind, Lex hurried off. Arriving at Phyllis' back gate, she stopped for a moment to put on the pose and facial expression she wished to present to her friend. Then she looked skywards and mouthed, 'Sorry, Lord, please forgive the lies I'm about to tell, but this is the only way I can think of to achieve what I want to.' Then she unlatched the gate and painfully limped into the yard.

Phyllis was most surprised to see who her caller was considering the time of day; it was an unspoken rule round here that between the hours of five and seven most families were sitting down to their dinner. Regardless Phyllis still gave her the usual warm greeting. 'How nice to see you. Come on in, gel.'

Limping over the threshold, Lex placed both hands firmly on the edge of the draining board as if supporting herself and said in a fraught voice, 'I'm sorry to call on you at this time, Phyllis, but I wondered if Derek was home from work, and if so could I have a quick word with him, please?'

''Course, yer can, ducky. I'll give him a call.' Before she did, though, she looked hard at Lex. 'Is there something wrong? You seem to be in terrible pain, and if I wasn't mistaken you were limping just now.'

'It's my back. It came on suddenly this afternoon. I think it's an attack of lumbago I'm suffering.'

Phyllis stared sympathetically at her. 'Oh, poor you. Hot water bottle should help ease it, and a good dollop of something alcoholic usually helps dull pain. I do hope it goes soon, lovey. Derek!' she shouted. 'Mrs Morton would like a quick word.'

Seconds later a pleasant-faced, soberly dressed young man appeared beside Lex. He seemed oblivious to the fact that he had a napkin tucked into the neck of his shirt and hanging down over his brown hand-knitted cable pullover, a style fashionable in the forties and fifties but which Lex's own fashion-conscious sons would baulk at wearing in what were starting to be termed the Swinging Sixties. 'Hello, Mrs M. Got a leaky tap or something? Give me five minutes to finish me dinner and I'll be round with me tools.'

He really was a nice young man, just the type for Mandy, she thought. 'It's nothing like that I've come to see you about, Derek. You see, I've arranged to meet a young lady tonight. I'm meant to be going to the pictures with her. Lovely young lady she is, Amanda Hopkins is her name. I only met her today, but we got chatting in a café and, you know how it is, one thing led to another so I agreed to go with her to see a film we're both keen on seeing. Mandy is really looking forward to it.

'Only, as I've just told your mother, I got this sudden attack of lumbago later this afternoon. I was hoping it would ease up but in fact it's grown worse. I know I won't be able to sit still and watch the film. In fact, it took me all my time to get myself here, the pain is so bad. Anyway, I don't know Mandy's address so can't get a message to her, and my two lads both had arrangements straight from work, and with things being the way they are with Mr Morton at the moment I can't ask him. So . . . well . . . you're the only neighbours who are speaking to me at the moment, the only ones I can ask this favour of. I'd hate to leave Mandy standing there, it wouldn't be right. I wondered if you'd be good enough to go and tell her what's happened and apologise to her for me letting her down? I'd really appreciate it if you could. I'd arranged to meet her at the Odeon on Belgrave Gate at seven-thirty.'

Being the gentlemanly sort of young man that Lex knew he was, Derek responded exactly as she'd expected. 'I'm sorry to hear about your back, Mrs M. No, it's certainly not right to let a young lady down. I'll deliver your message to her, don't worry. I'm off to my model-making group tonight. It doesn't start until eight so I'll have time to make a detour past the cinema.'

If her instincts were correct it looked like there would be one member of the model-making group absent tonight. Lex smiled gratefully at him and, after she'd given him a detailed description of Mandy, he went off to finish his dinner.

Phyllis was just seeing her out when a memory stirred. 'Oh, Lex, how did you get on with your interview today?'

She beamed broadly back. 'I got the job, start tomorrow.'

Phyllis was delighted to hear this. 'Oh, I *am* pleased. What sort of company will you be working for?'

'A marriage bureau.'

The older woman looked stunned for a moment before exclaiming, 'Well, ain't that right up your street, lovey?' Then another thought struck her and she asked in all seriousness, 'If you ever get a nice young lady in you think will suit my Derek, can you point her in his direction?'

After tonight Lex hoped that Phyllis' concern for him would be a thing of the past.

She was so pleased she had succeeded in her plan to instigate a meeting between the young couple that she completely forgot about her supposed attack of lumbago and sprang over to open the door, saying breezily, 'Sorry again to have disturbed your meal, Phyllis. Now, best hurry back, I haven't made a start on my own family's yet.'

As she briskly let herself out, a perplexed Phyllis stood staring after her, thinking that it must be her imagination that the woman just leaving looked nothing like the pain-racked individual who had arrived only minutes ago.

Back at home Lex was surprised to see that everything was as she had left it with no sign of either son. That puzzled her but regardless she was glad to see that her husband had returned. He was rinsing out his Thermos flask in the sink.

Gil looked both pleased and relieved to see her. 'Oh, there you are. I was beginning to think I'd boarded the *Marie Celeste* and you'd abandoned ship in the middle of your chores.' Putting his clean flask on the draining board, he came across to kiss her affectionately on the cheek and then asked, 'What's the reason both our lads' tool boxes are by the outhouse when they usually leave them in their lockers overnight?'

Lex looked as bewildered as he felt. 'I don't know, dear. Nor do I know why they aren't both here. I had a quick errand to do and left them both taking a look at the washer and vacuum as neither of them was working properly. Thankfully they said they knew what was wrong and could fix them for me, otherwise it would have been down to you.' But the unexplained disappearance of her sons wasn't as important to Lex as how her husband had fared that day. 'So how did your day go?' she asked.

'I enjoyed it very much. Des is a pleasure to work for. I detest the sort of boss who stands breathing down your neck, and always bore that in mind when I was one. Des tells me what he'd like me to do, then leaves me to it.'

Happy to hear this, Lex said, 'That's because he knows he can trust you to get on with it and do a good job. So I take it you're glad you accepted his offer?'

Gil nodded. 'But naturally I'll be even more so when enough work is coming in to pay me a decent wage. We had strong words today on that subject. He let slip he'd an appointment with the bank tomorrow to see about a loan to cover my wages. I eventually made him accept that if he kept that appointment, my agreement to work for him was null and void. He could see I meant business.' Gil looked at her in remorse then. 'I know this will be an awful financial strain on us but I just can't bring myself to take money from Des that he doesn't have.'

Despite the hardship this stance was going to cause them, Lex knew she was lucky to have a man with this much integrity. And they weren't in fact going to have to struggle too much financially as she herself would be earning now. She couldn't wait to lighten his load by telling him about her job, but out of respect for his feelings waited a little longer until he'd finished speaking.

Gil continued, 'The good news is that Des secured a couple of new clients today, recommended by the one who was so pleased with the job I did on his generator. He said he'd put work Des's way whenever he got the opportunity, and he's been true to his word. They're not big-paying jobs but new work all the same so things look pretty positive for us. Now, enough about my day. How was yours, love?'

'Well, apart from the washer and vacuum both letting me down, I had rather an exciting one.' Despite having wanted all the members of her family to be gathered together to hear her good news, the most important person was present and Lex was no longer able to contain herself. 'Oh, Gil, I'm delighted to tell you I got . . .'

She was abruptly interrupted by the back door flying open and both their sons charging in, faces lit up like beacons. It was plain they were desperate to divulge important news to their parents. Once again Lex would have to wait to tell her own.

'So what's lit your fires?' Gil asked.

'We've decided we're going into business for ourselves,' Matt announced.

Both their parents stared at them in surprise.

166

'You've what!' Gil exclaimed. 'But giving up perfectly good jobs with Brenton's to take such a huge gamble . . .'

Martin cut him short. 'Well, that's just it, Dad, we aren't employed by Brenton's any longer, not after what happened today.' At the expressions of shock on his parents' faces, he added, 'Look, I think you'd both better sit down and we'll explain how this has all come about.'

As he took a seat at the kitchen table, his wife sitting next to him, sons opposite, Gil said sternly, 'It'd better be a good explanation, lads.'

Matt allowed his elder brother to do the honours. After he'd related the events at work that had brought him and his brother to their decision, Gil's expression turned to one of regret. 'Well, now I know all the facts, I can't blame you both for walking off the job. I could be annoyed about the way you've covered up the trouble you've been having since my departure from Brenton's, but I should also give you credit for standing the abuse you've received as long as you have. The other men should be ashamed of themselves. What happened to me was nothing to do with you two, you just happen to be my sons. But then, when you're dealing with morons with a mentality such as Lawrence Stanton possesses, I doubt a saint would have lasted as long as you both did.' He looked at them both with open admiration. 'So, you're going it alone as domestic appliance engineers then?'

'That's the plan, Dad,' said an enthusiastic Matt. 'What happened with Mam's machines today gave us the idea.' He looked at his father earnestly. 'You do think it's a good one, don't you? That we'll make a living for ourselves from it?'

Inwardly Gil was worried that his sons were entering a precarious field where they'd be constantly battling against competition for the work that was on offer, never sure what amount they'd have in their pockets at the end of each week. It was precisely the same situation he himself was in, working for Des, so it wasn't as though he could provide them with a financial buffer meantime. But Gil wasn't the sort of father not to back his sons in anything they did.

Keeping his reservations to himself, he responded resolutely, 'With the right attitude, I certainly do. It's not the first time our washer or vacuum has had a problem that needed expert attention, but luckily for your mother she has her own band of household engineers to call on. Not many other housewives are as lucky, and if you charge reasonably for your services and do the best job you can your customers will always come back to you – and, more importantly, recommend you to others. And Des obviously thinks you're on to a winner as you say he's agreed to let you use his workshop as a base until you can afford one of your own?'

'He didn't need much persuading either, Dad. As soon as he'd heard our plan . . . we just missed seeing you as you'd left for the night . . . he said he'd do all he could to give us a helping hand,' Martin told him.

'Des is a good man,' Gil said with conviction. 'It's times like we're going through now when you find out who your true friends are. We're certainly blessed with ours. What are you going to do for transport? You'll be needing a van . . . one each actually as you can't reply on public transport for the kind of business you'll be operating.'

'We thought about that, Dad. We're hoping to be able to afford a couple of old jalopies to start, out of the savings we've both got and our last wages from Brenton's. We've our week-in-hand to come and some holiday pay so that gives us a bit more to play with. We reckon we can talk Tinkerbell into giving us a good deal on a couple of vans from his scrappy. Unfortunately his yard was shut by the time we passed after visiting Des, but we spotted a brown Morris van through the fencing which looked worthy of further inspection.'

Before his own troubles Gil would have offered to accompany his sons on such a mission, casting a fatherly eye on things and offering his advice, to satisfy himself his sons were getting a good deal from the likes of wily William Bell, an Irishman of gypsy origin nicknamed Tinkerbell by the locals. He was known for squeezing the last penny out of customers who were under the impression they'd got themselves a good deal, only to realise later that they'd paid well over the odds for the rusting scrap he'd sold them. He also bought vehicles that he knew would bring him in a good profit after a minimal amount of work was done on them, which he and his three sons tackled. Most of these vehicles hardly lasted the journey out of the yard before they failed again and the new owner then found himself facing a large bill to get his car running, but the odd one or two did actually prove useful as runabouts until the buyer could afford something better.

But excursions of this nature were out for Gil now. He must rely on the fact that he had taught his sons well enough to handle themselves with the likes of William Bell, without needing him to watch over them. It hurt, though, that he no longer had that freedom. Gruffly he said, 'I'm sure you're both old enough and wise enough to be sure of what you're buying before you part with good money.'

Both Martin and Matt would have liked nothing more than to ask their father to join them, valuing his experience and expertise as they did, but until matters changed for him, if ever, they would not embarrass him by asking.

'Don't worry, Dad, our money is staying in our pockets until we've inspected every inch of anything that takes our fancy,' Matt told him fondly. He then addressed his mother. 'You haven't said much, Mam? Look, I know we haven't exactly chosen the best time to go it alone. You're not angry with us, are you?'

Leaning over to pat his hand fondly, Lex told him, 'No, of course I'm not. When is the best time to make big changes, lovey? Better now than when you've both got the responsibility of a family to look after.' Like her husband she, too, was secretly worried about all the hurdles their sons would face, getting their venture off the ground. Regardless, she enthused, 'I know you're both going to make a great success of it.' Then a thought struck her. Eyes twinkling, she added, 'You never know who you're going to meet, doing a job like that.'

They both looked at her quizzically, then Martin twigged what she was getting at. 'Can you believe our mother, Matt? Here we are, excited by the prospect of making a decent living for ourselves, and all Mam can see it as is an opportunity to find ourselves nice girls to settle down with.'

Lex pretended to look aghast. 'I'm not,' she fibbed, and caught Gil looking at her as if to say, Yes, you are, dear. 'All right, maybe I am,' she reluctantly admitted. 'You can't blame a mother for wanting her sons to find nice girls to settle down with. And with all the customers you'll be getting, I was thinking it might just be a possibility.'

'How do you know I haven't already met someone who fits my bill, Mam?' Martin asked.

She gawped at him, her eyes filling with hope. 'Have you?'

His own eyes twinkling, he said, 'Don't worry, if I ever do meet someone I think enough of to give up my freedom for, I'll give you plenty of warning to get yourself a nice outfit for the wedding.'

The way her sons were both going, though, Lex felt she'd be too old to enjoy these events.

Knowing him as well as she did, Lex could tell Gil was itching to ask their sons how they proposed to get their new business off the ground, and offer them his own advice. She was immensely gratified by this as only a few short days ago he'd been so wrapped up in his own misery he wouldn't have had the stomach for it. But she had her own good news to divulge to them all, and if she didn't demand their attention now she might not get another chance until God only knew when.

Seeing Gil was about to speak, she got in first with, 'Look, before you start discussing the new business, can I please tell you my good news?' She took a deep breath and excitedly announced, 'I landed myself a job today.'

All the men looked stunned to hear it. Gil looked a bit put out, too. It was going to be hard for him, seeing his wife as a bread-winner, she knew, so hastily continued, 'I'll be working for a marriage bureau, helping to pair people up.' She was privy to the look that passed between her sons then. 'What did that mean?' she asked sharply. 'Don't you think I'd be suitable for such a job?'

'Far from it,' Matt told her. 'I know I speak for Martin too when I say the first thing that crossed our minds was that with you concentrating on fixing other people up, you won't have so much time to be concentrating on me and Martin.'

'I . . . I've never tried to do that,' she blatantly fibbed.

Martin flashed a look at Matt before he said, 'No, Mam would never try that with us, would she?'

''Course she wouldn't,' Matt readily agreed, though what he was thinking was another matter. 'Well, Mam, if that job ain't right up your street, I don't know what is. Don't you agree, Dad?'

It was obvious Gil was still struggling with the prospect. 'Well . . . er . . . yes, it is. I'm just worried about the extra strain it's going to put on you, Lex. Of course we'll all help out around the house as much as we can, won't we, lads?'

'Yeah, 'course we will, Mam,' they both agreed, although both privately dubious about having to tackle the housework from now on.

Lex couldn't help but laugh at their expressions. 'Don't worry, I'm not expecting you both to cook and clean. I can prepare the next day's meals the night before, and to quote Thelma, the house won't fall to bits if I don't Hoover and polish every day. But you can do more for yourselves by making your beds and being tidier around the house, and that will help me enormously.'

They looked relieved that this was all that was going to be expected of them.

Gil told her, 'I'm quite capable of putting the vacuum around, and I'm sure a bit of dusting isn't beyond me either.' Then he took her hand and said gruffly, 'I'm so proud of you, dear. The best day's work the firm you're going to be working for has ever done is to employ you.'

She was touched to the heart to hear this. To hide tears, she got up, saying, 'While you discuss men's things, I'll get cracking on the dinner. 'Cos if I know anything about my men, I know you're all famished.'

Lex was excited about starting her new job, couldn't wait to get stuck in and hopefully bring a new sense of purpose to her life. Several minutes later the Morton men were deep in discussion over the best way to get word around that a new domestic appliance engineering company was in operation. Lex, having put the potatoes on to boil, was just about to start frying the liver and onions when a loud crash resounded, to be followed immediately by the shattering of glass.

With a shocked cry, Lex clapped her bloodied hands to her face. 'What on earth was that!' she cried in alarm.

Jumping up, Martin exclaimed, 'It came from the living room.'

They all dashed into the front room to discover a large jagged hole in the top pane of the middle panel of the bay window. Shards of glass were strewn everywhere.

An ashen-faced Lex whispered, 'Who would do this to us? Is it not enough we're being treated like lepers and having nasty messages painted across the front door . . .'

The three men looked at her quizzically.

'What nasty messages on the front door?' Gil enquired.

Lex inwardly groaned. She had so wanted to keep that incident from her husband and sons so as not to distress them any more than was necessary. She had no choice but to come clean about it now. 'Oh, I'd forgotten about it,' she said unconvincingly. 'I found it on the front door the other day. Covered it up with paint I found in the shed.'

'And just what did this message say?' Gil demanded.

'Oh, I can't remember now,' said Lex evasively. But then she surveyed the chaos before her and her whole body sagged in despair. 'But who would do this?'

'A coward, in my book,' snarled Matt, stepping over broken glass to retrieve the house brick lying in the middle of the room. 'Not even the guts to tie a message to this, identifying himself.'

'Just let me find out who he is,' snapped Martin, his face thunderous.

His father glared meaningfully at him. 'And if you do, you'll do nothing. We Mortons do not believe in an eye for an eye, understand?'

A tight-faced Martin and Matt responded in unison, 'Yes, Dad.'

'Right, help me clear this up. I've some hardboard in the shed, enough to cover it, and I'll arrange for a glazier to come tomorrow.'

An expense they could have done without, thought Gil.

Seeing the worried look on his face, Lex realised she had to bolster him up or risk a return of his mood from earlier in the week. 'While you all clear this up, I'll carry on with the dinner,' she said matter-of-factly.

'Yeah, and I'm meeting a friend tonight so I need to get a move on,' Martin put in.

Lex couldn't help herself. 'Oh! Male or female?'

'Just a friend, Mam,' he responded cagily. He saw she was about to quiz him further but stopped her by saying, 'I'll go and give Dad a hand getting the hardboard out of the shed.'

As he disappeared Lex stared after him. He was meeting a woman, she instinctively knew that. But what was she like? Was this one in the same mould as his past girlfriends or had he really meant what he'd said and was looking for a new type, the marrying kind? Oh, she did wish she hadn't got it so wrong about Justine!

CHAPTER THIRTEEN

Lex had given very careful consideration to the way she wished to present herself to the clients of Cupid's Marriage Bureau. After a discussion with Thelma the previous evening, both women had decided she needed to set clients at their ease by looking competent and efficient. But it was equally as important she should appear, approachable, so that clients would open up to her about themselves, allowing her a clear insight into their thoughts and feelings. She strongly suspected that, Christine Landers had put people off with her austere appearance and manner.

Finally Lex settled on a plain navy blue kick-pleat skirt worn with a pale blue twinset and a tasteful diamante brooch, a present from her husband on their twentieth anniversary. She waved her hair gently to frame her face and applied makeup lightly, finally satisfied she had achieved the effect she wanted. She arrived promptly at ten minutes to nine, raring to go.

Her new boss looked relieved and extremely pleased to welcome her into the office.

'I'm so glad to see you, Mrs Morton. I worried last night you'd have a change of mind about coming to work for me. We didn't exactly get off to the best of starts, did we?'

Lex was taking off her coat to hang it on the stand in the corner of the reception area. 'Not all first introductions go swimmingly,' she said diplomatically 'I hardly slept last night from excitement, though, because I can't wait to get started.' Then she turned to face Christine and noticed the way the younger woman was scrutinising her appearance. Worried, Lex said, 'It's obvious I'm not suitably dressed, Mrs Landers. I'll go home and change . . .'

Christine herself was wearing the same sombre suit and sensible shoes she had worn yesterday although accompanied by a fresh white blouse. 'You look perfectly presentable to me, Mrs Morton,' she cut Lex's protests short.

And Lex realised then that Christine was comparing her own unduly severe appearance to her new colleague's and reaching the obvious conclusion. Which would save Lex having to raise the matter . . .

Christine said now, 'I've moved my personal items to the reception desk, ready for you to take over in the main office.'

Lex looked across at the reception desk. The only difference she saw from yesterday was the addition of a leatherbound diary and a fountain pen. Her immediate thought was that any new arrivals wouldn't think this was a busy office and might well doubt they'd have a varied enough list of clients on their books to be able to help the newcomer. Cupid's might well not have the number of clients they hoped for, but they could create the illusion they did meantime, to get those new clients through the door. The room itself was far from welcoming also and Lex felt that needed to be addressed.

'Er . . . I hope you don't mind me making an observation, Mrs Landers,' she began. 'It's just, to me this room is . . . well, my dentist's waiting room is more welcoming than this.'

Christine glanced around. 'Mmm, yes, it hadn't struck me before but you do have a point. What do you suggest?'

'Some pictures on the wall for starters.'

'I've some stored in the attic at home, nice scenic views of the Scottish highlands mainly. I've a lovely one of a majestic-looking stag on a hill. They were left me by my grandmother when she died last year.'

In the right sort of setting probably very tasteful pictures, but hardly conducive to the right sort of atmosphere, Lex thought. Diplomatically she replied, 'They sound lovely, but don't you think some pictures of happy couples together would be more appropriate, considering the business we're in? We could source them from magazines, cut them out and frame them, it shouldn't be expensive to do.'

To her relief Christine enthused, 'What an excellent idea. You're proving your worth to me, already Mrs Morton.' Then she noticed Lex was scrutinising the room again and asked what she was looking for.

'I just wondered where you kept the tea- and coffee-making facilities?'

Her new boss looked taken aback and responded shortly, 'Well, I don't feel the need for refreshments immediately on arriving for work, but if you do I've no objection to you slipping across the road to the café. It's what I usually do later.'

'Not for me, Mrs Landers, but to offer the clients.'

'Oh, I see. Well, I don't usually offer them any sort of beverage. Do you think we should, then?'

'I think it would be a nice gesture, especially to those who are very nervous. Help put them at their ease.'

'Again, you have a valid point. I'll see about sorting out the appropriate equipment and supplies. Thank you again, Mrs Morton. And anything else you can think of to help my business become successful, I'm very willing to consider.'

'Well . . . there is just one other observation. We don't exactly look as though we're busy. That reception desk is far too tidy, you see.'

Christine looked across at the desk. 'Well, it hasn't been used until now. I see what you mean, though, and I'll do something about it.'

Lex was gratified that her suggestions were being received so favourably.

'Anything else you think needs immediate attention?'

Lex smiled. 'Not for the moment. I'd like to know how you've been going about things, though?'

Christine gave her a knowing look. 'I've no doubt you'll have many more suggestions on that score, too, and I can't wait to hear them. Come through to my . . . no, your . . . office.'

Moments later the two of them were seated side by side behind what had been Christine's desk. Spread out before them were twenty or so white postcards on which was listed the name and address of each client, plus a brief description of them, along with an equally brief summary of the sort of person they were hoping to find.

There was a certain amount of embarrassment in her tone when Christine said to Lex, 'After what you said to me yesterday, I know you're going to suggest we note down much more information from clients.'

Not wanting to add to her discomfiture, Lex gave some serious thought to her reply. 'Well, it looks a bit basic, but presumably it was enough for you to successfully match some clients up?'

Her new boss shifted uncomfortably in her chair and said quietly, 'Well ... er ... actually I haven't matched any clients yet. To be truthful, the meetings I've arranged so far have all proved ... well ... disastrous. One client was so disappointed with the woman I arranged for him to meet, he cancelled his registration.'

Lex wasn't surprised to hear this in consideration of the haphazard way Christine was operating. Regardless she said encouragingly, 'Well, not all first meetings have people falling into each other's arms. A friend of mine only went out with a chap because a friend of hers liked his friend. She thought she was just making up the foursome until the other couple got themselves established, but after several evenings in his company she found she was really looking forward to seeing him. They've been very happily married for over twenty years now and have four children.

'A detailed questionnaire on registration should greatly help us to understand our clients better, then we'll stand a good chance of matching them up with people they're at least going to enjoy meeting. Them falling for each other would be a bonus.'

Christine looked bothered. 'Won't the clients think we're impertinent, probing so intimately into their personal lives?'

'In the circumstances, I should think they'll be expecting it. You can't expect a doctor to diagnose your illness correctly if you refuse to give him the symptoms, can you?'

'You're right, you can't. No time like the present to make a start on the questionnaire. We've two clients booked in today but not until the afternoon so we've all morning to work on it. There's a pad of paper and writing implements in the top right-hand drawer,' Christine informed her new employee.

Approximately two hours later four sheets of paper were filled with over thirty questions. Laying down the pencil she had been writing with, Lex said, 'I think we've just about covered everything we need to know now. We can always add to it later if we feel the need.'

'I wouldn't have thought of most of the questions you've come up with, Mrs Morton. Until you explained it to me, I would never have asked whether a man liked to buy a woman presents, but now I realise you can tell from his answer whether he's the mean type of man or a generous one. But what do we do if clients refuse to answer any of the questions?'

'Well, to my mind, only someone with something to hide would be evasive. In those cases we'll have to use our instincts, decide whether we accept them as clients or not.'

'You keep saying *we*, Mrs Morton, but it's you who's going to be doing the interviewing in future. I'm just the receptionist.'

'I know that's what you proposed yesterday, Mrs Landers, but there's a saying that two heads are better than one. So wouldn't it be better if we took it in turns to interview or chat generally to clients, during their wait in reception? That way we can both get a feel for them then put our heads together later when we're trying to pair them off.'

Christine smiled, seeming pleased that Lex had suggested she be involved in more than just a receptionist's capacity. She saw the sense of it, though. It was her business and she'd never become adept at running it otherwise. Then, should Lex ever leave her employ, God forbid, she'd be back in the same position as she was right now. Christine realised she'd found herself a very wise and compassionate employee and said a silent thank you that Alexandra Morton had come into her life. 'I'll see about getting the questionnaire printed at a local printers,' she said with a smile.

Lex was looking thoughtful. 'We will need to re-interview all the clients already registered when the new questionnaire is ready, won't we? We can tell them we've made improvements to our procedure in our continued efforts to offer our clients the best service. Can I ask you how you went about getting your original clients, Mrs Landers?'

'Through an advertisement run twice-weekly in the *Mercury* under the Personal column.' Christine moved back her chair to allow herself room to open one of the three drawers in the desk. She took out a newspaper cutting which she handed to Lex, saying, 'That's a copy of it. To be honest, I was expecting far more business to come in from it than I've seen up to now.'

Lex cast her eyes over the advertisement which was very brief. In bold print it read, *CUPID'S MARRIAGE BUREAU*, and then gave their address, hours of opening and telephone number, stating, 'Appointment Only'. She stared at it thoughtfully. It was a bit terse. Nothing about it to entice potential clients to give their services a try. Finally she said, 'Do you think we should add something?'

Christine looked at her quizzically. 'Such as what?'

'Well, something like . . .' She paused for a moment, deep in thought, then said, 'What about something like, "Let us help you find your perfect partner from our ever-growing list of people looking for someone just like you. Only genuine applicants should apply to register." The mention of our ever-growing list will let those who are unsure about trying a marriage bureau realise they aren't the only ones having difficulty finding themselves a partner. Then, hopefully, they'll come to us. The "genuine applicants only" will show potential clients we are serious about what we do.'

Christine looked most impressed. 'I'll get right on to the *Mercury*, make the changes right away.'

Just then the sound of the outer door opening reached their ears. Christine flashed a look at her wristwatch and saw the time was approaching eleven-thirty. 'I, wonder who that is? We've no clients booked in until this afternoon.' Getting up from her chair, she was about to set off to the reception area to greet the new arrival when she was stopped in her tracks by the sudden appearance in the office of an extremely large and severe-looking matron.

Before either Christine or Lex could address her, she boomed in a deep baritone voice: 'You the marriage bureau people?'

As the elder of the two women it was to Lex she naturally directed her question, so it was she who responded. 'Yes, that's right. This is Mrs Landers, the proprietress,' she politely introduced Christine. 'I'm Alexandra Morton, her employee.' She shot around the desk and held out her hand in greeting. 'Welcome to Cupid's Marriage Bureau. We're very pleased to meet you.'

Lex was surprised when the woman responded only by flapping one expensively gloved hand at her dismissively and snapping, 'Can we just get on with this? I've an appointment for lunch at twelve and haven't time to waste on pleasantries.' Then she looked around for a chair to park her bulk on.

Christine grabbed the back of the chair she had been sitting on and dragged it around to the front of the desk. Before she could politely ask the woman to take a seat, the visitor had done so. Over the woman's shoulder Christine looked at Lex as if to say, I'll leave you to it. Snatching up the questionnaire they had just devised, she left the office and closed the door.

When the Remington typewriter started clacking away in the reception office it became obvious Christine was wasting no time in drawing up the form. Lex opened her mouth to begin asking the new arrival her particulars but before she could utter a word, the large woman had launched into them.

'Aged between thirty and forty. Around six foot in height, masculine build, definitely not the whippet sort of man. Colouring isn't an issue but certainly not a redhead. Such pale-looking creatures, and I've never met one yet that I've found trustworthy. A professional man, of course, solicitor, doctor, accountant ... certainly *not* a blue-collar worker. Must be solvent and own his own house. No baggage of dependent parents, ex-wife or children. Must come from good stock for fathering purposes.' She paused and the piercing grey eyes almost lost above her chubby cheeks glared at Lex. 'You're not writing any of this down so I hope you've a good memory?'

Lex had been staring at her blankly, wondering if she could

possibly have heard correctly. This woman wanted a potential husband roughly half her own age and was intending to start a family? She must be sixty if she was a day! 'Er . . . yes, I do have a good memory and will certainly be noting down your requirements, but . . . well, you definitely wish there to be children from any future marriage?'

The woman flashed Lex a disparaging look. 'Isn't that the reason most people get married?'

'Yes, it is,' she readily agreed. The woman was obviously not as old as she looked then. Having hurriedly jotted down her requirements, and hoping she remembered all the questions she had just formulated with Christine, Lex smiled warmly and said, 'I'd like to know some personal details now, please. Your name is?'

Puzzled, she demanded, 'Why would you want to know *my* personal details?'

Lex looked back at her, equally as puzzled. 'So that I can do my job of matching you up with other clients who meet the criteria you're seeking and are in turn hoping to meet someone like yourself.'

The visitor huffed irritably, 'You stupid woman! I'm a married woman of thirty-five years' standing and have no need of the service you offer.'

'Oh, I see. Then . . . er . . . just why are you here?'

'To find a suitable husband for my daughter.'

'Your daughter? Oh! But with all due respect, Mrs . . . er . . . you didn't make it clear from the outset that it wasn't yourself you'd come to seek a husband for but in fact your daughter.'

'Because you never *asked* me who I was hoping you'd find a husband for. Now, can we get on? As I've already informed you, I've an appointment to attend shortly.'

Lex laid down her pencil and fixed the woman with her eyes. 'I'm sorry, I can't be of help to you . . .'

Before she could finish the other woman interjected, 'What do you mean, you can't be of help to me? Why ever not? This is a marriage bureau, isn't it? You are in the business of finding suitable husbands for women who can't find themselves one?'

'Yes, we most certainly are, but we do need to meet our prospective clients first. If you'd like to send your daughter in personally to consult us, we'd be only too glad to see if we can help her.'

The other woman's face darkened visibly. 'You imbecile! The reason I'm here on my daughter's behalf is because she's utterly incapable of finding a man for herself. Every boyfriend she's had has proved thoroughly unsuitable and it's cost her father a fortune to get rid of them – not that Cecile is aware of that – but we couldn't possibly have had any of them as father to my grandchildren or being introduced as our son-in-law. Cecile is approaching thirty now and time is running out for her. We've given up hope of her ever finding anyone but a complete rotter for herself. Now, I've told you what type I want for her . . .'

Lex cut her short, 'And I've informed you that if your daughter would like to come and see us personally, we'd be delighted to do all we can for her.'

Her face purple with rage, the woman hoisted herself from the chair and furiously boomed, 'Well, I certainly won't be recommending *your* services to any of my unattached associates!' With that she turned and stormed from the room. Seconds later the rhythmical clacking of the typewriter abruptly ceased and Lex heard the outer door give a resounding slam.

Christine came in, looking worried. 'Oh, dear, she didn't seem very happy. She gave me the most murderous glare as she left! When I first clapped eyes on her I felt we'd have trouble matching her up successfully, but your condition on taking the job here was that we'd never turn anyone away. I assume you did, though, and that's why she stormed out so furiously? So why did you turn her away, Mrs Morton?'

'That woman wasn't here to register herself as a client, Mrs Landers. It was her daughter she was hoping we'd find a husband for . . . without her daughter's knowledge.'

'What! Oh, my goodness, that's despicable.'

'Yes, it is. I feel so sorry for the daughter, having a mother like that. I wonder how she would feel if she ever heard what had been going on behind her back. I have to admit that my own mother did play a part in getting me and my husband together initially, but only with the best of intentions. Unlike that woman's.' She then looked remorsefully at her boss and said, 'I'm very sorry this means I've lost us a client but you do appreciate my reasons for turning her away, Mrs Landers? You wouldn't have liked your own mother to have hand-picked a husband for you, just to meet her own requirements in a son-in-law, would you?'

Christine stared at her frozen-faced for a moment then began gnawing her bottom lip anxiously.

'I . . . er . . . really think there's something I ought to tell you as it's not right I continue to mislead you, Mrs Morton.' She made her way to the chair the large woman had just vacated, sat down and clasped her hands tightly together. Obviously acutely embarrassed she said, 'You see . . . well, it's just that I'm . . .' she gulped before adding '. . . not married. It's *Miss* Landers in truth. I gave myself the title Mrs because I feared clients wouldn't think me capable of finding them a suitable spouse if I couldn't find myself one.' She stopped and looked enquiringly at Lex. 'You are actually *Mrs* Morton, aren't you?'

Lex nodded. 'I've been very happily married to my husband for twenty-five years. We have two sons, Martin is twenty-three and Matthew . . . Matt as we call him . . . is twenty-one.'

Christine gave a wistful smile then looked at Lex, clearly wondering whether to unburden herself further. She eventually decided to take Lex into her confidence.

'Actually, I've never had a proper boyfriend, Mrs Morton,' she admitted. 'Or any boyfriend at all actually. Bitter experience taught me that men don't want a plain woman on their arm.' She saw Lex about to speak but stalled her with, 'I've a suspicion you're going to tell me that beauty is in the eye of the beholder? Well, maybe there is a man somewhere who might find my kind of looks attractive to him, but I certainly haven't come across him yet.' She twisted her fingers together nervously. 'It's not just animals that have runts in their litters – my mother had one in hers.

'I'm the youngest of five sisters. All the others take after Mother in looks . . . she was a beauty in her day . . . still is, in fact, even though she's now in her sixties. My father too is such a handsome man. All the rest of our family ... grandparents, aunts uncles, cousins, et cetera, are all good-looking. Who I take after has always been a mystery.

'Please don't think for one minute, though, that I was made an outcast because of my plainness, Mrs Morton. My parents have always shown me just as much love and attention as my sisters, and they and I all get on extremely well together. But any boys who called at our house while we were all growing up ... well, it wasn't in the hope of finding me at home.

'I'm the only one still living there now as my four sisters are all happily settled. The saying, "Always a bridesmaid, never a bride", could have been written especially for me. Three of my sisters have children and the other is expecting her first next June. All the family are very excited, myself included.'

With an expression of longing she said, 'I'd love to be a mother, but I'm at the stage now where I've resigned myself to the fact that I'll never have my own mother furiously knitting matinée jackets for a grandchild from me. Not that she's given up. She's always telling me, "There's a lovely man for you, my darling daughter, it's just that you haven't met him yet." I smile at her as if I'm agreeing but I know it's not just my lack of looks that counts against me. I'm thirty-four in a couple of months and unattached men of around my age are thin on the ground, the ones that might look in my direction even thinner.

'With my family's encouragement, until about eight years ago I seriously believed that I'd meet someone and have that fairytale ending my sisters and friends did. I regularly attended social events, was a member of several clubs, it wasn't like I shut myself up at home, but my knight in shining armour never appeared and I was always the one making my way home alone. So you can imagine, I was beside myself when a man who worked at the same accountancy firm where I was a typist in the pool asked me if I was going to the Easter picnic. Gerald Rampton wasn't by any means the most handsome of men, a bit too much on the skinny side for my liking, but I still thought him attractive, though I wasn't conceited enough to think I was his type of woman. That hadn't stopped me having secret fantasies about him. Naively I thought this was it, I wasn't going to be a wallflower any longer, this was Gerald's way of asking me out.

'I told him I was going to the picnic and he looked really pleased to hear it, only then I realised how stupid I was to be thinking he was interested in me when he went on to ask me if I was aware that we could bring someone with us, and was I bringing the woman he'd seen meeting me out of work most nights? He was referring to my sister Margaret who worked for an insurance company in the same road. We journeyed back and forth to work together. I can't tell you how disappointed I was to know it was Marjie he was keen on, not me. Anyway, she was delighted to come with me to the Easter picnic ... I didn't tell her that Gerald Rampton was interested in her ... and I tried not to gloat secretly when she made it clear to him almost from the minute he introduced himself that she didn't find him in the slightest bit appealing.

'It wasn't just that incident that led me to resign myself to spinsterdom. A short while after the picnic I'd been given the task of restocking the stationery supplies and was in the cupboard making a list when I heard two people talking outside in the corridor. It was the owner of the firm and one of the senior accountants. They were discussing the fact that the senior accountants' secretary was leaving and needed to be replaced. Obviously they didn't know I could hear them. The accountant was complaining about the fact that over the last seven years he'd had five secretaries who had left to get married or to start families. Mr Babcombe, the firm's owner, suggested he look for an older woman to fill the post, or perhaps the plain Jane from the typing pool because he'd never seen her bring a male companion to any of the firm's dos.'

Christine paused for a moment; it was apparent that the memory of this incident still cut her deeply. She said quietly, 'I realised Mr Babcombe was referring to me as I was the only woman never to have brought a male escort to an office party. I was summoned by the senior accountant the next day for an interview and offered the post. I eventually resigned to start this place up, so Mr Babcombe was right, I suppose. No danger of me leaving because I was getting married or having a baby.'

She looked hard at Lex. 'In the light of what I've told you, Mrs Morton, you must be wondering why I chose this business when I found myself in a position to after receiving a small legacy from my beloved grandmother. She left the same amount to all five of us. I was undecided what to do with it at first. Then I went round to one of my sister's babysitting one night while she and her husband were out. I was watching a film on the television and there was a scene in it where two of the main characters were standing in a street in London under a sign advertising a marriage bureau. I wasn't even aware at that time that such bureaux existed. I knew people had always made matches, but to see someone actually opening a business doing it intrigued me.

'I felt quite excited about the prospect of bringing people together who wouldn't otherwise have met. I'm not bitter about my own lack of success – not at all. If there wasn't a marriage bureau already in Leicester, I decided it was a good way to use my inheritance and earn myself a living at the same time. Of course, I realise now, thanks to you, that there's far more to operating a business like this successfully than I'd ever realised. I came very close to wasting my grandmother's legacy, but hopefully now I have you guiding me that won't happen.

'I have never kept any secrets from my family before but I haven't told them anything about this. I know that if I did, every evening I went home my mother would quiz me about my own prospects – asking if some nice man had come in to register. I couldn't bear to keep disappointing her. So as far as my family is concerned, I still work for the accountants.

'Anyway, that's what has brought me here, Mrs Morton, and I feel better for having told you. I do hope that our association will be a long and productive one, and I can't expect you to prove a loyal and trustworthy employee if I'm not entirely straight with you, can I? I do think I've done the right thing calling myself "Mrs" before the clients, and would ask that you continue to do that in front of them.' When she received no response from Lex, she urged, 'Mrs Morton?'

Lex was lost in the sadness of the story she'd just heard and gave herself a mental shake. 'Yes, of course I will,' she confirmed.

Christine got to her feet. 'I'll get back to typing out the questionnaire then. If you wish to pop across to the café for a cup of tea or coffee, please feel free.'

Lex thoughtfully watched her boss make her way out of the office. Seconds later she heard the typewriter resume. It couldn't have been easy for Christine to divulge such personal details about herself to a virtual stranger. Lex was now looking at her in a different light. Christine wasn't the cold fish she had first appeared to be. It took a big-hearted woman to offer to help people achieve something she had missed out on herself and thought she had no hope of ever accomplishing.

Still, Christine may not have found a man as yet, but that didn't mean to say she wouldn't in the future. Lex was going to keep a lookout there. She was concerned, though, that due to previous hurtful experiences Christine had lost the ability to think of herself as eligible for love in any way, Lex sincerely hoped something would happen to open her eyes to the possibility of romance.

At just approaching five-thirty that evening Christine put the last letter she had typed into an envelope and used a moistened sponge to glue it down. She sat back in her chair, gave a tired sigh, and said to Lex, who was putting stamps on all the envelopes ready to drop in the post box on her way home, 'Well, I've done a dozen copies of our questionnaire as an interim measure until we get the proper printed ones, and all the letters requesting existing clients to make an appointment to be re-interviewed. I hope I haven't been too optimistic in ordering two hundred copies of the questionnaire from the printers, they don't come cheap.'

'I'm sure once the new advertisement is run in the *Mercury* we'll be flooded with new applicants to register and will need more printed,' Lex assured her, praying she was right. She felt she was, though, now that the advertisement had been reworded to encourage unattached people from all walks of life to give Christine's service a try.

'Well, thanks to you, Mrs Morton, two new clients have registered with us today. They didn't seem to mind being quizzed so personally about their private lives either, so that's a good sign, isn't it?'

Two such desperate women too. One was a forty-year-old widow of twenty years' standing. During that time while single-handedly raising her three children she had not had another relationship, but was now terrified at the thought of spending the rest of her life on her own once her children had all flown the nest. The other woman was in her thirties and had not had any social life of her own so far as all her spare time had been taken up since her early teenage years with caring for her much-loved, terminally ill mother. Sadly she had died a couple of months ago. Both very pleasant women from working-class backgrounds, were pinning all their hopes on meeting someone special through the bureau, and had willingly handed over a hard-earned ten pounds, entitling them to six introductions each. Should these proved unsuccessful through no fault of the bureau's then a further ten pounds would be due if they wished to continue.

'I have to admit, I would have turned both those women away before you made me realise it was wrong of me to pick and choose,' Christine admitted. 'Thank goodness you did, and at least these women today were spared the hurt of any rejection from me. I do hope we can help them.' She smiled at Lex. 'Well, if you want to get off, I'll lock up and look forward to seeing you tomorrow. First job for me in the morning is making sure we can offer a drink to our clients, and it'll save us making trips back and forth to the café across the road every time we want one ourselves.'

A thought struck Lex. 'My sons might be able to help there, Mrs Landers. They've just started up their own business as domestic engineers. I'm sure it wouldn't be beyond them to source a small electric stove for us and fix it up wherever you'd like. I've a spare kettle at home and a china teaset I could bring in for us to use,' she also offered.

'I'll be happy to put business your sons' way, Mrs Morton, and I'd like to accept your offer of the teaset and kettle. You're proving such a godsend to me.'

A while later Lex was just approaching Phyllis' house when Derek came out of the entry into the street. He spotted her and waited for her to join him.

'I was just coming to see you, Mrs M, to let you know that I ran that errand for you last night. Glad to see your back seems better now,' he added observantly.

With her mind on settling into her new job all thoughts of Derek and Mandy had temporarily been pushed into the background. It wasn't until Lex had turned the corner of the street she lived on that she'd started to wonder what had happened at her instigation. She had been going to call in at Phyllis' under the pretence that she was informing her friend how she had got on in her new job, as she had promised she would, but now Derek had saved her the trouble. She would call on Phyllis at a more convenient time when the two of them could have a proper catch up.

Lex smiled a greeting at the young man. 'It's much better today, thank you, Derek. I really appreciate you taking the time to explain to Mandy why I was letting her down. Was she terribly disappointed about missing the film?'

'Er . . . well, she was but then she wasn't.' Redness crept up his neck as he continued, 'You see, I offered to accompany her.'

He had told Lex exactly what she was hoping to hear. Choosing her response very carefully so as not to make him aware she had purposely cajoled him into it, she said, 'That was very thoughtful of you, Derek, giving up your model-making meeting like that. I'd have hated to let Mandy down. I hope missing your meeting wasn't too much of a loss to you?'

'Well . . . er . . . actually, I enjoyed what I did much better, Mrs M. After the picture finished we went for a coffee at the Wimpy Bar. I can't believe I've finally found a woman who likes doing the same sort of things I do, and is a really nice person too. We're meeting again on Saturday evening for a meal.'

190

Lex struggled not to show her delight and elation. In this case at least her instincts had been spot on. Not too far in the future, she felt sure, Phyllis would see her wish granted and her only son happily settled. Lex just hoped she got a well-deserved invitation to the wedding. Never, though, would she divulge the part she'd played in getting Derek and Mandy together. That would remain her secret.

Casually she said, 'I don't feel so bad now about not going myself. I do hope you two have a nice evening on Saturday. Well, better get home and feed my hungry men. Oh, and will you pass on a message to your mother for me? Please tell her I got on very well today, thoroughly enjoyed myself in fact, and I'll be around to tell her all about it as soon as I can.'

Once Derek had assured her he would, they went their separate ways.

Lex arrived to find her husband and sons had arrived ahead of her. To her great surprise Gil was at the stove, saucepan lid in one hand, looking intently into a pan. Boiling water was spurting madly out, hissing as it hit the hot plate. A strong smell of burning permeated the air. Martin and Matt were setting the table.

Looking mortally relieved to see her, Gil said, 'Hello, love.' Then he added, 'I'm glad you're home. I thought it'd be nice for you to arrive to the dinner all cooked ready for a change, but I think I've ruined it.'

'Dad's obviously a better engineer than he is a cook,' Martin quipped as he placed knives and forks on the table.

'From the smell that's coming from the oven, I think he's killed that pie you made last night,' Matt laughed, putting salt and pepper pots in the middle of the table.

Lex went over to join her husband at the stove, peering down into the saucepan and hiding her mirth when she saw the burnt-looking remains of the potatoes inside. Not wishing to hurt his feelings she said, 'I knew those weren't good potatoes when I bought them yesterday, but I had no choice as they were all the greengrocer had.' Then she noticed the oven was set at its highest mark so no wonder the pie was burning. She quickly turned down the heat then grabbed an oven towel and opened the stove door, relieved to find the pie was only blackening around the edges. They could be scraped off so all was not lost there.

Straightening up, she smiled appreciatively at her husband. 'The pie is fine, so well done you considering you've never cooked one before.' She stretched up and kissed him. 'I really appreciate what you tried to do for me.' Then she turned to look at her sons. 'If you both think you can do better than your father, then you cook the dinner tomorrow night.' She saw the expressions of horror on both faces at this suggestion, which was just what she'd expected, and added, 'Better thank your lucky stars I'm not serious. And think twice in future before you berate your father for trying to achieve something you two haven't a hope in hell of doing.'

She was very keen to hear how her men had fared that day, and to relate to them how her own day had gone, but getting them fed was her priority and the fact was she could do justice to a meal herself. 'Now why don't you all go through to the living room and leave me to . . .' She just stopped herself in time from saying, 'salvage what I can from this mess' and instead said, '. . . finish off what you started, Gil.'

Thankfully there were potatoes left from the supply she had purchased the previous day. Lex quickly peeled these and chopped them into very small chunks so they'd cook quicker. Half an hour later she placed steaming plates of buttery mash, wedges of succulent meat pie, sliced carrots and tinned garden peas in front of her ravenous brood. They all appreciatively tucked in.

Between forkfuls Gil asked her, 'So how did you get on today, love? Think you'll stick it?'

'Yeah, Mam, just how many misfits did you manage to fix up?' Matt piped up.

She flashed him an annoyed glance. 'Those misfits, as you unkindly referred to the bureau's clients, are just ordinary people like you and me who unfortunately, for a variety of different reasons, don't find it as easy to meet people of the opposite sex as you and your brother do.'

'I find it easy, Mam, but our Matt's been free and single since he chucked his last girlfriend so he obviously doesn't,' piped up Martin. Then he looked at his brother meaningfully. 'Best go down and register with Mam unless you want to end up a crusty old bachelor.'

Matt shot him an incredulous look. 'That's a bit rich coming from you, considering . . . OUCH!' Leaning down under the table to rub his leg he angrily snarled, 'There was no need for that.'

Martin snapped back. 'Yes, there was, you were about to blab . . .' He suddenly stopped talking, a horrified expression flashing across his face before he said to Matt in a more cordial voice, 'Can you pass me the salt, please, broth?'

Lex and Gil were looking at them both suspiciously.

It was their mother who asked, 'What's going on between you two?'

Matt gave her an innocent look. 'Nothing, Mam.'

'Stop playing games with me,' she snapped. 'Martin kicked you under the table to stop you divulging something. Well, we don't have secrets in this house,' she reminded him.

Busily shaking salt over his food, Martin said, 'My foot slipped, that was all.' He addressed his brother. 'Sorry, mate.' Then asked his mother, 'Any more spuds left?'

Lex and Gil looked at each other. Whatever was going on between their sons, it was going to remain between them.

'Help yourself from the pan in the kitchen,' she told him.

Martin got up, picked up his plate and went off.

Lex smiled at her husband and answered the question he had asked her before being interrupted by the exchange between their sons. 'I got on just fine at work today, love. I was of the impression the woman who owns the business was a real cold fish but I've realised now it's just a front she puts on. I think I'll enjoy working for her, so yes, I'll be sticking it. I interviewed two new clients today and must have done all right as they registered with the bureau. Now, I want to hear how you all got on today.' Out of respect it was Gil she asked first. 'Good day for you, love?'

He nodded. 'Des and I were kept busy enough with what work came in. No new business unfortunately but it's early days yet.'

Which meant that he had actually earned no money as yet. Thank goodness she had landed a job so quickly. 'I'm sure it will come in soon enough,' Lex assured him. Then she addressed Matt. 'I expect you spent your day advertising the service you're offering now. I'm sure business will start rolling in soon enough for you both.'

Martin returned, having replenished his plate, and as he retook his seat, said, 'Actually we got our first customer today, as it happens.'

She was delighted to hear this and exclaimed, 'You did? Well, I expect neither of you expected to earn money on your first day of business. Congratulations!'

There was a twinkle in his eye when Gil said to them, 'I think you'd better enlighten your mother.'

She looked puzzled. 'Enlighten me about what?'

'About the fact that we didn't actually make any money,' Martin said gruffly, flashing his brother a look of disdain.

Lex was confused. 'You didn't? But why not?' She dearly hoped it wasn't because the customer was dissatisfied with their workmanship and had refused to pay.

'Well, when we got the call to fix an iron in the early afternoon, you can imagine how thrilled we were . . .' Martin began to tell her.

Gil cut in, 'Don't forget to tell your mother how you argued over who was going to attend to it, and who was going to stay behind in case anyone else telephoned meantime. Thankfully I'd returned to the workshop after overseeing the glazier who came to fix the living-room window. I was able to step in and suggest you toss a coin to decide.'

Matt grinned sheepishly. 'Yeah . . . well . . . we did act childishly, I must admit.'

Martin took up the story again. 'It was Matt who won the toss.' Then he addressed his brother. 'Now you can tell Mam why we never made anything on our first job as it's your fault. Bloody pushover, that's what you are.'

Matt glared at him. 'I couldn't bring myself to charge the old dear just for a wire coming loose from her plug. It took me less than thirty seconds to spot it and even less to fix and it was obvious by the state of her and her house that she'd hardly two pennies to rub together. Anyway she did pay me in kind. She gave me a cuppa and a slice of her homemade cake.' He looked at his mother. 'Good cake, but not as good as yours, Mam.'

She smiled at the compliment.

'We're businessmen, Matt, not a charitable organisation,' Martin shot back. Then added sulkily, 'You never thought to ask her for a slice of cake for your business partner, did you, when you were gorging yourself?'

Gil laughed. 'Oh, so that's what's really bugging you, Martin, and not the fact that your brother was showing his chivalrous side?'

He pulled a childish face. 'Well, we'd missed lunch putting business cards up all over the place, which had taken us ages to write out beforehand, and I was starving.'

'Actually what Matt did today will stand you in good stead,' Gil said to his sons. They both looked at him quizzically, wondering just how, so he explained, 'The old dear you didn't charge will be singing the Morton brothers' praises to all her neighbours and friends. Recommendation through word of mouth is the best you can ever have.'

Martin slapped his brother good-naturedly on his back. 'In that case, I forgive you, broth. Next time you get offered cake at a job, though, don't forget about me.' Then he noticed the time on the kitchen clock and pushed away his plate, still with food left on it 'I haven't time to finish this. Sorry, Mam, but I'm going to be late if I don't hurry,' he said, heading out of the kitchen towards the stairs.

Lex glanced thoughtfully after him. Nothing usually came between her son and his food except for one thing. She knew without a doubt that he had a date with a woman, and one he didn't want to discuss with his mother or father.

Gil leaned over and whispered in her ear, 'I'm guessing there's a woman in this somewhere.'

She looked knowingly back at him. 'I'm pleased he's so popular but he's keeping unusually tight-lipped about this one. It makes me wonder why . . .' A worried expression clouded her face. 'Is it because he suspects we wouldn't approve of her, do you think?'

'It's not a case of whether we do or not, dear, is it? We've raised our boys to feel free to make their own choices in life, and should either of them go wrong we'll always be on hand to get them through the aftermath,' Gil reminded her.

Lex affectionately patted her husband's hand and smiled tenderly at him. 'Yes, I know.'

The sound of the front door knocker broke in on them then. Since his dismissal from Brenton's Gil did not answer the door. Lex therefore made to respond but Matt beat her to it. Jumping up from his seat, he called back, 'I'll get it.'

'Probably one of his mates,' Lex said to Gil as she rose and began to stack dirty plates. She saw the look of worry flood his face and added, 'Male, Gil. Our Matt would never invite a woman friend over, knowing how you feel.'

When Matt returned there was a look of fury on his face. 'Got any old newspaper, Mam?' he demanded.

Both his parents looked puzzled.

'There's a pile on the floor at the back of the pantry that I keep for lighting the fire,' Lex told him, then asked, 'What do you want it for?'

''Cos some vile bast— er, person, has posted a pile of dog muck through the letter box, and I need the newspaper to clean it up.'

Lex gasped in horror and tears glinted in her eyes. Witnessing her distress, Gil leaned over to hug her close. 'I'm sorry, love. This is all my fault.'

She pulled away from his embrace to look at him sharply. 'It's *not*. You did nothing to Miriam Jones, and neither have you to all the people victimising us now. They're doing it of their own free will. I pity them, really. They have to be mindless bullies to take pleasure from such meanness. Obviously they've nothing better to do with their time.' A spark of defiance glinted in her eyes then. 'Well, we have. We've a future to build, and we're not going to let anyone hinder the progress we've made so far.'

With that she jumped up from her seat and went in search of the bottle of disinfectant she kept under the sink. Along with Matt, who had now collected an old newspaper, she went off to set things straight after this latest attack on them.

CHAPTER FOURTEEN

Three weeks later, Lex sat staring at the man sitting on the other side of her desk. She kept her face carefully blank. Should she have shown him what she was indeed thinking then he certainly would not be acting so smugly sure of himself.

Much to her relief, the revamped advertisement in the *Leicester Mercury* was paying off. On average ten requests a day from new clients were coming in. Both women were being kept constantly busy, their working day flying by. With the changes implemented, the bureau's fortunes seemed to be on the up. Martin and Matt had installed a small stove in the reception area to supply beverages to clients, and also to save Christine and Lex wasting precious time tripping backwards and forwards to the café across the road. But as matters stood at the moment, neither of them had time to mash themselves a brew using the new facilities, let alone to relax while drinking it, and consequently elevenses, dinner and afternoon tea breaks were rushed affairs.

'Just to recap . . .' Lex said to her potential new client, Horace Wiggins, a portly, balding, bespectacled man in his mid-forties. By his whole manner he clearly considered himself to be God's gift to women, but he was obviously not seeing what the mirror was reflecting. 'You work away during the week, travelling the country in your job as area salesman for a stocking company?'

He puffed out his chest importantly. 'That's correct, my good woman. I cover the north of England territory for Pex Hosiery Company of Leicester as far as the Scottish borders.' He gave her a smarmy grin. 'You women look up to a well-travelled man, and

I'm certainly that. There's not a town in Great Britain I don't know intimately.'

If a man told Lex he was well travelled she would usually assume he meant to foreign parts but she kept her thoughts to herself. 'And when you're at home at weekends, you spend all your time in the attic playing with your train set or else attend model train enthusiasts' meetings.'

He didn't look amused and snapped at her: 'Playing with my train set is not the term I'd use. Over the years I've built a miniature replica of the Leicestershire railway system. Not just the trains and tracks themselves but everything else, the stations, villages, landscape, et cetera. It's a masterpiece of ingenuity, madam.'

Lex forced herself to look impressed. 'I'm sure it is, Mr Wiggins. Now, the type of woman you're hoping to find. All you've stipulated is that she's between thirty and forty-five, the quiet type, neat and tidy, and a good cook. You have no objection if she's been married before but definitely no children.'

He pursed his thick lips. 'Definitely no children. I come out in a rash if I'm within fifty yards of one of the little blighters.'

Face still bland Lex confirmed, 'You've said you're not concerned about looks or hair colouring or a future wife's personal likes or dislikes?' His seeming unconcern about a possible partner's physical appearance or preferences bothered her.

He gave a dismissive shrug. 'Apart from what I've stipulated, nothing else about my future wife is relevant. I'm open-minded, you see.' He eyed Lex keenly. 'So, when can I expect to have my first meeting with a suitable candidate?'

She laid down her Bic ballpen, sat back in her chair and fixed her eyes on the man eagerly awaiting her response. 'Mr Wiggins, this is a marriage bureau and our aim is to help find our clients a suitable partner to enrich their lives. You don't appear to me to want that kind of partner. You're not after a wife to love and cherish and share your life with, are you, Mr Wiggins?'

He looked taken aback. 'What do you mean?'

'I'm of the opinion it's a housekeeper you're really seeking.

Someone who'll go quietly about her business of caring for you and your house, leaving you free to do whatever you want. You can easily advertise for one of those in the *Leicester Mercury*. Now, if you'll excuse me, I'm kept very busy helping people who *do* require the service this bureau offers.'

He didn't deny that she had perceived his true motive for visiting them. Giving a grunt of anger, he got up from his chair and hurried away. Lex followed him out to address Christine who was in the middle of typing some correspondence.

Christine was looking annoyed, bashing away on the keys of the Remington. 'What an ignorant man,' she exclaimed as Lex arrived before her desk. 'Mr Wiggins completely ignored me when I politely said good day to him, and I know he heard me.'

'Not a very nice person all round, Mrs Landers. His type we definitely don't need on our books. It wasn't a wife he was after but a housekeeper. I pity the poor woman that's fooled by him into thinking she's landed herself a good catch, only to discover that's she really let herself in for a life of unpaid drudgery. Anyway, as his interview was cut short and it's another hour before our next client is due, I wondered if you'd like to take advantage of the lull to go through the clients and work out some matches. But first I'd like a chat with you about Kathleen Overton.'

Christine gave Lex her full attention. 'You've heard how she got on with her introduction last night, I take it. Please tell me it proved more successful than the others we've arranged?'

Lex shook her head. 'Afraid not. I haven't had time to tell you but I took a call from her this morning when you were in an interview and I was doing reception duty. She told me she wouldn't be pursuing matters further with Mr Kite, although Mr Kite telephoned in just after to say he was rather taken by Miss Overton and would like to pursue matters further with her. We'll have to let him down gently about that. But that's the seventh introduction we've arranged for Miss Overton and each time she's made the same comment about the man. Just that he wasn't her type, she'll never be any more specific than that.'

Christine looked bothered. 'Well, maybe we made mistakes with the matches we chose for her and they just haven't been what she's seeking in a partner?'

'That thought has crossed my mind, but we're very meticulous when we do our matches. The men we arranged for her to meet were all in the right age group, white-collar workers not blue, height range and build, enjoyed the sort of social activities she did, and possessed the sort of outlook on life she says she wants a potential husband to have. The fact that she won't elaborate on the reasons why she doesn't want to pursue matters further . . . such as he talked too much or was far too quiet for her liking, a fussy eater or couldn't dance . . . like all our other clients do, well, that bothers me. I did try to probe but she wasn't budging. I know in some cases it could take a dozen or so introductions between our clients before there's a glimmer of hope, but I get the feeling that we could introduce Miss Overton to three dozen clients and she'd still not want to go any further.'

Christine looked pensive. 'So what do you suggest we do, Mrs Morton?'

'Well, I'd like to have a talk with her to try and find out where we're going wrong, if indeed we are. So what do you think about asking her to come in for a chat with one of us?'

Christine smiled warmly at her. 'I've learned to my benefit to trust your judgement, Mrs Morton, and if you're suggesting we get Miss Overton in for a conference, then that's good enough for me. I'll get a letter sent off in the lunchtime post asking her to telephone us to make an appointment.'

Just then there was a tap on the door and a smartly dressed, pleasant-faced man in his mid-thirties walked in. He was lugging a large case.

He smiled a nervous greeting at the two women looking him over. Putting his suitcase down, he said, 'Good morning, ladies. My name is Peter Reynolds and I'm a representative of Bowman's Stationery Company. I wondered if you'd be interested in seeing a selection of our products? If you're busy just now I could call back at a more convenient time to suit you.'

Lex appraised him. Peter Reynolds seemed the total opposite of the normal pushy salesmen who breezed in, full of false charm, geared up to use all the tricks of the trade to secure an order. That was just the type who represented the firm they currently bought their stationery from but Lex immediately warmed to this man, feeling she'd sooner deal with him any day. As she looked at him, though, what was most glaringly obvious to her was the fact that it was Christine his attention was fixed on, and by the mesmerised expression on his face Lex knew he was liking what he was seeing.

Christine herself seemed completely unaware of it. Despite having learned much from Lex in respect of her attitude towards their clients, this man was not asking to join the bureau and therefore she displayed her usual brisk business manner towards him. 'We're adequately catered for in that department, but if you want to leave a card we'll put it on file should matters change in the future.'

Any other salesman would not have accepted that response but would immediately have opened his case, proclaiming, 'I'm sure I can persuade you to change your mind when you inspect the quality of our products.' And before there was time to stop it happening a selection of the said products would be tipped out on the desk, the salesman quoting bribes of huge discounts for large orders. Peter Reynolds, though, just stood transfixed, not seeming to have heard what Christine had said, until he was shocked out of his torpor by her demand of, 'Did you not hear what I said, Mr Reynolds?'

'Eh! Oh, er . . . yes. Yes, I did.' Flushing with embarrassment, he urgently fished in his pocket for his card and handed it to Christine. 'I hope you'll consider giving our products a trial should your usual supplier let you down in any way.' Then he gave her a broad smile before adding, 'Good day to you.'

Picking up his suitcase, he turned and made his way out.

Christine added the card to a pile of others in the top drawer of her desk. 'The number of salesmen calling on us is beginning to match the actual clients. It's annoying how much of our time is being commandeered by them. I wish there was something we could do to stop them.'

'We could put a sign up outside saying "No Hawkers" but I doubt it would help much. Anyway, that man seemed pleasant enough. Very nice actually.'

Christine was shutting the drawer of the desk after putting away Peter Reynolds' card. 'Yes, he seemed pleasant enough.'

Lex smiled. 'Well, it was very apparent to me he liked what he was looking at when he was addressing you. I think you've a fan in Peter Reynolds.'

Giving Lex her full attention now, Christine snapped, 'Don't be ridiculous! The man was after a sale and flattery is part of his training. Now, you wanted to use the time we had between clients to do some matches. I'm ready when you are.'

Lex had long suspected that Christine was convinced her plainness would deter men from approaching her, and now her suspicions had been confirmed. Somehow Lex had to get it through to her that there were many men who *would* find her attractive, but if she refused to offer them even a glimmer of hope with her austere attitude, then she was definitely destined to die a spinster.

She was just about to tell Christine she would fetch what she needed from the office when a commotion broke out on the landing outside. They were both looking towards the outer door and jumped in surprise when it suddenly burst open and two men appeared, dragging a third between them.

The taller of the three, carrot-haired with a ready smile and startling blue eyes, spoke first. 'Do us a favour and work your magic on our mate. Find him a good woman,' he called across.

Christine was looking at the man struggling to free himself from his mates' firm grip on his shoulders. 'It doesn't look to me like he wants our help,' she said dryly.

His fellow kidnapper spoke up next. 'You're right, Duncan doesn't, and that's why we've had to resort to desperate measures to get him here.'

The carrot-haired young man explained, 'He's been free and single since his wife ... scheming bitch that she was ... divorced him over a year ago. Duncan reckons he's off women for good, but we know he doesn't really mean it.'

Finally Duncan found his own voice and furiously exploded, 'Why can't you two get it through your thick heads I *did* mean what I said when I got my decree absolute through? I don't care if I never see another woman again. I'm quite happy as I am, and have no intention of letting another woman mess up my life like Caroline did.'

Carrot Top said evenly, 'Now, Duncan, you're just scared of letting another woman into your life, but they won't all try and treat you like she did. Now, me and James and all the rest of your mates have tried without success to get you to go on a date – and with some damned fine women too. This is a last resort. Be warned, we aren't letting you out of this place until you've registered with these good ladies. You obviously didn't trust your mates' judgement so listen to the professionals. Me and James will be standing guard outside the door and none of us are going anywhere until you've done the business.' He addressed James then. 'Let's leave him to it.'

The two men departed but it was apparent they meant to stand guard until Duncan had done their bidding as their shadows could be seen through the glass in the door.

Lex smiled across at the angry-looking Duncan. 'Mrs Landers and I won't force you to register for our services against your wishes. As far as we're concerned, you're free to leave.'

He heaved a heavy sigh. 'My mates weren't joking. I haven't got a choice, really, they aren't going to allow me to leave until I've done what they say. I'm not daft, I know it's their wives that are behind this. Why is it that all women think a man can't survive on his own, eh?' He stood for a moment, assessing the two women before he spoke again. 'Look, not that I need your services, but just how exactly does it all work here? What I mean is, how do you go about getting people fixed up? Oh, I suppose I should introduce myself properly to you first. My name is Duncan Holgate.'

Lex smiled warmly at him. 'We're very pleased to meet you,

Mr Holgate. Well, in simple terms, we find out all about you by asking you to complete a detailed questionnaire and then we meticulously go through our clients and match you up as closely as we can.'

Christine continued, 'It can take several introductions before you meet someone who has that special something that makes you want to take matters further, but basically that's how the bureau operates.'

A look of interest filled his previously sullen face. 'Oh, I see.' There was a long pause before he continued, 'Well, if I'm honest, I've got to admit it's not much fun being the only singleton amongst my friends. I do feel a bit of an oddity when we all go out. Trouble is, I was badly burned by my wife and . . . well, my mates were right. I am scared of being hurt again, that's why I never gave any of the women they tried to fix me up with the time of day.'

'Well, just because your first marriage didn't work out, doesn't mean to say another won't,' Lex said.

He sighed again. 'No, I guess not. I suppose it wouldn't hurt me to give your service a try. At least I know the women you introduce me to have been vetted. So, what do I do then?'

Christine looked at Lex as if to say, You'd be better handling this one than me, and she took the hint. 'If you'd like to come through to the office, we can make a start now by completing our questionnaire.'

While Lex was interviewing the bureau's latest client, her husband was working contentedly away, rewiring an old generator belonging to a long-standing customer of Des's. He relied on it to power the lighting in the workshop where he ground tools for his customers. Presently he was working only by the light cast from a heavily laden sky but wouldn't part with good money unless he had absolutely no other choice.

Much to Gil's delight two telephone calls had come in that morning requesting his sons' services and both of them had gone off in their newly acquired vans. Des was also out, attending to existing business and doing his best to drum up new clients.

The sound of a voice behind him made Gil jump; the fact that it was a woman's voice made him freeze.

'Oh, hello, Mr Morton.' It was Julie Dawson, the bookie's wife. As usual she was dressed in garish tight clothes, stepping precariously over machinery and tools in her high stilettos while saying, 'I never twigged when I saw the card in the corner shop window advertising Morton Brothers Domestic Appliance Engineers. Your sons, eh? Mind you, until my hubby told me that's what I needed to find to fix our washer, I hadn't a clue what a domestic appliance was or what the blokes who fixed 'em were called. Anyway, I tried telephoning earlier but the line was busy.'

Spanner in hand, face streaked with grease, Gil was speechless with panic. This was just the situation he had been dreading. A woman finding him on his own, and no witnesses around to say he had not molested her.

Only a yard or so away from him now, Julie suddenly noticed the look on his face, and her own clouded over as she asked him, 'Are you all right, Mr Morton? You're looking at me like I've . . . oh!' She cast a quick glance down at herself and looked mortally relieved when she didn't see what she feared she might. Laughing, she said, 'For a minute I worried all the buttons on me dress had popped and I was displaying me wares.'

When Gil didn't laugh but still stared blankly at her she instinctively made to reach out and lay a hand on his arm to reassure him. She just about jumped out of her skin when her attempt at a friendly gesture had him raising the spanner he was holding in the air, waving it threateningly at her and shouting out, 'Get away from me! Don't you dare lay a finger on me.'

She stared at him, baffled. He was acting like a madman and she couldn't understand why. 'But, Mr Morton, it's me . . . Julie. Julie Dawson.'

He screamed at her, 'Get away from me, I said! Go. Leave now. Women aren't allowed on these premises.'

Des returned then. Hearing Gil's shouts and thinking he was in some sort of danger he had raced across the forecourt to burst through the workshop door, only to see his friend menacingly waving a spanner at an utterly shocked Julie Dawson. 'Gil,' he bellowed, 'what on earth is going on?'

Julie spun to face Des and cried, 'Mr Morton's having a dicky fit. I don't know why, honest. I didn't do anything to him but he's acting like he's scared of me. Why would he be scared of me, Mr Reader?'

Then it struck Des just what had transpired. Rushing across to Julie, he took her arm and said, 'I apologise for Mr Morton, Julie love.' He frantically fought to excuse Gil's behaviour and said the first thing that came into his head. 'He's a bit jumpy today. A generator he was working on blew a gasket.'

Julie gulped. 'Blew a gasket, eh?' she said, like she knew what a gasket was. She looked at Gil in deep sympathy. 'Oh, how awful for you, Mr Morton. It's lucky you wasn't blasted to Kingdom Come, ain't it?' Then she looked at the generator Gil had been working on when she'd arrived, which was frighteningly close to where she now stood. She was obviously terrified the gasket on that might explode too and hurriedly added, 'Best leave yer to it.' She made to depart out of harm's way but Des stopped her by saying, 'You came here for something, Julie love. Jack's shop generator playing up, is it, and he's sent you round to fetch me to look at it?'

'Oh, no. I came to ask if one of Mr Morton's sons would come and tek a look at me washer. It won't heat the water. Jack reckons the thermosummat has gone on it. Will yer get one of then to call on me, soon as they can, to have a look at it for me?'

Des smiled kindly at her. 'Yes, 'course I will, as soon as one of them comes back.'

He waited until Julie had disappeared through the door before addressing Gil, still shaking and holding the spanner aloft. 'Now look here, you've got to stop this madness, thinking every woman you come across is going to do what Miriam Jones did. Thank goodness it was Julie Dawson just now and not someone else who'd have insisted the police be called after your threatening behaviour towards them.

'Look, I know I promised that no women ever came in here so there was no need for you to worry, but that was before your lads asked me if they could use my premises as a base. I can't guarantee the odd woman won't call around like Julie did. Unless, that is, you want me to ask your boys to go and find themselves somewhere else? I will, Gil, if that's what it takes to prevent incidents like this.'

Gil stared at him blindly. He couldn't ask Des to do that. His sons had suffered enough over this dreadful affair without he himself ruining their chances of making a success of their new business. But nor could he work here any longer, terrified that at any moment there'd be a repetition of the situation with Miriam Jones.

Lowering the spanner, shoulders sagging in despair, he uttered, 'If anyone's leaving here it's me, Des. I'm sorry, but I'll have to let you down. There's got to be a job I can get that rules out any contact with women. I don't want to keep looking the idiot I did just now and risk losing my employer business. I can't promise not to act like that again, you see, Des. A nightwatchman's job would maybe suit me.'

Des looked appalled by his suggestion. 'But you're worth more than a nightwatchman's job, Gil. It's such a lonely existence and the pay is a pittance. Look, don't be hasty. I'm sure we can resolve this situation somehow.'

Gil shook his head. 'It can't be resolved unless you can guarantee that no women will ever come in here while I'm on my own, and you're already told me you can't.' He moved across to where his metal cantilever tool box stood and started packing his tools away in it. Task done, he heaved it up. 'Thanks for everything, Des.'

Gil made his way over to pick up his coat before walking out of the door; a mortified Des stood staring after him. The fact that Gil's resignation meant his own hopes of expanding the business were now over never entered his mind; his only worry was for the plight of his friend. Des had been so happy to oblige Martin and Matt when they had come to him for help that he'd never stopped to consider the possible consequences for their father. He was racked with guilt about the fact he had promised his friend that his workshop was a woman-free zone and he need have no fear here.

The thought of Gil reduced to sitting alone inside a tiny, freezing cold hut night after night deeply distressed Des. Fixing and maintaining generators was a job far removed from that of works manager, where he had presided over a workforce of three hundred men and all that went with it, but it was still a damned sight better than being a nightwatchman. Thanks to his own stand Gil might not have earned an actual wage yet, but judging by the couple of new jobs they'd already got in since his arrival, and from the feedback Des had received while touting for new work, they'd have reached the position where Gil was being paid in just a few weeks.

Des heaved a heavy sigh. He'd a generator to deliver back to its owner. As he picked his way back over to the door where the generator stood ready for loading an idea suddenly struck him and a broad smile creased his face. There was one way that Gil could still work with him and not be constantly worried about a repetition of the incident today. It wasn't ideal, would mean more work on Des's part, but Gil was his friend and if there was anything he could do to make life more bearable for him, then he would do it, no matter what the cost to himself. The good thing was that he knew Gil would be unable to find any argument against this proposal and would have no choice but to accept.

Only a matter of seconds after Gil had left the workshop, his sons arrived back from their callouts. They were leaning against one of the two brown Morris vans they had purchased from Tinkerbell's scrap yard and Martin was convulsed with laughter. Matt, though, wasn't finding things so funny.

'You wouldn't be laughing if it had happened to you!'

Martin wiped his eyes on the back of his sleeve. 'Oh, broth, I just wish I could have been there and seen your face when you were bent over that vacuum, clearing the blockage, and looked up expecting to see a cup of tea being handed to you ... and saw a naked woman instead!'

'It wasn't a pretty sight, let me tell you,' Matt growled, pulling a disgusted face. 'She was forty if she was a day, and what I glimpsed of her body, well, it resembled a ...'

'Don't tell me any more, you'll put me off my dinner,' Martin abruptly cut him short, shuddering at the awful vision his mind was conjuring up. Then he asked, 'What did you say to her?'

'I just told her she should be careful not to catch her death on a nippy day like today, and carried on with what I was doing.'

Martin creased up with laughter again. 'I don't expect we'll be getting her custom again once she's discovered we don't offer the extra services she's obviously received from other tradesmen.'

Matt chuckled. 'No, I don't expect we will.' Then he looked enquiringly at his brother. 'I haven't had a chance to ask you with all that's been going on lately, but how's it going then?'

Martin looked at him blankly for a moment then the penny dropped and he smiled. 'So far, so good. Shocked me, I can tell you.'

A mischievous twinkle sparkled in Matt's eyes. 'Not so much of a shock as it will be to our mam when she finds out.'

'That'll be an occasion to look forward to, won't it, broth?'

Matt nodded. 'Sure will. You just make sure you arrange it for when I'm there. I wouldn't miss it for the world.'

Matt fished in his pocket for a packet of Park Drive and a box of matches. After offering Martin one, he lit his own and drew deeply on it. Blowing out a long plume of smoke, he asked his brother, 'So how did you get on with the other callout we got?'

'Not as exciting as yours. Mrs Jelly was so grateful to see me that a cuppa was thrust into my hand and the offer of biscuits or cake made before I got over the doorstep. A sock had got stuck down the water pump. I soon cleared it. She was very pleased with what I did and promised to call us again if any of her other appliances played up, plus telling all her friends and neighbours

211

about us. I hope there's been some more calls while we've been out.'

Matt looked worried. 'So do I. Let's go in and put ourselves out of our misery.'

Stamping out their cigarettes, they were about to go inside Des's workshop when the man himself appeared in the doorway, struggling under the weight of a generator. They both ran over to offer their help.

'Why didn't you ask Dad to give you a hand with this, instead of struggling to load it by yourself?' Martin asked.

Lowering the generator carefully to the ground, Des replied, 'Well, that's just it, lads. Your father isn't here for me to ask. You see . . .' And he proceeded to tell them both what had transpired that morning.

When he had finished there was a murderous look in Martin's eye. Without a word he spun on his heel and made to storm off, but Matt caught his arm, pulling him to a halt and demanding, 'Where are you going?'

'Where do you think I'm going?' he snarled, wrenching free his arm. 'I don't care if Dad and Mam have warned us not to tackle that woman, I've had enough of this, broth. Before she did what she did to him, our dad was a man who never flinched from anything. He could face down three hundred warring men who didn't like a new rule old man Brenton was wanting to introduce in the factory. Now he's like a raving lunatic just finding himself alone in one woman's company. Well, I'm going to see her and . . .'

Des caught his arm. 'You're *not* going to see that Jones woman or do anything, Martin, you hear? If she didn't flinch from getting your father sacked for something he never did, then she isn't going to hesitate about having you arrested for threatening behaviour, is she?'

Martin's shoulders sagged in defeat. 'No, I suppose not.'

'It's not right, our dad reduced to doing a nightwatchman's job,' Matt said bitterly. 'Not that I'm calling men who do that sort of job no-hopers, but Dad is worth more than that.'

Des patted their shoulders. 'I happen to agree with you, and if I get my way he won't be earning his living as a nightwatchman.'

They both looked at him quizzically.

'What do you have in mind exactly?' Matt asked

He smiled. 'Help me load this generator on to the van and I'll tell you.'

CHAPTER FIFTEEN

Back at the bureau, Lex was feeling rather pleased with herself. Duncan Holgate had been impressed enough by what she had told him to pay for his membership and to say he trusted her and Christine to come up with some steady, reliable women.

Duncan wasn't the only one impressed by Lex that morning. Christine was too. 'If I was a betting woman, I'd never have put money on Mr Holgate signing up with us. When he was railroaded in here by his friends, he wasn't exactly in a receptive mood, was he? You certainly have a way with people, Mrs Morton, and I'm learning so much from you.'

Lex smiled with pleasure at her boss's compliment. 'I shall have to watch out or soon you won't need me at all.'

Christine looked appalled that Lex could even think that. 'I couldn't imagine running this place without you now, Mrs Morton. In fact, I doubt I'd have been running it for much longer if I hadn't persuaded you to come and work for me.' She looked thoughtful for a moment. 'I really should review your wages. Business is beginning to boom, and it's all down to your suggestions for improvements. Well, from this week on you'll be finding another two pounds a week in your pay packet, I hope that's agreeable to you?'

Lex felt she was already adequately paid considering this was her first job in over twenty years, but another two pounds a week on top of what she was already receiving would make a welcome difference to the Mortons' precarious financial situation. She responded delightedly, 'If you think I deserve the raise, then that's most agreeable to me, Mrs Landers. Thank you very much.'

Christine smiled. 'Then it's settled.'

A while later they were both sitting behind the reception desk, contemplating possible matches, when the door opened and a well-dressed man entered. Both women looked him over. He was the epitome of the tall, dark, handsome sort most women dream of being swept off their feet by.

Smiling charmingly, he said in a deep cultured voice, 'Good morning, I'm Sebastian Evans. I've an appointment at eleven.'

Despite her opinion that no man would ever look twice in her direction and she was in fact quite resigned to this, resentment raged within Christine that Mother Nature had denied her the opportunity to catch the eye of a man like this. She'd learned a lot from Lex about behaving welcomingly to clients but it was a real struggle for her with Mr Sebastian Evans.

'You're a little early, Mr Evans, but fortunately Mrs Morton is available to see you now.' Then she addressed Lex. 'If you'd like to take Mr Evans through, I'll bring in a tray of tea.'

'I'd prefer coffee, if that's all right,' he announced.

'As you wish,' Christine responded tartly, flashing him another tight smile.

Lex knew instinctively why she was acting like she was and her heart went out to her. Admittedly she didn't possess the sort of features that turned men's heads but how did she know that this man didn't find her sort of looks appealing? Why just assume he wouldn't? It was, in fact, Christine's turn to do the interviewing as Lex had just seen the last client but she was obviously passing him over because she didn't want to be reminded of her inability to attract someone so handsome.

Rising to her feet, Lex gave Sebastian Evans a welcoming smile. 'Would you like to come through to the office and we'll get started?'

Sebastian Evans informed her he was thirty-five and had been working in the Middle East for the last ten years. Constantly moving from place to place there meant he had not formed any permanent relationships. Now he was back in his home town for good he was looking to settle down and raise a family. As he'd lost contact with most of his old friends due to his prolonged absence abroad, and those he had kept in touch with were now all married, he had no single friends to go out with socially. Having seen the bureau's advertisement he felt this was the ideal route for him to take.

As Lex sat listening to him she realised with acute embarrassment that she was hanging on his every word, and gave herself a mental shake. He certainly had magnetism. Gil was an extremely good-looking man, even now in his mid-forties, but he paled before this new client. And Sebastian Evans didn't appear to realise what an effect he had on women, herself included, which only added to his charm as Lex felt there was nothing worse than being on the receiving end of the arrogance of a good-looking man. As well as his physical attributes, Sebastian had a well-paid job with good prospects, his own house, car, money in the bank. He was going to break a good few female clients' hearts before he found the woman to claim him. She'd better get a supply of tissues in.

What concerned Lex was what precisely Sebastian Evans was looking for. They had women of all shapes and sizes and looks registered, but at this moment in time they hadn't, she felt, one who would quite match up to this client.

Having finished taking his personal details, Lex prepared herself to disappoint him. 'What kind of woman are you hoping for us to introduce to you, Mr Evans?'

His answer surprised her. 'I'm open-minded, Mrs Morton. Brunette, blonde, redhead, well-made, stick thin or somewhere in-between . . . that's not important to me, and neither is their looks. It's whether you get on with a person and enjoy being with them that is paramount, don't you agree?'

She nodded. 'I certainly do.'

'There is just one condition, though. I would prefer the women you refer to me to be financially independent, then I can be sure that I'm wanted for myself and not viewed as a meal ticket.'

Lex felt that was fair enough.

A while later, after seeing Mr Evans out, she went to update Christine on their latest signing and hand over the fee she'd taken from him. Christine stopped typing, took one look at Lex and said, 'You've got such a look on your face . . . I can only describe it as surprised.'

Lex perched on the edge of the desk. 'I am, very much so. I never thought the perfect man existed, but it seems he does.'

'Mr Evans certainly seemed to have it all in the looks department, so I take it he's got everything else going for him too?'

'Certainly seems to have. Good job, own house in a good area, nest egg in the bank. He just needs a good woman by his side to complete the picture. We'll have no shortage of clients wanting to be introduced to him, that's for sure.'

Reminded that she herself would never so much as receive a second look from the likes of Sebastian Evans, Christine said tersely, 'I wish the same could be said for all our male clients. While you were interviewing Mr Evans, I took a call from Geraldine Smart. You remember we arranged an introduction for her with Donald Whittington last night? Well, it seems all he talked about was himself, she couldn't get a word in edgeways, and according to her he made it very plain when he stopped his car outside her flat that he expected to be invited in for . . .' She paused, fingering the neck of her blouse uncomfortably before adding, 'I'm sure you understand what I mean. Obviously she told me she didn't want to pursue matters with Mr Whittington any further. Actually her words were, "I don't care if I never see the little weasel again."'

Lex looked concerned. 'That's the second report of such a nature we've had about him. We gave him the benefit of the doubt last time, knowing Miss Caruthers has a tendency to over-exaggerate, but I don't think we can give him the benefit this time. Geraldine Smart is a very forthright sort of woman who doesn't beat about the bush.'

'Then I need to arrange for Mr Whittington to come in and for him to be reminded that it's a marriage bureau he's registered with, not a sleazy escort agency. Any further incidents like this and we'll have no choice but to strike him off our books. I'll type a letter to him and send it in the lunchtime post, along with the one for Miss Overton,' said Christine.

Just then there was a tap on the door and Peter Reynolds re-entered. He wore a highly nervous expression. Arriving before the desk, he gave a gulp and fixed his eyes on Christine. 'Er . . . I, er . . . couldn't remember whether I left my card with you?'

She responded matter-of-factly, 'Yes, you did leave it with us.'

'Oh, good. That's fine then. Yes . . . right. I'd . . . er . . . better leave you to get on then.' He turned and walked back to the door before he retraced his steps and once again addressed Christine. 'I'm new to Leicester, only been here for a couple of days. I was promoted by my firm, you see. Much bigger round. From what I've seen of it, this is a nice city and the people seem friendly enough. I know I'm really going to like living here . . .'

There was an irritated expression on Christine's face when she responded, 'Well, we're very pleased for you, Mr Reynolds. And your point is? We are rather busy and need to get on.'

A tide of red was creeping up his neck by now. 'Oh . . . yes, yes . . . of course. I just . . . well, I wondered if you could recommend a good place for me to eat at? The places I've been already . . . well, what they served up couldn't be classed as the home cooking they advertised.'

'Well, then, you'll have to do what most people would in your position – keep sampling different establishments until you find one that suits your palate. Now you really must excuse us.'

Lex had been observing the exchange between Christine and Peter with great interest. It was very apparent to her that he had not forgotten he'd left his calling card but had used it as an excuse to return and see Christine again. His question to her, Lex knew, was a prelude to asking her if she would like to join him for dinner. Christine being Christine had not realised that at all and by her dismissive attitude towards him she'd prevented him from issuing the invitation. Lex felt a great desire to give her employer a good shake and command her to open up her eyes and see what was staring her in the face.

Uttering an apology for taking up their precious time, it was a downcast Peter Reynolds who made his leave, Lex's heart going out to him.

219

Quite impervious, Christine was saying, 'I'd best get Mr Whittington's letter done. I'm meeting my mother for lunch at a quarter-past one. She's in town today shopping and I have to get over to Wellington Street which takes a good twenty minutes on foot from here.'

Lex knew that was where the firm she used to work for was situated. 'I take it you still haven't told your family of your change of job then?'

Christine had inserted a sheet of headed paper, carbon between and buff-coloured copy sheet underneath, into the typewriter and was now furiously tapping away. 'No, I haven't, for the reason I told you last time. It would be like a red rag to a bull. Mother would pester me constantly to find myself a man among our clients.' With a flourish she whipped the now finished letter from out of the typewriter, separated the copies, slipped the office copy into the filing tray to deal with later, then inserted a white envelope into the typewriter and began tapping out Mr Whittington's address. 'If you would pass me my coat off the stand while I put stamps on the morning post, I'd appreciate it,' she requested Lex, pulling the completed envelope free.

Lex was in a rush to get home that night as it was Thursday, the night she would normally have been attending the W.I. meeting had she not been forced to resign. Gil remained in ignorance of this, fortunately. She still missed being part of an organisation where she could contribute to the good works being done in the local community, and also the company of the other members who had treated her as one of them before Gil's troubles, but nevertheless there was some compensation to her expulsion which was that she and Thelma got to spend quality time together, catching up on all their latest news. She knew her friend would be waiting for her to arrive prompt at seven-thirty, pot of tea and plate of mixed biscuits waiting.

She was approaching Phyllis' house when she saw Derek hurrying towards her, seemingly so preoccupied he didn't notice

Lex until he was almost upon her. He had an excited air about him.

'Evening, Mrs M,' he good-naturedly greeted her. 'Hope yer don't mind but I'm in a rush. I've an engagement tonight and I don't want to be late.'

She patted his arm in a friendly way. 'No, of course, you get on, Derek.' As he hurried on his way, she couldn't help but call after him, 'Your engagement is with a nice lady, I hope?'

As he turned into his gate he called back, 'It is. It's awful of me to say this, Mrs M, but I'm so glad you had a bad back that night or I'd never have met Mandy, would I?'

As Lex hurried on her own way, she smiled to herself. She was very pleased she had played her part in bringing those two together. She felt positive her instincts were spot on as far as they were concerned.

Arriving at the short path that led down her entry, she was about to turn into it when she saw another figure heading towards her. It was Justine. As the young woman arrived level with her, Lex smiled a greeting and said, 'Hello, Justine. How nice to see you.' To her surprise, however, Justine appeared not to see or hear her as she hurried on past. Lex had noticed, though, that she seemed very bothered about something, and immediately worried that something was amiss with one of her grandparents. 'Is everything all right, Justine?' she called after the young woman.

The girl stopped dead in her tracks and seemed to hesitate for a moment before she turned back to face Lex. 'Oh, Mrs Morton. I . . . er . . . didn't see you. Yes, everything is fine, thanks. Best get off as . . . er . . . Gran'll have the dinner on the table and she doesn't half get grumpy at food being ruined.'

As she spun on her heel and sprinted the rest of the way to her grandparents' house, Lex felt perplexed. It surely wasn't her imagination that Justine had seemed desperate to get away from her, and her explanation that she didn't want to be late for her dinner, although as good an excuse as any, seemed to be one that she had plucked from the air. Lex wondered what she had done to the young woman to make her want to rush away like that?

Walking through the back gate into the yard, she was confronted by a large object covered by a tarpaulin standing by the outhouse. She wondered what it was. Entering the kitchen, she found Gil peeling potatoes. No sign of either of her sons.

Gil looked across at her. His lips were smiling a welcome at her but his eyes held a worried look.

'Everything all right, love?' she asked him.

'Yes, of course it is, dear.'

She knew he wasn't being truthful with her. A niggle of worry began to swirl in her stomach. Something was amiss with her husband.

Gil was saying to her, 'I assumed we'd be needing potatoes in some form or other for dinner so I thought I'd start peeling them for you.'

Putting her handbag and brown carrier of shopping on the floor, Lex took off her coat then went across and kissed his cheek. 'I appreciate that, thanks, dear. I assume because the lads aren't here they're still out working. Did they get lots of calls for work today? I do hope so.'

'Well, I'm ... er ... not sure exactly how many calls they got. I expect they'll tell you themselves when they arrive home. Do you think I've done enough potatoes or shall I do more?'

As she looked into the pan to check the amount, she wondered why Gil hadn't an idea of how many telephone calls their sons had received. He took some of the calls himself when the other three were occupied elsewhere. Something was definitely not right.

She responded, 'Couple more should be enough, thank you. Mash with corned beef sound all right?'

He nodded. 'I'll look forward to it.'

Thursdays would once have seen them sitting down to loin pork chops with homemade apple sauce, but cutting back on household expenses meant cheaper everything from cuts of meat to bars of soap, for the foreseeable future.

Collecting her apron from the back of the pantry door, Lex tied it around her.

'So how was your day, love?' she asked her husband.

Having finished peeling the potatoes, he was wrapping the peelings in newspaper to burn later on the fire. 'Great minds think alike. I was just going to ask you how yours was. You first.'

He was definitely avoiding talking about his day so whatever had happened must have had something to do with work then. Beginning to peel and chop some carrots, she told him, 'We signed up another two clients today, and Mrs Landers is ever so pleased at the way things are going. She's given me a pay rise of two pounds a week.'

'Really? I'm so proud of you, love.' It was said sincerely but the look in his eye told her he still hadn't come to terms with her having to go out to work.

'So how was your day?' she asked him again.

Gil still didn't seem to hear her question. 'I'll finish these off for you while you put the potatoes on to boil,' he offered, taking over with the carrots.

His obvious avoidance of the topic concerned Lex. She had no choice, though, but to be patient until he chose to open up to her. Suddenly she remembered the bulky object under the tarpaulin in the yard. 'Oh, just what is that under the cover by the outhouse, Gil?'

There was a slight hesitation before he answered her. 'Oh, that. It's ... a generator.' He turned on the cold water tap to clean around the sink before casually adding, 'The workshop is getting a bit congested, what with our lads using it as a base and more work coming in for Des and me. Des can't afford a bigger place at the moment so it's been decided that I'll be working from home from now on.'

Lex stood staring at him blankly. Gil only went out of the house these days to go to work. If he was working from home from now on then he would have no need to venture into the outside world at all. This was a terrible state of affairs. Hardly the way to aid him to get his confidence back. What on earth was Des playing at, asking Gil to work from home, regardless of how short of space at the workshop they were? It didn't make sense to her, though. As far as she was aware, Des was as eager to see Gil

223

become his old self as she was. She needed to confront Des and find out his reasons for doing what he had. He might already have left for the snooker hall by the time she arrived to spend the evening with his wife so best she go now, to make sure she didn't miss him.

Untying her apron and placing it on the back of a kitchen chair, Lex said, 'I've just remembered, the meeting at the W.I. is starting early tonight as there's a lot to discuss. Best get off. You can manage dinner, can't you, Gil?'

Before he could respond she had grabbed her coat off the hook, snatched up her handbag and rushed out, leaving a bemused Gil staring after her.

Thelma didn't at all look surprised by her early arrival. 'Come on in, love, we've been expecting you.'

Almost leaping over the threshold, Lex demanded, 'Why has Des suggested that Gil . . .'

She was silenced by a warning hand and a stern, 'Come on through and let Des explain how this all came about.'

Charging through to the back room, she found him eating his dinner. Normally Lex would have apologised profusely for disturbing them but she was too fired up to consider etiquette tonight. 'What's going on, Des?' she demanded. 'I can't understand why you've suggested Gil should work from home in future. You must know it means that . . .'

He interjected, 'Lex love, I'm well aware that Gil's working from home is the last thing he should be doing, as matters stand, but it was either that or he was leaving my employ to take up a job as a nightwatchman. You see, he had a turn this morning. He . . .'

She gasped and blurted out: 'Turn! What do you mean by that, Des?'

Thelma came in then and placed a steaming cup of tea in front of Lex along with the sugar basin so she could help herself. 'Hang on to your patience until Des has finished telling you, love, or we'll be here all night.'

'I'm sorry, Des. Please continue.'

'Well, I say Gil had a turn but hysterical fit would best describe it. You see, Julie Dawson popped by the workshop to ask one of your lads to take a look at her washing machine. We were all out at the time so Gil was on his own. Luckily, though, I arrived back just then – to find him waving a spanner at her and yelling at her to leave him alone and get out. I was able to cover his behaviour to Julie by telling her that a generator had blown a gasket earlier and Gil was still in shock over it. Thankfully, Julie's the type, bless her, that'd believe the sky was pink if you told her it so. She went happily on her way with a promise from me that one or both of your lads would pop in to see her as soon as possible.

'Gil had calmed down by this time and was mortified by his own behaviour. He insisted on giving me notice to quit because he said he couldn't promise not to do the same again should another woman come into the workshop while he was there on his own. He informed me he was going to look for a job as a nightwatchman as it was the only way of avoiding any repetition of today.

'I did my best, Lex, to persuade him to rethink his decision. I even told him I would ask your boys to look for somewhere else to run their business from if it meant he'd stay, but he was adamant that if anyone was leaving it was him. Finally I had no choice but to stand aside while he packed up his tool box and watch him leave. Thankfully, though, I had a brainwave. If Mohammed won't go to the mountain, then the mountain must come to Mohammed.' He chuckled when he saw Lex's face. 'I had to explain what I meant to Matt and Martin too.'

Forgetting her promise not to interrupt again, she blurted out, 'My sons both know about this and yet neither of them thought to fetch me from work, or at least wait for me here so they could explain?'

Thelma patted her arm and told her firmly, 'Just bear with Des, Lex. He'll tell you why it was felt best you were left in the dark.'

'It had better be a damned good reason then. We've never kept secrets from each other in the past.'

Thelma smiled kindly at her. 'You were living a totally different life in the past, Lex, with no need for secrets. I'm sure once you've heard Des out you'll appreciate why Gil was trying to keep this from you.'

Des continued, 'What I meant by that expression was that if Gil wouldn't come to the workshop to work, I'd take the work to him to do at home. Martin and Matt had returned to the workshop by this time and you can imagine how upset they both were to hear what had happened. They gladly accompanied me when I went to persuade Gil to accept my offer for him to work from home from now on. He was very reluctant at first, worried about all the extra work it would cause me, having to bring the generators to him, but thankfully I managed to convince him that I'd sooner have that extra work than lose him. I don't need to tell you, Lex, Gil's very embarrassed and ashamed about his behaviour today and feels you've enough on your plate without adding this on top. So he asked me, Matt and Martin to keep it from you.'

She sighed. 'Gil already feels he doesn't deserve his position as head of the house, without thinking he's been demeaned further in my eyes by incidents such as today's with Julie Dawson. So, yes, I can appreciate why he wasn't honest with me about all this.' Eyeing Des with deep affection, she leaned over to squeeze his hand. 'I should have known you'd have a damned good reason for suggesting he work from home, and I'm sorry I charged in here like a bull at a gate, thinking the worst of you.' She could feel the tears welling then and her bottom lip tremble as she said, 'I really thought that Gil working for you at the workshop was going to help him regain his confidence. I thought he'd be able to hold his head up in public again so we could at least have some social life together, but that's never going to happen, is it? Not unless he can clear his name, and there seems no chance of that ever happening.'

And Des and Thelma felt powerless to reassure her on that score.

CHAPTER SIXTEEN

Lex was finding it very difficult to accept that her beloved husband's life was never going to be the same again, but three days later, as she sat and listened to the sorry tale of the woman before her, it did bring home to her that the well-used expression 'There's always someone worse off than yourself' did have substance to it. The Mortons' lives might not be what they once were, but at least Lex wasn't caring for her bedridden husband's every need while she slowly watched him lose his battle with life through an extremely painful wasting disease. That was what was happening to Kathleen Overton.

In her early-forties, she was a pleasant-faced woman of medium build. She wore her light brown chin-length hair loosely waved, and was dressed in an off the peg tan and cream flower-patterned shirt-waister dress. The expression on her face was one of deep shame.

'I really, really didn't set out to deceive you or Mrs Landers, Mrs Morton. You must believe me, I didn't. It just got out of hand. I saw your advertisement and thought it sounded like a wonderful way to meet members of the opposite sex for the occasional evening out. I only intended to do it the once but I so enjoyed my evening with Mr Wilson I thought just once more wouldn't hurt if you or Mrs Landers happened to find a client on your books who was suitable for me and me for him, which you did . . .' She heaved a deep mournful sigh before admitting, 'For a few hours once in a while I wanted to be reminded of how it feels to have a man find me attractive again.

'It's been many years since my husband looked at me as anything more than his nurse, because of his dreadful illness, let alone performed any husbandly duties. I do love my husband, Mrs Morton, although I have to admit not in the same way I did on the day we married. It's a caring sort of love now, me worrying whether Ralf's comfortable, has had his painkillers on time, been turned regularly to avoid bedsores ... that's the sort of love I mean.'

Her eyes glazed over. 'Life has been very unfair to us both. When we married seventeen years ago, we were so much in love, had so many plans for our future. Ralf and I had only been married a year, hardly had time to make our house ready for the large family we planned to have, when the first signs of his illness began to show themselves. Before the next year was out he was wheelchair-bound, and for the last five years he's been completely bedridden and unable to do anything for himself. Thankfully, he had an inheritance from his maternal grandmother when he was young. It had been invested wisely by his parents and so we've been able to manage a reasonable standard of living on the interest since he was forced to retire from work or I dread to think how we'd have coped for money. Ralf's father is dead now but his mother is still very much alive and sprightly for her age. She gladly sits with him to allow me the odd evening to myself, visiting my female friends as she thinks.' She paused then, looking at Lex beseechingly. 'Surely as a woman you can understand why I've done this? I haven't hurt anyone, have I? I never continued with any of my introductions, so what harm have I caused?'

Leaning her arms on the desk and clasping her hands together, Lex looked at her sympathetically. 'Miss Overton ... or should I address you as *Mrs* Overton?'

She cast her eyes down and guiltily admitted, 'It's Mrs Greenwood actually. Overton was my maiden name.'

'I see. Well, Mrs Greenwood, I can't deny that life has treated you cruelly, you and your husband, and I do understand why you've done what you have. But when all's said and done, you blatantly lied to us on your application form about your marital status. And maybe you didn't lead on any of the clients we introduced you to, but regardless you were deceiving them in the first place as we all believed you were in a position to meet a potential husband. I can vouch for all the gentlemen concerned that they were very disappointed when you made it clear you didn't wish to take matters further with any of them. You do appreciate we cannot allow this state of affairs to continue now that we're aware of it?'

She gave a sad sigh and uttered, 'No, of course I couldn't expect you to.' Collecting her handbag from the side of her chair, she gave Lex a sad smile and walked out.

With a heavy heart Lex watched her departure. She should have felt proud of herself for bringing a fraudulent client to task for their deception, but she didn't. What she did feel was guilty for snatching away the few hours of pleasure which broke the monotony of Kathleen Greenwood's otherwise joyless existence.

'Miss Overton scuttled out of here with what I can only describe as a guilty look on her face,' Christine commented as Lex went out to join her in the reception area.

Lex told her boss everything then. 'Miss Overton is actually Mrs Greenwood. Overton was her maiden name.'

Christine looked blank for a moment as she digested this information before the significance of it hit her and she exclaimed, 'She lied to us about her marital status? So *that's* why she looked so guilty just now. You found her out in her deception and informed her she's to be struck off our books? Clever you for sussing her out, Mrs Morton, and saving the good name of the bureau.' She pulled a face. 'And she comes across as such a nice woman too.'

'She *is* a nice woman, Mrs Landers. In fact, I feel very sorry for her.'

Christine gawped at her in astonishment. 'How can you say that when she's been so deceitful?'

Lex told her Kathleen Greenwood's story.

When she had finished Christine snapped, 'Well, I admit life hasn't been fair to Mrs Greenwood, but she wants to be thankful she has a man of her own to care for, regardless of his terrible illness. Some of us will never be that lucky.' She snatched up her handbag from under the desk then pushed back her chair and got up. 'We've no one due in until two-thirty and the telephone is quiet so I'm going to take an early lunch. I want to shop for a new pair of shoes. You don't mind holding the fort until you close up for our official dinner hour?'

Lex smiled in answer then shook her head in frustration as Christine headed off. She was clearly the type of woman who would never betray her man, no matter how tough the going got, and wasn't at all sympathetic to those who did, no matter how good their reason. Lex was in no doubt, though, that Christine *could* have a man of her own to fuss over if only she'd open up her eyes and see what was being offered her by the likes of that very nice stationery representative, Peter Reynolds.

For the next half an hour Lex busied herself tackling a backlog of filing. It was only the rumbling of hunger in her stomach that set her glancing at the clock and seeing it was just on one o'clock. She was halfway across the room to slip the catch on the outer door when it opened and a nervous-looking Peter Reynolds entered.

'Hello, Mr Reynolds. You've just caught me as I was about to lock up for lunch. I'm afraid nothing has changed regarding our stationery requirements since yesterday.'

He was staring past her at the empty reception desk. Lex realised that the reason he was back here had nothing to do with any hope of obtaining a stationery order, and it certainly wasn't herself he was hoping to see. 'Mrs Landers is out, I'm afraid. It was her you called in to see, wasn't it, Mr Reynolds?'

He stared at her blankly for a moment before giving an embarrassed gulp. 'It . . . er . . . was, as a matter of fact. I'll call back another time and hopefully she'll be here . . .' Then something Lex had said seemed to register with him. 'You said, *Mrs* Landers?'

She nodded. 'Yes.'

He seemed to shrivel before her eyes. 'Oh! Well, I'd best be off. Appointments to keep. It wouldn't do to be late for them. I'm so very sorry to have disturbed your dinner hour.'

A troubled Lex stared after him. It was apparent to her that

Peter Reynolds was very keen to ask Christine out, and judging by his highly nervous state when he had arrived it had taken him all his courage. What a dilemma she was in! Did she let this man go away under a false impression or did she risk raising the wrath of her boss and the possible loss of her own job by proving to Christine that there were in fact men who found her attractive? She had promised not to divulge the fact that Christine wasn't actually married. But then, it was the clients who weren't to know that. And Peter Reynolds was not a client.

Darting to the door, Lex rushed across the landing and leaned over the stair rail. Spotting her quarry on the second-floor landing, making for the next flight of stairs, she called urgently to him, 'Mr Reynolds?'

He stopped abruptly and looked about him bemused. 'Did someone call me?'

'I did, Mr Reynolds. It's me, Mrs Morton, from Cupid's Marriage Bureau.' When he leaned over the rail and looked up at her questioningly, she added, 'May I trouble you to come back. I'd like a word, please?'

'Oh, er . . . yes, of course.'

He disappeared back inside the stairwell and she heard his footsteps pounding back up the stairs. He was wearing a hopeful look when he walked back in. 'You've changed your mind about placing an order with my company?' he asked.

She shook her head, then took a deep breath before saying, 'Look, Mr Reynolds, the reason I wanted a word . . . well, the last thing I would wish is to embarrass you but it's very clear you're interested in my employer in . . . well . . . more than a business way?'

He stared at her blankly then a look of acute mortification flooded his face and he exclaimed, 'Oh, God, did I make my admiration of her that obvious?'

Lex smiled kindly at him. 'To me, yes, but Mrs Landers to the best of my knowledge isn't aware of it.'

He looked mortally relieved to hear that, then gave a miserable sigh, slapping his hand in annoyance against his forehead. 'What an imbecile I am not to have realised a woman like that would already be spoken for. I've always mocked the notion of love at first sight but now I know without a doubt it's true. Since I first clapped eyes on her, I haven't been able to get her out of my mind. I've never felt like this about a woman before. It's ridiculous, isn't it, that I should feel like this for someone I've barely spoken more than a dozen words to?'

And her words would hardly have given you any hope that your feelings were reciprocated, Lex thought. Other men would have been put off wanting to get to know Christine better by her offputting manner, but Peter Reynolds was obviously not. 'None of us can control our feelings, Mr Reynolds,' she said sympathetically.

Regardless of Lex's attempt to make him feel better, he looked shame-faced. 'I don't suppose Mr Landers would appreciate knowing that another man took one look at his wife and for him it was like the whole world stopped and he had a devil of a job stopping himself from scooping her up in his arms and running off with her?' He paused, sighed, and said wistfully, 'Mr Landers is a very lucky man.'

'And I'd be in agreement with you, Mr Reynolds, if indeed there actually were a Mr Landers.'

He looked perplexed. 'I don't understand?' Then the significance of what she'd said registered with him and he ventured, 'You mean, Mrs Landers is a widow or a divorcee?'

'Well, neither, actually. You see, there never has been a living and breathing Mr Landers. Mrs Landers is actually *Miss* Landers. She only calls herself Mrs for business reasons.'

His face lit up like a beacon. 'So there's nothing stopping me then from asking Mrs ... Miss Landers if she'd like to join me for an evening out?'

Lex shook her head. 'Nothing at all.'

The sound of a key being inserted into the Yale lock on the entrance door made then both spin round.

Christine entered then, shutting the door behind her and snapping down the snib. 'The door wasn't locked, did you forget to ...'

As she turned around mid-sentence she spotted Lex was not on her own. Eyeing Peter Reynolds, she asked him, 'What have you forgotten this time, Mr Reynolds? I know we haven't called you back in as we have all our stationery; you've already checked that you left your card with us earlier today; you didn't leave your sample case behind the last time you left, so I cannot imagine what else could have brought you back here.' By now she had joined Lex and Peter by the reception desk and put a bulky Lilley and Skinner carrier bag down on it, while fixing Peter's eyes with hers and waiting for his answer.

Lex flashed a look at him as if to say, Now's your chance, before saying to Christine, 'Mr Reynolds would like a word with you, Mrs Landers.' She felt it best in the circumstances to make herself scarce, free them both from the embarrassment of a third party being present at such a personal time. 'If you'll excuse me, I'm just going to pop across to the café for a sandwich. I forgot to bring my lunch in today.'

Christine looked at her strangely. 'I can assure you, you didn't, Mrs Morton. I saw you myself put your lunch box in the desk drawer when you first arrived this morning.'

'Oh! Oh, silly me, yes, I did. Well, I ... er ... made .myself salmon paste which I did have a taste for this morning but ... well, now I haven't.'

With that she spun on her heel and hurried out.

Lex was so excited by the prospect in store for Christine that she only just stopped herself in time from stepping out into the road in front of a car. The driver wasn't at all happy to have to do an emergency stop which sent a bag of shopping on the front seat flying. He shook his fist angrily at her before revving up and continuing on his way.

Over in the café a polite young waitress asked Lex for her order and it was only then that she realised she'd been so anxious to leave Peter and Christine to it, she had forgotten to pick up her handbag so had no money on her. The waitress looked at her bemused when Lex told her she had changed her mind, she didn't want anything after all. Back out on the pavement she was just about to take a walk up the street and window shop when she spotted Peter coming out of the building. Well, obviously no time had been wasted after her departure. Even if he didn't possess the qualities to attract Christine, she would at least have been asked out by a man. Things had to be improving for her, surely.

Without further ado Lex dashed back across the road and ran up the stairs, arriving breathlessly to find Christine seated behind the reception desk, idly thumbing through a magazine as she ate her lunch.

At the sound of Lex's return, Christine lifted her head and looked across at her. 'I had no choice but to leave the door unlocked. You didn't take your handbag when you left so I knew you hadn't your key with you. You wouldn't have had any money on you either to pay for a sandwich. I've saved you one of mine. I hope ham is to your taste?'

Lex smiled appreciatively at her as she walked across to accept the sandwich Christine was offering, feeling slightly guilty for the fact that her boss was going without in order to feed her when she had a perfectly good sandwich of her own in the box in the desk drawer. 'I appreciate your thoughtfulness, thank you, Mrs Landers.' Lex was disappointed that it didn't appear Christine was going to volunteer any information.

'Er . . . Mr Reynolds gone, has he?' Lex ventured.

Taking a bite of her sandwich, Christine flashed her a look as if to say, Well, isn't that obvious? She said matter-of-factly, 'It never ceases to amaze me what lengths reps will go to to secure an order. Discounted prices are one thing, bribery another.'

Lex enquired faintly, 'Bribery?'

'He asked if I'd like to have dinner with him tonight. Of course I sent him packing, and in no doubt that I wasn't open to such backhanded methods of gaining business. I warned him if he tried anything like that again, I would make an official complaint to his company.'

Lex was completely flabbergasted. It had never entered her head that Christine would view Peter Reynolds' request for her company in such a light. 'Mrs Landers,' she enquired, 'did you not stop to consider that Mr Reynolds' offer to take you to dinner wasn't by way of a bribe but because he actually wanted to spend some time with you?'

Christine flashed her a scathing look. 'Mr Reynolds might not be in the same league as Sebastian Evans, but I cannot imagine him being so stuck for female company he's reduced to asking out the likes of me. His offer was nothing but a bribe. Couldn't have been anything else.'

She went back to eating her lunch and thumbing through her magazine.

Lex sighed heavily, quashing the urge to grab her by the shoulders and give her a good shake for not seizing any chance of possible happiness that came her way. Then a sudden thought struck her. In a way, wasn't her own husband doing exactly the same as Christine, by allowing the incident with Miriam Jones to curtail his freedom? How you got people like Gil and Christine to stop allowing traumatic events to colour their daily lives was the problem. As far as Peter Reynolds was concerned, though, she doubted they'd see him again after Christine's misguided response to his invitation.

Both of them jumped then as the outer door unexpectedly opened and in strode the man himself.

Christine hissed under her breath, 'Damn, we forgot to lock the door after him when he left. What on earth could he be wanting now?'

Before either of them could address him, to their surprise Peter announced, 'I'd like to register as a client. Is it possible to see me now, I've a free hour before my next appointment?'

Both of them were looking at him dumbstruck. This was the last thing they'd been expecting him to say.

It was Lex who gathered her wits first. 'I'm sure we can arrange that, Mr Reynolds,' she said, getting up and checking the appointments book. Then she realised Peter was looking at her meaningfully and understood what he was trying to convey. She turned to address Christine. 'Would you mind conducting Mr Reynolds' interview? I really do need to pop to the shops for something for my family's dinner. I'll make sure I lock the door after me and be back to cover reception at two.'

The look Christine shot her would have wilted fresh flowers. It was most apparent this was one potential client she would have preferred Lex to interview, after the episode with him earlier. Rising to her feet, she said briskly, 'Would you like to come through, Mr Reynolds?'

As he followed Christine into the interview room, Peter Reynolds flashed Lex a smile. She smiled back. She liked this man. He might appear to be the mild-mannered, studious sort, but he certainly had enough backbone to go after what he wanted and not concede defeat at the first setback. What a clever idea of his, to come and register as a client. She assumed his hope was that by interviewing him, gaining an insight into him as a person, Christine would no longer see him as Peter Reynolds, stationery representative, but Peter Reynolds, a man with many other facets to his character. Hopefully than she would warm to him enough to want to take him up on his offer.

Peter came back out of the office forty-five minutes later. Lex would dearly have loved to have asked him how the interview had gone, but all she could do was nod him farewell as she was on the telephone, listening to a very excited Marie Noble telling her that her evening last night had gone really well and Sebastian Evans had asked to see her again tonight. He must be keen to want to see her so soon, Lex thought, and from the bureau's point of view she and Christine had obviously got that one right.

Christine emerged from the office moments later, clutching Peter's application form and registration fee which she placed on the desk for Lex to deal with, saying, 'That was a little unfair of you, Mrs Morton. I thought the arrangement we had was that we took it in turns to do the interviewing, and as I saw the one previous client then really you should have seen Mr Reynolds.' She could not fail to notice the expression on Lex's face, though, and continued, 'All right, I admit I am being a little childish, but I would rather not have interviewed Mr Reynolds after what happened between us this morning. I'm still offended that he thought he could bribe me into giving him an order.'

Lex bit her tongue, quashing the urge to set Christine straight in no uncertain terms. But, after all, this was her boss she was talking to. Instead she took Peter's registration form and looked it over. 'So, Mr Reynolds is originally from Manchester and has been with his firm since leaving school. He recently moved to Leicester after being promoted. Shows he's a very reliable man,' she said, impressed. 'He's living in lodgings at the moment but looking to buy a house when he's got to know the city better and decided what area he'd like to live in. He has lots of interests, including astronomy. His favourite programme on television is *The Sky at Night* with Patrick Moore. During his spare time he does all his own maintenance around the house, likes to go to concerts, reads, gardens, and is a member of his local Round Table. Well, he seems an active and interesting man, doesn't he?'

Christine responded, 'I do already know all this about Mr Reynolds, Mrs Morton. I wrote it all down, remember.'

And you still can't see a decent man when he's slap-bang in front of you, thought Lex. 'Oh, silly me, yes, of course,' she answered. 'Right, what sort of woman would he like us to introduce him to . . .' She scanned her eyes over those details on the form. 'Oh, he's very specific, isn't he? Mr Reynolds obviously knows what he's looking for. Aged in her early-thirties, preferably slim build and about five foot five. Not worried about hair colour but finds light brown especially flattering on a woman with grey eyes. Pretty.' She looked at Christine and said, 'This could be you, Mrs Landers.'

Christine gave an irritated click of her tongue. 'Yes, I admit I am in my thirties, on the thin side and have mousey-brown hair and grey eyes, but Mr Reynolds also stipulated, *pretty*. By no stretch of the imagination could I be described as that.'

Lex wanted to scream at her, Oh, don't be so blind! To Peter Reynolds you *are* pretty. Instead she suggested they go through the cards together to select those female clients they thought he'd like to be introduced to, although Lex severely doubted any would match up to the woman he'd already set his heart on. Christine was not going to prove an easy nut to crack. Lex dearly hoped Peter was prepared to go the distance.

Unfortunately for Lex her bus broke down on the way home and by the time she finally got in it was past seven o'clock.

She met Martin . . . well, collided with him as she was coming in at the entry while he came rushing out of it. 'We've all been worried about you, Mam, you're not usually as late as this. Anyway, glad to see you safe and sound. Got to dash or I'm going to be late myself.'

'But what about your dinner?'

'I'm having dinner out tonight. Sorry, forgot to tell you this morning.' He kissed her affectionately. 'See you later. Oh, but you'll probably be in bed by the time I get home, so see you in the morning.'

She glanced after him as he galloped down the path and into the street. He did look smart in his trousers, shirt and leather jacket, hair carefully groomed, skin closely shaved with no nicks. He whiffed of men's cologne, too, and not the cheap sort either. Just who was he eating out with? Dressed and groomed like that, it was obviously a woman he was seeing. The same one he'd been seeing for a few weeks now or someone new? Obviously his worry over his mother's lateness hadn't been strong enough for him to cancel his own engagement, so whoever he was meeting was important to him . . .

Lex was met in the kitchen by an anxious Gil. 'Oh, lovey, I'm glad to see you home. At first I just thought you must be working late, but then as time wore on . . .'

'The bus broke down,' she cut in, going over to kiss him. As she took off her coat and hung it up, she continued, 'The next three that arrived were full and there was a stampede by the passengers to get on the fourth . . . well, anyway, I'm here now.' She gave a sniff. 'Is that the casserole I made I can smell now?'

Gil nodded. 'I hope I did right by putting it on a low heat in the oven at five?'

She smiled. 'That's exactly right.' But it was two hours ago so she prayed his idea of a low heat was the same as hers or it'd be dried up by now. She glanced at the oven setting and was relieved to see that it was. 'Getting to be a dab hand in the kitchen, Mr Morton, aren't you? I could get used to this.'

Gil looked pleased by the compliment. 'Well, I told you I'd try and help out as much as I could while you're having to go out to work. They weren't idle words on my part.'

Lex smiled tenderly at him. 'I know you better than that, darling.'

He looked a bit ashamed then. 'I must admit, since doing these few jobs around the house by way of helping you, it's dawned on me that being a housewife isn't the cushy number we men seem to think it is. I'd always believed you had it easy at home, pottering around the house. But it's not really pottering, is it, more like hard labour. I have no idea how you managed to keep this house spick and span, with all the cooking, shopping, washing, ironing and what have you, while at the same time looking after the boys as babies.'

Lex laughed and jocularly quipped, 'We women have a natural ability that all men lack. We can do several jobs at one time, while a man can only do one at a time.' Then she spied the pan of potatoes sitting on top of the stove. 'Oh, you wonderful man, you've even peeled the potatoes ready for me to pop on, which I will do right now.' As she busied herself finishing off the dinner and Gil was setting the table, she said to him, 'I bumped into Martin on his way out.' Having turned on the heat under the saucepan of potatoes she faced her husband. 'Any idea who he's meeting?'

Gil gave a shrug and shook his head. 'Whoever it is, he's keen on her judging by the way he's spruced himself up, that much I do know. I could smell his aftershave down here in the kitchen while he was still upstairs.' He laughed. 'We know what to get him for Christmas, don't we?'

Her motherly concern coming to the fore again, Lex just wanted to be introduced to the new woman in her son's life, to put her own mind at rest.

'Matt upstairs getting ready to go out after he's had his dinner?' she asked, opening the oven door to check on the sausage casserole.

Gil was in the pantry collecting the cruet set to put on the table. 'He's not home yet. Martin told me that a frantic customer called about ten minutes before knocking off time . . .' He paused, cocking his ear. 'That's the gate so it'll be him now.'

The door opened and Matt entered. 'Brrr, it's turning chilly out there. Hello, Mam, Dad,' he greeted his parents as he shut the door behind him and wiped his shoes on the mat.

'I was in the middle of telling your mother about the call-out you got just before knocking off time,' his father told him.

'I volunteered to do it as I knew our Martin was off out tonight.'

His mother asked, 'Did you manage to fix the customer's appliance then?'

Matt shook his head. 'She'd completely blown the motor on her vacuum. Silly woman hadn't a clue that they're intended to suck up fluff and dust, not builder's rubble. Her husband had knocked a wall down in the lounge and she was cleaning up after him. Mrs Williams got quite bolshie when I told her there was nothing I could do. She's damaged it so badly it wasn't even worth me offering to buy it off her to salvage any parts.'

'Some people think engineers are miracle workers,' Gil agreed. 'Oh, I've just remembered, I need to telephone Des to ask him to bring me some soldering iron tomorrow. I forgot when he was here earlier. I won't be long.'

'Please tell him to give Thelma my love and I'll see her Thursday evening.'

'Will do,' he said as he went off.

Matt was looking hungrily at the bubbling pan on the cooker. 'Have I time to go and change out of my dirty work clothes and have a quick swill before you dish up, Mam?'

'If you hurry. You'll be wanting to eat up quick ready for going out, I take it?'

He grinned cheekily at her. 'No, I'm looking forward to a cosy night in with my old folks tonight.'

Lex glanced after him as he shot out of the kitchen and up the stairs. She was comforted to know that her twenty-one-year-old son was happy to spend time in his parents' company, when most young men of his age would baulk at the very idea. But it bothered her too that he hardly went out socialising with his friends these days. Was it because he was still being relentlessly taunted by them over what had happened to his father, or was he just keeping a low profile of his own accord until it all blew over?

Gil returned then. 'Des is going to get some and bring it over as soon as he can in the morning. And some good news – it looks like I'll start getting a wage next week as he's had a couple of telephone calls from new customers, looking for us to maintain their generators regularly.'

Lex's face lit up in delight. Gil had been working for Des for nearly a month now and their savings were just about gone. Although neither of them had spoken openly of it, they were both secretly worried about how they were going to manage financially very shortly as her wage and what their sons handed over did not cover everything. 'Oh, Gil, that's great,' Lex enthused.

He smiled. 'Yes, it is. Of course, it won't be a full wage I'm earning yet, but every little helps.' Then he looked at his wife thoughtfully as she strained the saucepan of cooked potatoes over the sink. 'Er . . . Lex?'

Her mind on her task, she mouthed, 'Mmm?'

'You never told me next-door was leaving?'

Resting the saucepan in the sink, she turned to look at him. 'Oh, did I forget to mention the Higgins had given up their tenancy? I didn't realise they were moving so soon, though.'

'A bit sudden this move, isn't it? When I was talking to Frank at the Websters' daughter's christening a couple of months ago, he was telling me how happy they all were living around here, and saying he hoped his landlord didn't suddenly decide to reclaim the house.' He paused for a moment, eyeing her, and said quietly, 'The Higgins are leaving because of me, aren't they, Lex? Jane Higgins sees me as a threat. Did she think I was going to leap over the garden wall and drag her into the outhouse when I spotted

241

her in the yard? Or creep into her house when her husband wasn't home . . .'

'Gil, stop it!' cried Lex. 'I'm not going to lie to you . . .' But she was. It was bad enough her beloved husband believing that all the women roundabout feared him now, which actually wasn't the case though how it could be proved to him when he wouldn't go past the yard gate was beyond her. But she would sooner he think the Higgins had scurried off because Jane feared for her own safety than hear the truth: that it was their two young daughters they feared he might harm. '. . . it's true the Higgins have moved away because of misguided fear. But, Gil, *we* know the truth, which is that you're no more a threat to Jane than Phyllis Watson's cat is!'

She wagged a warning finger at him. 'You're not to take this to heart, you hear me? We aren't going to let the Higgins' move set us back. One thing is for sure: wherever they've moved to, they won't get such good neighbours as us, helping them out in all sorts of ways. Now, can you go and give Matt a shout to hurry up, please? I'm going to mash the spuds then dish up, and I don't want his going cold.'

Gil eyed his wife blankly. He had removed himself from the public eye, never venturing further than the yard, in order that all the women in the vicinity could move around freely without fearing they were in any danger. But now neighbours were actually going to these lengths to avoid being near him. What else could he do to make people believe he posed no threat to them? Nothing he could think of, when he was already living under virtual house arrest.

Feeling subdued, he went off to do his wife's bidding.

Over in the Reader household, Des returned to the living room after taking the telephone call from Gil and sat back down in his armchair.

His wife, sitting opposite, in the process of knitting a matinée jacket to add to several other items awaiting the arrival of her first grandchild, looked over at him with a delighted glint in her eyes.

'Oh, that's good news, love. Why haven't you told me first, though?'

He looked back at her. 'Told you what?'

'About what I heard you discussing with Gil just now on the telephone.'

He sighed. 'Oh, you mean about the new work coming in and how from next week he can't refuse to take a wage packet from me?' His face clouded over guiltily. 'Well . . . I was actually lying to him, love.'

Thelma looked bemused. 'Lying to him?'

He nodded. 'New work *has* come in but not the amount I was hoping for. It's actually only one new customer, put my way by the chap Gil did his first job for. But I know it will pick up, love. It just takes time for word to spread that I'm expanding. Gil's been working for me nearly a month now, and he might be comfortable about doing it without pay, but I'm not. It's not right, love. A man should be paid for the work he does, even if I can't pay him the proper rate as matters stand. I'm fully aware that what savings they had must be running low by now, and they've only got Lex's wage and what their lads hand over to manage on. I was going to speak to you about it as soon . . .'

'As you plucked up the courage?' Thelma finished for him. Laying down her knitting on the arm of her chair, she leaned forward and clasped her hands together in her lap. 'So how *do* you propose to pay Gil, when we're only just getting by on what you bring in already? What I earn goes towards our high days and holidays, but it's hardly a king's ransom, is it?'

Des shrugged, looking at her helplessly. 'I don't know. I just feel I can no longer continue pocketing money for work Gil is doing on my behalf.'

Thelma sat back in her chair, looking at her husband tenderly. 'You're a wonderful, man, Desmond Reader, and that's why I love you as much now as I did when we said our vows. Right, I'll tell you how we're going to work this. We'll cut down on our outgoings plus, as luck would have it, one of the part-timers at work is leaving to go full-time at the chemist's. I'll ask my boss if he'll

243

make me a full-timer there. It'll save him looking for another member of staff, and I've been a good worker, never given him any cause for complaint, so I don't see why he'd turn me down.'

Des smiled at her gratefully for solving his problem for him, while at the same time feeling sorry that his dear wife would soon be working even harder.

Knowing her husband as well as she did, Thelma realised what was going through his mind. 'I've every faith that you will secure enough new work to support both families, like you say you will, so me working full-time won't be for long, love. And it wasn't like we were going on holiday next year anyway, not without Lex and Gil, so what I was putting aside for that can now go into the housekeeping.' She shook her head at him. 'But we mustn't tell them about this. If they got even an inkling what we're having to do to afford Gil's wage, neither of them would stand for it. Regardless, we'll do it, whatever it takes to get them through this terrible time. We know they'd do the same for us.'

'Yes, they would,' her husband replied with conviction.

CHAPTER SEVENTEEN

Lex was looking thoughtful as she replaced the telephone in its cradle and looked up as Christine entered the inner office, cup of tea in hand. 'Just what the doctor ordered. Thank you.'

'My pleasure. We're running low on supplies so I shall pop out in a moment for replenishments, if you'll be good enough to hold the fort?'

Lex gave her boss her due, Christine Landers never abused her status as owner of the bureau by using her subordinate as her lackey but always took her turn in seeing to the more mundane tasks. 'Yes, of course I will, but I was going out at lunchtime as I need to do some grocery shopping. I could get what we need at the same time, if you'd like me to?'

A sheepish expression crossed Christine's face. 'Well, you've caught me out. I was using it as an excuse to visit Lewis's before the lunchtime rush. They have a sale on and I'm in need of new underwear. You can't browse for clothing when you're being pushed and shoved out of the way by other customers, can you?'

Lex shook her head, laughing. 'No, you can't. I'll gladly hold the fort. Oh, by the way, that was Miss Noble on the telephone . . . a rather upset Miss Noble, in fact. She was informing us she's back on the market as her evening with Sebastian Evans didn't end as she'd hoped it would and he hasn't asked to see her again. I expect Mr Evans will be telephoning at some stage today to inform us that Miss Noble isn't for him after all, and to ask us to sort out another introduction for him. Anyway, to add to Miss Noble's woes, apparently she arrived home after her date with him to find that her flat had been broken into.'

Christine was horrified. 'Oh, my goodness, how dreadful for her. Was much taken by the burglar?'

'Nothing, apparently.'

'Thank goodness for that. Obviously Miss Noble disturbed the thief when she arrived home, before he had a chance to do his worst.'

'That's what the police think. Thankfully all the damage that was done was a broken window-pane which the thief smashed so he could get in. Anyway, maybe we can brighten her day by telling her we've a nice man on our books to introduce her to.'

'Anyone immediately spring to mind or do we need to go through the cards together?'

'I was thinking of Melvin Cane . . .'

Christine frowned. 'Didn't he stress to us that he has an intense dislike of redheads, and Miss Noble is one.'

'Yes, I know, but she has all the other qualities he's looking for in a woman, and he's certainly got all she's looking for in a man – apart from the fact that she wants someone who owns a car so they can go for runs in the country at the weekend, and he doesn't drive. But then, there's always coach trips, isn't there? We might persuade her to overlook that one failing and him to ignore the fact that Marie Noble is a redhead.'

Christine smiled at her. 'If anyone can, it's you. I'll see you back here after lunchtime then.'

On Christine's departure Lex moved herself into the reception area to have access to the typewriter plus man the telephone and greet any possible new clients who called in on spec. Her typing speed had improved dramatically during the time she had been with the bureau, and after deciding how she was going to word her letters to Miss Noble and Mr Cane it only took her a matter of minutes to type them out. She was just in the process of typing the envelopes when the clatter of shoes across the landing reached her ears. The door burst open and a very pretty young woman dashed across to the desk.

'I'm not late, am I?' she breathlessly enquired. 'I'm so sorry if I am, only I was halfway out of the door when my boss called me back to type an urgent letter for him to post on my way here and then the ink ribbon ran out and I had to replace it and ... oh, it was just one disaster after another. I'm not late, am I?'

Lex was looking uncertain. 'What time was your appointment exactly, only we haven't anything down in the book until three this afternoon?' She glanced over at the appointments book, then brought her eyes back to rest on the girl. 'That's for a Mr Brian Francis and you're far too pretty to be him.' She was secretly bothered a mistake had been made while at the same time wondering why such an attractive young woman would ever need to pay a marriage bureau to find her a man.

Although the young woman looked perturbed by this, nevertheless she smiled at Lex's compliment. 'My appointment is for ten to one. It's just for a check up.'

Lex frowned in confusion. 'Check up?' Then the truth dawned and she heaved a sigh of relief. 'Oh, no wonder we've nothing in the appointments book for you. I believe it's the dentist you want, on the floor below.'

'Oh!' the girl exclaimed, then began to laugh. 'I was so keen to be on time that I ran up one flight of stairs too many.'

'Well, you're not late, it's only just coming up for a quarter to.'

'Thank goodness for that! It's all right when the dentist over-runs an appointment and keeps you waiting for ages, but woe betide you when *you're* late! Well, sorry to have bothered you.' She turned to make her way out but stopped as one of the pictures of happy couples hanging on the wall caught her eye. 'What exactly is it you do here?'

'We're a marriage bureau.'

The girl looked surprised. 'Really? People actually come to you to help them find a husband or wife, do they?'

Lex smiled and nodded.

'Oh, it must be so satisfying for you when a couple you have introduced like each other enough to want to get married.'

'It is. Well, it will be when it happens. We've only been in operation a couple of months so it's early days yet. We encourage our clients to take their time getting to know someone before they make such a life-changing decision.'

The girl looked impressed. 'Good advice. I've friends who've rushed into marriage and are living to regret it. So what sort of people come to you then?'

'All sorts, from all walks of life. Our list is constantly expanding as word gets around about what we do. Some people don't find it as easy as others to meet a partner and need the likes of us to help.' Lex smiled warmly at the pretty young blonde. 'I shouldn't imagine you have any problems in that area.' This wasn't a question but a statement.

She smiled back at the compliment. 'No, I have to say that I don't. But I'm a bit tired of the sort I seem to end up with, though. I've had some nice boyfriends and really enjoyed their company for a time, but none of them could offer me the kind of marriage I'd like to have. Not that I'm desperate to get married, but I want to eventually,' she hastily added.

'What kind of marriage would you like for yourself?' Lex asked her, interested.

'One where I'm not just my husband's cook, cleaner and mother of his children. It just seems to me from what I've seen that the majority of men, once they've put a ring on a woman's finger, revert to their bachelor ways and then the poor wife is just a drudge. There is no way I would even contemplate marrying a man if I thought for one moment he'd treat me like that.

'For a change I'd like a boyfriend who sees me as more than just an ornament on his arm, expecting me always to want to go where he wants, and not to cause a stink when he cancels a date because he's decided to go out with his mates instead or remembered he's a darts match or union meeting or whatever, and so expects me to sit around meekly waiting for him meantime. I want a man who'll make a proper relationship, one where we share things together.'

'I'm sure there are many young men out there who would jump at the chance to have you for their girlfriend and treat you with a lot more respect than your past boyfriends seem to have, from what you've told me.'

'I always think I've met someone like that when I start to date them, only to realise pretty soon they're just like all the others: far more interested in themselves than they are in me. I've not met a man yet who doesn't seem all interested to start with, can't do enough for me in fact, but once he thinks he has me where he wants me then the real man comes out. And I'll have wasted another few months, under the impression that I've finally met the man of my dreams, only to realise he was just like all the others. Well, I'm fed up with wasting my time, but apart from turning my back on men for good, how will I know when I've found someone genuine if I don't give him a chance to show his true colours?'

Then her face lit up as the answer struck her. 'Oh, I should give your bureau a try, shouldn't I? You would only match me with a man you'd personally vetted so you'd know he had the makings of what I'd like, wouldn't you? Of course, my friends would tease me mercilessly if they knew I was paying a marriage bureau . . . but I don't have to let on to them about it, do I?' She looked at Lex enquiringly. 'Have you any nice men on your list, just the sort I'm looking for who you think would like me?' She then added hurriedly, 'Not that I'm desperate to get married . . . not right this minute . . . but eventually. With the right man.'

'Well, at the moment we've no one of your age group on our books . . .' Lex's voice trailed off as suddenly a vision of a man she felt positive was just the right sort for this young woman blazed before her eyes. Her son Matt! Lex knew without a doubt that he would be bowled over by this pretty, vivacious young woman. He'd definitely want to ask her out. And, in turn, she knew the young woman would be bowled over by her tall, dark, handsome son, and that would be the perfect beginning. She had been wrong about Martin and Justine, but on the button with Derek and Mandy. All her instincts told her she was right this time too.

Orchestrating their coming together was going to be tough, though. It Matt thought he was being set up, he was capable of cutting off his nose to spite his face, turning his back on this eligible young woman just to prove a point . . . Lex had to get the pair of them together quickly as, being the attractive sorts they both were, there was a strong danger they could both very soon meet someone else and then this chance would be gone.

Then an idea struck her which she quickly decided was worth a try. She realised the young woman was saying something to her and gave herself a mental shake. 'I'm sorry?'

'I was asking you if there was any reason why you're looking at me in that funny way?'

'Oh . . . I am sorry, I was miles away. It's just I remembered something important I had to do, and was making a mental note of it. Where was I? Oh, yes, I was saying that we don't have anyone around your age on our books at the moment, but there's nothing to say the perfect man for you won't walk through that door the moment you leave here. Why don't I make an appointment for you at a more convenient time? You don't have to decide whether to take up our service or not until you're happy with the way we operate.'

The mention of an appointment reminded the young woman of the one she had on the floor below, for which she was now in danger of being late. Flashing an urgent look at her wristwatch, she exclaimed, 'Oh, my goodness, a minute to go! I'd better dash.'

Not before she had allowed Lex to put the first stage of her plan into operation! 'Oh, but what about making an appointment with us before you go?' she urged.

'Well, I work from eight-thirty until five-thirty, sometimes a bit later if I've something to finish, and I won't have enough time during my lunch hour as I work at the top of New Walk, a good fifteen-minutes away. Look, I really must dash. I'll telephone you to make an appointment when I can get some time off.'

But Lex wasn't wearing that. She wanted a firm commitment from this young woman before she left, for fear she would change her mind for some reason and then she and Matt would more than likely never meet each other. Coaxingly she said, 'What about tonight? I'm willing to stay behind for you. How about six o'clock?' She could see the young woman was hesitating and added,

'It would be a shame for you to miss out on meeting the man of your dreams just because you hadn't registered with us.'

To Lex's delight her parting shot made up the girl's mind for her. 'Okay, I'll be here.'

With that, she turned and rushed out.

'Oh, what's your name?' Lex called after her.

But in her rush to make her appointment she was already halfway down the stairs so the question was lost on her.

Lex then immediately picked up the telephone and dialled a number. It rang several times before a manly voice at the other end announced, 'Reader's Machine Maintenance and Morton Brothers Domestic Appliance Engineers, what can I do for you?'

It was Martin and she was most impressed by his telephone manner. 'Oh, Martin, what a wonderful telephone voice you have.'

There was a pause. 'Who's that?' Then he twigged. 'That you, Mam?'

'Yes, dear. Is your brother there, please?'

'He's eating his sandwiches.' There was a hint of worry in Martin's tone when he asked, 'Is anything the matter?'

'No, I'd just like a word with your brother. Can you put him on, please?'

'What do you want to speak to him about? Won't I do?'

Lex snapped, 'Martin, can you please ask your brother to come to the telephone?'

'All right, Mam, keep your hair on.' Lex then heard him shout, 'Matt, Mam wants a word.'

And Matt's shouted response, 'With me?'

'Well, if it was with me, I wouldn't be passing her to you, would I?'

'Oh. Well, what about?'

'Dunno, she won't say. I reckon you're in hot water for some reason, broth.'

Lex heard the sound of the telephone being put down on the desk, then two sets of footsteps coming and going across the work-shop floor, then the telephone being picked up and a wary Matt saying, 'What's up, Mam?'

251

'Nothing, dear. Would you come to the bureau at a quarter to six tonight and give me a lift home in your van, please? I need to get home sharpish as I've things to do.'

'Yeah, 'course. Either me or Martin will, depending what work comes in.' There was a pause for a moment before he added, 'But you could have asked Martin that instead of fetching me to the phone.'

'Well, I didn't because I'd like you to do it.'

Quizzically he asked, 'Why me? What does it matter which of us picks you up so long as one of us does?'

In her desperation to get her youngest son to the bureau at the same time as the young woman she wished him to meet, she hadn't prepared her answers to any questions he might ask. Lex's mind whirled, seeking a plausible explanation for why she wanted it to be him and not his brother. Then, to her relief, Matt himself came up with his own explanation.

'Ah, it's 'cos I'm a better driver than Martin and you feel safer with me, isn't it, Mam?'

Gil had taught both his sons to drive when they reached the age of seventeen; they had pestered him to do so. A careful and considerate driver himself, he had instilled in them the fact that anything with an engine in it was potentially a lethal weapon. Until he had been completely satisfied his sons had fully taken this on board, he wouldn't let them even sit in the driver's seat, let alone turn on the engine. Consequently Lex had never hesitated to get in a car with either of her sons behind the wheel.

'Please don't tell your brother,' she hissed, mentally asking forgiveness. 'I'll be waiting for you in the office at five-forty-five sharp.' Before he could ask why she was expecting him to climb up three flights of stairs to tell her he'd arrived, she put down the telephone.

Christine noticed the tension within her employee as soon as she returned from lunch. Hanging up her coat, she asked, 'Is everything all right with you, Mrs Morton? Nothing's happened while I've been out, has it?'

What mother wouldn't be anxious when she was positive she

was about to introduce her beloved son to a woman who could turn out to be the love of his life, and was very much the type of woman she would be happy to have as a future daughter-in-law? 'I'm fine thank you,' Lex said through gritted teeth. 'Nothing out of the ordinary happened while you were out. Oh, except that a young woman came in mistakenly, thinking we were the dentist on the floor below. The upshot is that she's keen to come and discuss registering with us. It's impossible for her to come during our normal hours so I've arranged for her to come at six tonight.'

Christine looked impressed. 'I really found a gem in you, didn't I? Very few employees would elect to continue working after hours in the hope of securing more business for their employer. Well, I shall stay behind too. I'll telephone my mother and say I have to work late and she should keep my dinner hot.'

Lex felt a certain amount of guilt for allowing her boss to believe this when in fact she was hoping that the young woman would not need to pay over good money to the bureau once Matt had been introduced. And if Christine stayed behind, Lex's plan wouldn't work. 'It's pointless us both staying, Mrs Landers. I'm happy to interview the young woman and lock up afterwards.'

Christine was putting her handbag away in her desk drawer. 'Mmm, I suppose it is silly for us both to stay behind. Well, if you're sure you're happy to handle it this time, then should the situation arise again, I'll do the honours.'

Lex felt elated. Her plan was going swimmingly so far and she had no reason to believe the rest of it wouldn't.

They were just settling down to match clients before their appointment was due in when Peter Reynolds arrived, armed with a large bouquet of flowers.

Standing before the desk, he held them out to Christine, saying, 'These are a thank you for what you are doing for me.'

It was obvious she had never received flowers from a man before. She looked very uncomfortable as she accepted them, saying stiltedly, 'There really was no need, we're only doing what you're paying us to. But they are lovely, thank you.'

Lex inwardly smiled. She knew that Peter had made this gesture by way of showing Christine he was a thoughtful man. In the most unpromising circumstances, he was trying his best to woo her.

He smiled, gratified. 'I'm glad you like them. Anyway . . . I was just wondering if you'd found anyone you think would like to meet me yet?'

She flashed a look at Lex. Christine had in fact suggested several women as possible matches for him but Lex had picked fault with each of them, not wanting to build up their hopes in respect of Peter when she was very aware that he had his heart set on only one woman connected with the bureau.

'No, I'm afraid we haven't,' Lex told him. 'We did say we would write to you when we had.'

'Oh, yes, you did, I'd forgotten that.' He looked downcast. 'I suppose it was presumptuous of me, but in anticipation that you might have done I bought tickets to see a one-night performance of *Blithe Spirit* at the De Montfort Hall this evening. I suppose I shall just have to go on my own . . .'

Christine sat looking at him while Lex held her breath. Christine had told her only yesterday that she was very disappointed to be missing that production as no member of her family had been free to go with her, and she didn't welcome the thought of going by herself. Seeing how disappointed she was, Lex was on the verge of offering to go herself, but then had recognised this golden opportunity to get Christine to agree to go out with Peter. Then, hopefully, she'd begin to realise there *was* a man who desired her and was worthy of consideration.

So a while later, when Christine had been busy interviewing a client, Lex had telephoned Peter's lodgings and left a message with his landlady, asking him to telephone her back at a certain time so they could talk tactics in private. Should Christine ever discover the part her employee had played in this play being acted out before her, Lex doubted she'd still have a job. But no matter how much she loved it, she was willing to jeopardise working here to bring Christine the chance of happiness that was so nearly within her grasp.

'Would you like the tickets for you and your husband, as my gift?' Peter asked Lex.

Looking as though this offer of his was a great surprise to her, she said, 'I'm much obliged to you but we already have plans for tonight.'

Then he looked at Christine. 'What about yourself and your husband, Mrs Landers?'

She looked uncomfortable. 'He's ... er ... away working at the moment.'

Peter looked thoughtful. 'I don't suppose Mr Landers would like it very much if you accompanied me to see the play in his absence, would he?' Then, quickly, before she could agree, 'But if he wouldn't, I'd be most honoured to take you, Mrs Landers.'

Christine looked shocked at that. He really did seem genuine, made it sound like a privilege to have her agree to accompany him. And she definitely would like to see the play. There was no telling when a production of *Blithe Spirit* would visit the city again. 'Well, if you're sure you don't mind my coming with you, then I'd very much like to take you up on your offer, Mr Reynolds.'

How Lex stopped herself from crying out 'Eureka!' was a mystery to her. How Peter stopped himself too was all credit to him. Neither of them had dared hope that Lex's plan would work so smoothly and achieve the longed for result.

Evenly Peter suggested to Christine, 'Shall I meet you in the foyer at seven, then we could have a drink in the bar before we take our seats?'

She nodded. 'That would be most agreeable.'

With that he made his departure.

Lex felt it best she didn't make any comment on Christine's arrangement for fear it could result in her getting cold feet. She had never been out with a man before, after all, and had only agreed this time as she was under the illusion that it wasn't in fact a date. Setting her up a second time might prove to be beyond even Lex's talents.

Thankfully she was saved from saying anything by the shrilling of the telephone.

255

Picking it up, she wasn't even allowed to answer before the wailing voice at the other end launched into a verbal assault. She had to wait until the caller had had her say before she could respond with, 'Well, I'm disappointed to hear that from you. Be assured, though, Mrs Landers and I will do our best to find you another suitable introduction as soon as we can.' Replacing the handset in its cradle, she said to Christine, 'Seems Sebastian Evans has broken another of our female clients' hearts. He made it clear to Vera Clayton at the end of their evening last night that he wouldn't be pursuing a relationship with her.'

Christine had just returned with the cleaner's galvanised bucket, half filled with cold water. It was obvious her mind was on other matters by her response. 'It was actually very kind of Mr Reynolds to bring these flowers in for us, wasn't it? I shall bring in a vase from home tomorrow so we can display them properly on the coffee table for the clients to enjoy as well as us.'

It was the first favourable comment she had made about Peter and Lex hoped this was a promising sign.

Usually the time she spent at the bureau sped by but today, because she was desperate for closing time to arrive, it seemed to crawl. Finally the hands of the wall clock moved to announce it was five-thirty and Lex immediately said to Christine, 'If you want to get off to ready yourself for tonight . . .' she was very careful not to make any reference to Peter Reynolds, not wanting to scare her boss off '. . . I can finish stamping the letters then run them over to the Post Office and be back well before my appointment at six.'

Christine smiled gratefully at her. 'I'd appreciate that as getting home, ready, then back to town for seven would be cutting it fine unless I catch the bus now.'

As soon as her boss had departed, Lex hurriedly stuck the rest of the stamps on the remaining envelopes and piled them all together, then rushed over to grab her coat off the stand. She put it on, then went back to the desk to retrieve her handbag from the drawer. Then she stood and waited for her son to arrive. When a quarter to six arrived and he hadn't, she impatiently drummed her fingers on the desk, muttering to herself, 'Come on, Matt, if you don't arrive before that young woman does, my plan isn't going to work.'

Thankfully seconds later the door opened and he walked in, grinning cheekily at her. 'Your carriage awaits, Madam.'

'Well, I appreciate that, but it'll have to wait a few minutes more as I have to run over to the Post Office with some urgent letters. Mrs Landers was in a rush to get off sharp tonight herself so she couldn't do it.' Lex rushed past him and out of the door. It was only when she was about to descend the stairs that she turned to look back at him through the open door and put on a horror-stricken expression.

'Oh, my goodness, I completely forgot. There's a prospective client coming in shortly who couldn't make it during our normal working hours. Please don't tell her I forgot about her, but give her my apologies for keeping her waiting and do your best to entertain her until I get back, please. I shan't expect you to wait for me while I interview her, dear. As soon as I return you can go home yourself. I'll catch the bus, and you'd better explain to your father why I've been delayed so he doesn't worry.'

She knew he would offer to go to the Post Office for her next, so in order not to give him the chance she rushed off down the stairs.

Arriving breathlessly on the pavement in the street below, she immediately headed in the opposite direction from that she knew the young woman would arrive, then circled around via back streets to get to Bishop Street where the Post Office was located. It was only when she made to drop the letters into the last post bag that she realised in her haste to leave the bureau she had left them behind on the desk! Thankfully none of the letters to clients contained critical information, and the remaining ones to suppliers only contained payments for bills, so it wouldn't matter if none were received tomorrow morning. Hopefully her son would only have eyes for the young client now and would not notice she hadn't taken them with her.

Lex slowly made her way back to the bureau, making sure that at least twenty minutes had elapsed, plenty of time she felt for

Matt and the girl to strike up a conversation, decide they both liked what they saw, and make arrangements to go out together.

She was so convinced there would be an immediate physical attraction between the couple, another setback didn't enter her head.

Back on the top landing – not breathless as she had made her way up slowly to kill time – Lex paused for a moment to ready herself for her next performance. Taking several deep breaths, she grabbed hold of the doorknob, turned it and burst inside, exclaiming, 'I'm so sorry to have kept you waiting only there was such a dreadful queue . . . Oh!' she exclaimed as it suddenly struck her that Matt, perched on the edge of the desk staring over at her, was the only occupant of the room. 'Where's the young woman I had an appointment with?'

'Oh, I'm not sure whether I was supposed to or not but the telephone rang while you were out. I picked it up and it was her, saying she'd changed her mind about registering with the bureau. She sent her apologies.'

A surge of acute disappointment flooded through Lex then. Her effort to introduce her son to the perfect young woman had been a total waste of time. All she could hope was that fate would somehow bring them together a second time.

Matt got to his feet then and came across to her. 'Haven't you forgotten something?'

Lex looked at him bemused. 'Such as what?'

He flashed a look at the pile of post back on the desk. 'The letters you said you'd posted at the Post Office?'

Lex looked across at them wide-eyed. He was more observant than she'd given him credit for. 'Oh, er . . . they're all for tomorrow's post,' she said dismissively, then urged him, 'Come on.'

As she headed towards the door she missed the look of amusement on her son's face.

CHAPTER EIGHTEEN

Thelma gave a broad smile of welcome when she saw who her next customer was. 'Morning, Mrs Watson. How are yer?'

Phyllis was rubbing gloved hands together. 'Glad to be out of the bitter cold for a few minutes at least, Mrs Reader. I reckon we could be in for snow this Christmas.'

Thelma pulled a grim expression. 'I hope not. Me and snow don't get on. Only one flake has to fall, and you can bet your life it falls at my feet and I slip on it. I can't believe it's only a week to Christmas. It seems only five minutes ago that it was this time last year and I was having the same worry I'm having now – that I wouldn't have everything done in time.'

Phyllis smiled her agreement. 'But somehow we always manage, don't we? Got all the family coming, have you?'

Thelma nodded. 'I was hoping that one of my married sons would have us all for a change, but it seems that hope was in vain as it's been taken for granted I'll be doing the honours as usual. Mind you, me eldest lad's wife is five months pregnant with my first grandbaby, so it's unfair of me expecting her to have us all, but me youngest son's other half could have offered.' She gave a wistful sigh. 'It would have been nice for just one year actually to enjoy the day, instead of being too tired. I haven't made me pudding yet or iced me cake.'

Phyllis looked at her sympathetically. 'Well, it'll be an extra strain on you this year to get everything done, being's you're working full-time. I know you told me you were only doing the extra hours until you'd got enough money to have a bathroom

259

installed, but no disrespect to you, lovey, you aren't getting any younger, are you?'

Thelma didn't need reminding of that. Working full-time was taking its toll on her, even though she'd been doing it for only three weeks. She had absolutely no regrets about helping her friends this way but hadn't realised what a difference an extra four hours a day standing behind a counter would make to her, even with her two daughters doing extra chores at home. All she wanted to do when she got home of an evening was collapse in the armchair, but she couldn't as she'd dinner to see to and whatever outstanding jobs she couldn't expect her daughters to tackle without giving up their social life, and she didn't want that. The time couldn't come quick enough when she could return to part-time hours, but the trouble was it was taking much longer for new work to start coming in than Des had hoped.

'The tin bath in front of the fire has served you all your life, so is a bathroom that important to you you're risking your health to get one?' Phyllis was asking.

Thelma was feeling guilty enough already about lying to people over her reason for upping her working hours so said dismissively, 'I'll give it some thought.' Then asked. 'Usual farmhouse uncut?'

Phyllis scanned her eyes across the trays of cakes behind the long glass showcase on the counter top. 'And I'll have a Chelsea bun to have with my afternoon tea.'

As she collected the loaf of bread from a shelf behind her, putting them in a paper bag, Thelma quipped, 'Splashing out a bit, aren't you, on a cake? Something to celebrate?'

Phyllis' eyes lit up excitedly. 'Actually, I have, Mrs Reader. My Derek announced last night he's getting engaged on Christmas Eve.'

Thelma was stunned to hear this. 'Well, I never. I bet you felt like dancing on the roof tops? I know you'd practically given up hope of seeing your lad settled before the Grim Reaper came to claim you. It's a bit sudden, though, isn't it? The last time we had elevenses with Lex, a couple of months ago, I remember asking you if your lad had got himself a lady friend yet and you said he hadn't.'

'He hadn't then. He met Amanda roughly two months ago. They haven't been seeing each other that long, admittedly, but long enough for my Derek to know he wants to spend the rest of his life with her, and she feels the same as him. If ever I saw a couple who were right for each other it's that pair, Mrs Reader. Mandy's such a lovely girl, just the sort I always hoped my son'd find himself. Me and her get on famously, and all the rest of the family like her too. We're having a bit of a do for them. Nothing fancy, sandwiches and sausage rolls and a few bottles of drink. They plan to get married next year and we'd sooner put what money we can into giving them both a good send off as, bless her, she's no family herself. But you and your husband are more than welcome to pop in to toast the happy couple.'

Then a sad expression clouded Phyllis' face. 'Only blight on the proceedings is that Alexandra won't be there, as I know she won't come without Mr Morton and I can't see things changing in that quarter before the engagement party, not unless a miracle happens.' She gave a heavy sigh. 'Alexandra really is responsible for my Derek and Amanda being introduced to each other, you know. If, the poor dear hadn't been suffering dreadfully with a bad back at the time they would never have met. The two lovebirds really do feel they owe her a huge debt of gratitude and I know they'd like to propose a special toast to her on the night, but they can't do that if she ain't there, can they?

'Alexandra has been so good to me over the years, and especially recently when I was incapacitated after my tumble, I can't think of a better way to repay her kindness than by coming up with a way to get Mr Morton to start mixing socially again. But despite racking my brains, I just can't seem to.'

'Apart from bodily dragging Gil out, kicking and screaming, blowed if I can either, Mrs Watson.'

'Well, I've nothing but admiration for the way Alexandra is coping with this. It's hard on all the family but it must be especially so for her. I'm not much for going out gallivanting these days, but to have no social life at all ... even down to my female friends being at liberty to call around for a cuppa and a natter when the mood took them ... well, it's no life for her, is it?' She eyed Thelma knowingly. 'This must have affected you too, Mrs Reader, as you two couples did so much together on the social front, didn't you?'

Sighing, Thelma nodded. 'We did, and I miss it all very much. Christmas Day we only had a quick pop in at each other's to toast the day because we each had our family to entertain, but I'm dreading Boxing Day as we always spent it together, alternate years at each other's house, having a cold buffet from the Christmas Day leftovers, downing what booze was left over while playing cards.' Tears glinted in her eyes then and she added, 'I just can't bear the thought that our Boxing Day get-together will never happen again. All the other things we did together too.' She realised she was on the verge of tears, gave herself a mental shake and handed over the shopping to Phyllis. 'That's two shillings and threepence, love,' she told her, holding out her hand.

Taking the bag, which she put into her shopping bag, Phyllis handed Thelma half a crown. 'I suppose things could be a whole lot worse than they are for the Mortons.'

Thelma looked at her in surprise. 'And just how exactly could matters be worse for them?' she demanded, selecting the correct keys on the till and pressing down hard on them.

'Well, just imagine how much of a struggle they'd be having financially if Mr Reader wasn't putting himself out to take the machines to Mr Morton so he could work at home.'

Handing Phyllis her change, Thelma said, 'Well, it was the least my Des could do after all Gil's done for him in the past. Besides, he really didn't want to lose Gil so he was happy to do whatever it took to keep him working.' Thelma frowned then, puzzled by the frozen way Phyllis was staring at her. 'What on earth is the matter, Mrs Watson? Oh, dear God, you haven't just realised you turned on the gas oven before you left and forgot to light it, have you?'

'Eh! No, I cook with electric.' Then a look of pure triumph

flooded Phyllis' face as she proclaimed, 'I think I've got it!'

Screwing her face up, Thelma asked, 'Got what exactly?'

'A way to get Mr Morton back into the outside world again. I've no idea if it'll work but . . .'

'Anything's worth a try,' Thelma finished for her. 'Come on, I'm all ears. Spill the beans.'

Completely ignoring the fact that a queue of customers had built up behind Phyllis, all anxious to be served, Thelma bent her head over the counter to listen intently to what she had in mind.

Over in the bureau, sighing heavily, Lex replaced the telephone receiver and shook her head in disbelief. Christine, a pile of client details in her hand, pulled a chair over to one side of Lex and sat down, proceeding to separate the male clients' records from the female ones.

'I can't believe the nerve of some people, Mrs Landers. That was a prospective client on the telephone. He seemed happy enough when I told him how we worked, but then told me there was a condition to his registering, and that was that he personally should interview all the women we decided fitted his requirements in this office before agreeing to take them on an evening out. He said he wasn't going to waste his precious time or good money on those we were wrong about.'

Christine looked far from amused to be hearing this. 'That's telling us he doesn't trust us to do our job. It's like having all your work checked by the supervisor when you're an office junior. Just who does the man think he is? Huh, I hope you told him we wouldn't even consider his proposal. Damned cheek.'

'I was halfway through doing so when he put the telephone down on me. I don't think we'll hear from him again.'

'Well, let's forget about him and concentrate instead on clients who do have faith in our abilities. The clients who are already paired up apart, I was thinking it would be nice if all of them had a companion for Christmas Eve. What I'm proposing is that we do our best to match up all the still unattached clients for that evening. We're not looking for perfect matches, but just so that they at least stand a chance of enjoying an evening in someone's company. Of course, some of our more reserved clients might not want to get involved, but I'm sure all the more adventurous types will. Maybe we should suggest to the female clients that in these circumstances they should offer to go Dutch with the men, just this once?'

A beam of delight was already lighting Lex's face. 'Oh, Mrs Landers, I think your idea is wonderful! I can't see many of our unattached clients turning down the chance of a date on Christmas Eve. I mean, otherwise they'd more than likely be spending it on their own or like a gooseberry among their attached families and friends.'

A wistful expression crossed Christine's face then and Lex could have kicked herself for not thinking before she spoke. She knew she had just described Christine's own situation over the Christmas period. But it needn't be so; if Christine would only allow herself to see what one person at least was trying to offer her, she need never be alone again, at the festive season or any other time.

After her evening at the theatre three weeks ago, Christine had come into work the next morning enthusing over the play. The only comment she'd made about Peter was that she had found him to be a very attentive escort, and had no doubt that the women they selected for him would too.

Since that night, by clever manipulation on both Lex's and Peter's part, they had managed to persuade Christine to accompany him on another five occasions, twice for a meal at different venues, to the museum, the cinema, and an art exhibition at a local gallery, all under the pretence that she was doing him a great favour by helping him acquaint himself with the city so as to prove a good escort for any potential partners the bureau found for him in future. Each time her boss had told Lex how much she had enjoyed her evening, and reiterated that in her opinion Peter would make some fortunate woman a more than satisfactory partner.

How to stop her from allowing past humiliation to blind her to the fact that Peter Reynolds was not in the least interested in being introduced to any other women but only had eyes for her, in fact? After six failed attempts, Lex was at a loss as to what to suggest to him next.

Half an hour later twelve couples had been matched. They seemed to have sufficient common interests and personality traits to hopefully afford them an enjoyable evening out together. Both Christine and Lex were confident of doing the same for at least half of the remaining eighty or so people on their books. They just hoped that the clients themselves would want to participate, so that all this hard work on their behalf was not in vain.

The next client whose details they inspected was Sebastian Evans.

Lex picked it up and said to Christine, 'I apologise, I must have filed this in the wrong place when I put it away. It should have gone in the "pending the outcome" not the "to be matched up" tray.'

Christine said, 'Just an oversight. It isn't as if we've had much time lately to file at our leisure, not since business started to boom. Not that I'm complaining, far from it. The more clients we have on our books, the more chance we have of finding each of them a suitable partner. Mr Evans is meeting Miss Robotham for the second time tomorrow night, isn't he? I wonder if it will go the same way as with the other two we've introduced him to or be third time lucky, so to speak? He did seem to be keen on seeing her again when he telephoned us yesterday after their first date, but then he seemed the same way after a first meeting with the other two, didn't he? I must admit I admire a man who takes his time getting to know a woman before he decides whether she has what it takes. Unlike some of our male clients, who instantly decide a woman isn't for them because of the colour of the shoes she's wearing or the way she holds her knife and fork! If it does turn out Miss Robotham isn't for Mr Evans and he's back on the market again, then because of his open-mindedness he'll be easy enough for us to fix up on Christmas Eve.'

'It could turn out to be Miss Robotham who decides Mr Evans is not for her,' Lex reminded her boss.

'Well, yes, of course, that could very well be the case, but judging by her exuberance on the telephone this morning when she called to update us I think not – I could practically see her jumping for joy while she was informing me that he had asked to take her to dinner on Thursday, so she's obviously very taken with him. He'd have to do something really off-putting to change her mind. I do hope we don't receive the sort of tearful telephone call from her we did from the other two.'

'So do I,' agreed Lex. 'The trouble with the majority of women, though ... and they can deny it as much as they like ... is that as soon as they meet a man they're physically attracted to, in their mind's eye they're steam-rollering ahead, planning the wedding and where they're going to live, how many children they're going to have and what they'll be called, and don't even stop to consider that the man himself might not see *them* as marriage material.' She put Sebastian Evans' details to one side to place in the pending tray later while Christine started to pick up the next client's details off the pile, but was stopped short by the outer door unexpectedly bursting open. A thrilled-looking Marie Noble came charging in to stand before the desk, excitedly exclaiming, 'Please forgive me for disturbing you but I just had to show you this!' She thrust out her left hand at them. On the third finger was a solitaire diamond ring.

They both stared at it dumbstruck for several moments before Christine exclaimed, 'You're engaged!'

Grinning from ear to ear, Marie nodded. 'Melvin proposed last night. Oh, it was so romantic! In the middle of the restaurant he suddenly got down on bended knee. Of course, I said yes. From the moment I met him, I knew he was the one for me. I've already planned where we we'll hold our wedding, what style of dress I'll wear, and where I'd like us to live ... near my parents so Mother can help with the babies when they come along, naturally. Natalie is such a lovely name for a little girl, don't you think?'

Lex looked at Christine as if to say, I told you so.

Marie was continuing, 'I love him so much, I don't care a jot that he doesn't drive. You have to realise how unimportant some things are in the big scheme of things, don't you? Melvin admitted to me that he used to hate the sight of red hair, but he says he loves mine. Anyway, the manager gave us a complimentary bottle of Champagne. Wasn't that nice of him? I haven't told my family yet as Melvin and I wanted you both to be the first to know . . . well, apart from all the people in the restaurant that is. Without you we wouldn't have met, would we? We're getting married next summer. You will both come, won't you?'

'We'd be delighted,' they said in unison.

'You know, I nearly said no to meeting Melvin when you suggested it to me. I was still so devastated that Mr Evans hadn't wanted to take matters further with me, but I'm so glad I let you persuade me.'

'And, of course, you were upset about the break-in at your flat too,' Christine reminded her.

'Oh, yes, it was dreadful coming home to discover that on top of everything else that had gone wrong for me that night.'

'Did the police ever find out who the culprit was?' Lex asked.

Marie shook her head. 'Well, they had nothing to go on, had they? No witnesses, and besides nothing was taken. Anyway, must dash as I don't want to keep Mel . . . oh, he's my fiancé now, isn't he? Mustn't keep my fiancé waiting.'

Christine said to Lex after their visitor had departed, 'Well, I never commented at the time as to be honest I thought you were exaggerating, but women really *do* start to make plans as soon as they meet a man they judge to be right for them – without the man having a say in it!' She eyed Lex, intrigued. 'If you don't mind my asking, did you when you first met Mr Morton?'

Lex laughed. 'Actually, I did.'

'Well, as it turns out, your planning wasn't in vain. Oh, but isn't it just the most wonderful feeling to know you're responsible for bringing happiness to two people who might never have met if not for you?'

Lex nodded. 'Very satisfying.'

'Right, well, let's see if we can bring happiness to a few more couples,' Christine said, picking up the next form from the pile. It was Duncan Holgate's.

Seeing whose details they were, Lex said, 'Well, you know my feelings on this one, Mrs Landers.'

Christine folded her arms and leaned back in her chair. 'I know you feel very strongly about introducing those two to each other, and it's the only time I've pulled rank on you and stopped you from organising it because for the life of me I just can't see them getting past the shaking hands stage, let alone spending a pleasant evening together. At least the ones we've matched up for Christmas Eve so far have a certain amount in common, but these two have hardly anything, and there's nothing about the physical appearance each has stipulated that they'd recognise. Mr Holgate informed us he likes his women slim, and Gemma Stone is most definitely what I would call curvy. Plump, actually. And she's got blonde hair when according to his details he prefers brunettes. She favours quiet intimate nights at home. He likes evenings out with lots of other friends. I could go on.'

'But they do have some common ground, Mrs Landers. They've both been terribly hurt by their ex-spouses. I'm in no doubt that the reason neither of them has formed a relationship through the introductions we have arranged so far is because they can't bring themselves to trust anyone, no matter how much they like them. It was only through being forced into it by friends that we have them both as clients after all, they didn't come to us voluntarily. To stand a chance of ever having a successful relationship in the future, both of them need to learn to trust again. And who better to help them do that than someone who has suffered the same ordeal as they have, understands what they're going through, and fears ending up in the same situation again, just like they do?'

Christine was looking at her thoughtfully. 'Mmm, I do see what you're getting at.'

Lex was very relieved that after all the attempts she had made to coax her boss into her way of thinking over these two particular clients, at long last she just might have.

'So you'll agree to us introducing them to each other on Christmas Eve?'

Sighing in resignation, she nodded. 'You win, Mrs Morton.'

'I'll arrange it,' said Lex, smiling at her as she added, 'I know I'm putting myself on the line by telling you this and could end up with egg on my face, but I have a very strong feeling that Christmas Eve is the beginning of a beautiful relationship between Mr Holgate and Miss Stone.'

'Well, we're in the business of helping people, so I hope you're right. Now, let's get on, shall we? I'd like to have got at least halfway through this task before our next appointment is due in.' Christine picked up the next of the client details from the male pile. They were for Peter Reynolds. She studied them for a moment before saying to Lex, 'Have you anyone in mind for Mr Reynolds that night?'

The tone of her voice made Lex look at her questioningly. 'You say that like I won't approve of anyone you might suggest?'

'Well, you haven't in the past, Mrs Morton. Every time I put someone forward for consideration, you seem to find fault with her. Some very pretty women too, in my opinion.'

'Well, yes, that's true. But then Mr Reynolds made it very clear to us on registering just what type of woman he sees himself with. I can't speak for him, of course, but I'm sure he's of the same mind as me – that it wouldn't be fair to get anyone's hopes up when we know they're a non-starter from the onset.'

'You have a point, I suppose. I'm surprised Mr Reynolds is so pernickety in his requirements, though. Having spent time in his company myself, he comes across as a very easy-going man. In my haste not to be late to meet him at the theatre, I'm ashamed to admit to you that I'd put on odd shoes. When Mr Reynolds noticed he laughed and told me not to worry, the most important thing to him was that I'd arrived safely. A pernickety man would have been mortified I'd turned up like that, embarrassed by what others might think of his sloppily dressed companion, but he wasn't bothered in the slightest. He's a very contradictory man, isn't he?' She paused just long enough to draw breath. 'We haven't anyone on our books at the moment who fulfils his exacting standards so do you think in that case there's any point in trying to fix up Mr Reynolds . . .'

'Fix Mr Reynolds up with what?' a male voice cut her short.

They both jerked their heads up to see the man in question looking expectantly at them from the doorway.

'A lady to take out on Christmas Eve,' Lex answered his question as he shut the door and came over to them. Smiling up at him, she continued, 'We're pairing up couples as best we can for Christmas Eve so that at least those who aren't attached at the moment aren't entirely on their own over the festive period.'

'What a wonderful idea,' he enthused. 'Have you anyone in mind for me?'

Christine responded matter-of-factly, 'To be blunt, Mr Reynolds, your requirements in a woman are so precise, with no room for discretion whatsoever, that I'm beginning to wonder if we'll ever find anyone who'll fulfil your needs in this bureau.'

He looked hard at her for a moment, seeming to be deliberating something, before he took a very deep breath and announced, 'You're wrong. There is a lady who fulfils every requirement I've ever wished for in a woman, and who is very much connected with this bureau.'

Christine looked bewildered. 'I don't understand? As far as I'm aware we haven't introduced to you any of our female clients yet.' She looked questioningly at Lex, sitting beside her. 'Unless you've arranged an introduction for Mr Reynolds and haven't informed me, Mrs Morton?'

Lex shook her head. 'You have my word that no such meeting has taken place.' Come on, Mr Reynolds, she silently urged him.

Christine returned her attention to Peter. 'I trust Mrs Morton implicitly so you must be lying to us, Mr Reynolds.'

He responded resolutely, 'I can assure you, I'm not.'

'Well, in that case, prove to us you're not by divulging just who this woman is?'

With a tender smile he placed his hands flat on the desk and, much to Christine's surprise, leaned forward so his face was within inches of hers as he said softly, 'You.'

She stared back at him thunderstruck. Then angry colour glowed in her cheeks and she snapped, 'You're mocking me, Mr Reynolds. Out of all the women a man like you could land yourself, you expect me to believe you've fallen for someone like *me*?'

Looking stunned, he righted himself and said, 'Someone like you? What's that supposed to mean?'

Christine was fighting back tears. 'I've no illusions about myself, Mr Reynolds. I know I haven't the sort of looks to attract men to me.'

He looked aghast at that. 'Well, let me tell you, dear lady, you're wrong. Your looks certainly have attracted me. In fact, I find you beautiful. The first time I clapped eyes on you something happened to me that I'd never experienced before. It was like a million fireworks going off inside my head. I felt this irresistible impulse drawing me to you. It took me all my strength of will not to embarrass myself by scooping you up in my arms and running off with you.

'Walking away from you that first day, and every time I've been in your company since, has been like leaving part of myself behind. I think of you every minute of the day and my dreams are filled with you when I'm asleep. I know this must be coming as a shock to you, but every word I speak is true. That you'll return my feelings I can't expect, but would you at least agree to spend time with me, see if there's a chance you could eventually?' He paused just long enough for a pleading note to come into his voice. 'Please, will you?'

Lex felt uncomfortable to be a third party to such an intimate scene, but at the same time she couldn't bring herself to leave. Twisting her hands together in her lap, she was willing Christine to accept Peter's proposal; for the first time in her life to experience what it felt like to be loved and wanted by a man for just who she was.

Christine herself was staring wide-eyed at Peter. Alone of a night, in the privacy of her own bed, she had often tried to imagine what it must be like to be the centre of a man's whole world, to be wanted so badly by him that his life felt meaningless without her. She'd always believed that this could never happen for her because Mother Nature had bestowed all the good looks on the rest of the family and had none left for Christine. But now, here she was, being told just what she had tried to imagine, and all she could feel was numb with the shock of it.

She felt a pressure on her hand and, dragging her eyes away from Peter, looked down to realise Lex was holding it. She slowly raised her head to meet her assistant's eyes and hear her implore, 'Don't deny yourself this chance of happiness because of hurtful experiences in the past. Mrs Landers, please, believe what Mr Reynolds is saying. Please give him a chance to prove himself to you. I know without a doubt that he's genuine.'

Christine shifted her gaze back to Peter's eyes. She had seen enough romantic films at the cinema to know when a man was looking passionately at a woman, and Peter's eyes definitely held passion for her, but there was also warmth and sincerity there, too, and she knew he was being honest with her. Incredibly, he really did find her beautiful. He deserved the chance to prove himself to her.

Taking a deep breath, she said softly, 'All right.'

Lex fought a great urge to leap up from her chair and dance around the room in joy, but she thought it better to withdraw discreetly, leaving them alone to start planning what she believed would be the rest of their lives together.

CHAPTER NINETEEN

Over in the Mortons' back yard, Gil emerged from the outhouse, looking skyward at the thick grey blanket of cloud while stretching his aching back. He hoped it was rain those clouds were laden with and not snow, which it certainly felt cold enough to be. A fall of snow, though, would only serve to add to Des's burden in bringing the machines round to him and collecting them when they were done.

This arrangement, though, as unconventional as it was, had proved successful for them both. Gil himself was managing to get through as much work as he would have in the workshop, if not more with no one to distract him. No Des constantly interrupting to ask his opinion on work-related matters or with friendly chit-chat; no having to break off to answer the telephone when everyone else was out; no listening to his sons' banter when they were on the premises or giving them advice when they came to him for it. No neighbours to either side ... the Huberts were still holidaying with their son down in Brighton and the Higgins having moved out of the area. As yet no one new had moved in to that side.

Working from his outhouse did have its drawbacks though. The space he had managed to cleared to work in was tight, and the fumes from his paraffin heater became overpowering with the door shut, so periodically he had to open it to allow fresh air to circulate. He was doing that now, in fact, and during that time the shed quickly became icy cold and he along with it. It was difficult to work with frozen hands and so he had to wait while they thawed out. But that was something he could cope with. What he was having the most difficulty coming to terms with was his sense of isolation.

Gil had always been an outgoing person, enjoying the camaraderie of his work colleagues, social outings with his family and friends, and taking an active interest in his community. The thought that this prison-like existence could go on indefinitely did not sit well with him, but he felt he had no choice but to endure it as he wouldn't ... couldn't ... change his mind over associating with women while they believed ill of him.

But what was really tearing him apart was the thought of how this was affecting his beloved wife. Not that Lex ever complained, and not that it crossed his mind for a second that she would ever leave him over it. He wasn't merely being complacent but knew without a doubt that their love and respect for each other were far too strong for this turn in their lives, as devastating as it was, to come between them. But it was no way for Lex to be living. She'd hardly any social life now apart from an occasional visit to her friends and weekly W.I. meeting. And it wasn't fair that she was having to go out to work to supplement their income. It deeply saddened Gil to know that the once bright and prosperous future they'd had to look forward to, the many plans they'd had of things they wanted to do together before they were too old, would never now materialise.

How had it come to this? Through hard work and determination he'd worked his way through the factory from apprentice machine operator to works manager, and achieved it without any back stabbing or deceit, in order to give his beloved family the best standard of living he could. People in his community and farther afield had respected and trusted him, readily turned to him for help on matters that they couldn't deal with themselves. At any social events in the community, the Mortons had always been top of the list of invitees.

Now, through the lies of Miriam Jones, he'd lost his job, his standing in the community, and been reduced to earning a living shut away like a hermit,

He wiped his eyes on the sleeve of his grubby overalls. Since that fateful day when his life had been so unexpectedly ripped apart, he had racked his brain for a reason why Miriam Jones should have done what she had to him. But whatever it was, it still eluded him. If only he could find out then at least he might feel she'd had some justification for her actions, while as matters stood he tormented himself daily with the fact that she hadn't.

Thinking of Miriam Jones and her connection to Brenton's stirred a memory. His face puckered up in thought. His sons had told him last night at the dinner table that, according to rumour, the firm was in financial trouble. The works manager that Maurice Brenton had hired in haste to replace Gil had not worked out well. He'd not possessed Gil's managerial skills or indeed come from the engineering background he had bluffed Maurice Brenton into thinking he had in order to get the job. As a result he'd lost them the order which Gil had been about to secure before his sacking. The replacement Maurice had subsequently hired, according to the gossipmongers, could be Hitler's brother. He was a little man with an ego bigger than he was, and strutted around the factory full of his own importance, antagonising the men without even saying anything to them. When he did, his manner was unpleasantly dictatorial. The men had no respect for him, and by way of showing the factory owner their displeasure had allowed the quality of their workmanship to deteriorate dramatically, and the production rate was badly down.

Gil's old loyalty to Maurice Brenton had vanished as he had walked out of his office for the last time, knowing that when it had come down to it all the thanks and praise heaped on him over the years meant nothing measured against his boss's bank balance. Regardless, Gil still cared about the workers there and would hate to see them lose their jobs should Brenton's go under, which if matters were allowed to carry on the way they were, he feared was quite possible.

Worrying about firms going under reminded him that he had a part to play in keeping Des's from doing just that. Better get back to it.

He'd grabbed hold of the outhouse door, meaning to shut it behind him as he returned inside, when a sound reached his ears and he stopped short, frowning. It sounded like an army was marching down the entry, the sound getting louder and louder as it neared his back gate. There were voices, too, many of them. Women's voices! Then the latch of the gate clicked up, it opened, and like water pouring through floodgates, women of all ages, shapes and sizes crowded into his yard, some carrying shopping, some infants in arms. It seemed to Gil there were dozens of them, and at the head were Thelma and Phyllis.

Sheer panic raced through him. He stared at them all frozen-faced far too stunned by their sudden appearance to try and fathom what they were doing here.

It was Phyllis who enlightened him. 'We never got the chance to tell you in person that we don't believe that woman's claim against you. You've shut yourself away inside your own four walls, so we've come to tell you here.'

'Yes, and you'd better believe us an' all, Gil Morton, 'cos to do so I've walked out of work, telling me boss I'd a headache. I risk losing me job if he finds out the truth,' said Thelma. 'So have Brenda and Eunice.' She looked around at the sea of faces. 'Where are you both? Oh, there you are. Give Gil a wave.' She turned back to see him cowering against the outhouse door and wagged a warning finger at him. 'Oi, and you can stop that. You've no more to fear from us than we have from you.'

'I know you're no danger to me, Mr Morton,' a voice piped up from the crowd. 'I've known yer years and yer've never stepped outta line in my company.'

'No, me neither,' piped up someone else. 'That woman's a liar,' she proclaimed.

'Hear, hear!' several voices shouted out in unison.

Kathleen Crouch stepped forward then. With a look of shame on her face she told him, 'I'm sorry for the way I was with you that morning in the street, Mr Morton. I'd just heard a rumour, you see, from the milkman about why you'd been sacked. I was shocked to hear it because I knew you couldn't possibly be guilty of that. I told the milkman so, and that he should be ashamed of himself for spreading such lies.

'When me and our Katie came face to face with you just after . . . well, please believe that I acted like I did because I wanted to tell you I didn't believe the rumour but then I was worried you might not have heard it as yet and . . . and, well, I didn't know what to do, I was in such a dilemma. Then you turned and ran back home before I could say anything. I'm so sorry, Mr Morton, if you thought I was terrified of you because I believed that rumour. Nothing could be further from the truth.'

Phyllis looked at him hard then. 'Now, if us lot aren't enough to convince you that you've no need to be skulking behind your garden gate any longer, then me and Thelma will round up another load of supporters and get them round too. You're an intelligent man, Gilbert. I'm not going to try and tell you that everyone thinks you're Mr Whiter than White, but what I can tell you is that there's far more as do than don't. So what's it to be? Are you going to stop this nonsense or do we keep having to pay you visits like this until you do?'

He stared back at her blankly, unable to comprehend that all these women had dropped everything in order to prove a point to him.

'Gil, do you really want to go on living like you are?' Thelma beseeched him.

He stared at her for a moment then slowly shook his head.

'Well then, that's settled,' said Phyllis, mortally relieved that her plan had worked. 'I'm holding a party on Christmas Eve to celebrate my Derek's engagement. I'll be expecting you to come, along with your dear wife, to toast the happy couple.'

'Your Derek's getting himself engaged, Phyllis? Well, I never knew that,' said a woman at the back of her.

While Phyllis was being congratulated by everyone, Thelma went across to Gil and put her hand on his arm. 'There's no time like the present to start getting yourself out and about, lovey. I'd be delighted if you and Lex would come and have a bit of dinner with me and my Des tonight. It'll only be a scratch affair – I don't

277

know whether he's told you or not but I'm working full-time until I get enough money together to have a bathroom installed, and I don't get home meself 'til just before six. Well, we've abused the Mortons' good nature for long enough with you letting us use yours sometimes, and don't think we ain't grateful 'cos we are, very much so. Anyway, I'll expect you both about seven.'

She left him to make her way over to Phyllis and said to her, 'Well, I have to say I was sceptical whether your plan would work or not, but it has a treat, gel.'

'As I told you, I can't take all the credit for coming up with it. It was your husband that gave me the idea. When Gilbert refused to work in his workshop any longer, Mr Reader took the work to him. So I thought that if Mr Morton wouldn't come out of his back yard, we could all go and tell him we didn't believe what that woman said. Dear Alexandra hasn't had much to smile about just lately, has she? This is bound to put one on her face.'

Herself smiling happily, Thelma nodded. 'Isn't it just?'

Lex arrived home at just after six to find Martin and Matt sitting at the table tucking into their dinner. There was no sign of her husband.

'Hello, Mam,' they both greeted her.

'Dad ain't half getting a dab hand at this cooking lark,' Matt told her through a mouthful of food. 'This pork chop and mash is quite tasty. Not as good as you do, but he's getting there,' he added, matter-of-factly.

She was taking off her coat, thinking it strange that Gil had cooked his sons their dinner and not peeled any potatoes for themselves. 'Well, you're both obviously in a rush to get out tonight, being as you've not waited to have your dinner with me and your father.'

Matt flashed a glance at the clock. 'I am, as a matter of fact. I'd better get a move on.'

She was pleased to learn her youngest son was starting to go out socially again. It must mean that the taunting he'd suffered had eased. She didn't bother asking Martin where he was going as just lately he always gave her the same answer when she asked and that was, 'to see a mate and won't be late'. She knew this so-called *mate* was a woman by the way he dressed and liberally splashed himself with aftershave. As far as she could gather from the scant information she had gleaned from him, he had been seeing this mystery woman for a few weeks now. Lex wondered if it would get to the stage where he would bring her home to meet his parents or else end like all his past relationships had.

How she envied Thelma, expecting her first grandchild, and how much she looked forward to the day she herself would hold one of her own in her arms.

A vision of Justine popped unexpectedly into her mind then. Lex suddenly realised she hadn't seen the young woman for a good few weeks now and hoped she was all right. Maybe she had changed her visiting time to her grandparents' now she was working, and that was why. Lex wondered if Justine had found herself a new man, one who would treat her right this time. Such a pity Martin and she hadn't hit it off. Pity too that Matt never got to meet that young woman at the bureau because she'd changed her mind about registering. She wouldn't have needed to register if she'd met him, Lex was positive there'd have been an instant rapport between them, and it would have gone on from there. Still, no point in dreaming about things that might have been.

Collecting some potatoes from the pantry, she tipped them into the sink. On her way to take a peeling knife from out of the cutlery holder, she enquired, 'Where's your father?'

Before they could respond Gil arrived in the kitchen, clean-shaven and looking smart in a shirt, jumper and casual trousers. It warmed Lex to see he had made an effort for her like she used to for him when their roles were reversed. 'Ah, there you are, love,' she greeted him. 'I've had the most wonderful day, I can't wait to tell you all about it. My boss has finally . . .'

'You can tell me all about it on the way. You need to hurry and get yourself ready,' he cut her short.

Lex wondered if she had heard him right.

Gil had been expecting her to be struck speechless by his

announcement. With a twinkle in his eyes, he said, 'You heard me right, love, we're going out. Thelma and Des have asked us to dinner. I know you'll want to hear what's happened to make me change my mind so I'll tell you everything on the way.'

Without further ado, Lex spun on her heel and rushed off. While she had been out at work a miracle had happened. Gil was leaving the confines of his own four walls to face the outside world again, something she had worried would never happen. She hadn't a clue who or what had brought all this about, and at this moment didn't care. What was all important to her was to hurry up and get ready before he changed his mind.

CHAPTER TWENTY

Although she'd had every intention of doing her best to celebrate, Lex secretly hadn't been looking forward to Christmas.
The fact that she hadn't the usual amount to lavish on fancy food
and expensive presents didn't bother her one iota, but missing out
on the social side of the festivities had been a gloomy prospect.
Lex saw Christmas as a time for sharing hospitality with very dear
friends and catching up with other people in the community. Now,
through the actions of two dear and thoughtful friends, she had
enjoyed the social side of the season after all and, more importantly to her, so had Gil.

When she had learned what Thelma and Phyllis had got up to
in their effort to make her husband Gil change his mind about his
self-imposed exile, Lex had been very touched, especially upon
learning that Thelma and several of the other women involved had
risked losing their jobs in order to participate. Through their
endeavours Gil was virtually back to his old self, albeit he never
would be completely while he still had that accusation hanging
over his head. But what a joy it was for her not to jump up any
longer to answer the door, and give an excuse to the caller, should
they be female, as to why she was unable to ask them inside. And
what joy it was to walk arm and arm down the street once again
with her husband, heads held high, after wondering if she would
ever have that privilege again.

Her sons certainly had not missed out on the social front,
enjoying themselves every night, and Lex was so grateful that it
appeared the rifts with their friends brought about by their father's
misadventure seemed to have healed.

The future might not be the one they'd once looked forward to, but it certainly seemed far brighter now that Gil was not shutting himself away.

There was still a minority who harboured a belief that there was no smoke without fire, and therefore would not reconsider their opinion of Gil. They never failed to make their feelings plain whenever paths crossed, but now Gil had been convinced that the majority of folks believed in his innocence, he was finding it possible to turn a blind eye to the odd dirty look or nasty comment. There'd been no further attacks on their property since the smashing of their front window several weeks before. The icing on the cake for Lex was when Gil had told her he was returning to work with Des in his workshop. She was so grateful he was no longer working in solitude in the cramped confines of the icy outhouse.

Most people weren't enthusiastic about returning to work after the festive break but Lex was. She was very eager to find out if all the clients had enjoyed the arrangements made for Christmas Eve. And, even more importantly, how Christine's relationship with Peter was progressing.

To her frustration, Christine had proved very tight-lipped on the matter so far. She had spent two evenings with Peter before they had closed up shop for the Christmas break, and all Lex had managed to glean from her after both occasions was that she had enjoyed herself and they were going out again. She dearly hoped Christine was going to prove more forthcoming over how matters had progressed over the Christmas break.

Her boss was already at work when Lex arrived prompt at eight-forty-five to ready herself for the commencement of business at nine o'clock. As soon as she walked through the door, Christine breezily enquired, 'Did you have a lovely Christmas, Mrs Morton?'

She smiled back as she took off her coat and went across to hang it up. 'Very much so, thank you, Mrs Landers. My husband and I never had a moment to ourselves, what with friends and neighbours popping in and invitations to theirs. A neighbour's son got engaged on Christmas Eve and what a party that turned out to be! Did you have a good time?' she asked keenly as she placed her handbag in the bottom drawer of her desk.

'Yes, it was very nice. My mother did her usual, which was laying on far too much food for us all to eat, and I received some lovely presents, and all my family were delighted with what I gave them.'

Lex was pleased to hear this but still hadn't been told what she really wanted to know. She decided to be bold and ask. 'Did . . . er . . . you see Mr Reynolds at all over the break?'

Christine paused for a moment before replying. 'Twice, in fact. Both occasions were very pleasant, thank you.'

Lex was itching for more detail and before she could check herself, asked, 'Where did Mr Reynolds take you? Are you seeing each other again?' Christine was staring at her blankly. Worrying that she may have overstepped the mark, Lex blurted out, 'Oh, I'm sorry, Mrs Landers. I didn't mean to pry into your private life. Please forgive me.'

Christine looked at her for several moments more before she said, 'There's nothing to forgive. You're hardly prying. I'm not green enough not to have realised the part you played in bringing Peter and myself together. If it wasn't for what you took it upon yourself to do, I never would have seen that he was interested in me. I owe you such a debt of gratitude for bringing him into my life.' A worried look then settled on her face and she gnawed her bottom lip anxiously. 'It's just that . . .'

Pre-empting what she thought Christine was about to tell her, Lex exclaimed, 'Is it that you can't return Mr Reynolds' feelings for you?'

'Oh, no, that's not the case at all. I certainly haven't found any problem returning his feelings. It's just that . . . well, you see, I'm still having difficulty believing Peter likes me in the way he does. I keep waiting to wake up and find it's all a dream. I worry that if I tell anyone about him and they ask to meet him, I'll look stupid when it all proves to be nothing much. You must think me pathetic?'

Lex could fully appreciate why Christine was struggling to accept that Peter Reynolds loved her. For years she had never dared allow herself to hope that a man might look at her in a romantic way. To reassure her Lex said softly, 'I can fully understand and appreciate why you are feeling like you are. But maybe it's time to let go and embrace what the future is offering you. Mr Reynolds is real, all right, and his feelings for you are real. I had absolutely no doubt of his sincerity when he was telling me all about them. If I'd doubted him for a moment, please believe me, I never would have tried to bring you two together.'

'No, I know you wouldn't have,' Christine told her with conviction.

There was a tap on the door then and a special messenger arrived, carrying a bouquet of white chrysanthemums. He looked expectantly at the two women. 'This is Cupid's Marriage Bureau?'

Christine replied, 'Yes, it is.'

'These are for Mrs Landers,' he said, handing them to her.

'They're certainly real,' Lex told her, looking at the bouquet in her boss's arms.

Christine hugged it to her, her pale cheeks colouring with emotion.

'I shall press one of the heads for a keepsake. Oh, there's a card,' she said, suddenly noticing it. She plucked it out of the middle of the flowers and read it, her cheeks turning pinker as she did so. Then, putting the card in her pocket, she said, 'I'll go and put these in water.' She went off to do it, leaving Lex intrigued as to what Peter had written.

She was so delighted to see that the relationship between the pair of them seemed to be progressing just as she had prophesied it would. Lex couldn't be happier for them. She had a strong feeling now that in the not-too-distant future Christine and Peter would be announcing their intention of marrying.

Much later that morning, Christine replaced the telephone receiver and said in surprise to Lex, who was putting a cup of tea before her, 'Well, this is unexpected. That's four couples now who had such a good time together on Christmas Eve they've been going out together ever since. Only one couple had a disappointing time.'

Lex was very pleased to learn this after all their hard work bringing it about. 'Well, I think we can call your idea a resounding success.'

Christine smiled back at her. 'Yes, I think so too. Should we offer all our unattached clients the chance to participate again on New Year's Eve? It'd mean a lot of extra work on our part . . .'

'I don't mind the hard work, knowing that so many of our clients will be out enjoying themselves instead of sitting at home on their own, especially on New Year's Eve. I'll go and fetch the client details.' Lex made to make her way into the other office where the records were kept then stopped as a thought struck her. 'Oh, have Jean Robotham or Sebastian Evans informed us yet how matters stand between them? Only I haven't taken a call from either of them, and nor has either of them called in in person, to my knowledge. Their second date was three days before Christmas.'

Christine shook her head. 'I suppose no news is good news. I hope so.'

Just then the door opened and Sebastian Evans himself entered, smiling charmingly at Lex and Christine.

'I hope I find you both well?' he asked.

To her horror Lex realised she was gawping at him like a besotted teenager would at her favourite film star. Giving herself a mental shake, she dearly hoped he hadn't noticed. He certainly was the most good-looking man she had ever encountered. 'I'm very well, thank you, Mr Evans.'

His charms were lost on Christine. She only had eyes for Peter and therefore asked quite matter-of-factly, 'I hope you've come to tell us that you and Miss Robotham are getting along famously?'

'Well, no, actually. Like the other two you introduced me to, I found her a delightful woman, but unfortunately not for me. We just didn't have that spark, I'm afraid.'

'Oh, I'm sorry to hear that,' Lex said sincerely.

'We'll immediately set to and sort out another suitable intro-duction for you,' Christine told him.

'Well, that's what I've come to tell you in person; that I won't be needing your services again.'

'Oh, you're not happy with the bureau?' Christine asked, dismayed.

'On the contrary,' Sebastian assured her. 'More than happy, in fact. I would not be dispensing with your services if it weren't for the fact that I've been offered another job and will be leaving Leicester shortly to take it up.'

Christine looked relieved. 'Oh, well, in that case I'm really pleased for you, Mr Evans. Should it not work out and you return to Leicester still single, I hope you'll come back to us.' She stood up, stretching out her hand across the desk to shake his. 'I know I speak for Mrs Morton in wishing you all the very best for your future, Mr Evans.'

'Thank you. The same goes to you both.'

'Off to break more hearts wherever it is he's going. I do hope he eventually finds a woman who suits him,' said Christine after Sebastian Evans had left. Then she noticed Lex was looking thoughtful and asked, 'Do you think he wasn't telling us the truth about his reason for dispensing with our services?'

'Pardon? Oh, I've no reason to disbelieve what he told us. It's just that I wonder why we haven't heard from Jean Robotham. She's been very prompt to report in on all her introductions in the past; in fact, was on the telephone as soon as we opened for business to tell us Mr Evans had asked to see her again. It's been several days since their second date. I'm just surprised we haven't heard from her one way or the other.'

'Mmm, that is a bit odd,' replied Christine. Then a thought struck her. 'Oh, you don't think she really fell for Mr Evans and his rebuff has upset her so much she's having trouble getting over it?'

'I do hope not,' said Lex sincerely. 'Introducing her to another man would help her get over the disappointment. I'm sure she'd get on very well with Mr Wallis who registered with us last week, and he'd certainly like her.'

'I agree. We could telephone her, saying we'd heard via Mr

Evans that he isn't pursuing matters with her and would she be interested in us approaching Mr Wallis? Actually, we could help ease her heartache by telling a little white lie, saying that the reason Mr Evans didn't ask to see her again was because he's moving away . . .'

Lex smiled at her. 'Yes, we could.'

'Well, no time like the present,' said Christine. 'Miss Robotham works from home making costume jewellery, so a call from us won't cause her any embarrassment. If you take care of that, meanwhile I'll man reception and see to a couple of bills that need paying. Then straight after that we can get down to matching people up for New Year's Eve.'

Jean Robotham answered the telephone almost immediately. Her tone of voice was on the subdued side and Lex presumed they were correct in their assumption about why she hadn't contacted them since her second outing with Mr Evans.

'It's Mrs Morton, from the bureau,' Lex told her. 'I hope I find you well? I'm calling because we've heard via Mr Evans that you two aren't pursuing matters with each other and we'd like to know if you wish us to make another introduction for you?'

The other woman sounded genuinely shocked to hear this. 'Mr Evans doesn't want to see me again? Oh! But I understood when he saw me into my taxi that he would definitely be making arrangements for us to meet again. You see, I had the most dreadful migraine come on very early in the evening . . . I do suffer with them from all the intricate work I do on my jewellery. I knew it wasn't going to go away just from taking a couple of Aspro so the only thing I could do was go home to bed and sleep it off.

'I must say, Mr Evans seemed most upset at the time that our evening was ending abruptly. He even offered to take me to the hospital to see if they could prescribe me something and then we could enjoy the rest of our evening together. He came across as most concerned when I insisted that the only treatment was for me to go home to bed.

'I was really looking forward to going out with him again. He's very good company and certainly knows how to treat a woman

. . . so attentive. Of course, it's really an ego booster for a woman to be on the arm of such a handsome man. Oh, well, I'm glad this has happened now and not further down the line when I was well and truly smitten. I hope he finds what he's looking for. As for me, well, I'd like nothing more than to tell you to go ahead and make arrangements for me to meet Mr Wallis, Mrs Morton, but I'm afraid I'm indisposed at the moment.'

'Oh, I'm sorry to hear you're ill,' Lex said in genuine concern. 'I do hope you'll get better soon.'

'Not ill exactly. It's just that I'm sporting a disfiguring black eye, and I'm sure you can appreciate that I don't want to go out in public unless I have to.'

'A black eye! Oh, goodness, how did you come by that?'

'From a hefty punch.'

'Someone attacked you? I hope the police caught the man.'

'It wasn't a man, it was a woman, can you believe? It happened the same night as my second date with Mr Evans. I arrived home to find a burglar in my house. My arrival disturbed her. I was incensed to say the least, finding her like I did going through my personal papers in the bureau. I didn't realise it was a woman until we got into a tussle in my attempt to apprehend her, and I pulled off the black woollen balaclava she was wearing. She got away by landing a punch on me, which I wasn't expecting, knocking me over. By the time I'd come to my senses she'd escaped through the front door. She got in by cutting a hole in my kitchen window big enough to slip her hand through and open the latch.'

Lex was aghast to be hearing all this. 'Well, you surprising her by arriving home hopefully stopped her from taking anything?'

'No, actually, it didn't. But why she wanted what she did is beyond me.'

Natural curiosity getting the better of her, Lex asked, 'What was it exactly?'

'A handful of my recent wage slips.'

Lex couldn't understand why anyone would want these either. 'What did the police have to say, Miss Robotham?'

'I never called them. My headache was bad enough before I was attacked so I was feeling pretty rotten afterwards. I secured the house as best I could then went to bed. I was going to go to the police the next day but I didn't really get a proper look at the woman, not enough to give them a good description. And it's not like she got away with anything valuable, thank goodness, so I didn't see the point in wasting their time. I'm just grateful, I did have a migraine that night or I dread to think what I might have come home to find later.

'I just want to forget about it all now. If you think Mr Wallis a suitable introduction for me then I'd like to take you up on it. The bruising around my eye should be completely gone in a couple of days' time.'

'Then I'll contact him and ask if he's agreeable to meeting you then. Would you like me to suggest New Year's Eve or have you other plans?'

'No, I hadn't actually. I was going to be spending it quietly at home by myself so I'd love some company then.'

'I'll be in touch when I have some news,' Lex assured her.

Putting down the telephone, she returned to reception and relayed the details to Christine.

When she had finished her boss was looking horrified. 'Oh, poor Miss Robotham. How terrible for her. Thank goodness she caught the thief in the act and nothing valuable was taken. But why would someone want someone else's wage slips?'

Lex shrugged. 'It was a mystery to Miss Robotham too. Anyway, I'll contact Mr Wallis and hopefully he'll like the sound of her enough to meet her on New Year's Eve. I'm sure those two will get on well together. Let's hope there's that special spark between them.'

The telephone rang then.

Christine picked it up and after a brief discussion ended the call and told Lex, 'That was a potential new client. Told me he was fed up being on his own, saw our advertisement in the *Mercury* and decided to give us a try. He's coming in tomorrow at eleven.'

She picked up a pencil and wrote the details in the appointments book. Then there was a knock on the door and a smartly dressed, pleasant-faced woman in her thirties entered.

'Cupid's Marriage Bureau?' she queried.

Why most people did this when they first came in always astonished Lex and Christine as there was a brass plaque on the wall by the door clearly stating the fact.

Christine nodded. 'We certainly are. Can I help you?'

'My friend is a client and absolutely sings your praises. You've introduced her to some lovely men and she's seeing one at the moment she's very high hopes of. I'd like to register too. Is it possible you could see me now?'

Christine said under her breath to Lex, 'It's going to be one of those days but I'm not complaining.' She smiled welcomingly at the new arrival. 'I'm sure we can squeeze you in.'

CHAPTER TWENTY-ONE

Gil gave a groan. His head was pounding as if a million hammers were beating rhythmically inside it, and he could hear ringing in his ears. Unusually his bed felt most uncomfortable. He turned over, pulling the eiderdown along with him, and to his shock felt himself falling to the floor, jolting himself fully awake. Then he realised he hadn't been in bed at all but on the sofa. This sofa, though, wasn't his. It looked familiar but at this moment he couldn't place it. Why had he been sleeping on someone else's sofa? He wished the ringing in his ears would stop, it was driving him crazy, accentuating the throbbing inside his head. With extreme difficulty he manoeuvred himself into a sitting position. With his back against the sofa, legs drawn up, he cradled his painful head in his hands and tried to search his memory for an answer. At the moment his brain seemed to be filled with a dense swirling fog.

Then he saw a foot alongside him and realised he wasn't alone. His eyes travelled up the leg, over the torso, to the face above. It was Des! Slumped most uncomfortably in the armchair next to the sofa, he looked dead to Gil, but thankfully wasn't as his chest was rising and falling.

How had they both come to be sleeping in Des's front room?

Gil tapped his ear in the hope that might stop the ringing in it then he'd be able to get his thoughts in order enough to remember. Oh, but didn't his mouth feel like the bottom of a bird cage? Miraculously the ringing stopped then and his brain was able to function just enough for a memory to stir. Raised glasses. Voices toasting a Happy New Year. Des saying, 'Just one more for the road ...' His memory came to an abrupt halt after that.

A voice made him jump and he jerked his head round to see Thelma, dressed in her nightdress under a quilted dressing gown, glaring over at him. 'Did you not hear the telephone ringing?' she barked, clearly annoyed. 'But then, how could I expect you to, or him either ...' she added, flashing a derogatory glance at her husband, still out cold in the armchair '... after the amount you two sank between you last night? If I heard my Des say "and just another for the road" once, he said it a dozen times. And, of course, you being his friend couldn't refuse him, could you?' Then her face softened and she added, 'I suppose, though, you can be forgiven for letting your hair down after all you've been through lately.'

Gil was staring at her during this tirade, feeling very much like a naughty schoolboy.

Thelma continued, 'Anyway, there's a man on the telephone wanting to speak to Des, urgent he said it was, but as I doubt you'll get any sense out of him for a few hours yet you'd better take it. Now I'm going back to bed. Oh, and if yer wondering where yer wife is, she's upstairs sharing my bed. You weren't the only one who celebrated, a bit too much last night.

With that she turned and left him. As Thelma climbed back into bed, Lex sleepily asked, 'Was that the telephone I heard ringing?'

'It was someone for Des, but as he's still out cold, I told Gil to answer it.'

'I'm surprised he's awake, considering the state he was in last night. Mind you, it was nice seeing him enjoy himself for a change. I certainly wasn't going to put a stop to that, considering how he's been for the last few weeks and me worrying I'd never see him out with friends again. It was a good night, though, wasn't it, Thelma? Only I've got a bit of a head this morning ...'

Her words were lost on Thelma as she snuggled back under the covers. She had fallen asleep again. Lex caught sight of the clock. It was only a quarter to six. Turning over, she pulled the covers around her and fell back to sleep herself.

Downstairs Gil had managed to struggle upright and make his way to the telephone.

In a husky voice, he said, 'Mr Reader isn't available, I'm afraid. My name is Gil Morton, can I be of help to you?'

The caller responded, 'Can you fix a generator, Mr Morton?'

'Yes.'

'Thank God for that! Can you get round here quick? There's a power cut on this side of town, no telling when it'll be back on again, considering what day it is, and I've a bakery business. I need the gennie to give me some light so I can finish off the loaves or no one will get any fresh bread today. Not everyone has New Year's Day off!' He gave Gil his address and asked him how long it would take him to get there.

Gil inwardly groaned. It had taken him all his strength to get to the telephone and this man's business was over two miles away. Thankfully he didn't have to walk, he could use Des's van to get there. He didn't want to turn the man down just because he himself was suffering from a major hangover, and nor could he risk tarnishing Des's business reputation by refusing to go.

Telling the caller he'd get to him as soon as he could, Gil made his way to the kitchen to dunk his head under the cold tap in the hope it would revive him.

When he returned three hours later, Des was still unconscious in his chair. Gil didn't feel there was any need to disturb him. The generator had been easily fixed and he'd left behind one very happy customer who'd promised to use Des's firm in future, considering the good service he'd just received. No other generator mainten-ance firm had even answered the telephone.

When Des found out what Gil had done on his behalf while he'd been sleeping off his night of revelry, he couldn't thank him enough. But then, he wasn't surprised, considering the kind of man Gil was. Once again he was very grateful his friend was working for him now and just wished he was in a position to reward him better financially than he was able to at the moment.

Little did he know that very shortly his wish was going to be granted, and he would be able to show Gil just how much he was valued.

Two days later Des found himself in the office of Victor Eldridge, owner of Eldridge Engineering, manufacturers of motors for use in washing machines and vacuums. They employed a workforce of approximately eight hundred people.

'I appreciate you coming in to see me at such short notice,' Victor Eldridge, a thickset middle-aged man with receding greying hair, was saying to Des. 'I'll get straight to the point as I've a meeting in twenty minutes with one of my customers. I've ten generators in constant use around the factory that need regular maintenance and new parts fitting. The firm we use at the moment does a reasonable job but there have been times recently when we've called them in urgently and they haven't responded until the next day or even after that. My factory manager is under the impression that they've grown complacent about our business, feel they can treat us just as they like and we won't do anything about it.

'Well, time is money to me. I can't afford to have generators out of action and my men standing around twiddling their thumbs until the engineers feel like sending someone in.' He paused long enough to draw breath before he continued, 'I assume you can see where I'm heading, Mr Reader. But before I go any further, can I just clarify something with you? I understand you have Gil Morton working for you. Is that the same man who was works manager at Brenton's?'

Des's mind was racing. He was on the verge of being offered a very lucrative contract with Eldridge Engineering, and once it was known he was contracted to such a prestigious firm there was no telling how much new work would flood in. Landing this contract could make him! Thelma could immediately give up her extra hours because there'd be more than enough coming in to pay Gil the wage he deserved. But it was obvious that being offered this contract depended on his answer to Victor Eldridge's question. Eldridge must have heard the rumour about Gil, not surprisingly as they worked in the same trade, and wasn't prepared to give business to a firm that employed a man of that reputation.

But Gil was his friend, and that friendship meant more to Des than furthering his own business.

He looked Victor Eldridge in the eye and said, 'Yes, the Gil Morton that works for me is the same man who was works manager for Brenton's. I'm not prepared to sack him just to land your contract, Mr Eldridge. Gil's innocent of what it's said he did, and I'll go to my grave standing by him. Apart from that, he's a first-class engineer and I'm lucky to have him working for me.' He rose from his chair, saying, 'Well, thank you for considering me for the work and I wish you good . . .'

'Sit back down, man, and hear me out,' ordered Victor. When a bemused Des had, he continued, 'I've been acquainted with Gil Morton a long time. I've been trying to poach him for years to come and work for me but he was too loyal to Brenton's even to consider it. If I hadn't had an excellent works manager myself at the time I heard he'd left Brenton's, I'd have been straight on the telephone to him, offering him a job. I never believed a word of what was said about him. That man is one of the most upstanding individuals I've had the privilege of meeting.

'When my brother-in-law told me how his generator failed him early on New Year's morning, and how he had almost given up on getting it fixed with all that would have meant to his customers, not getting their bread, he was full of praise for your firm. He was especially full of praise for the man who came out, a fellow called Gil Morton. Said he'd done a first-class job and strongly recommended I give your firm a try as he knew I wasn't happy with the one I was using.

'I couldn't be more pleased to hear it's the same man I remember from Brenton's. I'm happy to offer you all my work in future, if you'll accept it? And, by the way, I admire your loyalty. Now you've shown me exactly what kind of man you are, I'm doubly happy to put my work your way.'

CHAPTER TWENTY-TWO

Meanwhile, totally oblivious to the fact that the Mortons' lives were about to take another turn for the better, Lex was busy at the reception desk, typing a pile of letters to clients. Christine was making them both a cup of tea, having just finished speaking to a possible new client on the telephone, when without any warning Melvin Cane entered the room.

He looked dreadful. His usually immaculate attire was all crumpled, as if he'd slept in his clothes. His hair was wildly tousled, face drawn and sporting at least two days' growth of beard.

'I'm so sorry to bother you,' he stammered, 'but I didn't know who else might know, you see . . .'

'Know what, Mr Cane?' Christine enquired.

'Why Marie's broken off our engagement. She did it two days ago, without even giving me a reason. She won't see me. Won't even speak to me. She won't speak to her family either. She's locked herself inside her flat and is refusing to come out. She hasn't been to work . . .'

Lex and Christine were looking stunned.

'This is news to us, Mr Cane,' Lex told him.

'As far as we're concerned, Miss Noble was extremely happy that you'd asked her to marry you,' Christine added.

Melvin's shoulders sagged in despair. 'Oh, I was hoping you might be able to shed some light on all this. Well, sorry to have bothered you.'

Both deep in thought, they looked at each other after he'd gone.

'This is a strange turn of events,' said Lex, breaking the silence.

'Mmm, it is. Miss Noble obviously has her reasons for doing what she has, though.'

'I wonder what they are?' Lex mused.

'It's probably nothing more than pre-wedding nerves. In a few days it'll all blow over and they'll be back to normal,' said Christine

But it was far too early for pre-wedding nerves, thought Lex.

'Oh, it's lunchtime,' Christine exclaimed, suddenly noticing the time. Her plain face lit up with excitement. 'Peter is taking me out for dinner tonight and I'd like a new blouse to wear. I've seen such a pretty one in British Home Stores which will go really well with the new skirt I bought myself last week.'

Lex smiled to herself. Christine's wardrobe was rapidly expanding. Like all women in the early stages of a relationship, she liked to wear something different on every date. The arrival of Peter in her life had transformed Christine. She barely resembled the austere woman Lex had first met several months ago. In her place was a softer, prettier person, and one who definitely had more confidence in herself as a woman.

'See you after lunch,' Christine called as she left the office.

But Lex wasn't listening. Her thoughts were back with Marie Noble. Lex had been the one to interview her when she'd first registered with the bureau. She had found Marie a very pleasant person, down to earth, not the sort to break off a relationship for no good reason, and certainly not leave the man she had planned to spend the rest of her life with wondering why. Then an awful thought struck her. Had Marie discovered something about Melvin that had shocked and upset her so much she couldn't bear to face him or anyone else? If that were the case then she should enlighten them about it in case he decided to continue using the bureau. Lex was very concerned that their reputation could be in jeopardy if they did have a bad lot as a client, and that could turn the clock right back until it resembled the failing business it had been before she joined it.

She made up her mind to go and pay Marie Noble a visit, and no time like the present. She only lived a short bus ride away. Lex could get there and back during her dinner break.

She had to knock several times on the door and wait a good while before Marie would answer, the last time announcing who she was through the letter box to reassure anyone inside. She had almost given up and was about to walk away when there was the sound of a bolt being drawn back and finally the door opened just wide enough for the person on the other side to look out.

The eyes that met Lex's were red and swollen, the voice that spoke to her with the rawness to it of someone who had been crying for a very long time. 'Please don't think me rude, Mrs Morton, but I'm really not well enough to see anyone at the moment.'

'I'm so sorry to bother you, Miss Noble, it's obviously not a good time for you, but could I just have a quick word? I promise I won't keep you a moment,' Lex coaxed her.

Marie seemed to hesitate before opening the door a little wider and stepping back into the shadows of the dark hallway to allow Lex to enter. After she'd shut and bolted the door, Lex followed her into a tastefully furnished lounge, albeit a dark one as the curtains were drawn. It felt to Lex as if Marie was shutting out the outside world.

She indicated a comfortable-looking armchair to one side of the fireplace, sitting herself down in the one opposite.

Getting a good look at her now, Lex was shocked to see just how wretched she looked. It was apparent she hadn't slept for a while; didn't seem to have bothered to attend to her appearance either as she was very unkempt. 'I'm sorry things haven't worked out between you and Mr Cane, Miss Noble,' Lex began. 'He came to see us this morning and told us you'd broken off your engagement to him. He's very confused as he doesn't seem to know why. That is your private business, and I have no wish to pry, but I'm worried in case the reason you have called it off is because you've found out something worrying about Mr Cane. If so, we really ought to know about it in case we're putting another woman at risk by introducing him to her in the future.'

Marie was looking horrified by now. 'Oh, Mrs Morton,' she exclaimed, 'Melvin is the kindest, most considerate man I have ever had the good fortune to meet. There is nothing untoward about him, nothing at all. He'd have made me the most wonderful husband . . .' There was real distress in her voice when she added, 'I'm just so devastated that he'll never be mine now.'

'Then . . . may I ask, why have you broken off your engagement to him?'

A flood of tears filled Marie's eyes and her bottom lip was trembling as she whispered, 'Because how could I expect a respectable man like Melvin to saddle himself with a woman who suddenly finds she's responsible for a huge debt? It's for something I haven't even bought but no one will believe that, so it looks like I've no choice but to pay for it or go to prison . . .'

Lex was staring at her, confused. 'I don't understand?'

'I've had a job understanding it myself, Mrs Morton. I had no idea about any of this until two men called on me a couple of evenings ago, just after I got home from work, informing me I was behind with the payments for a car I was supposed to have purchased four weeks ago. A red Vauxhall Victor, costing just under five hundred pounds plus interest of nearly three hundred! They're returning at the end of the week to collect the outstanding arrears of twenty pounds plus the five-pound payment due to them for this week, which, they're saying I agreed to when I bought the car, otherwise I'm to return it to them and settle the outstanding arrears.

'I was flabbergasted when they told me all this. Then I thought someone must be playing a joke on me . . . but these men weren't the joking sort. I tried to tell them I had done no such thing, so then they showed me a copy of the Hire Purchase agreement in my name. The signature on the bottom of the document was nothing like mine but they said that didn't prove anything as people's signatures were never exactly the same twice. Regardless, they said they had my wage slips to prove my identity, given to them at the time I bought the car and kept on file in their records. But they couldn't have had my wage slips, I thought, as I keep them, along with all my personal papers, in a shoe box at the bottom of my wardrobe. I went to get them and check them out, clear up this problem once and for all . . . and that's when I discovered that a handful of my most recent slips had gone. The thief who broke into my house didn't leave empty-handed like I thought they did.

'I tried to make the men believe that I was the victim of a crime, but they wouldn't listen. They told me people told them all sorts of tales to try and get out of honouring their HP agreements, and if they believed everyone they'd end up bankrupt. As far as they were concerned, I'd bought the car and I was responsible for the repayments on it. In desperation, I begged them to check with the salesman what the woman looked like who came in to buy the car, thinking that would prove it wasn't me. They just said that the salesmen couldn't be expected to identify everyone who bought cars off them, weeks after the event. So, you see, I can't prove it wasn't me who bought that car and I've no choice but to pay for it or they'll take me to court and have me locked away.'

Marie heaved a shuddering sigh. 'I can just about manage to pay the five pounds a week as I have a well-paid job, but it's not going to leave me much to live on after I've paid my other bills. It's not fair, is it, that I should have to struggle for the next three years to pay for a car someone else has the use of? I can't expect Melvin to marry a woman with such a huge debt hanging over her, so much as it pained me to do so, that's why I've ended it between us. I daren't tell my family about this either. I feel so alone.'

Lex had been prepared to hear that Marie Noble had uncovered something terrible about Melvin Cane, but she wasn't prepared for anything like this. All she could find to say was, 'I'm very sorry. I just wish there was something I could do for you.'

'You could find the swine that's done this to me, Mrs Morton, that's what you could do.'

Lex had no doubt Marie was telling her the truth and that she was an innocent victim of a despicable crime. She hated leaving the other woman behind in the state she was in, unable to ease her plight at all, but Lex had to get back to work.

She was so consumed by Marie's troubles that she made her way back to the bus stop in a total daze. It wasn't until she'd arrived at the stop and sat down on a bench to await a bus that something occurred to her. Jean Robotham had told her only that morning that she had arrived home early one evening before Christmas to find her house in the process of being burgled. All the thief had got away with was a handful of recent wage slips ... Lex frowned thoughtfully. That was two people connected with the bureau who had had this happen to them. What if the slips that had been stolen from Jean Robotham were going to be used in the same way as Marie Noble's had been? If so, then very shortly Jean was going to receive a visit from bailiffs representing the firm who'd supplied expensive goods on spurious collateral. Jean Robotham also could find herself with a massive debt she had no option but to pay off else risk going to prison.

Were these incidents involving two clients of the bureau just coincidence or were they connected in some way? Someone must have known both women well enough to have known what nights they would be out, then taken the opportunity to break in and search through their possessions ...

So engrossed was she in trying to unravel this mystery that Lex did not notice the bus until it had gone sailing past her. By that time she was beyond caring because she thought she saw it all now. There *was* someone who had known exactly when both women would be out – because they'd been with him. If her suspicions were right, then he must be working with an accomplice. A surge of great anger filled Lex then. If this man and his accomplice were using the bureau as cover it had to be stopped before any more lives were wrecked in their heartless pursuit of money.

Then another awful thought struck her. If the man she suspected was indeed behind this wicked money-making scheme, then Marie Noble and Jean Robotham might not be the only women he'd targeted through the bureau. At least one other woman to her knowledge could be in immediate danger of being defrauded.

Desperate to get back, Lex had no patience to wait for another bus so kicked up her heels and ran all the way to the bureau.

At the reception desk, Christine looked relieved to see her and said, 'I was getting so worried about you, Mrs Morton. It's gone half-past two and you've never been late back from lunch before so I . . .'

Standing at the desk, red-faced and panting after her precipitate return, Lex cut her short with, 'I apologise for being late, Mrs Landers, but I need to talk to you urgently.'

A sense of foreboding swept through Christine, but she didn't hesitate.

'I'll put the snib on the door and take the telephone off the hook so we aren't disturbed.'

A while later she was speechless with shock at what she'd just heard. Finally she said, 'After all you've told me, I can only reach the same conclusion as you, Mrs Morton. If this man is using my business in order to feather his own nest then I want him exposed and imprisoned. I just can't believe he'd be capable of this. He came across as so honest and upright and charming . . . I feel a fool for being taken in so completely.'

'I was too,' Lex reminded her. 'So, you do agree, we have to go to the police with our suspicions and leave it to them to decide what to do?'

Christine said resolutely, 'Most definitely, Mrs Morton. It wouldn't be right for us to turn a blind eye and possibly leave this man and his accomplice at large to carry on defrauding innocent people. I'd sooner have to beg his forgiveness if I'm wrong than leave him free to do that. I'll get my coat.'

Gil knew something was wrong with Lex immediately she entered the house. She looked absolutely drained and he demanded she tell him why. Thankfully her sons chose that moment to arrive home, too, so she didn't have to go through her tale twice.

All of them were stunned when she had finished it.

Gil reassuringly patted her hand. 'You've done the right thing, love. You were morally obliged to report your suspicions to the police and then let them deal with it as they see fit.'

That still didn't stop her worrying, though. She'd seen at first hand how hard it could be for an innocent man wrongly accused of a crime.

'Did the police give you any idea when you would hear the outcome?' her husband asked her.

'They said they'd come and inform us at the bureau when they'd finished their investigations. So we just have to be patient.'

'Well, I'm proud of you, Mam. Took brains to work out what you did, and guts to do something about it,' Martin told her.

'I'm proud of you too,' said his brother.

The back door opened then and Thelma came straight in, smiling delightedly to see them all gathered around the kitchen table. 'Oh, I'm glad I've caught you together. I just popped around to tell you I'm having a celebration dinner on Saturday night and I'd like you all to be there.'

'What are you celebrating, Thelma?' asked a puzzled Lex. As far as she was aware there'd been no new developments in her friend's life to justify a celebration.

Thelma tapped the side of her nose, giving a secretive smile. 'All will be revealed on Saturday. Will I be seeing you as usual tomorrow night for our . . . W.I. meeting?'

Lex decided there and then that she wasn't prepared to lie anymore to Gil over where she went on a Thursday evening. 'Well, I wanted to talk to you about that, Thelma. You see, I've decided I don't want to continue being a member, not while Veronica Middleton is still Chairman and makes all the decisions without consulting the rest of us.'

Thankfully Thelma cottoned on to what she was doing. 'Well, great minds think alike, lovey. I'm of the same opinion. But we could still spend Thursday evenings together, take it in turns round each other's house while our men are down the snooker hall?'

Lex looked enquiringly at Gil. 'Will you be joining your friends at the hall this week, dear?'

Des and Matt were always reminding him that their crowd of snooker pals had always supported him, and were constantly enquiring when he was going to start joining them again. So far Gil had resisted. The men concerned were all well-respected, upstanding businessmen and he'd worried about them being tainted by association with himself.

Lex knew what her husband was thinking. Taking his hand, she squeezed it reassuringly and said, 'Darling, your friends wouldn't be insisting they want you back amongst them if they were worried it would affect their businesses and reputations.'

Gil knew she was talking sense. He flashed a look at Thelma then grinned and said, 'I dread to think what you and Phyllis will do if I don't agree to go.'

'Well, just you make sure you do and then you won't find out! I'll see you tomorrow night then, lovey,' she said to Lex. 'But, mind, don't bother quizzing me about what we're celebrating on Saturday night. As I said, all will be revealed then.'

CHAPTER TWENTY-THREE

Christine and Lex were most surprised the next afternoon to see Detective Brown walk into reception. He didn't look much like a policeman, slightly built, not overly tall, and with boyish good looks making him appear much younger than his actual thirty-nine years.

Christine smiled warmly at him. 'Good afternoon, Detective Brown. We hadn't expected to see you quite so soon. You policemen don't waste any time, do you? I trust you have some news for us or you wouldn't be here.' She addressed Lex then. 'Thankfully we've no appointments due in, so if you'd like to hang the sign outside the door and put the snib down, I'll take the telephone off the hook and then we can talk in private.'

A few minutes later, all seated around the large desk in the main office, each with a cup of tea, Lex asked the policeman worriedly, 'Have I pointed the finger of suspicion at an innocent man, Detective Brown?' She had spent a fretful night worrying that she had and about the possible repercussions.

'On the contrary, Mrs Morton, you're greatly to be congratulated. You're responsible for the capture of a couple of crooks that forces up and down the country have been trying to apprehend for years. Sebastian Evans isn't his real name, of course. It's really Sidney Harper. He's originally from Carlisle, and in his youth spent time in Borstal and later several terms in prison for petty crimes. Then he met his wife . . . Brenda Biggs. She's a seasoned criminal herself with a long string of petty crimes to her name. Perfect partners in crime, those two. Between them they came up with the idea of using Sid's good looks as a way to make their

307

fortune. While he kept the women occupied, Brenda broke into their homes to steal wage slips or other proof of ID. Then she'd pass herself off as them in order to buy expensive cars on hire purchase, which Sid Harper would sell on. They'd pocket the proceeds, leaving the innocent dupe with the outstanding debt. Having done this to several women in succession in a town, they'd pack up and leave for the safety of another before they could be caught.'

'How dreadful of them!' Christine exclaimed. 'I can never understand how people like that sleep at night. They must be aware of the devastation they have caused those poor women.'

'People like the Harpers have no conscience, Mrs Landers. All they think of is using their God-given assets as a way to make an easy and lucrative living for themselves,' Detective Brown told her. 'When you mentioned your suspicions of a client of yours, I was pretty sure he fitted Sid Harper's bill. Now Leicester police force will go down as the one that nipped his little game in the bud.'

'Detective Brown, forgive me for interrupting, can I just ask why you think Mr Harper took the time and trouble to come into the office to inform us he was dispensing with our services as he was leaving the area?' Lex asked.

'Just playing out the part of the charming, upright man he was conning you into believing he was. Then, should his crimes come to light before he and his wife had made their getaway, he'd be the very last person you would think was responsible. By the time you'd made the connection he'd planned on being in another town, living under another false identity. That's why no other force has ever got close to him.

'Anyway, once you'd told us your suspicions, we wasted no time in going straight to the address you gave us . . . not his own house, by the way, but rented for the duration . . . and couldn't believe our eyes! There were actually two men standing in the driveway by a very expensive-looking Triumph soft-top sports car, in the process of exchanging documents and money. There was a saloon car parked next to it, piled with belongings. It was apparent that as soon as the transaction was complete, the Harpers were off to their next destination. We caught them just in the nick of time, so to speak.

'We halted the transaction while we radioed back to check out the identity of the vehicle's owner, despite Harper and his wife both giving sterling performances of injured innocence. Lo and behold, the owner of the sports vehicle was registered as a Miss Jean Robotham. Well, Sid Harper couldn't talk his way out of *that* so he had no alternative but to accompany us back to the station where he confessed to everything. I'm afraid I can't say the same for Mrs Harper. She didn't come quietly. Apart from everything else, she's being charged with blacking a policeman's eye.'

'Oh, she's good at that,' said Christine dryly. 'She blacked Miss Robotham's for her when she was caught in the flat, stealing wage slips. And to think Sid tried his best to act like a knight in shining amour by insisting he took Jean Robotham to the hospital so they could treat her migraine! He must have been like a cat on hot coals, going home early to wait for his wife to return.'

'And that's why he always saw the women twice,' put in Lex. 'On the first date he'd obtain their address by gallantly offering to see them safely home or else overhearing them telling the taxi driver their destination. The second time he'd keep them entertained and out of the way while his wife did her stuff.' Then Lex looked deeply worried and asked the policeman, 'Will our clients still be left in debt for the cars they didn't buy?'

'Well, unfortunately, when a crime takes place someone always ends up the loser, Mrs Morton. The cars are actually owned by the hire purchase company until fully paid off so they will reclaim the cost from the new purchasers Harper sold them on to. Unfortunately it's they who will be out of pocket, not your clients.'

'I feel so stupid for being completely taken in by Sid Harper,' said Christine, looking ashamed.

'No more than me,' said Lex.

'You and dozens of others,' the detective told them. 'He's a professional conman, it's his job to fool people. Well, thanks to you he won't be doing that for a very long time ... nor Mrs

Harper neither.' He rose to his feet, saying, 'Well, I'd better get back to the station.'

Opening the door, Detective Brown made to go through it then stopped and looked back. To their surprise he said to them, 'Er . . . do you happen to have anyone on your books you think would be interested in me? My wife couldn't stand the hours I worked so she divorced me four years ago and went off with another man, taking our two children with her. Obviously I was devastated, it took me a while to get over it, but now I am ready to meet someone else. I've had a couple of relationships but neither of the women was prepared to put up with my unsocial working hours either. I was just wondering . . .'

Lex put her hand on his arm and interjected, 'Well, actually, we've several ladies who wouldn't be put off by that, if they liked a man enough.'

'In that case, when can I make an appointment to register?'

CHAPTER TWENTY-FOUR

'Before we eat I want to make a toast to Detective Morton here,' Thelma addressed the gathering the following Saturday night. Everyone was jostling for space around her table, all looking smart in their Sunday best, Gil and Des in grey flannel trousers, navy blazers and white shirts, Lex in a fitted boat-necked floral-patterned dress, and Thelma in a loose-fitting two-piece costume in a flattering lilac.

Squashed next to Gil, Lex blushed. 'Oh, stop it, Thelma. You've all gone on about nothing else since I told you about it.'

'Well, you are a heroine, Mam. The *Mercury* really sang your and Christine's praises,' said Martin proudly. 'It was you who worked it all out, though. Mrs Landers really only went to the police station with you, so it's you who deserves most of the credit.'

'Have you thought of running your own detective agency, Lex?' Des joked.

She snapped, 'I said, that's enough from the lot of you. I don't want to hear another word on the subject.' Then, eyes twinkling mischievously, she added, 'All right, just one more toast. Then that's it, thank you.'

They all raised their glasses. 'To Detective Morton,' they said in unison.

Putting down her drained glass, Thelma said to her, 'Want to give me a hand bringing the food in?'

'Oh, but aren't you going to tell us what it is that we're celebrating first?' Lex asked expectantly. 'I can't speak for the rest of us, but I can't wait to find out what this is all about.'

'Well, I must admit, I'm a little intrigued myself,' put in Gil.

Des grinned. 'Shall we put them out of their misery, love?'

Thelma grinned back at him. 'Okay.'

He rose and went over to the sideboard, taking from it a large brown envelope. Returning to the table, he sat down and passed the envelope to Gil.

Looking surprised, he accepted it, asking, 'What's this?'

'Why don't you open it and find out?' Thelma told him.

Gil pulled out a bound set of papers and scanned his eyes across them, then he looked up in shock at Des. 'It's a contract of partnership between you and me.'

Des smiled. 'That's right. It's never sat well with me, you working for me. I wouldn't have had a business in the first place if you hadn't encouraged me and stood guarantor with the bank. And I only landed Eldridge's contract recently because of your reputation. We'll split everything down the middle, fifty-fifty. Sign it, Gil, please?'

Des offering him a partnership like this had never entered Gil's mind. He was touched to the heart that his friend thought so much of him. Out of respect for his wife, he had to consult her, too. 'What do you think, dear?'

'Oh, darling, I don't know why you're even bothering to ask me that. If ever you were to go into partnership with anyone, I would want it to be Des. It would be very ungracious of you to turn down such a generous offer.'

'It would, Dad,' said his sons in unison.

'Have you a pen?' Gil asked his friend.

Des pulled one out of his trouser pocket. He'd put it there earlier in readiness. The document signed by both parties, Des put it back in its envelope and returned it to the sideboard, saying, 'I'll give this back to my solicitor on Monday and then it's all legal.' Back at the table, he replenished everyone's glass and then raised his own. 'Just one more toast, if you please. To Reader and Morton, Motor Maintenance Engineers!'

They all stood and raised their glasses. 'To Reader and Morton!' they shouted out joyfully.

Having drained a good measure from her glass, Thelma put it down on the table and said, 'Right, can we eat now? 'Cos I'm starving!'

CHAPTER TWENTY-FIVE

Three months later Lex was busy updating clients' records but her mind was not as focused on her job as usual. It was Christine she was thinking about instead. Over the months she had worked here she had learned to read her boss rather well, as usually happens when working closely with another person, and she knew that something was playing on Christine's mind; had been for the last couple of days, in fact. Several times Lex received the distinct impression that Christine had wanted to take her into her confidence, but then for whatever reason had decided not to. Lex only hoped that what was bothering her was nothing to do with Peter. As far as she was aware the pair of them were now inseparable, spending every spare minute they could together. Had something happened to sour things between them? Lex sincerely hoped not.

Christine came into the office just then wearing a very pre-occupied look. Lex smiled up at her expectantly, waiting for her boss to tell her what she'd come in for. Christine opened her mouth to speak, then seemed to change her mind, closed it and made to walk out.

'Erm . . . did you want me for something, Mrs Landers?' asked Lex.

'Oh, you're busy, what I have to say will keep.' She made to depart again then stopped, saying, 'By the way, we received a card in the morning post from Marie and Melvin Cane. They're having a wonderful honeymoon. I'm so glad things worked out well for them in the end. And I had a call just now from Miss Robotham. She and Mr Bickers are having another date on Saturday night.

That's the fifth so far, things are looking very promising there. Anyway, I'll leave you to get on.'

This wasn't the first time she'd started to say something then backtracked, and Lex felt enough was enough.

'What I'm doing isn't that urgent, Mrs Landers. Look, it's very apparent to me you've something on your mind. I do hope it isn't bad news?'

Her boss seemed relieved that Lex had paved the way for the conversation she knew she must eventually have. She sat down on the chair before the desk, wringing her hands nervously 'Well, you may take what I have to say as bad news. That's why I've been dreading telling you . . .'

A feeling of foreboding flooded through Lex then.

Taking a very deep breath, Christine announced, 'Peter has asked me to marry him, Mrs Morton.'

And this was bad news? Lex beamed in sheer delight as she exclaimed, 'Oh, how wonderful! I'm so delighted for you. I know you'll both be happy together. To think, you'll actually be the bureau's second marriage. Bet you never thought for a minute that would be the case when you opened up, did you?' Then she looked quizzically at Christine. 'How could you ever think I would view this as bad news, Mrs Landers?'

'That isn't the part I was dreading telling you. There's more, you see. I want to be a proper wife to Peter . . . keep our house nice, have his dinner ready for him when he arrives home from work every evening, slippers warming before a blazing fire in winter. And we'd like to start a family as soon as we're married as were not exactly spring chickens. I can't be the sort of wife and mother I want to be and still run my business, so I'm selling it.'

This news was indeed upsetting for Lex. She had very much enjoyed her job, all the highs and lows of it, and it saddened her to learn it would be coming to an end. But mixed with that was her joy over Christine's happy ending, and that was a great consolation.

'I will recommend you very highly to the new owners, and hopefully you will be kept on by them,' Christine was saying.

Lex stared at her thoughtfully. Did she want to be kept on? Gil and Des's business had really begun to take off since they'd landed Eldridge's contract and word had spread through the trade what a first-class firm Reader and Morton were. So much work was flooding in now that they were considering taking on another engineer to help out. Gil was, in fact, earning as much as he had at Brenton's, with the outlook for even greater financial rewards very bright indeed. Lex no longer needed the extra her sons had tipped up. In fact, now she refused to take more than the bare minimum from them since they had announced they wanted to start saving hard for homes of their own, for when they eventually got married. There was, in fact, no need for Lex to work any longer to supplement Gil's wage, and if she were honest working full-time as well as running a home, despite the help she received from Gil and her sons, was very demanding and took its toll on her.

Since she'd started working for Christine she had taken no holiday except for two days at Christmas and one at New Year. Maybe she should see this as an opportunity to go back to being just a housewife, recoup her energies and take her time deciding if she wanted to continue working or not.

She smiled warmly at her boss to reassure her. 'I've really enjoyed working for you, Mrs Landers. I've absolutely loved this job and it's brought me great satisfaction, helping our clients find their perfect partners. But I've decided to go back to being a housewife for the moment. I'll take my time about deciding if I want another job. I do thank you for offering to put a good word in for me with the potential new owners, but the day you leave is the day I do too. Until then I will work for you as I have always done.'

'I wouldn't have expected any less from you, Mrs Morton. And this isn't a goodbye for us, I hope? Peter and I have your name top of our wedding guest list. We couldn't get married without the woman who brought us together being there, so I won't accept any excuses.'

Smiling brightly, Lex told her, 'I'm already planning my outfit.'

CHAPTER TWENTY-SIX

Six weeks later, Lex took a long look around the office. Now tidied up ready for the new owner to come in at one that afternoon, it looked almost as stark as it had when she had first entered the premises over six months ago. Well, save for the walls which were now lined with strategically placed tasteful pictures of happy couples, and the client waiting area which now had far more comfortable chairs and a coffee table holding a selection of the latest magazines and some pretty pot plants.

Christine came in, glanced around and said, 'I've just come to give you a hand with the office, making sure it's ready to hand over to Mrs Patterson and her daughter, but it's already spotless.' Looking at it, she smiled with satisfaction. 'We've managed to bring happiness to a lot of people between these walls, haven't we, Mrs Morton?'

'We certainly have,' Lex agreed.

'Seen a lot of heartache too. But then, that's the nature of this kind of business. Mind you, if I hadn't had you working for me, I wouldn't be in a position today to sell on a thriving concern, nor be about to get married. Well, it's the end of an era for us, isn't it? All that remains is for me to take the keys round to the solicitor and pull that door shut after us ... Oh, how forgetful I am! I haven't put the vacuum around the reception area yet and I said I'd take care of that when we split the cleaning duties between us.'

'Well, I know you should really be the one to close the door for the final time since you're the owner, but I'll finish it off for you if you'd like me to, Mrs Landers?' Lex offered.

Christine smiled gratefully. 'I'm not worried about being the last to leave. To be honest, I can't wait to get on with what the future holds for me so I appreciate your offer. Well, see you and your husband at the wedding in three weeks' time!'

'You certainly will, Mrs Landers. We're looking forward to it.'

'I'm not your boss any longer, Mrs Morton, and we haven't any office protocol to abide by anymore, so I'm just Christine to you from now on.'

'As long as you call me Lex.'

The women were both starting to get emotional about this parting, and tears threatened to fall.

Christine felt it wouldn't do for her to arrive for her appointment all red-eyed and blotchy-faced so said briskly, 'Right, best be off.'

With that she grabbed her coat and bag of belongings and left Cupid's Marriage Bureau behind for good, to start her brand new life with the man she loved.

A short while later, having stowed away the vacuum, Lex took one more look around just to check nothing had been left undone. Satisfied it hadn't, she was about to collect her coat and take her own leave when to her surprise the outer door burst open and Duncan Holgate charged in, his face almost obscured by the enormous bouquet of flowers he was carrying.

Peering out from behind them he looked mortally relieved to see Lex. 'Oh, I'm so glad I caught you, Mrs Morton. I knew your last day of business was yesterday and you aren't actually open for business today from the letter you sent all your clients, telling us of the change of ownership, but I couldn't manage to come then. I thought I'd take a chance and call today. If I'd missed you, well, then I couldn't have done what I really wanted to.'

Lex was looking at him in bemusement. 'And what's that, Mr Holgate?'

He thrust the bouquet at her. 'Give you these.'

Her mouth dropped open in astonishment as she accepted them. 'These are for me? But what I have done to deserve them?'

He smiled at her. 'Just made me the happiest man, Mrs Morton, when I never believed I'd be happy again . . . that's all!'

She laid the flowers gently on the bare reception desk to one side of her. 'I take it that means you and Miss Stone are still getting on very well together?' Just as her every instinct had told her they would.

'I'll say! I asked her to marry me the night before last and she's accepted.'

Lex's face lit up. 'Oh, Mr Holgate, I'm so very pleased for you both.' She was so glad she had managed to persuade Christine that, despite the couple's seeming incompatibility, the experiences they had in common were enough to bond them. It seemed she had been right.

'No more pleased than I am, Mrs Morton. I have to tell you that when I first saw Gemma waiting for me as you'd arranged in the foyer of the White Hart Hotel, she didn't appeal to me at all. She looked the frumpy sort. I couldn't believe you were expecting me to spend an evening with her after I'd described my usual type in detail. I nearly turned round and went straight home, but I couldn't bring myself to leave the poor woman standing there so I put on a brave face and went and introduced myself. We went into the bar of the White Hart and I bought her a drink. To be honest, all that was on my mind then was how I could make an early escape. Well, we got talking and I learned she'd suffered badly through a failed relationship. The next thing I noticed it was gone eleven and . . . well, the rest is history.

'Oh, Mrs Morton, when I think that I didn't want to even come in here that first day but had to be dragged, kicking and screaming, by my friends! I knew they meant what they said and I couldn't expect you to lie for me so really I had no choice but to register with you or I'd never have got out. I'd vowed not to get involved with a woman again after what my wife did to me. She crucified me, Mrs Morton. Broke my heart and left me penniless.

'I should never have married Caroline in the first place. Everyone tried to warn me about how selfish she was . . . my parents, friends . . . but you know what it's like when you're young? You ignore good advice because you think you know better. Well, I came to regret that I'd chosen to ignore what people were trying to tell me. As soon as we married I found out what a mistake I'd made. She never told me she was giving up her job; never mentioned until after our honeymoon that she was expecting me to keep her. She spent most of the housekeeping on things for herself and hardly anything on food. We practically lived on baked beans! Caroline didn't believe in housework so it never got done unless I did it. In fact, she lounged about all day on the settee, reading romance novels, and then moaned that there was never any money for nights out. Well, my wages only stretched so far.

'I was shocked when she told me she wanted a divorce because I wasn't keeping her in the manner she'd expected. She made it plain, though, that she wasn't leaving empty-handed. In fact, she wanted the lot: the house my parents had generously bought us on our marriage and everything in it. When she realised I wasn't going to just hand it over ...' his face puckered up in hurt as painful memories surfaced '. . . she took steps to leave me no choice. I never realised that Caroline could be so wicked. I arrived home one night from work to find her and another woman talking in the lounge, just an ordinary-looking woman, like a normal house-wife, and before I'd even had a chance to ask who she was, Caroline dropped her bombshell.

'She told me that if I didn't sign over everything to her, this woman was going to go to the police and tell them I'd broken into her house one night and brutally raped her, then I'd go to prison. I told her I'd deny it. Caroline said I wouldn't be able to as she'd given the woman details of a birthmark on my abdomen, enough to identify me.

'I couldn't believe it. I asked the woman why she would do such a thing, I was a stranger to her, why would she want to wreck my life like that? She just said that she'd do anything if she was paid enough, which my wife was doing. Well, I was backed into a corner and I knew it. I had no choice but to hand over every-thing to my wife and go back to living with my parents. As soon as I'd signed over everything, Caroline put the house on the market and squandered all the money from the sale on a fancy car, clothes and a holiday. The last I heard, she'd married some other poor sucker. At the time this all happened I thought it was the end of the world for me, but now I look back, getting my freedom from her was the best thing I ever did . . .'

He stopped mid-flow as he realised that Lex wasn't listening to him but seemed to be staring into space. 'Er . . . you all right, Mrs Morton?' he asked in concern. 'Mrs Morton, I asked if you were all right?'

'Pardon? Oh, er . . . yes, I'm fine. Er . . . can I just confirm something you've told me, Mr Holgate? Did you say that your wife paid a woman to lie for her so she'd get her own way over the divorce?'

'Yes, that's correct. Why?'

'Oh, er . . . as you said, it's a very wicked thing to do. I wondered if I'd heard you right, that's all. I really appreciate the flowers.'

'My way of saying thank you for finding me the wonderful woman you have. Well, I can see you were ready to leave when I came in, and I must get back to the office. Goodbye, Mrs Morton.'

Lex wasn't being rude when she failed to respond, her mind was busy elsewhere.

When they had been trying to work out Miriam Jones' reason for falsely accusing Gil of molesting her, they thought they had covered everything. The only conclusion that had made sense to them was the idea that Gil had accidentally brushed against her while he'd been preoccupied with the urgent tender he'd been working on. But what Duncan Holgate had just divulged to her had made Lex think there could be another reason why Miriam Jones had done what she had.

Someone had paid her.

Her heart was thumping painfully. Oh, if she could somehow prove it, then Gil would be completely exonerated of any blame.

She needed to talk this over urgently with someone. Thelma!

Grabbing her coat, bag of belongings and the very thoughtful gift of flowers from Duncan Holgate, she left Cupid's Marriage

Bureau without a backward glance. She had other more important matters to think about.

Thelma was delighted to see her visitor. Noticing the flowers before she did Lex's face, she exclaimed, 'Oh, lovey, flowers for me? What on earth have I done to deserve those? The size of that bunch, it must have cost you a fortune.'

'Sorry to disappoint you but a happy client gave them to me just as I was leaving. I'll share them with you, though. We'll have half each.'

Thelma smiled appreciatively at her friend's generosity. 'I'll get a vase.'

Lex placed the bouquet on the draining board. 'No, that can wait. First I want your opinion on something important.'

By the urgent tone of her voice, Thelma knew it was serious. 'Oh!'

'Thelma, do you think it's possible that Miriam Jones was paid for accusing Gil?'

Thelma looked stunned. 'Eh! But who would have had that much of a grievance against him they'd pay good money to get him sacked?'

'I've no idea. But what if someone did? Look, I know it sounds like I'm clutching at straws here but if I am right, and we can find out somehow who it was, then Gil's name would be cleared.'

'I want his name cleared as much as you do, Lex, but it's not like Miriam Jones is going to admit to being paid, is she? So I don't see how we can find out.'

Lex's shoulders sagged. 'No, of course she's not just going to admit it. Maybe it is just a fanciful idea of mine anyway. Oh, I was so excited about proving Gil's innocence.'

An idea was occurring to Thelma and she stood staring at Lex, pondering it.

Noticing her friend's preoccupation, Lex asked her, 'What is it, Thelma?'

'Well, it's just an idea ... but maybe we *can* wheedle out of the Jones woman whether she was paid or not.'

'How? I mean, we'd have to be very careful choosing our words in case I've got this all wrong and then she could have us for slander.'

Thelma's eyes were sparkling. 'Are you up to a bit of play acting, lovey?'

'I'll put on the performance of my life if it'll clear Gil's name, Thelma.'

'And so will I. Come on, I'll tell you my plan on the way to Brenton's.'

'Why are we going there?'

'Because neither of us knows where Miriam Jones lives. We'll need to follow her home so we can pay her a visit later.' She grabbed her coat off the back of the door and urged Lex, 'Come on, the factory office staff finish at four on a Friday and it's half-three now.'

On the way to Brenton's, Thelma outlined to Lex what she had in mind. Lex was impressed. It was a good plan her friend had come up with. All she was worried about was whether they could both keep up the pretence until they had what they were after, and not give Miriam Jones any reason to suspect them and throw them out. They had agreed that Thelma should do all of the talking as Lex was too emotionally involved, desperate to hear what she wanted to, and in her need to find out the information might forget herself and give the game away.

As they approached the factory they were both astonished to see the whole yard full and men spilling out through the gates, hundreds of them. Some huddled together in groups, heads bent in deep discussion, engulfed by clouds of smoke from the endless cigarettes being smoked; some were lounging against the factory walls; some just aimlessly milling around. All were obviously waiting for something to happen, and all were angry judging by their faces. At this time of day on a Friday they should have been at home by now, leaving just the office staff to take their leave at any minute.

'Something's going on,' said Thelma. 'The men don't look happy, do they?'

A grim look on her face, Lex shook her head. 'No, they certainly don't.'

325

They had arrived at the edge of the milling crowd and Thelma accosted one of the workers. 'What's happening?' she asked.

'We're all waiting for the top union brass to arrive, to sanction an official strike.'

'What are you threatening to strike over?'

The man took a last drag from the cigarette he was smoking, threw it on the ground and stamped his boot on it. 'It's no bloody threat, missus. We're striking, make no mistake about that. Management is trying to get us to accept a three-day week 'cos we ain't got enough work at the moment to keep us going full-time. Try telling *that* to my wife when I can't give her enough housekeeping! They should get their fucking fingers out their arses and get the work in, else Brenton himself should pay our wages out of his own pocket 'til they do secure more orders.

'Since Gil Morton left, this place has gone to pot. The first bloke that took over as works manager was a waste of space. If one of us said "Boo!" he jumped a mile in the air. Us blokes used to take the piss out of him summat rotten. He spent most of his day hiding in his office 'cos he was scared of us all.

'He lost us that big order that Mr Morton was in the middle of tendering for when he left. They knew the tender that came in was a back-of-a-fag-packet job and unworkable, so didn't award it to us. Well, that ain't the men's fault, is it? Why should we be made to suffer by having our hours cut? That lost order would have kept us all working overtime for the next three years.

'The manager we've got now is n'ote more than a little Hitler, strutting around looking down his nose at us all on the shop floor like we was nothing better than dog shit, moaning that production is down and the stuff we're turning out is shoddy. And if that ain't bad enough, now we've got Brenton Junior lording it around the place. We've lost all respect for the management. I've worked at Brenton's me whole life and I've never seen things look so bad as they do now. There's no big orders in the offing at the moment, only bits and pieces, so if we don't land summat size-able soon I'd be most surprised if old man Brenton still has a factory this time next year. Then all us workers will be on the scrap heap.'

Maurice Brenton only had himself to blame, thought Lex. He should have stood by Gil instead of worrying about the workforce's reaction, which couldn't have been worse than this. Instead he'd seen works managers as two a penny, and to his cost found out that ones of Gil's calibre could make all the difference to a firm's profitability. Despite them neither standing up for her husband nor coming to see him with any kind words after his dismissal, Lex did feel sorry for the men now. Should this man's prophecy come true, then this time next year Brenton's factory would have closed its gates and they'd be looking for other jobs. Some of the older or unskilled ones might not find that easy.

Lex nudged Thelma when she saw several women barging their way through the men at the gates. 'The office workers are coming out.'

Thelma said to the disgruntled worker, 'Can you help us? We're looking for Miriam Jones. We don't know her by sight but we've got an important message for her from her sister.'

The man looked around, spotting a blonde-haired, thirtyish-looking woman pushing her way through the crowd a short distant away. 'That's her,' he said, gesturing in her direction.

Thelma thanked the man and she and Lex watched as Miriam Jones passed them by, only a matter of feet away, to hurry off down the street.

So that's the woman who wrought havoc in our lives, Lex thought. She hadn't actually visualised the woman, but hadn't expected her to look so ordinary either. Maybe to have some sort of wicked look to her . . . but she seemed like a perfectly ordinary woman.

Keeping a discreet distance away, they set off after her. Several back streets later Miriam stopped before a house, inserted a key in the front door and let herself in, shutting the door behind her.

A little further down the street, pulling Lex to a halt, Thelma said to her, 'Right, let's give her a couple of minutes to take her coat and shoes off then we'll make our move.'

A few minutes later, now standing outside the house they had seen Miriam Jones let herself into, Thelma asked Lex, 'You ready?'

She took a deep breath, trying to quell her thumping heart. 'I'm as ready as I'll ever be.'

Thelma purposefully rapped on the door

Presently they heard the slip-slop of slippers heading down the tiled passageway towards the door. Then it opened and Miriam Jones stood there, looking at them both enquiringly. 'Yes?' she asked.

'Mrs Jones?' Thelma queried, just to confirm they did indeed have the right woman.

'Yes.'

Both of them said a silent thank you that they had.

'Could we have a word in private?' Thelma asked.

'What about?'

'Well, it's not really fit for discussion in the street. Mind if we come in?' Miriam looked like she was going to refuse to Thelma added, 'It could prove financially beneficial to you.'

Her eyes lit up then. 'Oh! Have you come to tell me I've won something?'

'Look, if you'll let us in we'll tell you exactly what we've come about. It's . . . er . . . a bit chilly out here.'

Miriam stood aside to allow them both entry then led them down a dimly lit, dingy passageway and into a shabbily furnished back room where a fire burned in an old-fashioned grate.

She indicated for them both to take a seat on a lumpy-looking old moquette sofa. She herself sat down in an equally well-worn armchair. Taking a packet of cigarettes off the arm of the chair, she slid one out and lit it, blew a plume of smoke in the air then offered the packet to them. They both refused. Settling back in her chair and crossing her legs, Miriam said, 'Well, are you going to put me out of my misery then?'

Thelma took a deep breath. Here goes, she thought. 'Well, it's like this. We understand you helped a friend of ours with a problem they had and wondered if you'd be interested in helping us with one? We'd pay you, of course, like they did.'

Miriam narrowed her eyes at them both. 'Just what are you talking about?'

Thelma smiled at her knowingly. 'We both know what we're talking about, Mrs Jones.'

She was looking at Thelma very suspiciously now. 'Do we?'

'Yes, we do. You was paid to lie that a bloke at your work manhandled you in his office, in order to get him sacked.'

They both held their breath as her face paled, a look of horror filling her eyes. They weren't sure whether this was from indignation that two strangers could be accusing her of doing such a despicable thing or because she was mortified that her secret was out. To have a hope of ever clearing Gil's name, they prayed it was the latter. Side by side on the sofa, under the protection of their coats, they were gripping each other's hand.

Then to their elation Miriam replied, 'How did you know that?'

Lex froze. This woman had just confirmed her suspicions. It was taking her all her self-control not to leap across and throttle the life out of her for all the suffering she had brought on the Morton family. But they hadn't found out what they really needed to know to clear Gil's name, and that was who had paid her?

Thelma was addressing her again. 'Well, we're mutually acquainted with the person who paid you. They know my friend here is in a hole and needs the same sort of help. They said it might be worth asking you to help us.'

Miriam's face darkened thunderously as she hissed, 'He promised me when I agreed that this would be our secret. He wouldn't tell a living soul, he swore to me. Wait 'til I see him! I only agreed to do it for him 'cos I was so desperate for money. My husband had run off with his fancy piece, taking every last penny I had to my name and leaving me bills to pay. I'd started getting bailiffs calling.'

So it was a man who was behind this, thought Lex and Thelma.

'Well, don't be too hard on him, love. He could tell my friend here was desperate and he was only wanting to help,' Thelma said. 'So, are you interested in earning some extra cash by helping my friend or not? You have our solemn promise that if you do we won't breathe a word.'

Miriam looked at them both for several long moments, seeming to be mulling the matter over, before she said, 'Well, like most people, I'm always in need of extra money. As you can see, I'm not exactly living like a queen, am I?' she said, casting a scathing glance around the room. 'Depends, though, just what you want me to do and how much you're willing to pay me?'

'We'd like you to do the same as what you did to that bloke in the factory. Just tell my friend's husband that you'll go to the police and say he mauled you ... laying it on thick like ... unless he agrees to give her a divorce. My friend will be with you when you do it.'

Miriam looked thoughtfully at them for a moment. 'Well, I suppose I could. So how much are you willing to pay me then? I could do with enough to get a new suite. You can tell for yourselves, mine's not exactly comfy.'

'How much did you get paid last time?' Thelma asked her.

'Thirty quid. But I won't do it again for less than forty.'

Lex's breath was catching in her throat. She felt like a volcano about to blow its top. Didn't know how much longer she could restrain herself. This woman had been prepared to ruin a man and his family's lives for a paltry thirty pounds! She needed to get the rest of the information fast and be out of here before her self-control broke.

'We'll pay you forty,' she blurted out.

'Deal,' Miriam agreed, stubbing out her cigarette.

In total desperation now to get out of this house and away from this woman, there was no more beating about the bush for Lex. 'As a matter of interest, how did our mutual friend come to pick on you to help him out in the first place? I mean, it's not the sort of thing you approach everyone with. Was he a boyfriend or something?'

Miriam pulled a disparaging face. 'You having a joke? If you think I go for his sort, what do you think I am? For your information, he was passing by when I happened to be at the wages office hatch. He was on his way upstairs to cadge a lift home. He overheard me asking the wages manager for a sub of my pay and they wouldn't let me 'cos I'd already had one the week before. So are you going to tell me when you want me to do this?'

Thelma's heart sank. Miriam's changing of the subject meant it was going to look very suspicious if either she or Lex blatantly turned the conversation back to the subject of how she was acquainted with the man who'd paid her. It looked very unlikely they were ever going to hear the man's name now. So close and yet so far! Then, to her utter astonishment, she realised Lex was on her feet and heard her say, 'Right, we'd better be off.'

Thelma looked up at her in bemusement. As far as she was aware they hadn't yet gleaned from Miriam Jones the identity of the man who'd started all this. 'Eh?'

Lex grabbed her coat sleeve and urged her up. 'Come on, you need to get home, don't you?'

'Er . . . yes, all right,' she said, reluctantly getting up.

Miriam, too, was looking a bit bewildered. She'd agreed to do it but they hadn't as yet made any arrangements for when and where with her yet. 'I'll be hearing from you then, will I?' she asked.

Lex smiled at her. 'Oh, you most certainly will, Mrs Jones.'

'At least give me your names?' she requested.

'Oh, how rude of me not to have introduced us. This is Mrs Reader,' she introduced Thelma. 'And my name is Alexandra Morton. I'm Gil Morton's wife.'

Miriam's face drained of colour. She stood frozen to the spot as the two women saw themselves out.

Outside in the street, Lex immediately started to charge off in the direction of home. Thelma caught up with her and grabbed her arm, pulling her to a halt. 'Lex, why did you make us leave before we'd got out of her just who it was who paid her to falsely accuse Gil?'

'But she did tell us, Thelma.'

Her friend looked taken aback. Was she missing something? 'She did?'

331

'Yes. I know exactly who it was. I still don't know why, so he'd better have one hell of a good excuse,' she snarled. 'But better than anything is the fact that we're going to expose that man's lies in front of an audience. Come on, I need to get home.'

Gil looked pleased to see his wife arrive through the back door fifteen minutes later when he was putting on the kettle. 'Hello, love. I thought you were finishing at one today so I was surprised not to find you home. I've just got back myself. Was it awful saying goodbye to . . .'

'Gil, can you leave that and get your coat on?' she urged him. 'Thelma's fetching Des and they'll be waiting for us there.'

'What?'

She was tugging at his sleeve. 'I need you to come with me now. I was hoping our boys would be here too but . . .'

Just then they both arrived and before they could say anything Lex blurted out, 'Don't bother taking your coats off, we're all going out.'

'Where?' they both asked.

She shouted at them, 'Will you all stop asking questions and just do as I ask? I want to get there before the meeting is over. You take your father in your van, Matt, and follow me and Martin in his,' she ordered.

They all looked at her in bewilderment.

'Come on, lads, best just do what your mother is asking us. Then hopefully all will be revealed,' Gil told them.

He had no idea just how much was about to be made plain.

CHAPTER TWENTY-SEVEN

As Martin's van approached the gates of Brenton's Engineering, Lex was relieved to see the men still crowded together like sardines inside the yard. She could see that some of them were raising their fists angrily. As they got nearer voices became audible. Angry voices. Shouts of, 'Let's put this to the vote.' 'We ain't accepting a three-day week due to management cock ups!' 'Bring Gil Morton back before this place sinks!' Which warmed Lex's heart.

Martin had done his best to coax out of his mother during the short journey just what was going on, but she was keeping her own counsel, far too busy urging him on to get there before the men dispersed to bother answering questions. Pulling the van to a halt just before the gates, they bother jumped out. Gil and Matt behind them did likewise. Thelma and Des, who'd been waiting by the factory wall for them to arrive, came over to join them.

Lex asked Thelma, 'Have you told, Des?'

She shook her head. 'This is your moment, lovey. You ready for this?'

Lex smiled. 'More than ready.' She turned to the men then and instructed them, 'Follow us.'

With their confused menfolk following, Lex and Thelma went over to the gates and began pushing and shoving their way through the packed crowd towards the temporary raised platform by the entrance to the machine shop on which stood six men. Maurice Brenton was there along with his son Julian. There was also the current works manager, the shop steward Cyril Breville, the union representative from headquarters and his aide.

Maurice Brenton was standing before a mike addressing the crowd. 'Now listen to some sense. Please, hear me out.' He stopped short when he spotted Lex, Thelma, Des, but especially Gil and his sons, heading through the crush of workers, and watched, taken aback, as Lex clambered up on to an upturned crate to reach the platform. Before he could stop her, she had manoeuvred herself between him and the mike and was addressing the crowd.

'You all stood by and said nothing when my husband, Gil Morton, was thrown out of here like a common criminal despite protesting his innocence of any crime.' She turned to look at Maurice Brenton and pointed her finger at him. 'My husband worked for Brenton's since leaving school. He was your works manager, working closely with you, for over five years. You know what kind of man he is and that he's not the sort to abuse a woman, yet you did nothing to defend him but sacked him instead because you were afraid your finances would suffer if the men went on strike. Well, now I know that Miriam Jones was paid to do what she did. My friend down there witnessed Mrs Jones' confession,' she said, pointing to Thelma who stood looking smugly up at her, along with a bemused-looking Des, Gil, Martin and Matt.

Lex addressed Maurice Brenton again. 'Now, Mr Brenton, why don't you ask your son why he did it – because I'd love to know, and so would my husband, and so I'm sure would everyone else here too.'

Maurice Brenton was gawping at her like a fish. He turned to look at his son who was looking very pale by now. In an utterly astounded tone, he barked, 'You *paid* Miriam Jones to accuse my works manager of something he never did?'

Julian Brenton looked terrified, as he backed away from his father, but found he'd nowhere to go as he'd reached the back edge of the podium. He spluttered, 'But ... but I never, Dad, believe me. I don't know what Mrs Morton is talking about.'

Maurice Brenton grabbed him by the scruff of his neck, pulling his shorter son up so they stood eye to eye. 'Don't lie. I know when you're lying, and you're lying now. Why, Julian? Why?'

Lex was aiming the mike stand towards them so everyone could hear this conversation.

'Because . . . because I wanted to get back at him for what he did to me.'

His father shouted, '*You what?* What the hell did he ever do that was so bad you had to destroy him and his family – and lose me the best damn' manager I've ever had?'

'He . . . he caught me driving one of the forklifts with my four friends on the back one Saturday afternoon. I didn't know he was there and I'd brought my schoolfriends in because we were bored and wanted some fun.'

Maurice Brenton was so shocked by this that he loosened his grip on his son and pushed him away.

From where he stood before the platform, looking up at the scene being played out before him, Gil couldn't believe what he was hearing. He shouted up to Julian, 'But I was only trying to stop you killing yourself and your friends! You were about fourteen at the time and speeding around on that forklift without the least care or attention. If you'd collided with any of the machines, I dread to think what could have happened.'

Julian glared down at him and shouted back, 'But you made me look a fool in front of my friends, ordering us off the premises like we'd no right to be there. I had *every right* to be there. My father owned the factory; you were just his paid worker with no authority to order me about like you did. I was the butt of all my friends' jokes for weeks after that.' As he seemed to forget where he was and who was listening, Julian's eyes blazed with hatred. 'I vowed then I'd get even with you for what you did to me, and I did, didn't I?'

Gil was struck speechless.

The whole meeting also had been stunned into silence by this shocking turn of events. The workers who'd chosen to believe the accusation, making Martin and Matt's lives a misery at every opportunity while they'd still been employed at Brenton's, were sporting guilty expressions, even Loz Stanton and his cronies.

Gil felt a tug on his arm then and turned his head to see his wife standing beside him.

'I think we've done all we need to here. Let's go home, love,' she said.

She hooked her arm through his. As they made to move off, she felt a tap on her shoulder and turned round to see Thelma looking at her in consternation. 'Just how did you know it was Brenton's son?'

Lex smiled. 'Because Miriam Jones said *he passed her on his way up to cadge a lift when she was at the wages office hatch*. I know from Gil that only the boss's private offices are on the second floor of the building. His secretary hasn't a car because I know Gil used to offer her a lift home if he ever saw her waiting at the bus stop in bad weather. Well, I know no one working at the factory would ever have the nerve to ask the boss for a lift home, so it had to be his son, didn't it?'

As she walked along proudly beside her husband, their sons to either side, Thelma and Des following close behind, the crowd parted to allow them free passage. The men all bowed their heads in shame as Gil passed by. Lex noticed that the defeated stoop to his shoulders had finally gone and he was walking erect and purposefully, as he used to before.

What the Mortons as a family had suffered through Julian Brenton's spiteful revenge had tested them all almost beyond endurance. They had all had to find strengths they had never known they possessed, but had stood firm and survived together, to become stronger, more united, than they had ever been. And friends too . . . very dear friends . . . had showed them what lengths they were prepared to go to prove that friendship. Their future before today had looked bright, but at this moment it paled into the background. Lex's heart was soaring. She'd got her husband back again.

CHAPTER TWENTY-EIGHT

Several weeks later, the Readers and Mortons were gathered together, once again, for dinner.

'You've got two extra places set by mistake, shall I clear them so that we can all shift round?' asked Lex

Thelma looked at her blankly for a moment. 'Oh . . . er . . . well, leave the place settings as they are, eh? Take those spuds through before they get cold then come back for the veg.'

Arriving back in the room with a dish of potatoes, Lex noticed that Martin had disappeared. Putting the dish in the centre of the table, she asked no one in particular, 'Where's he gone?'

'He needed to use the telephone,' Des responded.

Who would Martin suddenly decide he needed to call just as they were about to eat? He returned so Lex immediately asked him.

'Oh, I just remembered I had to tell a mate something,' he answered dismissively. 'Those spuds look good . . . nearly as good as yours, Mam,' he said, licking his lips.

She knew he was changing the subject, hiding something from her. Her thoughts were interrupted by the arrival of Thelma carrying a meat plate on top of which sat a large joint of beef which she set in front of Des. 'Start carving, ducky,' she ordered him, then said to Lex, 'You on strike or what? There's plenty more needs fetching from the kitchen.'

Finally all the dishes of food had been set on the table, succulent thick slices of beef carved, and they were just about to start helping themselves when the front door knocker resounded.

'That's them,' said Matt to Martin.

337

Lex looked at her sons, perplexed. 'Who's *them*?'

Both sons scraped back their chairs and stood up as did Thelma who went off to answer the door.

Martin fixed his mother with his eyes before announcing, 'We've a surprise for you, Mam.'

She looked bemused. 'A surprise! What sort of surprise?'

'Well, we thought it was about time to introduce you to the women we're going to marry.'

This unexpected announcement shook Lex rigid. 'What! The ... the ... women you're going to *what*?' Then a wave of panic rushed through her. 'But ... but ... shouldn't you have warned me that I was about to meet my future daughters-in-law so I could at least have prepared myself?' Then anger overtook her. 'Didn't me and your father at least deserve the courtesy of being told you were both courting seriously before it got to this stage? To spring this on us like this ... well, it's ...'

She was cut short by Thelma returning to the room, ushering two females along with her.

Lex gasped in recognition. 'Justine!' she exclaimed.

Justine grinned back at her. 'Hello, Mrs Morton.'

Then a voice asked her, 'Do you recognise me, Mrs Morton?'

Her eyes flashed over to the other girl with the beautiful blonde tresses. 'Of course. I do. I tried to introduce you to my son Matt, but it didn't work out.'

Thelma laughed. 'Maybe it did.'

Lex was staring at them all furiously. 'You're all in on this. Gil, Thelma, and you, Des. I'll speak to you all later ... but first, will someone please tell me what's going on?'

'Our sons couldn't resist springing this surprise on you, love, and roped us all in to help them,' Gil told her.

She frowned. 'But why did they have to surprise me?'

'Because you couldn't resist poking your nose into our love lives when you knew how strongly we felt about you keeping out of it,' Martin told her. 'I'm my own man, same as my brother, and we were going to find our own wives without any help from our mother, no matter how clever she is about knowing when a woman

338

is right for us.' He put his arm around Justine and pulled her close. 'Though, thank God you did ignore us, Mam. I dread to think what I might have missed out on if you hadn't been responsible for bringing me and Justine together. Mind you, I never cottoned on at the time just what your game was.

'You knew we were right for each other and you were so frustrated that I wouldn't even look twice at her, let alone consider her as a possible girlfriend. So in order to get me to spend time in her company, so I'd see for myself just what a wonderful woman she is, perfect for me in every way, you did your best to manipulate me into taking her out by lying that she needed cheering up after her boyfriend dumped her. At the time I'd sooner have mucked out a stable full of horses than take a kid like Justine out and have my mates see me and take the mickey. You've our Matt to thank for finally persuading me otherwise.'

He took up the story. 'What you were up to was so obvious to me, Mam, I got to thinking that with you having such a knack for knowing when people are right for each other, maybe there was a chance that our Martin and Justine were. So I took him into the back room and told him what was on my mind, made him see that he had nothing to lose by going to find out.'

'I knew he was the one for me the first time I clapped eyes on him when you moved into your street, but he just saw me as an unsophisticated student and I'd given up all hope by the time he knocked on the door to ask me out. By the end of that first night, you knew I was the one for you, didn't you, sweetie?' Justine said, looking at Martin tenderly.

Looking back at her, love brimming in his eyes, he nodded. Then he told his mother, 'I just couldn't bring myself to give you the satisfaction of saying "I told you so", that's why I wouldn't let on we were seeing each other, and that's why Justine avoided you every time you met up, although she wasn't happy about doing that, until I was good and ready to let you in on it.'

Matt spoke up then. 'I knew immediately I walked into the bureau and saw . . .'

'Me, Mrs Morton,' cut in the girl Lex had met in the bureau.

'You fell instantly in love with me, didn't you, darling?' she said to Matt.

He laughed as he put his arm around her and pulled her close. 'Yes, just like my mother knew I would and that's why she manipulated me into coming there that night at the time she did.'

The girl held her hand out towards Lex. 'In the circumstances, I ought to introduce myself properly to you. After all, I'm going to marry your son. My name is Joanna Upton. I'm so pleased to meet you properly at long last, Mrs Morton.' Then she looked at Gil. 'And you too, Mr Morton.'

'I'm very pleased to meet you, Joanna, and welcome you into our family,' he responded sincerely.

As Lex grasped Joanna's hand and shook it, she said, 'So you did keep your appointment that night after all?' Then she looked accusingly at her youngest son. 'You lied to me! You told me Joanna never showed.'

'And you didn't lie to me to get me there in the first place?' he accused her back.

'Well, I . . . all right, yes, I did. But would you have come if I'd told you that a woman was going to be there I very much wanted you to meet because I knew you'd be perfect for each other?'

'No, I wouldn't have.'

'And I knew that, so I had no choice but to lie then, did I?'

Matt smiled. 'I knew immediately I saw Joanna came into the bureau that night just what you were up to, Mam. And although I thought, My God, she's gorgeous, I was so mad with you, I told her that we'd been set up by my mother of all people and apologised. Jo wasn't mad at all. She said that she felt honoured that a mother thought her good enough for her own son, and if *she* was so convinced that we were suited, then the least we could do was go for a drink and see for ourselves whether she was right ot not. Thankfully, I agreed and here we are.'

Martin asked her worriedly, 'You aren't cross with us, are you, Mam, for springing this on you?'

At that moment all Lex wanted to do was cry with happiness because she knew without a doubt that her sons were indeed going to have themselves wonderful new lives with the women they had chosen to settle down with ... or rather, the ones *she'd* chosen for them.

'Time for another toast, do you think?' suggested Des.